TINKER, TAILOR, Schoolmum, Spy

Faye grew up in Essex before running away to drama school. She worked on the West End as a stage carpenter but decided to get a 'proper job', for reasons which are still unclear but may have been influenced by Rachel from *Friends*. After a decade working her way to the heady heights of middle management, Faye met her husband and moved to Dubai where she ditched corporate life for good in favour of having a baby, performing improvised comedy, and gaining an MA from Falmouth University.

Now back in London with her family, Faye divides her time between performing in musicals with her local theatre company and working as a freelance copyeditor, but her real passion is for writing novels about (and for) kick-ass middle-aged women. *Tinker, Tailor, Schoolmum, Spy* is her first novel, and won the Comedy Women in Print Unpublished Prize 2020.

Keep in touch with Faye on Twitter and Instagram.

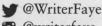 @WriterFaye
 @writerfaye

TINKER, TAILOR, Schoolmum, Spy

FAYE BRANN

HarperCollins*Publishers*

HarperCollins*Publishers*
1 London Bridge Street
London SE1 9GF

www.harpercollins.co.uk

HarperCollins*Publishers*
1st Floor, Watermarque Building, Ringsend Road
Dublin 4, Ireland

Published by HarperCollins*Publishers* 2021
1

A catalogue record for this book
is available from the British Library

ISBN: 978-0-00-847961-9

This novel is entirely a work of fiction.
The names, characters and incidents portrayed in it are
the work of the author's imagination. Any resemblance to
actual persons, living or dead, events or localities is
entirely coincidental.

Set in Sabon by Palimpsest Book Production Limited, Falkirk, Stirlingshire

Printed and Bound in the UK using 100% Renewable Electricity at
CPI Group (UK) Ltd

For Louie

Chapter One

Victoria Turnbull ran up the hill, panting with effort, willing her body to keep moving. Shots echoed around her as she sprinted towards the shelter of woodland ahead. Only a few metres stood between her and the sanctuary of the trees, but if they got a lucky shot she'd be finished.

She dodged one way and then the other, blazing a kamikaze trail that even a trained marksman would have difficulty keeping up with, squinting into the trees to try and spot any sign of an ambush. Nothing obvious. She dived into the foliage, landing badly and rolling to a crumpled stop at the foot of a tree. The noise of gunfire was behind her; she was safe, for now.

She stood up slowly, taking stock of the situation and trying to control her breathing. The combat trousers she wore gripped her thighs like sausage casings; love handles spilt through the gap between her top and bottoms. She wasn't as fit as she once had been; the years had taken a toll and she was regretting any number of lifestyle choices as sweat leaked into every crease and crevice. She leant against the tree trunk for support, legs shaking, and checked her weapon.

She needed to get to her team. She'd tried to tell them to spread out, to divide and conquer, but they hadn't taken her seriously and had ended up cornered. Such were the perils of working with amateurs. Her eyes flickered with annoyance. Currently, as far as she could tell, she was the only person from Yellow squad who was still operational. Even so, her ankle was hurting from that badly timed roll. She tested the weight; she could still run on it, although not as fast as she would have liked. With a bit of luck, her attackers would assume she was already down, though, and she would be able to circle around and make her way back to her team without the need to sprint there. She listened hard and scanned the woods. Everything was still. Except—

She cocked her gun. There was a small movement deep in the trees and she thought for a moment she had seen something. But after a few minutes of intense staring there was no more movement and she relaxed her finger off the trigger. A squirrel, probably.

A battle cry came from the clearing in the small valley below. She took a deep breath and began making her way out of the cover of the trees. As she approached the brow of the hill, a hulking figure of a man ran up and over, towards her. Not an ally. She fired straight at him without hesitating. He staggered backwards, a look of surprise on his face, before falling away. She jogged on, not stopping. It was only a bit of paint. He would live.

Paintball. Who the hell has a paintballing party for their fortieth, anyway? Jon, that's who: the youthful-looking, athletic husband of her best friend Kate, and the last one of their group to hit the milestone. Her friends had been moaning about it for weeks: why couldn't he have chosen something more civilised, like a weekend in the country? Why would they want to run about shooting people with fake bullets full of Dulux's finest, when they could be doing shots in some swanky West End bar? Vicky crouched low behind a small bunker and assessed the situation below her. Granted, by the time the younger ones in their social circle came to celebrate the big four-oh, they'd all agreed something a little less run-of-the-mill was required to coax people into spending yet another fifty quid on witty cufflinks or a Jo Malone candle, plus drinks. But *paintballing*? She had rather liked the idea herself. There was something a bit thrilling about firing a gun, even if it did only have paint in it.

Jesus, her trousers were snug. She needed to move on again before the waistband deprived her lower body of oxygenated blood. Evaluation over, she moved forward and saw a second enemy team member making their way up the hill. Vicky shot off another round of acrid gloop and heard the satisfying yelp as she hit them in the chest. Maybe she needed to unwind, or maybe it was hormones, but shooting people until they were covered in bright-yellow gunk was extremely enjoyable.

From her vantage point she had seen that her remaining enemies were occupied with the assassination of her team, who were cowered at the far side of the valley like sheep in the rain. It was the best time to strike; slowly, sniper-like, she moved around the site, stalking her victims with silent and deadly precision. She spied a member of Blue squad hailing paint pellets from behind a tree and positioned herself to shoot. Quickly, she took aim at the back of his knees, ran forwards, and fired as soon as she was in range. He doubled over and looked up to see who had taken him out.

'Bloody hell, Vicky! That really hurt.'

It was Chris. Dressed in a decade-old set of waterproofs bought for a hiking holiday in the Lake District, he rolled about on the floor like an overgrown Boy Scout.

'Get up, you big baby.' There was no time for tea and sympathy. In any case, she suspected his pride was more injured than anything else.

Chris got up. 'What did you do with my wife? Should've gone to the bloody pub.'

Vicky gave him a quick wave and turned back to the job in hand. She headed towards another bunker, reloading her gun and keeping her eyes open for imminent threat. Blue team's attention had, for now, been diverted to killing off the remainder of her team; but it wouldn't be long before they escalated their attack on her. As if to prove her point, a shot whizzed by her right ear and she dodged out of the way before leaning left of the bunker to fire back in the direction it had come from. She span towards a stack of crates and waited. Outsmart them, be elusive, stay in control. That's what would keep her alive.

She carefully made her way towards the black cab randomly parked up on one side of the clearing, keeping her eyes peeled for any immediate threat. Once she'd reached the cab, she lay flat under the chassis. From there, she could see the legs of another Blue team member straight across from her. Bang. Clean shot to the ankles.

'Dead man walking,' came a female voice. It was Kate. Vicky got up and sat tight behind the wheel of the cab, waiting for a good moment to move. But Blue team were on to her position now, and her only option was to tempt them forwards and out into the open where she could get them before they got her. She whipped round at the sound of footsteps and hit someone right in the chest. Another two, approaching on the right, got pelted in the stomach. She paused to reload, feeling the sweat rolling down her cleavage, and listened to the 'dead man' cries of her enemies and the victorious cheers of her team. It was then that she realised she'd shot everyone.

She remained engaged until the ref called the end of the game. 'You can put that down now,' he said, placing his hand on top of the gun muzzle and lowering it gently. Vicky unpeeled her finger from the trigger. Her heart was pounding from the exertion, but inside, she felt the calm of a job well done. It had been a long time since she'd last had that feeling.

She turned to see Chris hobbling over, accompanied by Jon and the others. Feeling a little contrite, she ripped off her helmet and goggles and slung the gun over her shoulder.

'That was some sharp shooting, Vics.' Chris gave her a kiss and covered her in yellow paint.

'Traitor!' Jon yelled.

'Well, she is my wife,' Chris said, 'and she did do a pretty good job against all of us.'

'Nice one, Vicky.' Her friend Becky gave her a hug and Vicky saw Kate limping up behind her, spattered in yellow paint from the knees down.

'Vics, you were awesome.'

'Sorry I shot you,' Vicky said. 'I got a little bit carried away.'

'It's only paint,' Kate replied. 'Mind you, I don't think

the boys were expecting any of us ladies to have such killer instincts. You should have seen their faces. Poor darlings.'

'I'm sure they'll get over it.' Why was everyone so surprised that a woman could shoot a gun? Vicky wiped her hands through her sweaty helmet hair. She was in dire need of a shower, but it would wait until after a drink. 'Shall we go to the pub now?' she said.

'We certainly can,' Chris replied.

'Winning team buys the beers, right?' Jon said, followed by a chorus of cheering.

They crowded into the nearest old man pub with crap beer and chalkboards advertising pie and mash and a pint for £5. Vicky stood at the bar waving her debit card, taking orders. Her girlfriends Becky, Kate, and Laura bagged a table in the corner and waited for her.

The four women had known each other since their eldest children started school. Playdates and birthday parties eventually led to family barbecues, dinner parties, and weekends away; the children, ranging mostly in age between eight and thirteen, were more like siblings than friends.

Vicky and Chris were the only ones with three kids. Ollie was thirteen, Evie was eight and several jugs of sangria were to blame for James, who had made a somewhat surprise appearance nearly six years after Evie was born, when they were already in their forties. They'd done their best to embrace the situation, but, as much as she loved James, Vicky longed for a bit of freedom again, to go back to work, or at the very least to have a nice, long, uninterrupted bath.

Now James was at nursery, things were easier. But after such a long time as a stay-at-home mum, she was virtually unemployable in the traditional sense, and, with three kids to run around after, it was impossible to imagine how she would hold any kind of job down, never mind a full-on career like before. She dreamt of bagging a job in the school office, which would at least give her convenient hours and holidays off, but so far without much luck. While she was busy imagining various ways to bump off the existing school admin assistant without anyone noticing, her friends were attempting to persuade her to join the PTA. Vicky didn't know why; she'd never shown the slightest bit of enthusiasm for it. She was happy to support the PTA by buying Christmas wrapping paper or offering up a batch of sorry-looking, misshapen bake sale items once in a while, but she resented working for free, and knew from years of experience that she was an executor, not an organiser. In any case, she despised the politics surrounding the whole thing.

The main source of contention was the Chair, William, who had ruled the PTA for the past eleven years while a never-ending stream of his children were farmed through the school. A recently retired accountant, William was the very definition of a middle-aged, middle-class misogynist, and Vicky was still bemused as to why no one had taken an axe to his head, or at the very least removed him from his seat of power. As of this summer, however, the last of his offspring had finished Year Six, and William had reluctantly, though not without enormous fanfare, stepped down.

With William gone, Becky had assumed the role of Chair, and she and the others were pressuring Vicky to join them. She wished they wouldn't. Saying no to her friends made her feel bad, but, frankly, a night at Guantanamo Bay was more appealing. On the other hand, she was running out of excuses and she needed to start doing something for herself. Would the PTA be enough though? Second-hand uniform sales and school discos were hardly compensation for—

'Congratulations, Victoria.' The soft roll of the 'r' and the smell of expensive perfume told her that Matisse, another mum from the school, was right behind her. She turned with the tray in her hands and gave an awkward smile.

'Oh, thank you, Matisse. Can I get you a drink?'

'Non, non, I am fine, thank you.'

There was a pause while the two women wondered what else to say.

'Did you enjoy the paintballing?' Vicky asked.

'I did not play,' she replied.

'No, of course not.'

Matisse was attractive, toned, immaculately dressed, and Botoxed to within an inch of her life despite still only being in her early thirties. She was a polite woman, nice enough, but there was something a little off about her. Or, more to the point, with the man she was married to, Sacha Kozlovsky.

Sacha and Matisse had appeared out of nowhere with their son, Dmitri, about six months ago. The Head of Year Three had announced, just before the Easter holidays, that Dmitri would be joining Evie's class, even though everyone knew for a fact there were no more places. Dimitri was a small, skinny kid with a personality to match and took up very little space, so in the end no one minded very much. But, unlike his son, Sacha ate up the room. The man was in his fifties, with a strong Russian accent and tattoos

8

adorning both arms, and everyone wondered who he was, what he did and what he'd done. Vicky did her best to ignore the curiosity nibbling away at her, but couldn't let it go. She'd Googled both Sacha and Matisse and found very little on either of them through any normal channels. It was out there though, she knew it.

On the rare occasions he did put in an appearance, Sacha never let his wife stray far. Vicky saw him now, drink in hand, smiling as he made his way over to them; on arrival he put a possessive arm around Matisse's shoulder.

'She's not bothering you, is she?' he rasped.

It was almost a threat. Vicky held the tray in front of her like a shield, although her arms were beginning to ache.

'Not at all,' Vicky replied. 'We were just . . . catching up . . .'

'Excuse me,' Matisse said, and sharply shrugged Sacha's arm off of her. She headed straight for the ladies' loo without saying another word. Sacha watched her go, his face ruffling for an instant before he turned back to Vicky and raised his glass.

'You played well today,' he said, smiling. His Russian accent cut through his words like gravel on bare feet. 'You shot me right in the heart, you know.'

'Did I? Gosh, I'm sorry.' Vicky swallowed.

'Did you enjoy it? The shooting, I mean?'

'Yes . . . I suppose so.' She relaxed her shoulders a little. 'I didn't think I'd have as much fun as I did, but once they put the gun in my hand . . .'

'Did you ever shoot a gun before?'

'Yes – er, no—' With some effort, she dragged up the

memory of a weekend away from twenty years before. 'I mean, an old boyfriend and I went clay-pigeon shooting once, years ago in Scotland somewhere, but apart from that . . .'

'Well, you were really very good. Very talented.' He held his fingers in a gun shape and fired at her, making her flinch. The bottle on the tray wobbled. Sacha gave a smoky laugh and disappeared.

'Vicky! Are you bringing us those drinks or what?' A shout from the table in the corner cut through her jitters and she smiled at Becky, who was making room for her on the padded seat. Vicky finally made her way over and sat down to join the conversation.

'Making new friends?' Kate nodded towards Sacha.

'How come they're here anyway?' Vicky said.

'Oh, Jon said we couldn't invite everyone else from school and leave them out or Sacha would probably poison our cornflakes,' Kate said. 'As it happens, Sacha was a pretty sharp shooter. Could give you a run for your money in a duel, Vics.'

'Maybe. I still shot him first though.'

The girls laughed.

'I had no idea you were so competitive,' said Becky. 'I feel like we've seen a whole new side of you today.'

Vicky shrugged her shoulders and picked up her wine. 'Well, I don't know about anyone else, but all this talk of Russians and guns is making me thirsty.' She raised her glass a little higher. 'Cheers, everyone.'

'Cheers!'

*

The white wines began to stack up and Vicky quickly forgot about Sacha. In fact, she forgot almost everything, including her own name, over the next couple of weeks. The autumn term began and organising the activities of three children of disparate ages and personalities pulled her in every conceivable direction, making Vicky feel like she'd picked up a job as an unpaid Uber.

On a sunny Thursday afternoon in late September, with Evie and Ollie at school and James safely ensconced in front of the TV, Vicky decided to have a bit of 'me' time and took herself and her phone off to the bathroom. The kids had long ago bought into the lie of 'Mummy's doing a poo' and Chris knew better than to challenge her over it. So, it was right in the midst of enjoying the sanctity of the downstairs toilet, knowing that she had umpteen episodes of Peppa Pig (courtesy of Netflix) to keep James distracted, that she saw the email entitled 'From a friend' in her ancient and rarely used Hotmail inbox.

She stared for a second, wondering whether to open it. There was no 'from' address and Vicky briefly suffered from the dilemma of how to sate her curiosity versus inviting cyber-crime into her phone, before deciding to open the message anyway. To her relief, the screen didn't dissolve *Matrix*-style, melting her phone and taking half the planet with it. Instead, the message read, simply:

WAKE UP

There was no signature, but it didn't take more than a second for Vicky to realise it wasn't spam. It was a message meant for her, and she knew exactly who it was from.

She heard a sound at the front door. *James*. Vicky hiked

up her pants and jeans and rushed to check on him. To her relief, he was still sitting grinning at the TV, exactly where she had left him.

Except, in contrast to before her trip to the loo, a plain brown padded envelope lay on the floor by his feet.

'What's this, James?' she said.

'A man came,' James said, preoccupied by muddy puddles.

Vicky's stomach lurched. 'Don't. Move.'

She moved quickly to the kitchen to grab a knife, silently checking the ground floor for the intruder with the blade held outstretched and ready. Downstairs was clear. She made her way upstairs, watching for movement in the back garden from Evie's bedroom window and in the street beyond their tiny front yard from hers while she checked the wardrobes, behind the doors and under the beds. She could see nothing and no one; whoever had paid them a visit was long gone. She breathed a sigh of relief and went back downstairs. The house was hardly Fort Knox, but she hated that someone had got in so quickly and with James at home too . . . if she hadn't been in the bathroom when he arrived, if she'd had to defend herself in front of her son . . . it didn't bear thinking about. Vicky replaced the knife into the block with shaky hands and ripped open the package. She pulled out a burner phone and instructions on a typed note, reading:

GILBERT HOUSE, MONDAY 10 A.M. RSVP.

Gilbert House was the official headquarters of a little-known branch of British intelligence, the Joint Operations Intelligence Services, or JOPS for short. Access was by invitation only, and the spies who worked there were the cream of the crop, skimmed from MI5 and MI6 to perform special ops across both foreign and domestic territories.

Vicky Turnbull was one of them.

Chapter Two

Fourteen years earlier, Vicky walked into her boss's office at JOPS HQ clutching a small black-and-white image of her unborn son.

'I have to say, Victoria,' Jonathan Cornelieu crossed his arms and leant back in his plush leather chair. 'I'm slightly surprised. You don't exactly strike me as the maternal type.'

'It surprised me too, sir. But it's not going to change anything.'

Jonathan sighed. 'I appreciate your intentions are good, but I know from experience that, for most women, things don't always go according to plan when it comes to having children.'

Jonathan was a great boss, but could be a bit of an arse on occasions. This was one of them. Vicky tried to keep from sounding testy so he didn't accuse her of being hormonal. 'With respect, sir, I'm not most women.'

'Well, that's true, but—'

'I'm trained to expect the unexpected. I got this job because I can keep things under control in the most extreme of circumstances. I'm smart, I'm driven and I'm an excellent intelligence officer and there's no reason for that to change just because I'm having a baby.'

'You trained hard and you're an asset to the team, Victoria. Officers as good as you don't come along often. But the unfortunate incident with the Russian tells me that you aren't *always* in control of your emotions, and when a baby comes along—'

'I've learnt my lesson about letting feelings get in the way of work, sir.' Vicky cursed herself for the millionth time. The past year, she'd been on a case building evidence against a Russian crime ring suspected of people trafficking. She'd gotten involved romantically with an asset and convinced herself and everyone else that he would do anything for her, including betray his own countrymen. She was wrong.

Her love life cost the actual life of one of their own – Adam, an undercover operative, shot dead in the back alley of a Moscow casino acting on bad intel she'd been the one to gather. The case fell apart, leaving Jonathan facing the wrath of Number 10 and Vicky babysitting diplomats at the Foreign Office for the best part of six months. And now here she was, standing in front of him with yet another piece of bad news and Vicky could see the irritation written all over his face.

'I'll be back as soon as I'm cleared for duty, sir. The doctor said six weeks, eight if it's a c-section.'

'Well, I was planning to reinstate you at JOPS now the dust has settled, but you can't be on active duty now. You may as well stay with the FCO until you go on maternity leave.' Jonathan shuffled some paperwork on his desk unnecessarily. 'We'll sub in Gemma to take your place here, effective immediately.'

'Gemma? The one from MI5?' She failed to keep the jealousy out of her voice. Their most recent recruit had the makings of an outstanding JOPS officer, but Vicky didn't like the idea of a young, ambitious spook getting comfortable with her caseload while she was desk-bound for another six months.

'She's young, but with a bit of guidance she'll be fine. And she hasn't pissed off the boss lately, either.'

Vicky didn't reply. Jonathan's scowl was replaced by a look of horror as a new thought occurred to him.

'It's not . . . *his?*'

She felt herself redden. 'No, sir. It's . . . well, I met someone else, not long after . . . it put things into perspective, sir. We're very happy.'

'Does he know, the new chap? About what you do?'

'No. He thinks I'm an art appraiser. And I'm happy to keep it that way.'

'Are you sure? If you really are planning on returning to work after the baby's born, it might be better for you if you had a bit of support at home.'

When would he understand that she wasn't some fragile flower in danger of being squashed underfoot by the prospect of having a child? 'Thank you, sir, but I'm fine. If I decide differently at any point, I'll let you know.'

Jonathan nodded and stood to signal that the meeting was over. 'Well, good luck.'

She stood to leave. 'Yes, sir. Thank you, sir.'

He stared at her belly. 'An art dealer, you say?'

'Appraiser.'

'Hmm.' Jonathan scratched his chin. 'Second thoughts, maybe we should find you a real job, as one of these appraisers, so you can stay below the radar altogether.

Especially once you, you know, have a—' He made the shape of a bump with his arms. 'If anyone catches a whiff that you're expecting it might make life very difficult in the future.'

'I don't see why it would. It's only a bloody baby.' Vicky wondered if he'd be saying the same thing if she was a man.

'I just thought you might be concerned about the safety of your new family, Victoria,' Jonathan said dryly. 'The information gets into the wrong hands, you never know how they'll use it.'

She worried for a moment that he might be right, but dismissed the notion. She couldn't be the only spy to ever have a baby; there had to be protocols in place. She just had to read up on it, maybe take some time to go and see HR. But what she wasn't going to do was give her boss the satisfaction of thinking he'd rankled her.

'I think I'll be fine, sir.'

Jonathan shrugged. 'Well then, stay at the FCO. And if – or rather *when* – we go live again with the Russians, we'll have to consider how to integrate you back onto the case.'

'Thank you, sir. I'll be ready.'

In the end, things had happened just as differently as Jonathan predicted. After a difficult first few months of motherhood, Vicky finally returned to Gilbert House when Ollie was six months old, cleared for duty again by the JOPS doctor as well as their psych evaluator and PT officer. She'd made sure she was ready to go straight back into the field; she'd worked her job at the FCO up until she went on maternity leave and knew already that she couldn't handle the idea of sitting at a desk all day when she went back.

The drudge of it was so depressing; she'd rather be at home with the baby. But it quickly became obvious that a return to full-time operational duty wasn't on the cards. Trying to juggle agent handling, covert surveillance or sniper duty with looking after a baby was completely impossible; and besides, she got the distinct feeling she wasn't welcome. She'd hoped that time would heal the sick feeling she got every time she thought about Adam being shot in the back of the head, and she'd assumed, a year and a half down the road, that everyone else at JOPS would have forgiven, if not forgotten, what happened. It was the nature of the job, after all; you lost people – people you liked, people you trusted, good people – and you made your peace with it. But from the way people looked at her, the stilted conversations and sideways glances, it was clear she hadn't been forgiven for letting her personal feelings cloud her professional judgement. People didn't trust her. And you couldn't do this job if people didn't trust you.

She needed to talk to someone desperately. Not Jonathan: he would be unlikely to show any sympathy over the set of circumstances she'd got herself into, and consider it a sign of weakness if she admitted it was upsetting her. Vicky toyed with telling Chris the truth about her job, just to relieve some of the pressure, but she couldn't bring herself to do it. There'd never been a right time; they met not long after the Russian case collapsed and everything had been so raw that she'd found the lie easier than the truth: that she'd got a man killed because of her own selfish stupidity. Later, when they knew each other better, she could never find the right moment and after a while she convinced herself it didn't matter. So what if Chris thought she spent her life studying fusty old bits of canvas? It was a cover story, sure, but she'd graduated in Art History before she was recruited to MI6 and then JOPS, so, in that sense, she wasn't really lying . . . and now, with a small child in tow, she was even less inclined to reveal her real job and risk Chris loving her less because of it. Besides, whatever Jonathan said, it was easier for her to protect him and the baby this way. The less Chris knew, the less interesting he would be to anyone wanting to harm her.

She thought about resigning from the service altogether. It was, really, the best solution: she wouldn't have to lie anymore, her family would be safe, and it seemed like no one wanted her around anyway. But it was hard to imagine walking away from a career she loved and had worked so hard for. She really did want to be back in the field, where she belonged. In the end, she decided that she simply needed more time. Ollie needed her too much at the moment, but one day he'd be older and at school and leaving him would be easier . . . and, eventually, she could make things right with her team. She met with Jonathan who was surprisingly helpful, and they agreed she would go on indefinite leave and return to JOPS properly, as and when she was ready and able. It was with a certain amount of sadness that she saw the relief in his eyes as she left.

She hadn't counted on having more kids. Or on the fact that they needed her more, not less, as they got older. And she hadn't even considered just how much she would love them, or how much fear would sit in the pit of her stomach every time she thought of not being there for them. She stuffed the burner phone into her handbag and headed to the kitchen to torch the note over the gas hob. Even though she knew that there was always the risk of being recalled from inactive service in response to a direct operational requirement, she'd convinced herself years ago that it would never happen. But maybe she'd been kept buoyant by the idea that it might . . . She held the note until the flames reached her fingers and then dropped it onto the metal surface. It was frightening and thrilling at the same time, to notice how automatic the action was. It had been so long since Vicky had thought about being a spy.

JOPS wanted her back. And the temptation was enormous, to say yes, to feel like she was back where she belonged again and to be truly herself for the first time in so many years. But what did 'being herself' even mean? She wasn't the same person she used to be. Having a family had meant she was forced to make changes, but she'd got used to them, and, these days, found comfort in the rhythm and security of family life. Everything about her had softened around the edges in the past fourteen years – her body, her mind, and her soul. Going back to a job where everything was so . . . critical . . . the idea of starting over again with fake back stories, stakeouts, and clandestine meetings left her feeling excited but exhausted, and while her pulse quickened just thinking about the thrill of the chase, she wasn't sure she had either the time or the energy to resume living life as a split personality. It was hard enough these days remembering not to swear in front of the kids.

She scooped up the ashes of the note from the hob and rinsed them down the sink before heading to the living room. On the TV, Peppa's family jumped in muddy puddles and giggled to the strains of the familiar theme tune. As she watched James leaping about with delight along with the characters on the screen, her decision was made. To just expect her to drop everything and come running was typical of the JOPS, but a hell of a presumption. *Pursue the objective, outsmart everyone, and take control.* Well, two could play that game.

'Come on, James, time to go and get Evie,' she said, ignoring his protests as she swept him up from his spot. She grabbed her handbag, hoped he didn't need the toilet, and left the house.

'Mummy, where are we going?' James asked from the back seat as she turned on to Putney High Street and headed out of town. 'Where's Evie?'

'Mummy's just got to run a little errand first,' Vicky said, glancing back in the mirror. James smiled at her and she smiled back, although really she'd been looking to check she wasn't being followed. It occurred to her that the JOPS must have had tabs on her for a while before they made contact. What had they seen, where had they been, and how much of her life had they dug into, to make their decision to recall her? Was it weeks, or months, or years? *They'd been in her home.* A wave of resentment boiled up inside her. They could have rung the bloody doorbell.

She drove a short way down the A3, swung into the car park behind the big Asda, and pulled up by the recycling bins. Leaving the engine running, she removed the SIM card from the burner phone and cut it in half with a pair of nail scissors from her bag, threw the pieces in a couple of drink cans and stuck them in one of the bins. Then she placed the phone under the wheel of the car and, to James's amusement, pulled forward a few inches to crush it, then backed up and buried the remains deep in one of the trainers Chris had worn for paintballing. She opened the hatch of the clothes bank and dropped them in, along with a set of Evie's outgrown dresses and her own grotty black vest top, still splattered with yellow paint. She hesitated slightly before grabbing the combat pants, then stuffed them in as well. There would be no need for combat pants, none at all. Half a dozen wine bottles and a stack of pizza boxes later and they were on their way, back up the A3 to pick up Evie. And that, she decided, was that.

It was Laura's birthday and the girls were going out for a drink that night, so when Chris got home from work the handover took place with the usual chaotic haste.

'Evie needs to do some piano practice before she goes to bed, James needs a bath and Ollie's due home at eight,' Vicky shouted over the hairdryer.

Chris gave her a peck on the cheek. 'Leave it with me,' he said. 'Just go and have a good time with the girls.'

She stopped the dryer for a minute and smiled at him.

'You're a good man, Charlie Brown,' she said.

'I know.'

'You know I love you, right?'

'Of course.'

'Good. Just checking.'

Evie's voice floated up the stairs. 'Mum, James just did a poo.'

James appeared at the foot of the stairs.

'Wipe my bottom please, Mummy.'

'Just get out of here,' Chris said, heading to the rescue. Vicky smiled gratefully and put the finishing touches to her hair. She eased her wedges on, and then stopped mid-second foot . . . maybe it would be better to swap them for flats in case she needed to move quickly. She growled, annoyed at herself again for slipping so quickly into old patterns of thinking. What would she need to run from? She shoved her heel inside the wedge, turned out the bedroom light and trod carefully through the debris of toys, books, and clothes scattered liberally on the stairs.

It was a gorgeous September evening; a cool breeze blew as the sun went down in a blaze of autumnal glory. She slipped on a red mac she'd bought years ago at a Top Shop pop-up party, before pop-ups were even a thing. On the back of a younger woman, it used to draw a fair bit of attention in a city teeming with stock colours of black, navy, and grey, but these days she could be naked under it and no one would notice. Just as well she wasn't though, given it was a little on the snug side now. She decided against doing the buttons up and grabbed her keys.

'See you later, love you!' she said, and shut the door. She made her way down the road, striding purposefully towards Putney High Street in her wedge heels and making a deliberate effort not to look around her. The van on the corner was *just* a van on the corner. The girl on her phone was *just* a girl on her phone. No one was watching her. Chris hadn't suspected anything was wrong. She'd reached a good decision and would stick to it. She felt guilt and relief wash over her and tried to ignore the tiny shudder of paranoia as a man in a suit walked past and caught her eye.

*

'So, William called Becky up and started offering her "advice" about how to manage the Christmas Fair,' Kate said, taking a swig of her beer. She put her arm in the air to signal a passing barman and gestured to Vicky. 'Want another one?'

Vicky looked at the empty jug of sangria in front of her and nodded. 'Go on then.'

'Careful, Vics, that sangria is stronger than it looks,' Becky said.

'I need it, having to listen to all this PTA talk,' she replied. The girls all laughed, even though she was only half-joking. She took the last glug of her drink and all the ice fell onto her face.

'That's karma for being a snarky cow,' Laura giggled. She turned to Becky. 'So, what did you say to William?'

'Well, I tried to be polite—'

'Too polite,' interrupted Kate. 'I don't know why you didn't just tell him to piss off. I think, after all these years, you know what you're doing.'

Becky and Kate had both served on the PTA since their children first walked through the door. It was a full-time job for Becky, who'd been Vice-Chair for almost five years before she took the Chair at the start of that term. Kate, a consummate politician and master events organiser, had been a class rep for both her children twice already. Vicky still couldn't quite believe they put up with William all that time – or how much work they put in, and yet they never, ever, asked for anything back, not even thanks.

'He is such a prick,' Vicky said, pouring herself a drink from the newly arrived jug of sangria. 'He always has been. I wouldn't mind, it's not exactly rocket science, is it?' She looked at her friends and realised she'd just massively insulted them. 'What I mean is, it's not like you aren't absolutely capable of doing the job.'

'We could still do with more help though. What about it, Vics?' Becky challenged. 'It's not rocket science, just like you said.'

Vicky took a long sip of her sangria. She wasn't entirely sure she should have ordered another jug. Things were going a bit blurry.

'To be honest, I *had* been thinking about going back to work,' she said. She wished she could be really honest about it. It would be such a relief to tell someone about what had happened and ask their advice. *But then she'd have to kill them.* She sniggered.

'Assuming you aren't actually laughing at the idea of getting a job, it's not the worst idea in the world,' Laura said. She'd escaped the PTA altogether when her daughter moved on to secondary school and she had since returned to work as a receptionist at the local dentist. 'I mean, I wouldn't say I've hit the big time quite yet – I'm earning about the same as a teenager in Pizza Hut. But at least it keeps Steve from moaning at me about what the hell I do all day. And, you know, the kids see that their mum works too: feminism and all that.'

Working as an underpaid skivvy clearing up magazines to the heady stench of antiseptic and the sound of children screaming in pain didn't feel like feminism to Vicky. But it was probably a bit closer to what Gloria Steinem had in mind than the PTA.

'Yeah, but with three kids and no family nearby?' Kate said. 'It doesn't make financial sense, Vicky, not while James is still little. You'll spend more money on childcare than you earn.'

'It's not about the money, though,' Laura said.

'Of course it's about the money,' Kate said. 'Why would you go back to work otherwise? It's not like any of us are rolling in it. We can't all be Matisse Kozlovsky.'

'Thank God.' Vicky chuckled. 'She's living proof money can't buy you happiness. Although I'd quite like her boobs.'

'I'm sure she could tell you where she got them,' Kate cupped her chest and they all laughed.

'Well I know for me, having a job is about the satisfaction of doing something for myself,' Laura persisted.

'Are you saying the PTA isn't that?' Becky's shoulders tensed.

'No,' Laura replied, 'Not at all. I just prefer doing something that's just for me – without the kids involved.'

'Easier said than done when you keep on having them,' Kate grinned in Vicky's direction.

Vicky acknowledged the joke with a rueful smile of her own. 'If I'm honest, I'm with Laura here: it would be nice to go back to work,' she said, her voice a touch wistful. 'But you're right, Kate, it doesn't make sense, logistically or financially. And I mean, I'd hardly win Employee of the Year right now. I'd be useless. I'm so out of practice and I'd be worried about the kids all the time.' She tried to imagine herself defusing a bomb without crying and failed miserably.

'Didn't you used to be an art dealer?' Laura looked confused.

Vicky stared into her glass. 'Appraiser.'

'Well it's not like the technology has moved on, or it's too physically demanding to do in your forties. I would have thought it was the ideal job to go back to.'

Vicky couldn't argue with that logic. Laura might have

a different view of things if she knew the truth. 'I'm not sure I'd want to go back to my old job,' she glossed. 'It was pretty full-on, I'd be at the beck and call of clients all the time and go from wanting time away from the kids to never seeing them.' She took another sip of her drink. 'I just want to do something, I suppose.'

'Well then, join the PTA!' Kate and Becky cried triumphantly. Everyone laughed, and Vicky felt herself weaken. Really, what was the harm? William wasn't there anymore to make her think murderous thoughts. The kids were all out of the house. And she'd just thrown a job offer from JOPS into the recycling.

'*Alright*. Fine – I'll do it.'

'Yay, that's great! Our girl is on the PTA. I say cheers to that.' Kate raised her glass.

'Cheers!' Vicky drained her drink again before getting up from the chair in the style of a zero-gravity astronaut. The room was beginning to spin, and her words were slurring.

'Actually, ladies, I think I might have to call it a night. Becky was right, those sangrias are pretty strong.'

'Nooooo!' they chorused.

Don't be a wet blanket!' Laura shouted.

'We'll all go. We can share a taxi.' Kate made a half-hearted attempt at waving down a waiter to get the bill.

'No, it's okay – you girls stay and finish your drinks. I could do with the fresh air.'

She left them at the bar and lurched up the high street, wobbling on her wedges and wishing she'd worn flats after all. Halfway home, the sangria hit her with its full force and she threw up in the bushes. She made it back to the house and sat for a few minutes on the sofa, the room spinning. What a day. She'd walked away from her career at JOPS for the second time in her life and had instead signed up to something so easy and safe it made sitting on the sofa look like it needed a risk assessment. But it was a good thing, wasn't it? The past should stay in the past; she wasn't that person anymore.

So why did she feel so full of regret? Could she honestly say she didn't want to go back and prove herself, to fix what she broke? Not that anything she did could ever get Adam back. Nausea threatened to overwhelm her again and she closed her eyes and tried to wish herself unconscious. Maybe the easy option was all she *should* be okay with. She had other priorities now, other people to think about. For God's sake, she was a forty-six-year-old mother of three who couldn't keep a jug of sangria down, not James bloody Bond.

Vicky woke to the sounds of the bin men crashing and banging outside the window. She sat up slowly from the sofa, head pounding, and gulped the fresh water sitting across from her on the coffee table. Upstairs, she could hear Chris in the shower – he'd obviously been down and found her. She winced, half in pain, half in shame, and hobbled into the kitchen to make a cup of tea for both of them. Her hands were shaking, and she felt distinctly queasy at the sight of a dirty pan soaking in the sink.

Not sure if she'd be able to keep down a bit of toast, she decided it was probably a good idea to try anyway. She popped a slice of bread into the toaster and looked at the clock. Shit. She'd never get James and Evie dropped off in time. Chris would have to take Evie this morning, and she'd walk James to nursery.

Ollie appeared at that moment, bleary-eyed, dressed for school and with his rucksack slung over one shoulder.

'Morning, Ollie,' she croaked, thankful her teenage son wouldn't notice the state she was in, or care.

'See you later, Mum,' came the reply. He disappeared again, clutching two breakfast bars and a banana. She shuddered as the front door slammed and on cue heard James calling out for her. She cleared her throat and tried speaking again.

'Coming, sweetheart. Just a minute.'

She pulled the teabags out of the mugs and grabbed one to take with her. As she started up the stairs her husband appeared at the top, wrapped in a towel, the smell of soap and deodorant and aftershave wafting towards her and making her feel fifty times as unclean as she already did.

'Big night?' He grinned.

'What gave you that idea?'

'How were the girls?'

'Fine,' she said, 'although I was the first one to leave. God knows what state they were in—' She groaned. 'Oh God. I said I'd do the PTA . . .'

Chris's grin got even wider. 'Well, I think that's great,' he said. 'Especially now that tosser, Will, is out of the way.' He took a breath as she wafted past him and whistled. 'Will PTA meetings involve quite as much alcohol each time?'

'Is it that bad?'

'Just don't breathe on anyone. Seriously, though, I think it's great that you're doing something again now James is at nursery.'

'Well, the PTA is a good place to start, but, to be honest, I'd quite like to go back to work.'

'Would you?' Chris looked surprised. 'I mean, you've always said you were happy at home.'

'I think we'd both agree that sometimes it's not all it's cracked up to be.'

On cue, James appeared from his room with pen all over his hands and face.

'Mummy, I did a picture,' he said, holding up a blackened piece of paper with several holes worn through.

'That's beautiful, sweetie,' she said, and looked at Chris. 'I rest my case.'

'Fair point.' Chris chuckled.

She guided James to the bathroom to minimise the pen stains. Her head was pounding. 'I guess I'd better attempt to get ready and get James to nursery. Will you do Evie?'

'Sure,' Chris said. 'Can you pick up that parcel from the Post Office for me today though? I think it was something I ordered for Ollie, but it would save me the trip on Saturday morning.'

'I'll do it after I've been to the supermarket.' What a fun morning she had stretching ahead. Vicky took a sip of her tea and mentally prepared for the day. It was going to be a long one.

Chapter Three

She dropped James off at nursery, making excuses to avoid getting caught in conversation with the younger mums hanging out in the reception area. It wasn't that she didn't like them; they seemed nice enough, but her years of wanting to discuss toddlers and their various quirks were far behind her, and she always felt the odd one out. Plus, today in particular, their effervescence was making her feel quite ill.

She walked down to the high street and grabbed a coffee and croissant to go from the hipster-ish place on the corner. A few of the mums from Evie's class were in there and gave her a wave; she remained hopeful she didn't look as bad as she felt, but didn't make any moves to engage. The first rule of the middle-aged hangover, obviously, was that you were guaranteed to run into as many people as possible who you knew while suffering from it.

A message came in from Becky reminding her about the first PTA meeting. Vicky sighed. From spook to school mum. How had her life drifted so far off course? She stuffed the croissant in her mouth and half-heartedly beat the crumbs from her chest. There was no objective, that was the problem. There was just stuff to get done before the kids got home from school, and dinner to cook, and homework to help with and laundry and it was one relentless journey from a fixed point – childbirth – to nowhere. She gulped at her coffee. Maybe the objective was simple: to raise your kids well and be happy. But it seemed too big, too broad. She still needed to find validation beyond that.

It was unlikely she'd find it at Sainsbury's, but she still had to go. Resigned to her lot, she decided to skip the shower for now and get her chores over and done with. She drove straight to the supermarket and managed to find a space mercifully close to the entrance. It was unusually quiet in the car park. She was glad; it meant fewer people to negotiate. Her headache was slowly dissipating, though, and there was the faint glimmer of hope that the remainder of her morning would pass without incident and that the sights and smells of the fish counter wouldn't make her too nauseous.

Twice on her way round the aisles she felt queasy, this time with the prickle of presence rather than alcohol. A young woman dressed in innocuous grey athleisurewear walked by. It was the third time she had been in Vicky's proximity. Was she following her? Vicky did a few double-backs for fish fingers and tinned tomatoes, but then saw the woman was at the checkout bagging her goods and decided she was being paranoid. In any case, if the woman was following her, she was having the most impossibly boring morning.

At the Post Office collection point there was the usual assortment of people in the line, all looking as if the happiness had been sucked out of them on the way through the door. Vicky joined the queue and waited for her turn. What was it about the Post Office, in particular, that made people who were probably perfectly normal and nice in real life, so utterly miserable? Even the man working at the desk wore the contemptuous scowl of someone heinously wronged. A glance at his co-worker in the back told the same story.

She reached the front of the queue. Her headache was coming back, and she needed the loo. She gave a weak smile to the man behind the desk.

'Got your ID?'

'Yes, good morning, here you go.'

He raised his eyebrow at Vicky's driving licence – it was a nine-year-old photo and definitely time for a new one. 'Got the delivery card?'

'Here it is – oh, there's two.' She could have sworn Chris only gave her one earlier. The Post Office worker turned without another word and disappeared into the parcel room. She waited, watching herself on the TV behind the counter. The security camera pointed down at an angle that made her realise she *really* needed to get her roots done.

The man came back and pushed a package and an envelope, wrapped in elastic bands, across the counter.

'Sign here please.'

Vicky looked at the envelope. It was addressed to her. So she wasn't just imagining it. The woman in the supermarket must have planted the delivery card in her bag.

'Oh, no, there's some mistake: this isn't for me.' Vicky didn't want any part in this. She pushed the envelope back towards the man, who looked at it, and at the cards that she had given him, and at her driving licence.

'You are Victoria Turnbull?'

35

'Yes, but—'

'Then it's yours. Sign please.'

He turned away with the receipt and left her standing there, alone and yet not alone, as the camera recorded her movements, watched her pick up the bundle, and walk slowly away. Back in the car she removed the elastic bands. The top parcel was for Chris. The second item, an envelope, had her name and address printed, but no other markings. She tried to keep her breathing steady. Another message could mean only one thing: her boss was ignoring her ignoring him, and if she wanted him to stop, she was going to have to find out what he wanted.

She checked out of the windows for any sign of movement, then eased her finger under the opening of the envelope and pulled out the paperwork. Her final JOPS report spilt out; the one that had gone so wrong. A bunch of photos were clipped to the top right-hand side and she flicked through them. Her heart skipped a beat as she saw a photo of Anatoli Ivanov: Russian art dealer, her asset, and her ex-lover.

She looked more closely at the photo, taken, at a guess, around the time they first met. His blond hair was freshly cut, fringe left slightly long; the sides sheared to the shape of his face, accentuating his chiselled cheekbones and grey-blue eyes.

She felt a kind of detached affection, mixed with mild curiosity, followed quickly by exasperation. First they break into her house, now they send her photos of ex-boyfriends. Anyone with a basic understanding of the human psychology – and anyone with a basic understanding of Vicky – would know it wasn't the way to win her over. She'd spent a long time coming to terms with everything she'd done; the lies she'd told and the secrets she had kept – was still keeping –

from the people she loved. And now, fourteen years later, JOPS decide to open up Pandora's box and let the ghosts out.

Seeing Anatoli's photo again after all this time was strange, though . . . despite herself, Vicky flicked through the report. The words sounded odd to her now, the formal language depersonalising the situation, boiling things down to operational error. She shook her head, remembering it all like it was yesterday. It was all *very* personal at the time.

From the beginning of their relationship, she and Anatoli had a chemistry which had tempted her to go beyond the usual conventions of asset recruitment. They'd become lovers and friends; even at the time, she knew she was treading on dangerous ground. When she revealed who she really was, he'd been so angry: he couldn't get over the idea that she'd used him to get what she wanted, put him in harm's way, and, worst of all, that she'd suckered him into a relationship that was, in his eyes, nothing more than a huge lie. Anatoli left London and left her; upset, she neglected to pick up on intel that would have alerted her to a leak, and their JOPS undercover operative, Adam, had been killed in Moscow shortly after. The operation folded, the department was in disgrace and Vicky even more so. She'd been put on desk duty immediately and threatened with an internal investigation. The whole thing had been one huge, embarrassing mess.

Vicky closed up the report. Jonathan been right all along, of course. Russians very rarely betrayed their own, despite what you see in the movies. She'd been so naïve, so over-confident in her own abilities. If she could do it all again, things would be very different. She traced her fingers over Anatoli's photo one more time. Where did he end up? Was he married, with children, or still a bachelor with a penchant for English art appraisers? Or was he dead, another body to add to the list? Maybe he was still making a tidy living working for Russian oligarchs and Saudi princes, and they wanted to try and recruit him again. *Surely* Jonathan wouldn't pick her for the job though? He'd be in for a shock if he thought a forty-six-year-old in double Spanx and a granny bra would seduce an asset when the twenty-something version hadn't been able to.

She stuffed the photo and reports back into the envelope. She couldn't do all this again. She would call Jonathan on Monday and tell him that, whatever it was, they needed to find someone else. She'd get rid of the paperwork over the weekend, and that would be that.

At pick-up time, she was waiting with James for Evie to appear when there was a tap on her shoulder.

'And how were we feeling this morning?' Kate's grin told her she had already anticipated the answer.

Vicky made a face.

'Same here. Oh my god, though, you should have seen the state of you trying to leave the bar. It's a miracle you made it home.'

'Barely, to be honest. I threw up, then fell asleep on the sofa.'

Kate laughed; a great big belly laugh that caught the attention of the mums all around before the other women went back to their various conversations.

'Anyway, I'm glad we got you drunk enough to say yes to the PTA. Good news – we got another new recruit today as well,' Kate said, glancing back at the crowd of gossiping mums and waving at someone. 'A rather unexpected one . . .'

Matisse sashayed over.

'Hi, Matisse. I was just telling Vicky you're joining us on the PTA.'

'Oui, yes, I am,' she replied, giving them both a stiff smile. 'I decided that now we are settled and the house refurbishment is finished, I want to do something more with my time.'

'Well, I know Becky is really pleased to have you on board,' Kate said. 'All these new recruits! It's like buses, isn't it, Vicky?'

Matisse looked confused. 'Buses?'

'Yes, you know, they all come at once . . .'

'I never took a bus before.'

'How could you live in London and never get on a bus?' Vicky was incredulous.

'It is not so difficult. Sacha has his driver for the days I do not want to drive.'

Of course he did. Vicky exchanged glances with Kate. No one knew what Sacha did for a living and though Vicky had a couple of ideas, none of them were good.

The school doors opened and Dmitri bounded towards them, saving everyone from any further stilted conversation. Matisse reached out to him and gave him an enormous hug. It was the first time Vicky had ever noticed her smiling.

'Bonjour!' she said to him, bending down to hold his face. 'My golden boy! How was your day?'

'Is Papa home? Do you have a snack?' Dmitri rummaged in Matisse's Hermès bag, looking for treats.

Matisse switched to Russian. 'Papa is making a deal in his office today, and he says it is very important to stay quiet when we get home, or he will be angry.'

'Oh, okay.' Dmitri's face fell. Vicky's mind drifted absently to the photo of Anatoli, and to the file she'd pushed under the passenger seat of the car earlier. It was a long time since she'd heard Russian spoken out loud.

Matisse switched back to English to address Vicky and Kate. 'Well, we have to go. Have a nice weekend.' She waved farewell and, as her shirt sleeve rode up, Vicky noticed the faint impression of a series of finger-shaped bruises around her upper arm. When his wife didn't do as she was told, how angry did Sacha get, exactly?

It was none of her business. And yet, the Kozlovsky family obviously had secrets they didn't want anyone knowing about. She would keep an eye on Matisse from now on. Vicky felt adrenaline kick in at the idea and found herself thinking about Anatoli again. What had he done – or what was he about to do? Her heart sped up and her head filled with possibilities.

'Erm, hello, Mum?' Evie was standing in front of her, waiting for some sort of sign of acknowledgement.

'Sorry, darling, hi, I didn't even see you.' Vicky waved at the teacher standing by the door and grabbed Evie's bulging rucksack from her. 'How was your day?'

'It was great, I got a golden scroll in assembly today for my writing. And me and Isobel are going to be playing in the netball team next week as well, Miss Burnwood told us today in P.E.'

'Wow, that's great, Evie,' Vicky said. 'Well done. When's the match?'

'It's next Wednesday after school. We're getting a bus there and back, but Miss Burnwood said you can come and watch too, if you like. Where's James?'

'Well I'd love to come if that's okay. I'll have to bring

James too, of course.' She registered Evie's question. 'Where *is* James?'

'I just said that,' Evie said, looking around.

Vicky's eyes darted towards the open gate where parents were leaving hand in hand with their kids. No sign. She felt herself panic. They'd been in the house. They'd found her at the supermarket. What if they'd been trying to warn her of something . . . what if James had been —

'Mum, look, he's playing in the playground; I can see him just over there.' Evie pointed, and Vicky saw with some relief that her little boy was giggling and running about on the padded green area by the climbing frame. She exhaled and waved at him.

'Can I see if Isobel's mum is coming too?' Evie said.

'To what?'

'To the netball match, Mum. God you're so *embarrassing* when you're being dumb.'

'Watch your manners, Evie. I don't appreciate your tone.'

Evie refused to offer an apology, folded her arms, and stalked across the playground towards James, leaving Vicky to trail after her.

'Evie!' James's chubby face lit up at the sight of his sister and he ran over to them both. To his delight, Evie picked him up and swung him around.

Vicky couldn't help herself; she loved them even when they were being revolting. She loved them more than anything. 'James, sweetie, don't run off to play in future without telling Mummy where you're going.' She gave his hair a ruffle. It still had that lovely baby-soft feel to it. 'And Evie?' Evie gave her a sideways glance as Vicky moved to make peace. 'I'm really proud of you, making the netball team, and for your golden scroll.'

'Thanks, Mum.' Dispute over, they all walked hand in hand to the car. She unlocked the doors and lifted James into his seat before going around the other side and risking a kiss on her daughter's cheek. As Vicky started the engine, Evie spoke again from the back.

'What did you do today, Mum?'

'Oh, the usual groceries and stuff,' she said. She didn't mention the bit about being recalled to the Secret Service while she was on the toilet.

'Katie says her mum's going back to work after Christmas,' Evie said.

'Good for her.'

'I heard you talking about going back to work, with Dad. Why don't you go back to your old job, that you did before we were born?'

'Because there's three of you to think about, and my job before I had you was pretty full-on.'

'Can't you just do it for three days a week or, like, just work when we're at school? Or work from home? Loads of other mums do stuff like that.'

Vicky briefly imagined trying to negotiate a Secret Service job-share. 'I don't know, Evie. It's not as easy as it sounds, to do the kind of job I used to do with you three kids to look after as well.' She signalled and pulled out of the parking space. 'But in the meantime, I'm doing the PTA.'

'Isobel's mum doesn't like the PTA; she says it's for people with nothing better to do.'

'Well, Isobel's mum doesn't know everything,' Vicky said, slamming on the indicator with so much force she thought the lever would fly off.

'I know, Mum. Calm down.'

Vicky paused and tried to think of another way to explain things to her daughter.

'The PTA is an important part of the school life, and the people that do it give up their time because they are good people who want to help,' she said.

'I get it, Mum.' There was a pause before Evie spoke again, in a hesitant voice. 'If you're doing the PTA, does that mean you're going to be in school more?'

Vicky sighed. 'You won't even know I'm there, Evie. I promise.'

In the ten minutes or so it took to get home through the swathes of after-school traffic, she thought about her conversations with Evie, with Chris, and the girls last night, and all the feelings she'd had since last Thursday when she'd first got the message.

Whatever she chose to tell herself, there was no doubt she was tempted by the idea, intrigued to know why JOPS wanted her, and flattered they'd asked. The PTA seemed a poor substitute for the Secret Service, as far as doing something meaningful with her time was concerned. But the problem remained; that her job was never – could never be – part time. It was the most full-on, full-time job you could get. It would mean years of her life wiped clean and re-invented. Lying to everyone she loved about who she was and what she did. Being constantly vigilant in case someone was out to get her or her family . . . the thought niggled her, that maybe someone *was* out to get her family. Maybe not Anatoli himself, but someone associated with him, who'd found out about her somehow and was close by. She couldn't bear the thought of putting Chris and the children in danger.

The art world was full of crooks of all shapes and sizes – drug smuggling and money laundering were the usual points of entry – but she'd gained information that led to arrests for far greater, more gruesome crimes committed by all sorts of terrible people. Anatoli's refusal to help and the disappearance of the Russian crime ring she'd been targeting . . . she'd been lucky, he'd obviously never breathed a word to the wrong people about who she really was – but it occurred to her for the first time, that she might not always be so fortunate. Crooks had long memories. But surely Jonathan would have been explicit about a threat? In which case, it might be that he really did want her for an operation.

She could be kicking ass again. She nearly laughed out loud. It was more likely she'd get her arse kicked. How could she go back to being a spook? She'd be a laughing stock at best and, at worst, dead. Her daughter wasn't even ten and found her embarrassing. Anyone her age should be getting their kicks from school assemblies and too much sangria on a school night, not chasing terrorists and arms dealers. And, yet, JOPS had sought her out. They'd contacted *her*.

By the time she pulled up at the house, curiosity and ego had got the better of her. She grabbed the envelope from under the front seat.

'Evie, can you get James a drink of water and get yourself a snack? I just need to use the bathroom,' she called on her way up the stairs. She shut the bathroom door and went to the ancient medicine cabinet that hung over the sink. She pressed the two light switches under the cabinet simultaneously and a thin A4-sized panel shot out to the side of the cabinet. Amazed it still worked after all these years, Vicky blew the false back of the cabinet free of dust, dead insects and who knew what else. She placed the envelope inside and slid the panel back, flushed the toilet and went downstairs.

'Who wants pizza for tea?' she asked and put the oven on. Her daughter might not want her around anymore. But JOPS did. It wouldn't do any harm to hear what her boss had to say. She got a flutter of excitement at the idea of being undercover again. Ironic, really, after fifteen years away, that she'd be better at it now than ever. After all, what's more invisible than a middle-aged housewife going about her daily routine?

Chapter Four

Very few people outside of the security services knew the Joint Operations Intelligence Services even existed. According to all official sources, MI5 worked to protect domestic interests and MI6 took out threats from abroad. They were two different entities with two very different approaches who did their very best to stay out of each other's way. No one mentioned the small but extremely effective department that sat between the two. This could be mainly attributed to sour grapes; despite JOPS being considered as a uniting force for good by the few senior government officials who created the department in the first place, MI5 and MI6 were both bitter about the best of their operatives being ripped away from them and did their level best to ignore its very existence.

JOPS was certainly the more successful department of the three as far as retaining anonymity was concerned, by a long way. Saddled with the worst acronym ever, it lacked the street cred that Five and Six enjoyed; as a result, it was never the subject of any TV shows or movies, and the general public had mostly never heard of it. The closest it came to a big reveal was in April 1996 when the Queen Mother unveiled a memorial in Westminster Abbey honouring a bunch of fallen operatives who hadn't actually fallen at all, but were, in fact, a list of JOPS officers working so deep undercover they were presumed dead by the rest of the world. The plaque gave everyone cause for concern until it could be removed and melted down, but by some miracle (or other, darker powers at work), it never caught the imagination of the media or enemy states. Indeed, JOPS was, by design, a forgettable entity, sitting in the forgettable depths of the Watford countryside, far away from the more visible wings of the Secret Services. And from there, it operated out of sight, out of mind, taking assignments and working across borders and boundaries, with surprisingly little interference from anyone.

Jonathan Cornelieu waited in his office in the underground bunker below Gilbert House, watching Victoria on the security cameras as she made her way through the hotel car park towards the formal gardens and wooden area beyond. The building itself was a stately Victorian manor that had originally been home to a famous poet and playwright. Following the death of his son in the late 1960s, it was sold off and did a stint as a rehab centre before becoming a Best Western Hotel that served a very decent afternoon tea. Since 1947 it had also housed various branches of one intelligence agency or another in a secret underground complex on the edge of the estate, disguised as an electricity substation. On its formation, JOPS had assumed occupancy, and was still there thirty years later.

The inhabitants and employees of the house had always been very good about it; those that weren't in the employ of military intelligence to begin with were carefully vetted and happy to sign the Official Secrets Act, and often came from Thames House or Vauxhall Cross to take a break from city life and serve scones in a country house while the JOPS ops went about their day far beneath them.

The cameras continued to catch Victoria as she strode onwards down the tree-lined path, past the pond, towards the metal gate that sat within the perimeter of barbed-wire fencing surrounding the station. Jonathan watched as she stopped outside the gate marked DANGER. LIVE ELECTRICITY. DO NOT ENTER. It swung open as she was buzzed in and after one final check behind her, she walked through the deceptively decrepit door of the old brick substation.

Jonathan's office was down a long flight of stairs and at the end of the corridor, in the same place it had been since he'd taken the job two decades previously. Not the most luxurious of offices; his peers in the city had views of the river while he was stuck in a concrete bunker at the arse end of nowhere. But it was home to him.

The clutter of fax machines and oversized desktop computers Victoria would remember had been replaced some years back with the minimalistic trappings of twenty-first century life: slimline monitors and three phones graced his desk, and an obligatory Nespresso machine sat on the sideboard where the daily papers used to be. The shelves that used to creak with reports and reviews were now stocked with photos of Jonathan's prolific family – a family which seemed to expand with each passing year. Much like Jonathan. He was rather more thick set than the last time he had seen Victoria, with puffy jowls and creases around his eyes. His wife had bought him a dog a few years ago to get him out of his chair once in a while, but he wasn't convinced it had made much difference.

Victoria appeared at the door, and Jonathan took off his glasses and stood in greeting. They said hello and shook hands, and then sat, each assessing the other in a million tiny ways. He may have changed physically over the years, but now she was facing him and not a figure on a security camera or trussed up in combat trousers and a paintball gun vest, he could see Victoria was most definitely not the same person who walked into his office two decades ago either. She was nervous, vulnerable, and unpolished; her hair was brushed but not freshly washed, her shoes were on the scruffy side. She was still wearing that bloody red raincoat too, even though it didn't do up anymore.

Jonathan had always thought of her as a chameleon, someone who could blend into any situation. As a young woman she'd been pretty, but not too attractive; sexy, but not overtly so; clever, but not bookish. And she was funny: he'd always liked that about her. She'd been their top operative in her day, taking on high-risk undercover work to take her targets down any which way she was able. Orphaned in her early twenties, Victoria was the original tough cookie, throwing herself into any situation, determined to succeed, and less prone to caring about herself than the average person with parents at home to worry after them. Despite being a woman, or maybe because of it, she was unusually talented at finding her way into an operation, reaching her objective, and extracting herself unscathed. Most of the time the terrorists, arms dealers, and other garden-variety hostile threats she took on never knew what hit them.

Jonathan took a good, long look at the forty-something

Victoria that now stood opposite him. In middle age, she'd become a tired-looking, doughy, clapped-out version of her earlier self. Now she wasn't a chameleon: she was completely anonymous. With all the same wiring. Which made her perfect.

They exchanged pleasantries and sat down. Victoria shuffled in her seat, looking about as comfortable as a turkey at Christmas. He tried to put her at ease.

'Before we start, I wanted to say how pleased I am to see you. I mean, we're glad you've come back.' He smiled, and her shoulders relaxed a fraction.

'Thank you, Jonathan.'

'So, how are things? It's been a long time. How is the family?'

'They're fine. Ollie is a teenager now and Evie and James are . . . well, you know exactly how they are already, sir.'

Jonathan ignored the dig. 'I suppose you'd like to know why we contacted you?' He picked out a file from his desk drawer. 'An associate of Anatoli Ivanov has come to our attention, and we need your help.'

He watched carefully for a reaction, but got nothing.

'We believe they may be involved in the illegal export of weapons to the Middle East,' he continued. 'The chatter is that they're doing a big deal of some sort over there. A big enough deal to need extended credit lines and their own slow boat from China.'

'Isn't this basic MI6 turf?'

'It's a crossover case.' He opened the dossier. 'HMRC identified an unusual transaction last month: a third-party distributor in the UK who bought a container full of guns. Big guns. They're on the move, and MI6 have been watching to see where the shipment went next, to make sure it's all

51

legit. They're still on standby in the Middle East, but it's been handed to us because we have . . . better resources.'

Vicky smiled. 'Bet Six weren't happy about that.'

Jonathan continued, ignoring her comment. All would become clear to her soon enough. 'They think the guns are headed to a Jihadi terrorist organisation based on the border of Syria.'

'Islamic State?'

'They're old news these days. The power base has shifted to Africa. But there's been trouble brewing in the Middle East again in the past six months or so that we can't afford to leave alone. Our sources suspect a new Al Qaeda training camp has been set up on the Syrian border and we think that's where the guns are headed.'

Victoria nodded, her face still impassive. 'How come you want me? Surely you have operatives who could do this in their sleep.'

He tossed the file across the desk. She took it and, this time, he got a twitch of the eye. He smiled, satisfied that he'd managed to surprise her a little.

'Sacha Kozlovsky.' She looked up. 'I suppose I should have guessed.'

'To be honest, I'm a little disappointed you didn't.'

'So, basically, you want me to entrap a dad from my daughter's school for illegal arms trading and catch a bunch of Al Qaeda terrorists in the process?'

'That's the general idea.'

Chapter Five

Vicky opened the file. 'I take it Sacha's got prior?'

'He's been running shipping and air freight companies for the past twenty years, selling weapons on to third parties in the Middle East and Africa and washing the money before it hits his bank account. Nothing we've ever been able to prove unfortunately. The goods leave Europe, allegedly on their way to legit buyers – governments, army that sort of thing – but he routes a lot of stuff via Russia, the Ukraine, and China, where the paper trails start to get more difficult. No agency has ever had enough proof to arrest him for any illegal activity and he's been clever enough not to get too greedy or too political. He "retired", for want of a better word, a few years back. That's when he moved to the UK and started investing in property instead of guns.'

'But he's back in action?'

'We believe so. We think this deal is too good to turn down and he's a greedy son of a bitch. But we need more intel to pin this on him. That's where you come in.'

'What's this got to do with Anatoli?' Vicky asked. 'Assuming that's why you sent me that old file.'

Jonathan paused a moment. 'We know that after that whole – *fiasco* – Anatoli went to Dubai for a while. He met Sacha at an art fair and, by all accounts, they hit it off; Anatoli needed money and Sacha was looking to build an impressive art collection as befits a Russian oligarch – and it proved a mutually beneficial friendship. Sacha used his contacts to help Anatoli open a gallery there, and, as well as helping Sacha spend his ill-gotten gains on priceless masterpieces, Anatoli became something of a trusted advisor.'

'So, he's involved with the deal too?'

Jonathan nodded and shifted in his seat. 'A major player. Victoria, I know this must all be a bit of a shock, asking you to come back and work on this. But we didn't really ask you because of Anatoli; that was just to get you in the room. We asked because of pure dumb luck. When we discovered you were a parent at the same school as Sacha, we knew you were in a great position to get us what we need. We believe if we can fill in the gaps and figure out when and where this deal is happening, we can get the evidence we need to catch Sacha with his pants down. And then we can follow the guns all the way to the people they are intended for. All we need from you is information.'

'That's all you needed last time. Look where that got me.'

The first time she'd approached him, Anatoli had been in a South Kensington wine bar, across the road from the auction house where she started work a few weeks previously, to establish her cover. Anatoli was a Russian art dealer selling Russian art to rich Russians who made their money – and spent large swathes of it – in London, in any number of ways, ranging from mildly immoral to downright wanted-by-Interpol illegal. It had come to the attention of JOPS that a particular group of these Russians were a small subset of another group associated with their case; Vicky, with an impeccable track record and a solid 2:1 in Art History, was tasked with gaining intel and exposing the UK wing of the people-smuggling operation. Anatoli, innocent of his clients' side hustle, was the way in.

The bar was busy, drinkers spilt on to the street to enjoy the early summer sunshine. Beautiful people, for this area of London didn't encourage anything else: young, carefree office workers stopped for their after-work tipple; well-to-do tourists left the various museums looking for something a little more upmarket than the nearest All Bar One. But Anatoli still stood out – a handsome man with no clear mission and happy in his own company.

As Vicky made her way inside, she could see him perched on a stool, flicking through a glossy A4 auction catalogue, a glass of something fizzy resting on the bar, possessive fingers wrapped around the stem. She barely recognised him from the rather drab description given by the surveillance team of 'a tall, slim man in his early thirties, plain but well dressed'. He was, in her eyes, elegant, and exotic. Dressed in a smart suit, her hair smooth and sleek, she was perfectly matched. It relaxed her a little, knowing that they'd got her position on the power ladder just right. He might just find her attractive enough . . . not that anything was expected of her in that respect, far from it.

Inside was just as busy as the street. She edged her way

towards the bar, her heels click-clacking, and prayed she would reach it without sliding across the polished wooden floor. She'd put heels on as a last-minute touch, knowing that the first encounter would dictate everything. She wasn't intending to work the honey trap angle, but it didn't hurt to be prepared, and although she wasn't a natural in stilettos, she was a highly trained spook and would bloody well make it across the room without falling on her backside.

She found a place at the other end of the bar to where Anatoli sat.

'A glass of rosé, please.'

The barman, another JOPS officer working undercover, caught her eye in subtle recognition before glancing down toward Anatoli. She nodded in reply. 'Dry.'

The sunlight coming through the windows lit up the particles of dust as they danced through the air and wrapped around the Russian's golden head like a halo. Miraculously, the crowd of drinkers between them took their leave and Vicky grabbed her glass and made her way towards him. She sat down at a newly available leather-topped stool and placed her bag on the hook under the bar.

'It's a beautiful piece, isn't it?' she said, acknowledging the page of the catalogue that captured his attention.

Anatoli looked startled, interrupted from the deepest of thoughts. He traced his fingers over the picture.

'Yes, it is.'

'I always think there is such hidden depth to Kandinsky's abstract work. . .' she laughed. 'Forgive me. Victoria Anderson.' She stuck out her arm.

'Anatoli Ivanov.' He took her hand and shook it gently.

'I work at an auction house down the road.' Vicky leant into him. 'We have some pieces similar to this one that I'm sure would be to your liking, if you would like to see them sometime.'

He kept his hand on hers and looked her straight in the eye, his own twinkling with mischief. 'Victoria? This name, it's so prim and proper . . . and, forgive me, but you don't look prim *or* proper. Giving me the hard sell when you barely know my name.' He kissed her hand, lips soft and slightly parted. She withdrew her hand and smoothed her hair, smiling.

'Well, Mr Ivanov, I can assure you I am extremely proper and have even been known to be prim. Especially with people whose names I barely know.'

'Well you know my name now . . . and I would like it very much, Victoria, if you'd join me for another drink so we can get to know each other a little better. Maybe something with a little more fizz?'

Clearly he wanted her to think he was the kind of man who called the shots. She could play along. 'Do you have something to celebrate then, Mr Ivanov?'

Anatoli smiled and held up the catalogue, pointed at it, and then at her. 'Something old and something new are coming my way, I believe.'

He had balls, she'd give him that. But she didn't want him to think she was a pushover. He'd lose interest too quickly or suspect there was an ulterior motive. So she handed him a crisp white card with her number printed on it.

'I'm afraid I'm not really in the market for anything fizzy today. But do call me if you'd like a private viewing of our collection some time. I'd be glad to show you around.'

He took the card, brushing her fingers with his as he did so, and tucked it into the inside pocket of his jacket. She felt a warmth spread inside her, from the physical contact, or the success of the subterfuge, or maybe somewhere between the two.

'Goodbye, Victoria. See you again sometime.'

Vicky turned away. He'd be in touch soon.

After the operation went so badly awry, her initial feelings of rejection were replaced by massive humiliation and guilt as she finally realised the magnitude of what she'd done. Time and again she would replay the moment when, days after that initial meeting, she had first kissed him; the memory of that exquisite electricity was now replaced with nauseating shame and remorse. Anatoli's departure and Adam's death had been a lesson to never mix business and pleasure again.

At first, she couldn't even imagine having another relationship. But a few months later, when she met Chris, she realised that wasn't true. She wanted someone to love, to see the good in her, and make her feel less alone. She liked Chris's company. She fancied the arse off of him. Anatoli had been the fantasy, but Chris was the real deal. And no, he had no idea who she was or what she'd done, but maybe it was better that way: a clean slate, and she could make sure this time that there were no mistakes. It hadn't stopped her from feeling guilty about lying to him. But, over the years, the lie softened and melted away. The youthful spy that once climbed into bed with an exotic Russian stranger played like an old movie in her mind; she could almost imagine it had never been her life at all. . .

Vicky snapped to attention. What did they want her to do, anyway? Seduce Sacha? God, no. . .

'Sir, if you want me to – I mean, I don't think that—'

'Don't worry, Victoria, I'm not going to ask you to pick up where you left off. I'd like to take a difference approach to the undercover work this time. We'd like you to use your relationship with the wife to see what you can dig up and—'

'Well, I don't really have a relationship—'

'But you do. You're both parents at the school. It's an easily workable angle, Victoria.'

Vicky sighed and sat back in her chair. And then leant forward again.

'My family cannot be involved. I won't compromise on that.'

Jonathan smiled. 'We appreciate that. We're not asking you to make them part of it. Matisse doesn't work, she's around in the daytime. You can easily forge a friendship with her away from the children.'

'But they're still involved. We all go to the same school. Evie and Dmitri are in the same class.'

Jonathan's jaw clenched briefly. 'Well look at it this way, would you rather be in control of the situation or me send in someone else to deal with it, who might not be quite so personally invested in keeping things clean?'

Vicky quickly played out several scenarios in her mind and shuddered. It didn't bear thinking about, having some spook with nothing but an objective to fulfil and a target to take down, infiltrating their lives. Far safer for her to take control of the situation. She had a fleeting memory of Adam, the operative who'd lost his life all those years ago. This time she would make sure no one got hurt.

Jonathan continued. 'You can report back on a weekly

basis to me, we'll arrange a dead letter box and a meeting point and agree some codes so that if you can't get to me, you can send us an encrypted email through a secure VPN.'

'Eh?'

'Email, Anderson. I assume you've heard of that.'

'It's Turnbull now, and yes, very funny . . . but I don't know what a VPN is.'

Jonathan sighed. 'Christ, maybe we should get you caught up on a few things. It's a secure part of the internet, where you can send and receive messages.'

Vicky nodded slowly. 'Oh, right.'

'Talk to my secretary about getting yourself an induction on IT and comms. And while you're at it, maybe some refresher courses in subterfuge and strategic diplomacy—'

'No need for that. I have three children. Subterfuge is a necessary tool in my house if I want to know anything that's going on in their lives. Strategic diplomacy is what happens when I find out.'

Jonathan shook his head. 'A lot has changed since you were last here and you can't do this old school. Get yourself up to speed. Read up on the dos and don'ts. And assuming you haven't been assassinating the milkman in your spare time, refresh your firearms license.'

Jonathan picked up the desk phone to dial a number, but Vicky cleared her throat.

'Yes?'

'One more question. What made you decide to wake me up, get me back on board?'

'I already told you, it was serendipity. You happened to be a parent at the school—'

'Yes, but let's face it, it's been a long time, Jonathan. How do you – or I, for that matter – know I'm going to be capable of this?'

Jonathan replaced the handset. 'Honestly, Victoria, I wasn't sure. All the intel said you were the best-placed operative, but I needed to make sure you would cope with being back on the inside.'

'What made up your mind?'

'Paintballing.' The hesitation in Jonathan's voice was replaced by certainty. 'You should have seen you in the field, Turnbull. When the pressure was on, you were on *fire*.'

Vicky grinned. 'I didn't realise I was at an audition.'

'Well, you got the part,' Jonathan said. 'Question is, will you take it?'

Vicky paused. She thought of Chris, and the kids, and Matisse and Sacha, and then finally she thought about herself. There was really only one answer she could give him.

'Mission accepted, sir.' She saluted him and Jonathan rolled his eyes.

'Welcome back, Turnbull.' He waved in a tall, lanky man in his thirties who was clutching a laptop case. 'This is Mike. We call him Inspector Gadget, even though he hates it.'

'I don't mind it that much,' Mike smiled at Vicky, and held out the bag. 'In here is your computer; it's got a VPN function and I've messaged the codes to one of the burner phones I've also included in the pack. Try not to go through too many phones; there's been complaints lately about us going over budget and we don't want to piss them off too much in case they cut our spending.'

Vicky flushed, remembering she'd run over one of them already. She took the bag. 'Thanks.' It weighed a ton.

'There's also a smart phone with a thermal imager in

there and a couple of other goodies too: a stunner, WASP injection knife and a cell jammer. Oh, and here's the remote control for the bag itself.'

Vicky took the small innocuous-looking box he was holding and opened it, revealing a small key fob inside. 'What does it do?'

'Standard contact electrocution and alarm when deployed. The safety latch is on the side, I've made sure it's completely child-proof. I can have the bag retrofitted for tear gas too if you like, but I wasn't sure you'd want it.'

Vicky hastily put the lid back on the box. 'Not necessary.'

Mike looked at Jonathan. 'Is that all, sir?'

'Thanks, Mike.' Jonathan turned to Vicky again. 'You'll be assigned a gun, too, but you need to get your license renewed first. Having seen you in action, I don't think you'll have any problems with that, though.' He passed her a card with a phone number on it. 'There's a range out in Egham where you can requalify. Call and make arrangements.'

'Yes, sir.'

'We still have eyes on the shipment and it will be a few weeks before it docks in China, but there is plenty you can do in the meantime. Get the lay of the land, maybe get inside the house if you can. Send us updates as necessary and if you need to see me, email the address Ops give you and ask to borrow a book from the library.'

'I'll check my passport's in date too.'

Jonathan paused. 'Maybe I didn't make myself clear. Your objective is to get intel from the Kozlovskys on the deal – and only that. A risk assessment has been done, we've carefully considered—' Jonathan seemed to struggle a bit, '—we've taken your . . . situation into account, Victoria, and especially after such a long time away, we don't think it's appropriate for you to go beyond that objective. We will have other operatives to deal with our targets in the Middle East. I'm relying on you to do what you've always done and get what we need without drawing attention to yourself. You, as you are now' – he gestured – 'you're perfect for the job. No one is ever going to think you're any more than . . . well, than what you are. A housewife, a school mum; a nobody.' He brightened, apparently pleased with his assessment of her. 'Just be yourself. Okay?'

'Yes, sir.'

She didn't look at him or Mike as she left. She needed to process what had just happened and get out of the building before she said something she would regret. Had she really just been through all that to say yes to what amounted to a babysitting job? Was it really *not appropriate* for her to be anywhere near the real action? She noticed she was stalking across the path back to the car and slowed her pace. He wanted her *just as she is now.* So, basically, they were happy to have her do the grunt work but thought she was too old and too out of touch to dance with the big boys. And maybe they were right. She got in the car, holding back the torrent of emotions until she was clear of the cameras lining the road and then, when she was safely away from prying eyes, parked in a layby and finally let the hot tears trickle down her face. All the excitement of saying yes had dissipated in the face of Jonathan's comments. He'd managed to make her feel like a fool for believing she could just walk in after fourteen years and pick up where she left off. She wiped her face. *A nobody.* She was fully aware that she wasn't the Victoria Anderson of old; she didn't need him to remind her the current version wasn't altogether the usual stuff JOPS officers were made of. But that didn't mean she didn't still have what it took, or that the years in between hadn't taught her anything. She sniffed and wiped the tears away again, angrily. Fine, so it was just information gathering, but she would very quickly make Jonathan *and* Sacha realise just how foolish it was to underestimate her.

Chapter Six

That Friday, Vicky arrived at Becky's house shortly after school drop-off, for her first PTA committee meeting. To buy herself a little more time she rang the bell, even though she knew the door would be unlocked. She was nervous. She was sure some of the mums there would be familiar from the school gates, and sitting drinking coffee with them wasn't something that would usually have fazed her. However, everything was very different this morning. She couldn't afford to have a single piece of information pass her by.

She had sought Matisse out at pick-up yesterday, to check she was coming to the meeting. 'Maybe us new girls will work together on something,' she said, hoping to get her onside. The faster they became friends, the easier it would be to infiltrate the Kozlovsky home and figure out what Sacha was up to, quickly, and with the minimum of fuss. But it meant she was going to have to make a supreme effort to befriend the French woman and appear to be *fully* engaged with PTA activities, if she was to be effective.

*

Entering Becky's living room, she encountered a sea of smart-casually clad women, all clutching reusable water bottles and flashing impeccable teeth. The noise was like seagulls on Margate beach: high-pitched squawking punctuated by shrieks of laughter.

Vicky stood like a meerkat in the bush and looked around with silent alarm. Who were these women? Were they mums at school? She prided herself on being observant, but she was *sure* she'd never seen half of them before. Why was everyone dressed up like they were on an Instagram feed? Becky's house on the Costa del Putney was very nice, but it wasn't exactly The Berkeley Hotel. The fear spread through her, curling in tendrils along her faded sweatshirt and creeping into the soles of her battered Converse. This really wasn't her sort of thing – actually it was her nightmare – but she was going to have to dig deep and get over herself. She had an objective and Jonathan had little enough faith in her as it was—

'Victoria.' Matisse appeared out of the flock and the rest of the women turned in unison, presumably expecting someone else. Only two people in the world called her by her full name: the woman who did her bikini wax and her boss. But Matisse didn't believe in being familiar, and, as if to prove it, gave her a couple of air kisses, one on each side of her face.

'Hello, Matisse. Hi, everyone.' She offered a weak wave in the direction of the yummy mummies.

'Hi!' they said, one by one or all at once, or something in between. She really couldn't tell. She was busy trying not to break into a sweat. She gave what she hoped passed for a smile and hovered at the door, hoping there might be some sort of emergency exit to an alternate dimension through the polished wooden floor. The floor, in the usual style of floors, remained stubbornly in place.

'Good morning, everyone,' Becky breezed into the living room carrying a steaming mug. 'There's tea and coffee and breakfast in the kitchen for those that want it – we'll start in just a few minutes, okay? Oh, hi, Vicky.'

Vicky spun Becky around and they scooted back through the living room door and into the hallway.

'I'd forgotten how much I really don't like all this,' Vicky whispered.

'You'll be *fine*, Vicky, stop being so miserable. Remember you volunteered to come – you can always leave again. It's not a job.'

Vicky could hear the passive aggressiveness coming from Becky loud and clear, but wasn't about to get into PTA politics with her best friend. If she needed validation for what she did, she would have to get it from someone else. Vicky had a job to do.

'So, what's on today's agenda?'

'The Christmas Fair.'

Vicky groaned, put her fingers under her chin in a gun shape and mimed pulling the trigger. It was at the completely wrong angle to kill yourself, but Becky wouldn't notice. 'Sounds fun,' she said.

Becky swiped Vicky's hand away from her throat, holding onto her fingers with her right hand and patting them with her left. 'It might be if you stop being such an arse about it. Come on, hurry up and get yourself a drink and let's get started.'

Becky twirled back into the living room and left Vicky to meander towards the kitchen. She grabbed her mug of coffee, added a spoon of sugar, and debated slipping in a shot of the Baileys she knew Becky kept at the back of the pull-out pantry, before deciding she should probably keep her wits about her. Also, it was only 9 a.m. It didn't seem like a great idea to celebrate her return to undercover life by getting pissed at her first PTA meeting.

She headed back into the living room, where the women now nibbled demurely on mini chocolate croissants and listened to Becky plot out the festive fair to end all fairs.

'We're going to have local business vendors in this year, to boost footfall. I thought the Year Fives might take this on? Then there's the grotto and the raffle, that's Years One and Two.' Becky paused and consulted her list. 'That leaves games for Year Six, security Year Three, Reception will do the barbecue – the bacon butties are hugely popular with parents who may have a little Saturday morning post-Christmas party hangover – and, finally, the Grand Christmas Bake-off and charity cake sale will be Year Four. Matisse and Vicky, I know you're both new to this, but would you be able to coordinate?'

Everyone looked at them. Vicky had a mouthful of croissant and was finding it difficult to speak.

'Mmm,' she said, with what she hoped sounded like enthusiasm but was actually her trying not to choke. *Catering*? What was Becky trying to do to her? More to the point, what was she trying to do to everyone else? She was literally the world's worst baker, a fact of which Becky was fully aware. Vicky had a licence to kill, sure, but would rather not commit cupcake genocide at the PTA Christmas Fair.

Matisse came to her rescue. 'Oui. Yes of course,' she said.

Was that a smile on her face? Vicky couldn't quite make out Matisse's expression through the layers of cosmetic filler, but it looked like it might be.

'Fantastic, thank you.' Becky picked up a bulging binder from beside her coffee and held it in the air. 'I think that's it, for now. Any questions? I'll be setting up a WhatsApp group and sending emails out to each year group with details of what you need to do, but if anyone wants to come and take a look at this Christmas Fair bible while they're here, it's got all the information in it from previous years.'

The noise started up almost instantly as a rabble gathered around Becky and her bible. Not feeling quite so enthusiastic, Vicky took another bite of her croissant and chewed on it carefully, before swallowing and turning to Matisse.

'I can't believe Becky's put us in charge of cakes. I have to warn you, Matisse, I'm not exactly good at baking.'

'No matter, I am,' Matisse replied. 'It is the perfect job for me.'

Vicky stopped for a second. Jonathan had said not to go too far, too fast, but it was right here for the taking . . .

'Well, we are supposed to be doing it as a team, Matisse. Maybe you could teach me how to bake a cake?'

Matisse blinked slowly. 'I suppose so. Where do you live?'

Vicky spoke casually, trying to keep her voice light and airy. 'Well I thought I could come to yours, seeing as you probably have all the stuff we need, like cake tins and so on. Otherwise you're going to have to bring it all with you. Plus, my oven is crap.'

Matisse looked at her with a blank expression. Vicky tried to read her eyes: this woman really was an enigma. Maybe she'd pushed her luck and gone too far, too fast. Maybe Matisse didn't want her to come to the house. Maybe she was hiding something.

She waited for Matisse to answer.

'I am sure that will be fine.' Matisse gave a tight smile.

Come to my house next week. I have a big kitchen, there is plenty of room for us to make our cakes.'

'Great.' Vicky agreed a date with her for the following Wednesday and gave herself a mental high-five. She had a foot in the door. She'd send a message to Jonathan later that night, when she'd worked out how to fire up the laptop.

Which was easier said than done. Vicky sat in her onesie in the kitchen, hunched over at the table trying not to swear, simultaneously listening for any signs of Chris or the kids coming down and finding her *in flagrante* with her new laptop. The secret compartment in the bathroom cabinet was really only useful for paperwork so she'd hidden all the IT kit in the utility room – the laptop fitted neatly in the gap between the washing machine and the worktop above it and was perfectly camouflaged – not that it mattered, given no one except her ever went near it anyway. The charger and the rest of the paraphernalia that accompanied the main device was, for similar reasons, crammed at the back of the drawer containing clean tea towels. She'd stashed all the other stuff – the stunner, knife and cell jammer – at the top of her wardrobe, behind a mass of old skiing paraphernalia where she knew no one would ever go. The laptop bag was in the boot of the car for easy access, but the remote control that operated its more lethal functions remained in the box, inside a sewing kit that was gathering dust in the cupboard under the stairs. All safely out of reach of the kids and in places no one in her house would ever think to go looking for anything.

She'd waited patiently in front of the TV for Chris to go to bed before she'd snuck into the kitchen and started the computer up. All she wanted to do was get online and send an untraceable, encrypted email, but you'd think she'd asked the damn thing to solve the meaning of life. Vicky cursed under her breath. There was a dog barking from down the road somewhere, and, as the night cooled off, every creak the house gave out made her jump with so much guilt she couldn't think straight. She admitted that when Mike had issued her laptop, she may have glossed over her general levels of IT incompetence. Any sign of this VPN that was supposed to let her know she had a secure connection remained elusive and, in the end, after a few more minutes of frustrated finger jabbing, she slammed the lid shut and shoved the laptop back under the counter, taking care that any flashy lights weren't pointing out for eager little eyes to see. On top of all the other catching up she needed to do, she'd have to admit her stupidity and go in for some IT training.

Was she really up to this job? She couldn't even work a laptop, for God's sake. She was woefully out of practice when it came to surveillance – she'd dismissed that woman in the supermarket, a rookie error – and she wasn't sure if she had the memory these days to retain important information long enough to share it. As for protecting herself . . . shooting a paintball gun was one thing, but running a suspect down or even throwing a decent punch was beyond her right now. Jonathan said to 'be herself' and she'd been annoyed and upset at the implications of that, but the truth was, she was quite possibly past her sell-by date. Mike was half her age – well, okay, maybe a bit more than that – but still, she felt so *old*. Old and stupid and useless and a bit ridiculous. What was she chasing? An objective, a crook, or her youth? She needed to get focused before she failed at all three.

Vicky headed for the fridge to get a glass of wine. Old photos adorned the door, held on by alphabet magnets and willpower. Chris kissing her bump on their wedding day, her standing outside hospital a few months later with Ollie in her arms . . . it all seemed so long ago, and her life before that even more so. There was no point in getting upset over growing older, but she couldn't help herself. She was hot, too, from faffing about with that computer . . . was it the computer or a hot flush? Please God don't let this be the menopause on top of everything else.

She drank her wine and waited a few minutes, thinking about what to do. She had to sort herself out. She couldn't keep on running back to Gilbert House whenever she felt overwhelmed, but she at least needed to start from a good place. Vicky grabbed one of the new burner phones out of the bottom of the peg basket and messaged Mike. 'Visit to target residence confirmed. Be in on Monday for IT lesson,' she wrote, and pressed Send. At least she knew how to do that.

The weekend passed in a heady mix of chaos and alcohol. Vicky had booked a babysitter for the Saturday night weeks before, thinking they'd find something to do with someone, and then she'd forgotten to arrange anything, so she and Chris ended up in the Italian down the road, splitting a bottle of red and stuffing their faces with pasta.

It was nice, spending the evening together. The restaurant was decent – stone floors and dark wood and a welcoming bar at the front. Not too posh, but a step up from the Pizza

Express next door. It wasn't so busy tonight that the service suffered either, their waitress buzzing between their table and the foursome who had sat down next to them at the same time. Carrying trays piled with pasta to and fro, she was like an ant marching its prize across the floor, the ease and speed with which she moved at odds with the weight and size of the tray. Vicky watched her sailing towards the couple sitting behind Chris, carrying a steaming plate full of fried calamari and a rather less-exciting salad. The woman took the salad and began to pick at it, eyeing up the calamari her date was shovelling into his mouth. Her lip curled as he sniffed and wiped and crunched his way through his food. Watching your partner eat was certainly a make-or-break business. She turned her attention back to Chris, who was ladling a gargantuan forkful of spag bol into his mouth and splashing red sauce down his front in the process. She shook her head in amusement. It was like having dinner with James.

'So, how was work this week?' she said, snapping out of her thoughts. 'Did you find a new account manager?'

Chris swallowed his mouthful. 'No, not yet. There are plenty of qualified people who could do the job, but I can't seem to find anyone who fits.'

'Well it's a small office, I suppose.'

Chris was the Managing Director of a marketing agency based down the road in Richmond. When Vicky met him, he was working as a graphic designer at the V&A and still living with his mum and dad. A friend who worked in the curatorial department introduced them at the opening of one of the galleries there, and, despite her misgivings, Vicky found she liked Chris immediately. He was so different from Anatoli: an open book, with a pithy sense of humour and a way of saying the right thing. It turned out he liked her, too; the night ended with both of them pissed on too much free prosecco and frantically getting off with each other in a side alley opposite the Natural History Museum. The rest, as they say, was history. Or natural history, as Chris had joked to anyone who'd listen.

'What about you?' Chris said. 'Anything exciting happening with the PTA?'

'Not much.' This was one of those times when Vicky wished she could talk about work. The conversation would be far less one-sided. She wondered if Chris ever found her boring.

'I'm baking cakes with Matisse on Wednesday.' Well if he didn't before, he would now.

'Baking cakes?'

'Yeah, it's for the Christmas Fair. Becky put me and Matisse in charge of the Bake-off competition and the cake stall. It's like now she's got me involved, she wants to humiliate me as much as possible.'

Chris chuckled. 'You're not cut out for this PTA lark, are you?'

'I feel there might be better uses of my time.'

'Like what?' Chris took a sip of wine. 'You said the other day you were thinking about going back to work.'

Vicky felt her heart speed up. 'I was. I am. But it's complicated. Logistically.'

'What do you want to do? Something new? Or go back to what you were doing before the kids?'

'Not exactly . . . but yeah, pretty much.' The lie was already sticking in her throat.

'Well I'm sure it's nothing we can't figure out, if it's what you want to do. Hopefully you still have some contacts to get a foot in the door.'

'I'm worried I'm past it.'

Chris shook his head. 'You're not dead yet. And there's a bunch of people getting paid for doing a job when they can barely put one foot in front of the other. You know your stuff. You'll be fine.'

She smiled at him. That was Chris. Since the day they'd met, he'd been on her side. He had a knack of settling her and making her feel safe, even when the rest of her world – a world he had no idea about – was in complete turmoil. Her affair with Anatoli had been exciting and dangerous, but it was short-lived and would have burnt out quickly enough naturally, regardless of the situation. Her and Chris – well, it sounded corny, but he really was her soulmate. She thought back to what Jonathan had said. Maybe she *should* have told Chris about JOPS all those years ago. It would make this conversation much easier now.

He swallowed the last of his pasta. 'Why don't you see how you feel after Christmas?'

She nodded. 'Good idea. After all, I'm busy with a mission to bake cakes right now, and I won't rest until it's complete.'

'Well, I hope Matisse knows what she's let herself in for.'

Vicky mopped up the last bit of sauce on her plate with some bread. 'She doesn't know the half of it.'

Chapter Seven

Mike leant back in his chair and raked his hands through his hair in a slow movement.

'Vicky, no offence but where the hell have you been that you literally know *none* of this shit?'

Vicky blushed. 'Erm . . . parenting?'

'Yeah, but surely you've got a laptop? Everyone's got a laptop. I mean, how do you do anything without one?'

She looked out of Mike's glass-walled office at the rest of the tech department. The windowless grey room was filled with screens, smartphones, and swiping; the small team of workers faced forward, tapping away as if their lives – or, more accurately, other people's lives – depended on it. But for the occasional bit of banter during a slurp of coffee or a mouthful of sandwich, there was silence. The white noise of it all threatened to overwhelm her.

'I'm pretty sure people existed for thousands of years without all . . . this. I can Google, send emails. I know how to get the shopping delivered. To be fair, I haven't needed to do much else.'

'But what about your smartphone – transferring photos, downloading music, syncing your calendar?'

Vicky bowed her head. 'I never needed . . . my husband did it all, and then my son . . .' She thought about the past thirteen years. When had she stopped learning things? What the hell *had* she been doing with her brain all this time? She looked up at Mike. 'I had three kids. It's not a very good excuse, but it's the only one I've got.'

Mike softened his gaze. 'I get it. My wife's going mental trying to "have it all". I keep saying to her, she needs to stop trying to be perfect all the time.'

'You have kids? You're only a kid yourself.'

'I'm thirty-two,' Mike smiled. 'Our son just turned one. Mandy went back to work three days a week last month, after maternity leave finished, and she was in tears by the end of the second day. I mean, I help out when I get home, putting him in the bath and stuff if it's not too late, but she's juggling much more than me and getting paid less for the privilege.'

'It gets worse,' Vicky said. 'Well, not worse . . . different. They start school and have playdates and after-school clubs and homework; you feel like you should be there for all of it, making sure they are happy and fulfilled and growing up into good people. It's a full-time job all by itself, never mind once you add in actual work on top, and staying married. What does she do?'

'She's in Projects.'

'Here?'

Mike nodded. 'If you ever want to talk to someone. I mean, I know your circumstances are a bit different, but, you know, I'm sure she would be happy to . . .'

'Thanks, Mike. I appreciate that. I think I might just depress her though. Ghost of Christmas Future and all that.'

Mike chuckled. 'You might. Maybe lay off on the whole relentlessness aspect of the whole thing. Now, let's get back to basics, and see if we can get you IT savvy by lunchtime.'

They turned back to the computer and Vicky tried to relax. By the time one o'clock came around, she could set up a VPN, upload photo files to HQ's server and encrypt an email.

'Thank you, Mike, for spending all this time on me.' She began packing up her laptop into her bag and eased on her coat.

'You're welcome, it's what I do.' He grinned and shook her hand, giving her a slap on the shoulder. 'You'll be all right, you know. It just takes time.'

'Yeah, I know. But it's time I don't have. I don't want to spend hours figuring stuff out I should already know. I don't want to feel like the new recruit. Or worse still, the granny on the team.'

'You're not a granny, Vicky. You're a fast learner and a perfectionist, and, from what I've heard, a bit of an all-round rock star.'

'Maybe fifteen years ago.'

'Nothing stopping you from doing it again.'

'I suppose so.'

She hurried back to her car, taking a more direct route through the woods than was strictly encouraged, conscious of the time and the fact that she needed to pick up James from nursery in less than an hour. It was drizzling, and she tried in vain to do up her jacket against the cold. Winter was on the way, skulking like a teenager outside a chip shop, and she really did need a new coat. Maybe with her first pay cheque she'd treat herself. She'd opened up a savings account for each of the kids, and most of her money would go to them in the long run. But she could siphon off a little bit for herself here and there.

She started the engine and pulled out of the car park onto the main road, checking to make sure she wasn't followed. Just because she'd been out of circulation for a while didn't mean she couldn't do the job. She drove, keeping watch for any activity; the loyal staff of Gilbert House had done a good job of keeping their secret over the years and, as Jonathan had proudly reported in their meeting, they were yet to suffer a security breach in this quiet corner of North West London countryside. But it never hurt to be cautious.

The windscreen wipers pushed away the rain and dead leaves from the screen in droning tones, an unwanted eulogy to summer. As she passed through Harrow and Wembley, then south towards the river she checked her mirror again, and then again, to be safe. This time, she saw something. A motorbike sat, uncharacteristically patient for a bike, two cars behind her on the dual carriageway. It had been behind her for a while, she realised. Intuitively, she kept her speed constant. While other cars overtook her, the bike stayed exactly in position, matching her speed and making no attempt to pass. Definitely a tail. Another one of Jonathan's tests or something more sinister? She searched her sat nav for a suitable detour and came off the main road at the next junction. To her surprise, the bike carried straight on. Not a tail, then. Unless there was more than one of them. . .

She stopped at the top of the road as she hit the traffic she'd have avoided by taking the main road. She'd probably added twenty minutes onto her journey thanks to being paranoid. She shook her head and tried not to get frustrated by the stop-start of traffic lights that now lined her route back. A combination of adrenaline and irritation prompted her to shout into her rear-view mirror.

'Why would anyone be following you? You haven't even done anything yet.'

Yet. It was a word – a disease – that was creeping into her subconscious more and more often.

'I haven't told a barefaced-lie to my husband about where I am or who I'm seeing. *Yet.*'

'I haven't put anyone's life in danger. *Yet.*'

'My children and my family aren't involved. *Y—*'

No. There was no getting around it; her family were already involved, by the very nature of the case. Evie and Dmitri were in the same class at school. Short of moving in with them, you couldn't get much closer to home. But it would have always been that way, no matter who'd been put on Sasha's tail. At least this way, she could control the narrative and know that, with her on board, JOPS would do everything to make sure Chris and the kids were protected. But she didn't expect it would come to that, given she wasn't exactly risking life and limb herself – and, in fact, had been given very specific instructions not to.

Vicky walked into the reception area at the nursery and checked the clock. She was nearly twenty minutes late. James stood, backpack on his shoulders, his smiling-but-clearly-pissed-off teaching assistant behind him.

'Sorry I'm late!' she said, bending down to receive her little boy's embrace and lifting him up onto one hip. She saw Mrs Goodwin, the nursery manager, marching down the hallway.

'Oh, that's okay—' The TA passed James' bag to Vicky

and hesitated, about to speak when the nursery manager reached them.

'Mrs Turnbull, good afternoon.' Mrs Goodwin nodded at the TA, dismissing her, and then turned to Vicky. She was smiling, but it appeared strained. Vicky noticed her foundation was pooling in the lines around her eyes. She looked like she needed a good night's sleep.

'Mrs Turnbull, I need to politely remind you that although we have no issue with offering supervision after hours in the case of emergency, our staff have to prepare for the next day and should not be expected to provide a day care service on a regular basis.'

Vicky was taken aback. Gail Goodwin had never been all that friendly for a nursery teacher, but she hadn't expected a lecture. After all, she'd been working, not got carried away at a bloody yoga class. But under the intense gaze of the teacher, she began to feel extremely uncomfortable. She might be the one who could torture a prisoner in seventeen different ways, but Mrs Goodwin dealt with toddlers all day long and would wait for an apology as long as was necessary. Besides, she had a point. Vicky decided not to be difficult.

'I'm really sorry. I know it's not on. I promise it won't happen again.'

Mrs Goodwin smiled, victorious. 'Thank you, Mrs Turnbull. I appreciate it.' She turned to James. 'Good afternoon, James. See you tomorrow.'

She turned to go and Vicky, suitably chastised, bent down to give her son a squeeze. 'Hello, gorgeous boy.'

'Hello, Mummy.' He gave Vicky a huge smacker on the mouth, hugging her like a snake suffocating its prey. She took in the moment, knowing it wouldn't be too much longer before he was too big to carry and too old to dole out such unrestrained affection.

'Mummy didn't get to go to the supermarket this morning. Would you like McDonalds for lunch, James? Burger and fries?' The Band-Aid solution of guilty mothers everywhere: junk food. James's face lit up.

'Burgers, yeah!'

'It'll have to be our secret though; if the others find out we've had a sneaky burger for lunch they'll be super jealous.'

'I'll keep the secret, Mummy, I promise.'

And with that, she'd recruited her youngest son into her semi-complicit world. They sat stuffing their faces with shoestring fries and Vicky tried to ignore the shame leeching its way into her heart. Her youngest beamed at her, blissfully ignorant.

'Mummy?'

Vicky paused her thoughts. 'Yes, sweetie?'

'I like having secrets. They're fun.'

'Well, yes, they can be. But it's good not to have too many.'

'Why?'

'Because too many secrets make you lonely, James. If you have too many secrets to keep, you end up not being able to speak to anyone about anything.'

'But it's okay to have a few secrets?'

'A few are fine. You just have to make sure you pick the right ones to keep.'

'Do you have a secret, Mummy?'

She chewed the last bit of burger and swallowed it down.

'Of course I do.'

'Really? What is it?'

'It's a secret, so I can't tell you.'

'But it's *your* secret, Mummy. So, it's up to you who you tell it to.'

'Yes, that's the good thing about them,' she said, relishing the simplicity of three-year-old logic and realising there was no reason not to apply it to her own circumstances. 'If they get too much to keep then you can always tell them to someone.'

'You can tell it to me.'

'I would probably tell it to Daddy, if I needed to,' she said, wiping James down and removing all traces of ketchup. 'Because you're far too little and cute and we already have a secret we're sharing.' She zipped up his jacket, gathered his hand in hers and they set off towards the car. 'Now, come on, we need to stop at the shops before we go and get Evie from school.'

They stood outside in the pick-up area with the other mums, nannies and siblings of various ages, waiting for Evie. The rain was still spitting, the wind had picked up, and the grey sky did nothing to make the playground look less neglected.

Vicky walked over to Matisse, whose red lips matched the Lulu Guinness umbrella held high over her head.

'Hi, Matisse. Are we still okay for Wednesday? Is there anything I can bring?'

'Non. I have asked the housekeeper to make sure everything we need is ready.'

'Okay,' Vicky said, wondering how she would ever get any intel from someone with no facial expression and no conversation. 'Well, I'll see you after drop-off then . . . about nine?'

'Oui, yes, this is fine. Do you need directions?'

'No, I have your postcode from the contact sheet. I'll just plug it into the sat nav.'

'Use the buzzer at the gates when you arrive, I will let you in.'

Gates? Who the hell has *gates*? She'd have to get some intel from Jonathan on the Kozlovsky residence because, obviously, Matisse's house wasn't anything like the Victorian terrace she resided in. Not that she was bothered; Vicky loved where she lived. She loved that her home looked the same but different to all the other houses on the street. She loved hearing the voices of people walking past on the rickety pavement outside but never saying hello; she loved the comforting drone of the planes overhead, the idea that people might look down and wonder what she was doing. Arguably, she liked the idea of being able to keep an eye on everything and everybody. Living life behind a gate, driving in and closing off the world, didn't appeal to her at all. But it probably rather suited Matisse.

She needed to figure out the best course of action based on this new information. 'Is there space for me to park inside the gates, then?'

'Non. My husband does not like his car to be blocked in. So maybe it will be better for you to park on the street outside.'

'Oh okay,' Vicky kept her reply bright and breezy despite Matisse's curt response. Maybe the gates weren't just to shut the world out. Maybe they were to keep the secrets *in*. 'Is Sacha not at work then? I don't want us to disturb him or be a nuisance.'

Matisse gave an empty laugh. 'I am making a career out of being a nuisance to my husband, Victoria. I do not know if he will be home or not. It doesn't matter.'

'I suppose not.'

Well, actually, it did matter. Vicky had assumed Sacha would be out of the house when she was there, but now she was going to have to make a contingency plan or else the baking session would be a waste of time.

How much did Matisse know about her husband's world? Was she in on his secrets or completely ignorant of them? It wasn't unfeasible that Sacha kept all but the essential information from her; after all, Vicky was doing the exact same thing with her husband . . . the thought made her squirm. She was definitely not cut from the same cloth as Sacha.

Evie appeared, rucksack slung over her back, chatting animatedly to her friends as she came out of the door. She turned to acknowledge Dmitri, who'd come out at the same time. 'Bye, Dmitri. See you tomorrow.'

'Bye, Evie. Thank you for helping me today.'

'No problem.'

'Helping him?' Vicky asked.

'Oui, Dmitri tells me that Evie has been aiding him a little with his English comprehension,' Matisse said.

'Oh . . . that's great.'

'Yeah, and he said maybe I can go over to his house one time. He's got a massive TV and a PlayStation, Mum.'

'Has he now?' It was time to leave, before she was forced to make any kind of commitment. 'Well, maybe some time you can. Okay, time to go. Bye, Matisse. Bye, Dmitri. See you tomorrow!'

Evie, James and Vicky headed out of the school gates and towards the car.

'I like Dmitri now, Mum. I didn't used to – I thought he was a bit odd – but he's actually really nice and funny.'

'Mummy's got a secret,' James said, out of nowhere.

'James!' Vicky felt herself flush red and her heart sped up.

'We had a burger for lunch.'

'What? Mum, you *never* let me have a burger for lunch. That's so unfair—'

They squabbled good-naturedly all the way home, Vicky pacifying Evie with the promise of homemade burgers for tea instead. James was smug that he'd be getting burgers twice in one day, even though he'd spilt the beans and told their secret. Vicky was happy to sink into family life again and left all thoughts of Sacha and Matisse behind.

Chris Facetimed while they were having dinner to say he was going to be late.

'I've got a client presentation in an hour and they've asked us to dinner afterwards,' he said. 'Sorry, guys, Dad's not going to make it home before bedtime.'

James and Evie moaned with disappointment, and Ollie grunted, which they assumed was teenager-speak for 'I don't give a toss' but could have just as easily meant 'damn, Dad, I was really looking forward to having some father–son time later while we played guitars in my room'.

'Dad, are you in your office?' Evie said.

'Sure am.' Chris flicked the camera round so they could see, and Evie and James both left their chairs to stand by Vicky and get a better look.

The bare-brick wall at the rear of the office could be seen through Chris's glass office doors, and Vicky could see a young account exec flapping outside, waiting with a stack of print-outs bearing a leaf–shaped logo in various colours and sizes. A predictable request by a client to try to appear 'green' or 'healthy' and a predictable response by the design department. The account exec was right to look tentative; Chris was going to hate the leaf.

Chris's face appeared back on the screen. 'I've got to go. Sorry.'

'No problem. I've got a few things I need to do anyway this evening.'

'Oh aye, what are you up to then?'

'Nothing major,' she said, averting her eyes.

'Okay. Don't wait up. Think it will be a late one.'

'Okay. Love you.'

'Love you, too.'

After James and Evie had gone to bed and Ollie was safely ensconced in his room playing Fortnite online with his mates, Vicky slid out her laptop from the top of the washing machine and fired it up. Mike had suggested she try sending a message to him tonight, to reinforce what she'd learnt and make sure she remembered how to do it when it came to sending a real report. This time she would get it right. In less than ten minutes, she'd scrambled her VPN, encrypted an email, and was sat waiting patiently for a reply. Minutes later, she received the following message:

Congratulations! Not as useless as you thought!

Vicky smiled and deleted Mike's email out of existence, logged off and shut down. She was going to be just fine.

Chapter Eight

Sacha Kozlovsky was not a happy man. Russian obscenities exploded from him, rumbling under the door and out of his office. The kitchen, where Dmitri and his mother were having breakfast, was two floors below, but, as they sat eating, Matisse winced at the echoing tirade her husband was unleashing down the telephone and wondered who was going to suffer more; them or her.

'Is Papa taking me to school this morning?'

She looked at her son. Even at eight years old, he was still so small and innocent. His papa shouldn't be a thug, a menace, a person to be frightened of. He should be Papa the hero, who smelt of nice cologne and had a big belly laugh; Papa who could throw him a ball in the garden or have a kick-about in the park; Papa who told him all about the adventures he had in Russia when he was a boy. Maybe one day he would be all those things, but she doubted it.

'I don't know, petit chou, we will have to ask him when he is finished with his call.'

She stood up from the table, leaving an empty bowl and

a half-finished cup of coffee where they were. Once they had gone upstairs to get ready for the day, Magda, her housekeeper, would appear from her room tucked away behind the utility area, and tidy things.

'Come on, Dmitri, let's get your teeth brushed.'

Dmitri raced up the helical staircase that twisted, resplendent, through the centre of the not-inconsiderable house. Matisse followed at a more ladylike pace, taking pleasure from the smooth wooden stair rail that ran beneath her hands, and casually marvelling at the footlights that sensed her steps and lit her way on her grey marbled path upwards. She paused on the first floor, to listen; Sacha had stopped shouting and the conversation was now reduced to a low hum. She could make out a couple of words here and there – something about Dubai, and an agent. She assumed this was a second call; his ominous tone didn't bode well for the first caller. She carried on going up, and away from the door before he caught her listening. The last thing she wanted to do was antagonise him.

Matisse reached the second floor and padded into her room; the deep pile of the carpet wrapped itself around her bare feet as she slipped her house shoes off. She walked into her dressing room and slid back the doors, revealing the numerous racks of dresses, trousers, and shirts at her disposal. It was getting cooler every day now; a slow, steady march towards the short days and miserable weather that would smother everything until around May next year. But she wasn't ready for winter clothes just yet, and, anyway, today she was cooking; she wouldn't want to wear anything too warm.

Having rejected several options, Matisse decided on a bronze Marc Jacobs shirt and a pair of skinny-fit dark denim jeans. She placed some ankle-breaking black leather knee boots on the floor by the door, and a fitted wool Chanel jacket on the padded chair beside her, before adding a silk scarf to keep off the morning chill. It was unlikely Sacha would be taking Dmitri to school this morning, and she liked to be prepared.

She heard the office door swing open; when there was no noise – no slam – she exhaled the breath she'd been holding and went to her dressing table to pick out her lipstick. His mood must be a good one, after all.

Sacha appeared as she began preparations to take a shower in the palatial en suite that sat at the south end of the master bedroom.

'I have to meet someone for coffee in South Kensington at nine, so I'll be leaving in a minute.'

'Will you take Dmitri to school?' She hated asking him, but it would give her some time to make sure Magda had prepared the house for Victoria's arrival. She should probably prepare Sacha as well in case he was coming straight home after his meeting. She didn't want him shouting and swearing in front of her guest. They all talked about them enough at the school, without adding fuel to the fire.

'And I wanted to remind you, I am baking cakes this morning with Victoria from the school,' she said, pulling her hair into a ponytail. She would put the rather unattractive shower cap over the top once Sacha was gone. Why were beauty routines so ugly? Shower caps were right at the top of the list of things Matisse would rather not acknowledge the existence of, along with foot scrubbers and teeth retainers.

'Ah yes, the famous baking lesson for the lady with the guns. Well, I will try not to scare off our sharp shooter.' He came behind her and put his hands on her shoulders, looking at her in the reflection of the mirror while he pushed his hands downwards towards her breasts. She could feel his hard-on poking into her back. 'But she stays in the kitchen, okay? I don't want strangers wandering about the house.'

'Of course,' Matisse said. 'Only the kitchen.'

'I have someone coming to collect a package at midday. It would be better if she were gone by then.'

He uncapped his hands from their grip and patted her shoulders like a dog. She hated it when he did that, like she was something to be owned.

'Dmitri, I'm taking you to school, let's go.' Sacha dropped his hands and rearranged himself, before turning away and heading to the door.

'Bye, Mama!' Dmitri bounded up to her side and gave her a big kiss on the cheek.

'Bye, darling. Have a lovely day and don't forget your bag.'

'I won't. Bye!'

Matisse listened as the front door opened and shut and the engine fired up on the Maserati sitting in the driveway. They didn't usually use that one for school, preferring to maintain a little discretion and drive the Range Rover instead. But, occasionally, Sacha liked to be the big man; this morning's call had obviously put him in the mood. Clearly it had put him in the mood for sex later, too. Sacha was nothing if not predictable.

She started the shower running and stepped in, her hair encased in its plastic protector. Smooth and blemish-free thanks to hours of intensive lasering, lifting and sculpting, Matisse gently massaged her skin with a body scrub before rinsing off and stepping out. The oil content of the scrub made the water slink off her body before she'd even looked at the towel; still, she dried each leg slowly, checking for any signs of imperfection, before moving upwards to her torso and finally to her arms, hands and face.

She rubbed a large quantity of expensive moisturiser all over her body, admiring the tautness of her skin, before smoothing high-class anti-ageing serum on to her cheekbones, throat and forehead. Ageing was not on Matisse's agenda. It was something that happened to other people, but never to her. It hadn't been easy, though. She'd been in her late twenties when Dmitri was born, so had the advantage over many of her older peers in that her body was more willing to spring back to where she wanted it, but, eight years on, it didn't bow to her wishes without a daily workout, a personal trainer, and an increasing number of procedures, surgical and non-surgical. While she attempted to freeze time, Sacha got older; of course, this was expected of him, and allowed. His tattoos, some nearly as old as her, stretched and faded across skin that was more fat than muscle these days; his hair was disappearing and his face was in danger of becoming one giant crease. But he was a man, and a powerful, rich one at that. It didn't matter that he'd aged, in fact it probably did him a favour. For Matisse, the only way to stay even the slightest bit powerful was to stay young. It wasn't fair, but it was the way life worked. And Matisse needed to stay powerful, especially when it came to Sacha.

She returned to her dressing room to put on the clothes she had laid out, before releasing her hair with a small shake. She hung her jacket back on the rail and placed the boots in their box; she wouldn't need them now Sacha had taken Dmitri to school. A lick of mascara, a light dusting of face powder, and a dab of the lipstick she'd picked out earlier, and she was done. Matisse looked in the mirror with satisfaction. She looked exquisite, as always.

She went downstairs to ready the house for her guest. On her way, she shut Sacha's office door. The shaft of light that lit the hallway was reduced to a thin, glowing sliver. She thought about the first caller again and wondered if he or she would have any kneecaps left by now. She shrugged it off, and continued downstairs to her own office space, next door to the kitchen, to close up that room as well. She turned the lock and pocketed the key; there were things that she didn't want anyone poking around in either, business of her own that she would prefer to keep away from prying eyes. And despite the fact that Victoria came across as the sort of person who wouldn't notice anything very much, Matisse wasn't buying it. Victoria may project an image of the archetypal domesticate, but Matisse had seen her watching the room during the PTA meeting and she wasn't sure it was the whole story. She knew from years of perfecting her own veneer that there was more to Victoria than meets the eye.

The doorbell rang a few minutes past nine and Matisse set her coffee cup down.

'I'll get it, Magda,' she said, dismissing the older lady, who went shuffling back to her room muttering Hungarian curse words under her breath. Matisse wound her way back up the stairs and checked her reflection in the gargantuan hall mirror before pasting a smile on to her face and opening the door.

'Bonjour, Victoria. Welcome.'

'Wow! What a lovely house.'

'Thank you very much. Please, come in.'

'Sure. I didn't see Sacha's car. Is he out, then? I parked on the street anyway . . . I'll just take off my shoes . . . oh wow! Look at that staircase, that's beautiful. Did you do all these renovations? Bloody hell, it must have cost a fortune.'

Matisse narrowed her eyes. These sorts of outpourings were usually a symptom; a way to deal with the surprise of just how rich the Kozlovskys really were. People were so unrefined when it came to money. She had seen it before from the few people who came and went from their home. But there was something about the way Victoria spoke that wasn't quite genuine. It could be nerves, but to Matisse it sounded almost . . . rehearsed?

While she took off her shoes, Victoria pestered her with questions.

'How long have you lived in Wimbledon? Was it a whole house when you bought it? I thought they were all split up into flats on this road. I didn't realise people still owned *whole* houses on the Common!'

'We bought it when Dmitri started at the school. It's convenient, but we had a lot of work to do before we moved in, to get it how we wanted it. I think someone died in it, before. It was like a museum but with none of the beauty; everything old or broken or ugly.'

'Well not anymore, clearly. You have beautiful taste, Matisse.'

She let Victoria enjoy the full vista from the hallway, watching her take in the sheer scale of the place. Carefully curated paintings hung from the walls in tasteful gaps between the impossibly grand windows to accentuate the space. The view straight ahead revealed a library, with embroidered armchairs set facing the manicured garden to the rear. To either side of the hallway, the door to the living and dining rooms on the ground floor were placed strategically ajar to reveal a tantalising peek of paintings, ornaments and fine furniture – a sliver of their lives designed to intimidate and seduce each visitor who came through the doors. But not too much. She ushered Victoria towards the stairs.

'Shall we go down?'

'Downstairs?'

'Oui, to the kitchen.'

'Oh, yes, of course.'

Matisse noted the disappointment in Victoria's voice and was glad she hadn't offered to do a full tour. For once, Sacha had been right to limit her visitor to the kitchen. They didn't need anyone poking around.

'How do you find having a kitchen in the basement? I imagine getting the shopping downstairs is a bit of a bore.'

'We have a service lift at the back for deliveries to the lower ground,' Matisse said, waving in the general direction of the lift and the CCTV screens tucked discreetly in the basement hallway.

'A lift? Bloody hell!'

They rounded the last step into the kitchen. It was an impressive sight. To the right, the state-of-the-art room stretched the entire depth of the house, an array of shining appliances mingled with tasteful cream and gold kitchen units. To the left, a smaller area displayed a glossy black dining table, laid ready as if for a photoshoot. An enormous circular kitchen island was in the centre of the room, the countertop resplendent in black and gold marble.

Even Matisse would admit, she *had* outdone herself when it came to the kitchen remodelling. She had spent much of her adult life in Paris, where the streets brimmed over with stick-thin women living on a steady diet of coffee and cigarettes, but as a girl she grew up in a village house in southern Provence where food was king. It was in that kitchen that her mother had taught her how to cook, not stopping until Matisse had a full repertoire of recipes tucked securely under her belt, ranging from the simplest jus to a perfect meringue. These days, of course, they had a chef come in to cook for them most of the time. But that hadn't always been the case, and Matisse was secretly looking forward to her baking session with Victoria this morning.

'The first, and most important, ingredient for any good cooking is that you take pleasure in the place where you create the dish,' she said. She poured two fresh coffees, slipped an apron over her head and handed an identical one to Victoria. 'Let's get started, shall we?'

The two women spent the morning in clouds of flour, whipping eggs and butter and sugar together to produce a plethora of sponges and cupcakes that Mary Berry would have been proud of. They talked about art, which surprised Matisse; she thought, given a captive audience, Victoria would be the type to prattle on endlessly about her children with little else to say. But, despite her initial assumptions, Victoria had turned out to be an entertaining baking partner. And she really didn't have a clue how to make a cake; Matisse had enjoyed showing her how to beat the butter and sugar and then gently fold in the flour so that the mixture stayed light and airy in the tin.

They made good progress. By eleven-thirty, the aroma from the kitchen had wound its way through the entire house, tendrils of sweetness wrapping around the staircase and sneaking under the doors.

'You're an excellent teacher, you know,' Victoria said, as they sat on stools drinking a celebratory coffee. 'Some people have that knack, don't they, for helping other people be better at something?'

'I am not sure anyone has said this about me before.' Matisse gave a half-smile, wary of taking the compliment and glanced at the cakes that were cooling on a rack on the counter. 'Sacha wouldn't agree with you. He does not like it when I try to help him.'

'Well, I'm useless. I can't teach anyone anything without taking over. I always said, the kids are going to have to learn to drive from Chris. He says they don't have to learn; I can just sit in the back seat and drive the car from there like I usually do.' Victoria laughed. 'Men though – they're all the same, aren't they? Don't want to be told how to do anything.'

'That is certainly true of my husband. He does not want me involved in his life. He says it is interfering. I say, maybe I would do better than him and this is what he is afraid of.'

There was a small pause and Victoria put her mug down. 'Would you mind if I used the loo quickly?'

'Not at all. It's upstairs by the front door.'

She watched Victoria leave. She had given a little too much away, maybe; Victoria had seemed glad of the excuse to interrupt the conversation. While she sipped her coffee and waited for Victoria to return, the front door slammed. Sacha. Matisse heard him go straight to his office but knew it wouldn't be long before his stomach got the better of him. Sure enough, within a few minutes, she heard him heading downstairs.

'Smells like you've both been hard at work,' he said, striding into the kitchen.

Matisse wasn't sure how he could smell anything with a cigarette dangling from his mouth. She nudged a crystal glass ashtray towards him as he placed the cigarette packet and his gold Cartier lighter down on the counter.

Sacha inhaled deeply. 'Where is she?'

'In the bathroom, Sacha. She's been here since nine. I couldn't deny her a trip to the toilet.' Matisse kept the irritation out of her voice, not wanting to rile him with a lit cigarette in his hand. She still had the scars from a previous incident where she'd not been quite so careful.

Sacha shrugged and exhaled. 'Fair enough. I guess we all have to piss.' He stubbed out the cigarette, letting it sit folded and half-smoking in the ashtray, and picked up a cupcake from one of the wire racks standing on the centre island. He took a large bite, making a satisfied noise as he swallowed it down. 'It's just as well you don't do this too often,' he said, patting his stomach. 'Otherwise I would get fat.'

Matisse didn't say anything. Sacha helped himself to another cupcake and began peeling the casing away. His phone pinged, and he checked the message, typed a reply, and hit Send, before turning his attention back to Matisse.

'So, are you all finished here then? What time will she be leaving? Remember, I have someone coming at midday and, anyway, I don't want her hanging around. She's been here long enough already.'

'I know. Don't worry, she won't.' Matisse heard his office phone ringing. 'Aren't you going to answer that?'

Sacha grunted and jogged back up the stairs. Matisse put the extractor fan on and busied herself with clearing away the mixing bowls into the sink for Magda to wash. She heard the soft rumble of Sacha's voice signing off the call and his heavy footsteps coming back down to her.

'Matisse!' He hissed at her from the foot of the stairs. 'She's still in there. How long does it take to go to the bathroom?'

'Well, you know, maybe she had to. . . Well, you know what I am saying, right, Sacha?'

Sacha screwed up his nose and made a sound of disgust. 'Bloody English. Why can't they wait to take a shit in their own house?'

'Hi, Sacha.' Vicky appeared behind him, and, to Matisse's satisfaction, Sacha's cheeks glowed a faint red.

'Hello, Victoria,' he said. 'The baking has been a success, I hear.'

'If Matisse is even half as good at teaching as she is at baking, everyone might just survive my cakes long enough to enjoy Christmas,' Vicky said. 'Matisse, I hate to be rude, but I have to cut and run. I have to be at nursery to pick up James shortly.'

'Oh, no need to worry, I understand,' Matisse said. At least the awkward issue of getting Victoria to leave the house had been taken out of her hands. 'Would you like to take some of the cakes for the children?'

'Are you sure? They'll be so surprised.'

'Of course.' Matisse counted out a dozen of the cakes and put them into a Tupperware standing by on the counter. Vicky took them from her and began to back out of the kitchen.

'I can't tell you how relieved Chris will be to see I've produced something edible at long last. Well, good to see you, Sacha.'

Sacha nodded a curt goodbye, his mouth full of the remnants of his third cupcake.

'I'll see you out,' Matisse said.

The two women mounted the stairs and Vicky placed the cakes down to get her shoes back on before standing up again and giving Matisse a rather unexpected kiss.

'Thank you, Matisse. I had fun.'

'Me too,' Matisse said. And, weirdly, she meant it. 'I'll see you at pick-up.'

'Sure, see you then.' Vicky waved and Matisse pushed the button to open the gate and let her out.

Matisse shut the door just as Sacha was coming back up the stairs.

'I'm working in my office the rest of the day. The courier's coming to the service door so tell Magda to buzz me when he arrives, and I'll send the package down in the lift.'

'Okay.'

She watched as he moved up the stairs, his large backside swinging from side to side like a rhino, his breath heavy with effort. The office door swung shut behind him. Matisse took off her apron, smoothed her hair, and went back downstairs to give Magda her instructions. It really had been a fun morning. She should do it more often.

Chapter Nine

Vicky allowed herself a small sigh of relief as she got into her car that she'd parked on a side street to the left of the Kozlovsky's house. She had been lucky earlier, when she found the space; it was perfect for her to see through their small wrought-iron gate to what she assumed was the service door. There were no windows on this side of the house past ground level, and she'd checked the CCTV screens on her way up the stairs from the kitchen and knew they were focused on the entry points to the house – the service door, the main door and the gate – rather than the grounds and surrounds, so she was confident she would be okay to sit here for the short while she needed to be. She guessed that the courier Sacha had mentioned would be sent straight around, so she sat, the smell of the cupcakes wafting from the passenger seat, and waited with her phone in her hand. From a distance, she'd look to anyone like she was consulting Google Maps for divine intervention. But the camera was ready to snap the visitor, when he or she arrived.

It had been an interesting morning. She was genuinely

bowled over by the house, which was beautifully put together. Despite being an art-lover, Vicky's budget only stretched to framed prints bought from museums and galleries; and her own interior design attempts stopped a long way shy of *Homes & Gardens*. Upgrades to the Turnbull family home mainly consisted of getting Chris to repaint the living room once every few years and paying a visit to John Lewis once in a blue moon to buy some new cushion covers and a fig-scented room diffuser. The Kozlovsky house was something else, though. She hadn't been inside a house like that in a long time – certainly not at the invitation of the owner, anyway.

She hadn't expected to be shunted straight off to the kitchen, though. She hoped Matisse might be the sort to want to give her the guided tour of the house renovations, so she could get the lay of the land and maybe see something that might not have been on the schematics JOPS had procured. But Matisse seemed cautious and suspicious of her gushings about the house (which were, on the whole, completely genuine), and Vicky had quickly deduced she was either under instructions to keep Vicky in a restricted area or had made that decision for herself for some reason. It wasn't a big deal and she didn't want to push her luck, but it did mean she would need to work a little harder to create an opportunity and gain access to the rest of the house.

It had taken a while, but she'd got there in the end. She'd just asked Matisse if she could use the loo, intending it as a ruse for a quick recce of the house, when Sacha arrived home. She was in the hallway near the front door and about to take a look around when she heard the sound of a key in the lock. Quickly locking herself into the hallway bathroom, Vicky waited to see if she'd missed her moment. Sacha was muttering something; she heard him light a cigarette and smelt the smoke as it leached under the door. The clip-shuffle of his feet on the stairs told her that Sacha had gone upstairs to his office. Right where she'd been headed. Damn. She waited a moment longer and was just about to give up and flush the toilet when she heard him come back down again and continue to the kitchen. It was an opportunity too good to resist, despite the risk. Vicky left the light on and exited the bathroom, using a coin in her pocket to ease the lock shut again from the outside. Anyone who came back up would assume she was still in there, if she was quick about it. She paused for a fraction; her nerves were shredding themselves like cheese through a grater. She could hear voices downstairs and knew she wouldn't have long – a couple of minutes, maybe, at the most. It was now or never. She took a deep breath and headed for the stairs. Lucky for her she'd taken off her shoes when she arrived, and she moved quickly upwards, sockless and silent, until she reached the now-open door.

Sacha's office. There were paintings lining the panelled walls and shelves near the windows that housed books in Russian, French and English. The laptop sat there, resplendent, in the centre of a regal desk made of carved wood. It was empty aside from the computer and a notepad; Vicky didn't dare go around the back to check the drawers. She worked quickly, taking an external drive from her pocket and plugging it into the laptop to download the malware that would give them access to Sacha's every digital move. While it downloaded, she took a panoramic photo of the room with her phone, just as Mike had taught her, and then bent over the laptop and took a photo of that too. As an afterthought, she snapped the notepad as well, and carefully ripped the top page off, folding it and putting it in her back pocket. It was empty of any notes, but a blank page often revealed more than was intended—

The phone on the desk began to ring. *Shit.* Vicky looked around for a hiding place but all that was available to her was under the desk or behind the door. She chose behind the door; it was a better position from which to attack or escape. Her heart thudded and she waited for the sound of Sacha's footsteps. Two rings, three rings, four . . . finally, the phone stopped ringing and she heard Sacha's voice in the hallway downstairs. An extension. *Thank God.*

'Privet.'

Vicky listened through the crack in the door as Sacha switched from Russian to speaking English through what sounded like gritted teeth.

'I told you not to call me here.'

He lowered his voice even further and Vicky strained to catch anything of the conversation. Who was he on the phone to? *Was it Anatoli?* A rush of old feelings threatened to surface, followed quickly by shame. What did it matter? He was a traitor, Sacha's right-hand man, not the person she had known. And, anyway, it wasn't him; they would be speaking Russian, not English.

She switched her focus to her current predicament. How on earth she was going to get back, Houdini style, into the downstairs cloakroom while Sacha stood in the hallway? Her eyes wandered back to the laptop and she realised she'd left the external drive in the side. A rookie error; if that phone call hadn't stranded her in the office, she'd still have blown the whole operation.

She still might. Vicky edged her way to the middle of the room, petrified that the slightest creak in the floorboards might give her away. Finally, she reached the laptop and had just grabbed the drive when she heard Sacha's voice, loud and clear.

'I will see you on Monday at the club. And don't call me at home ever again.'

Vicky heard the phone being slammed onto a surface and stood stock still in the middle of the room, waiting for signs of movement.

'Matisse!'

Vicky breathed a sigh of relief as she heard Sacha's voice travelling towards the kitchen. She silently raced back down the stairs from the office, opened and closed the bathroom door and flushed the toilet. Her heart was pumping out of control, and she was pretty sure she'd broken a sweat. She opened the door again, audibly this time, and went to join them. When she got back to the kitchen, Sacha made it clear it was time for her to leave.

But she'd accomplished a lot while she'd been here. The spyware was installed, and they had access to Sacha's laptop. She'd overheard him reminding Matisse about a visitor, and she knew he had a package to give him and a service lift to send it down in. She'd seen the lift doors in his office, forming part of the wood panelling on one wall in between the bookshelves, where a fireplace would normally be. She'd seen the layout of the house already, of course, but now she was starting to get a better idea of how it was all used by the Kozlovskys: the kitchen basement, the maid's room, utility room; the ground floor with the living and dining rooms and study; the first floor with Sacha's office. There were other rooms leading off the hallway – maybe a less formal family room or something – Dmitri must hang out somewhere. The plans suggested the top two floors contained the main concentration of bedrooms, five of them, and a few bathrooms too. It was a sizeable house, and that wasn't counting the indoor pool, linked by a glass-panelled hallway on the front corner of the plot. Whatever Sacha had done in the past, he had done it awfully well.

And what about Matisse? Vicky had watched her carefully during the course of the morning. She was mistrustful of strangers, that much was obvious. There was fear, too, of Sacha; and a little bit of defiance. The comments she had made about him and the palpable tension between the two of them once he got home made Vicky suspect Matisse wasn't just a pretty face and that Sacha liked to make her pay for that. Whether she was involved or not, Vicky couldn't say for certain yet. She was keeping secrets, that was for sure. But the phone call, and Sacha's reaction to being called at home, suggested that maybe they weren't Sacha's.

At two minutes to twelve, Vicky saw a bike pull up in front of the Kozlovsky's side gate. She noted the plate, make and model and realised with horror that it was the same bike that followed her from JOPS HQ.

'Shit.' Maybe Sacha was on to her after all. She scrabbled about in her glovebox, wishing she'd brought one of the weapons stashed in the top of her wardrobe. Finding nothing except the car manual and a few empty crisp packets, she began to panic. The rider removed his helmet; keeping one eye on him as he approached the car, she looked around her for anything to defend herself with. She breathed a sigh of relief as she caught sight of Evie's skipping rope lying in one of the rear footwells. It wasn't perfect, but it would have to do. She grabbed it, pulled it taut around her hands and slid low in her seat.

The man was tall and slim, moving with an easy stride. He headed towards Vicky's car and she tensed herself for action.

But instead of stopping, the man headed for the Kozlovsky's gate, checking the number on the entry buzzer and then pushing the button. Vicky relaxed her fingers and let the blood flow back into her hands. He was just a courier. It was coincidence. No threat to her at all. But it wouldn't hurt to know who he was anyway. She dropped the skipping rope and reached for her phone, taking pictures in bursts just like Mike had told her to, so that she captured as much information as possible.

The gate swung wide, and the man slipped inside and waited at the lift service door. After a few seconds, it opened. Vicky strained to see what or who was inside, but she was too far away. Instead she waited until the gate opened again. The man walked through with a new carrier bag in his right hand, threw his helmet on and headed towards his bike.

Vicky cursed. She wouldn't be able to follow him in the car – bikes were too nippy – and she really did have to pick James up from nursery on time today. She wished she didn't have to interrupt things when she was on such a roll. But Jonathan would be happy with the office photos and the intel on the house and on Sacha's visitor, and maybe she even had enough to get a match on facial recognition, if the guy had a record already. She assumed they had that technology. *CSI: Miami* had had it for years. Bloody hell, even Facebook tried its best, though it repeatedly tried to tag James as the wife of someone Chris went to university with. But it seemed likely the people in charge of a top-secret military intelligence agency might have access to slightly better software.

Vicky put her phone away and started the engine, easing away from the house. She wove her way through a few side streets to reach the main road again a little further down, not wanting to pull straight out in case Sacha or Matisse happened to look out of the window. As she drove, she burst into a big grin. She'd completed her first proper piece of undercover work in fourteen years, and, bar the odd slip up, it was like riding a bike.

*

The darkening evenings and misty mornings told Vicky that half term was nearly upon them already. She'd decided to cook spag bol for dinner; it was chilly today and she felt like some comfort food. While she prepared the vegetables, Vicky thought about the operation. Since their baking session, Matisse seemed to have relaxed a little. She was still reluctant to indulge in idle chatter at pick-up, but Vicky persisted and, slowly, the odd stilted greeting had been replaced with warmer exchanges. Vicky could see herself growing to like the Frenchwoman. She had a wry sense of humour and a way of seeing through people that Vicky liked a lot. But this was a job, not a friendship. She didn't want to get to know Matisse any better than she needed to.

The sting of the onion hit her eyes as she chopped and Vicky swept it to one side of the board, blinking away the tears. Grabbing a stick of celery, she cut it in half lengthways and began dicing. Jonathan would be meeting with her tomorrow to talk about next steps. But she was facing a week of school holidays with three kids of disparate ages and interests, locked up in the house watching the rain come down. She had little to no idea how she would ever juggle that with the demands of a surveillance operation.

Vicky grabbed a handful of mushrooms and hacked them up into pieces in a rather cavalier fashion. In the normal scheme of things, she wouldn't have minded, but for the first time ever she resented having to put the kids first. She was loving being back in the saddle – even now she could still feel the buzz. Jonathan seemed happy with her too; she felt – there were so many words running through her mind – *useful, wanted, important*. She stuck the knife into the board and picked up the vegetable peeler and a carrot. That sounded so disrespectful to herself and her life as it had been, yet she couldn't help herself. The battle lines between 'working mum' and 'stay-at-home mum' were drawn and erased, then drawn and erased; one half of her asking why she should feel bad about doing something for herself for a change, the other asking what was so bad about her life up until now that she was bandying about words like *useful, wanted* and *important*, as if she wasn't all those things before? In any case, surely, she could have the best of both worlds?

She didn't realise she'd taken the skin of her thumb off with the peeler until the blood dripped onto the cutting board. 'Shit.' She grabbed a piece of kitchen roll to stem the bleeding. At least it wasn't her shooting hand. Not that she needed it; she'd gone to the range the day after she'd been to Matisse's house and requalified as easily as Jonathan had predicted, but her gun was still waiting for her at HQ. Fashioning garrottes out of skipping ropes and having a stun gun buried in her ski socks was one thing; but a gun . . . she couldn't bring herself to have it in the house.

'I can hardly keep it in the knife drawer,' she said to Mike, when he called to find out why she hadn't signed it out. 'Although maybe it would solve the issue of whose turn it is to load the dishwasher.'

Mike chuckled. 'We'll install you a safe to keep it in,' he suggested. 'That way you have it if you need it.'

'Thanks . . . but what good would a gun do, locked in a safe? And it's just another thing to have to lie about. I really don't think it's necessary, Mike. It's not like I'm on the takedown team; I'm hardly likely to encounter a shootout on Wimbledon Common. Besides, I'm trained to improvise. I've become quite the entrepreneur; you should see the handbag I'm packing.'

She was rummaging in a drawer for a plaster when a ping on her phone interrupted her thoughts. She read the message and smiled.

Becky and Simon are having a Halloween Party! Saturday 30th October, from 8 p.m. Theme: Crime fighters.

Well, that couldn't be any more appropriate.

'Did you get the invite to Becky and Simon's Halloween party?' Kate said, later that afternoon at the school gates.

Vicky nodded. 'I've not been to a party on Halloween in years. Chris always insists we dress up and go out trick or treating with the kids, but Ollie's getting too old, Evie's too embarrassed, and James is better off without the sugar rush. This party gets me off the hook very nicely.'

'I have never been to a fancy-dress party in England before,' Matisse said, joining their conversation. Kate looked a little surprised.

'Oh, er, hi, Matisse. We were just . . .'

'It's okay, I have been invited by Becky to her party,' she said, putting Kate out of her misery. 'I think she invited the whole PTA. It's husbands too, yes? Sacha loves to dress up.'

Vicky very much doubted that, but maybe she was doing Sacha a disservice; after all, even Russian gunlords were allowed to let their hair down occasionally. Becky was a saint. A party meant Sacha and Matisse would both be out of the house, meaning there would be a perfect opportunity for JOPS to get in.

'What are you going as?' Kate asked, her eyes darting from one person to the next. Vicky grinned. Kate was as competitive as hell and probably figured a little due diligence would give her a head start on procuring a suitable costume.

'I leave that sort of thing to Chris,' she said. 'You know what he's like with stuff like this: wind him up and watch him go. He'll come up with something. I'll probably end up as Scooby-Doo.'

'I think Sacha and I will go as James Bond and a Bond girl,' Matisse said.

'You'd make an amazing Bond girl.' Kate looked sick with jealousy.

'Thank you, Kate, you are very kind.'

'Although it might be a bit cold for a white bikini and a hunting knife,' Vicky added. Kate laughed.

'Do you think so?' Matisse said. 'Hmmm. Well, in that case, maybe I will go as a Bond baddie. A PTA assassin.'

Vicky squirmed. Was Matisse trying to tell her something?

'A PTA assassin,' Kate said, 'that's hilarious. Although we've already got our own personal assassin right here, don't we, Vicky?'

She swallowed uncomfortably and tried to sound

light-hearted. 'I can't believe you're still bringing that paint-balling party up.'

'My husband is still wondering how you were so good,' Matisse said. 'He says that—'

'Mum! Guess what? I got made captain!'

'What?' Evie was pointing at a small enamel badge on her PE kit.

'I'm captain of the netball team!'

'That's brilliant, Evie!' Vicky gave her a huge hug, delighted for her daughter. She didn't waste too much time wondering what Sasha had been saying about her. Some things in life were more important. 'Seems we've got some celebrating to do,' she said. 'Come on, we can stop at the shop on the way home and you can choose a choco-late bar as a treat. My superstar!'

'Muuum!'

'Whoops!' Vicky rolled her eyes knowingly at Kate and Matisse, who were smiling. 'I'm being embarrassing. Sorry.'

They said their goodbyes and began walking to the car, Evie attempting to maintain her sulky disposition but failing miserably. At eight years old, she was already halfway to womanhood, but Vicky was glad she wasn't a tweenager just yet. While she liked having her nails painted and knew the words to all the One Direction songs, her room was resplendent in pink, and her favourite soft toys still lurked on her bed.

Vicky was in no hurry to change that. She was never one to look back and wish her kids younger again; she believed in enjoying the journey and had done just that with Ollie. But with her daughter, it was different. More and more, she felt herself trying to hold on to Evie's youth, to have as many years as possible without caring about what other girls were wearing, or doing, or thinking, or whether she was too thin, or too fat, or too tall, or too short; without worrying about bras or when her period would start, or boyfriends or marriage or whether children would ruin her career, or if she should go back to work or stay at home with the kids . . . she wanted to stave off the whole thing so Evie could just be free of it for a little longer.

Girls were so difficult in comparison to boys. Ollie had just got bigger, eaten more, and at thirteen, almost to the day, he had become mute. He was still her son: a polite, intelligent and happy boy with an intense love of football and computer games who didn't want to talk to her very much right now. She was fine with that; she knew eventually – around about seventeen or eighteen she supposed – he'd come out the other side.

But Evie . . . Vicky knew it wouldn't be the same. She was doing her best to make sure she was an ally to her daughter, paving the way already with shopping trips and crafting sessions, saying yes to sleepovers, and keeping an eye on bad influences. Her own teenage years had been difficult; her parents strict and uncommunicative. After her dad died of a heart attack, her mother had been so depressed and angry; by the time Vicky had left for university, she'd felt nothing but relief. She often wondered, had she known then that neither of them would be around to see her grow older, would she have been more tolerant, more generous, more forgiving? She doubted it. Teenage girls tended not to view the world in that way and Evie would be no different. Vicky sighed. Just as she was embracing the idea of working again, she needed to turn her attention back to parenting. She wondered if there would ever come a time when her loyalties wouldn't be so divided.

Chapter Ten

The next day, after drop-off, she headed to a small park in the depths of West London to meet Jonathan for an update.

'New coat? Looks nice,' he said, as she walked up and kissed him on both cheeks. Vicky bent down to pet Jonathan's dog, in a bid to stop the pooch from jumping on her with muddy paws.

'Thanks.' She'd bought it last week, with her first pay cheque – a sensible quilted navy number from John Lewis that cost a fortune but went through the wash and was a lot like wearing a duvet. Not what you'd call cutting edge. But between Jonathan's comments and her own realisation that she'd been hanging onto some things for far too long – mainly her youth – it was with much reluctance that she had finally proffered the red coat to the charity donation pile.

Jonathan and Vicky started off along a path together, like any normal friends, breathing clouds of white as they spoke into the cold morning air. The dog galloped around them and Jonathan played fetch with him as they walked.

'Your little visit to the Kozlovsky house gave us solid intel, Turnbull. You can consider your maiden voyage a great success.'

'Well, the cakes certainly turned out well.'

'Victoria,' he chastised. 'Report. How have things been since then?'

'Sorry. Matisse is warming up, but I'm still not sure how much she knows. They don't like each other; there's tension – a lot of it. Sacha has no respect for her. But they seem to be on the same page when it comes to their privacy. Maybe she knows some of what's going on, but not all of it. Or maybe she's just scared of him and does what he says. He's obviously a violent and volatile man.'

'Keep digging. She could be useful – and less suspicious than her husband. Might give something away without even realising, if we're lucky.'

Vicky wasn't so sure. Matisse seemed wilier than Sacha, in her opinion. But Jonathan was stubborn and she knew him well enough not to question the order.

'What about Sacha?'

'He tolerated my presence in the house, just about. He took a call while I was there, arranged a meet. I couldn't tell who, but figured you were listening in.'

'We couldn't trace the call. But we're sending surveillance to the golf club on Monday just in case.'

'It's half term next week. I'm not sure I'll be able to—'

Jonathan cleared his throat. 'Actually, we're sending someone else. A woman at a golf club would stick out like a sore thumb and there's no way he'd buy you casually bumping into him there. We need someone unknown to him, who can blend in better.'

Vicky rolled her eyes. She agreed that it would be better

to send someone Sacha wouldn't recognise, but didn't really understand why, in the twenty-first century, they had to have a penis. She moved on. It wasn't worth the fight. 'What about the laptop?'

'Search browser seems to be used primarily to download porn. Pretty average porn at that – nothing deviant. All the saved files were his onshore financial statements, property documentation and so on, and clean as a whistle. If he was keeping anything on there, he's not any more. But we suspect there's an external drive or server somewhere that has more on it. Mike is searching the laptop to see if he can find a back door.'

'So, what do you need from me?'

'Mike took a look at that page of the notepad you brought back, and we managed to determine imprints saying "Jebel A." and "21DEC". We believe this might be the missing link between MI6 intel and HMRC's. According to the paperwork, the guns are due to dock in China at the beginning of December. MI6 report that Kozlovsky has a small ship waiting there but the trail goes cold after that. We think he has plans to pay off the third party and take possession of the cargo, then move the weapons to the Middle East and meet the new buyer there. The imprint from the notepad gives us the place – Jebel Ali Port in Dubai – and, better still, the date they are due to dock.'

'That makes sense. So, what now?'

'We need you to get us access to the rest of the house. Easier said than done, I know, but—'

'Anything specific? We already have the phone and the laptop tapped.'

'We need eyes and ears. I want the place bugged from top to bottom in case one of them talks. And I want a tracker on Sacha. I want to know where he's going at all times. And I want to find whatever it is that he's using to communicate this deal.'

'I'll see what I can do.' Vicky paused. 'What about the courier?'

'The courier?'

'The guy who picked up the package from the service lift entrance. I'm sure I've seen him before; he was tailing me after I left JOPS.'

Jonathan looked down, pursing his lips. 'Ah.'

'Jonathan?'

'His name is Jacob Zimmerman. He's a courier, twenty-eight years old, arrested for petty theft and carjacking as a minor but no major priors.' He paused. 'Well, that's his cover story, anyway.'

'He's one of ours? What was he doing tailing me?'

Jonathan scratched his head. 'The thing is, Victoria, we didn't know how – how *proficient* you'd be, after all this time. Jacob, well, let's just say he's been looking after your best interests.'

Vicky felt the fury rise up inside her. 'You mean *your* best interests.'

Jonathan didn't say anything.

'You've been spying on me, to make sure I can do my job properly?'

'It's not like that exactly; we just wanted to make sure you didn't run into any trouble you couldn't get yourself out of.'

'You were testing me. When he tailed me, to see if I could shake him off. And when he was at Sacha's house, what was that?'

'You'd made contact so quickly, we were concerned you weren't ready—'

'I don't need a babysitter, Jonathan.' She thought about how she'd nearly blown up the whole op by leaving the thumb drive in Sacha's laptop, and pushed the memory aside. 'You can tell your little spy pup to stand down.'

Jonathan sighed. 'Look, I know you think you have something to prove, but you really don't. You made one mistake, and it was such a long time ago. . . Jesus, most of the people who were there are retired, or dead, or don't even remember you. You were a good spy. One of the best. But you're rusty, Victoria. You haven't done this in years. And you've got a family you care about now, and that will naturally make you feel more cautious and vulnerable. It's not that we can't trust you—'

'Well it feels an awful lot like you don't.'

Jonathan glanced at his watch and called the dog to heel. 'You've done a brilliant job so far, Turnbull. Take Jacob's lack of interference as a good sign and maybe start considering him as an asset. You're part of a team. Start acting like it.'

He checked his watch. 'Time to go.' He leant in and gave her a peck on the cheek as if to say a fond farewell. Vicky played her part and kissed him back, even though it was the last thing she felt like doing.

'Signal when you have something for us.'

'Yes, sir.'

That evening, after they'd finished dinner and the kids were in bed, she got her phone out and tapped in a message to Matisse.

> Would Dmitri like to come for a playdate during half
> term next week? Monday? Bring him over after lunch,
> I can drop him home again later. Vxx

She knew what she was doing was totally hypocritical, even
as she hit Send. Her whole justification for taking this
assignment was to make sure the kids were kept out of it.
But she was still smarting over her meeting with Jonathan
and desperately wanted to prove she could do what he
needed. And, really, Dmitri coming to their house wasn't
putting any of them in danger. She'd thought about it from
every angle: there was literally nothing about having this
playdate that could be construed as suspicious by anyone;
it was just a playdate, and, in any case, given the lack of
attention Sacha paid to his son, it was unlikely he'd even
register it was happening. Vicky ignored the nagging guilt
gnawing away in the pit of her stomach telling her she was
wrong. It was fine, it was perfectly safe and it would get
her what she needed: access to the house.

She waited impatiently for the reply, though she suspected
Matisse wasn't the sort of person whose fingers hovered
over her smartphone. Even if she'd seen the message, she'd
most likely wait before she answered. Vicky would just have
to be patient. She tucked her phone into her jeans pocket
just as Chris sneaked up on her from behind to nuzzle her
neck. Vicky spun around, elbows flying, and just about
managed to stop herself from drop-kicking him in the face.

'Whoa! Calm down, tiger.' Chris backed off a few feet and
fell onto the sofa, hands up in front of him. 'What was that?'

'You surprised me.'

'I don't usually get karate chopped. Where did you even
learn how to do it, anyway?'

'Sorry.' Vicky kissed him apologetically. The last thing she needed was for him to get suspicious. 'I think I've been watching too many action movies.'

She sat down next to him on the sofa.

'Maybe we should stick to a bit of *Location, Location, Location* tonight instead of all that blood and guts you usually like watching.'

'It's not all blood and guts, but, yes, I'm fine with a bit of Kirstie and Phil for a change.' She snuggled into her husband and put her hand on his thigh.

'This is nice,' Chris said. 'It feels like we've been a bit busy for each other lately.'

'What do you mean?'

'Well, me with work, and you with the kids, and the PTA – you seem to be rushing about a bit these days – and we just don't seem to have had much time for us.'

Vicky held her voice steady. 'I don't think it's been any different to usual.'

'You've just been a bit . . . preoccupied, I suppose. And tired, maybe. We haven't talked as much as we usually do. I feel like I don't know what's going on with you at the moment.'

The last thing she needed was Chris getting suspicious. 'I'm just a bit busy with the PTA. No wonder Becky says it's a full-time job for her.'

'I supposed we'd better get used to it if you end up going back to a full-time job of your own,' Chris said. He put his arm around her shoulder. 'How will you ever find time for Kirstie and Phil?'

'I'll always have time for Phil. And you.' She gave him a peck on his cheek. He kissed the top of her head in reply and a rush of affection came over her. She was so lucky to have found Chris. He'd given her balance and taught her compassion, two things she never even realised she was missing until they met. She was loyal and full of tenacity and grit, but the measure of what made a good or bad human had been dramatically skewed by what she did and the people she worked for. Looking back, Vicky would admit that she really hadn't been a nice person a lot of the time. She lacked patience or empathy and was often very selfish thanks to an extreme survival instinct. But Chris saw her differently; and, over time, that made her see herself differently, too.

She slumped down a little further on the sofa and pulled out her phone from her back pocket to get comfortable. She put the phone on the little wooden nest of tables next to the sofa and focused on the young couple on the TV who were waiting tentatively by the phone while Phil and Kirstie made their offer on property number two. Work – and Matisse – could wait. Tonight, she would enjoy some quality time with her husband.

Chapter Eleven

Somewhere on the other side of Wimbledon Common, Matisse was also otherwise engaged. She heard the buzzing of her phone on the nightstand and looked over to see that a message had arrived. From where she was, on all fours in the centre of the bed, she couldn't see who it was from; she'd have to reply when they were done. Which wouldn't be long. Matisse took a glance at her watch as Sacha's great heaving lump of a body knocked into hers from behind. His 'lovemaking' was getting quicker and quicker as time went on. Not that she cared. She preferred things to be over, with minimal fuss.

Flashbacks of cheap, sticky leather and the thumping of Eurotrash dance music flitted into her mind as Sacha continued to pump himself into a frenzy; the memories of the nameless, faceless men she had danced for, sat for, laid down and bent over for crowding into her head. Sacha's fat fingers grabbed at her still-slender hips and she thought about the girl she had been back in Paris: her body young and firm, writhing in unknown faces, her hands running down unknown bodies, her mouth closing around unknown cocks. She'd enjoyed it; enjoyed the anonymity of it all, enjoyed arousing the strangers who wanted her before they, and she, moved on. But when Sacha had come into the club the first time, and then the second, and the third, she saw a glimpse of an alternative way of life.

Sacha had eyes only for her. He found her amusing, thought she was smart, and she was happy to entertain this rich, important man, talking to him in Russian, whispering in French, and fucking him in silence, just how he liked it. Her boss didn't like it – he thought clients who were attached to one girl were bad for business – but Sacha was an imposing figure who had money and power at his disposal, and, if he asked for Matisse, he got her.

He visited the club for nearly three months, every time he was in the city. His compatriots – other rough-looking men with dangerous faces and flexed muscles – threw money at a different girl each time; for Sacha it was always her. She was his property, and, in an odd way, he was hers. One night, while she was straddled on his lap in a quiet room backstage, he muttered into her ear that he would like to see her away from the club.

'No,' she'd said.

'I will pay you. Name your price,' Sasha replied, his greedy crotch rubbing against her. 'What do you earn here that I could not give you ten times over?'

'What if it's not about the money?' she said, moving her hand down to unzip his flies.

'Of course it's about the money,' Sacha said, closing his eyes. 'It's always about the money.'

He asked her each time he saw her, while she was dancing for him, or while she led the way to the private suite, but she would always simply laugh and put a finger to his lips, knowing the fate of girls who fell for rich men in dancing clubs did not always turn out well. He wouldn't stop asking though and finally, one day, she agreed to listen to what he had to say.

'Matisse, you are a good dancer and I like fucking you. But I want someone loyal who I can depend on for more than just dancing and fucking. Am I wrong to think this is you?'

'Are you in love, Sacha?' She tweaked his nose playfully, but he grabbed her wrist, held onto it hard and stared into her eyes.

'That's not what this is about.'

'Why do you need me then?' She yanked her hand away. 'Why do you need anyone?'

Sacha reached into his jacket pocket and pulled out a cigar. 'In my line of business, it is good to have a person to watch your back. Men can stand guard with guns, but women see and hear much that men do not. Plus, men are weak around a beautiful woman. That can be useful to me.'

'And if you pay me enough, you get blow jobs whenever you want them.'

'It was wrong to offer you money as if you were a common whore. I like you, Matisse, and I should have made it clear that this arrangement will be mutually beneficial. You will have a better life, with not just money, but security and status too. I will have a beautiful woman on my arm, who can keep her ears open and her mouth shut.'

'I will think about it.'

He clipped the cigar, lit it, and exhaled heavily. 'Matisse, experience has taught me that if someone offers you a better life that the one you currently live, you should take it. You are attractive now, of course, and if you look after yourself you will stay that way for a long time. But a few more years of this shithole and you will be all fucked out. And then what will you do?'

She left the club the next day. Sacha, true to his word, bought her an apartment to live in while he travelled between Moscow and Dubai, always returning to Paris, and to her. Within six months she had transformed from a girl massaging his crotch in a club to the woman he wanted to come home to. Despite what he said, Matisse was sure that Sacha had fallen a little bit in love with her, but she knew he was still holding back. There were things he didn't tell her; meetings and money and men that he hid from her. And Matisse knew that, to be safe, she needed him to completely trust her. She needed a ring on her finger.

She resolved to make it happen through saying nothing. She didn't ask questions about his money, didn't comment on the stream of unsavoury guests coming and going from their apartment when he was resident, and kept quiet about the conversations she overheard. She focused on becoming a confidante rather than an inconvenience, a figure of strength, not subservient. She never complained, never did anything that would tarnish his reputation; she allowed him to use her as decoration for his arm, and his cock, whenever the mood suited him, but never flattered him enough to think he had complete power, either. Soon enough, she became the sort of woman he *would* like to marry, and so they did.

*

Pulling herself back to the present, Matisse looked at her watch again. It was time to wind things up. Stay silent for too long and he'd run into problems these days, which would just end badly for everyone. She adjusted their rhythm, made all the right noises and tossed her hair around, listening as the grunting got more intense and the pace of his thrusts quickened until finally it was over, and he slumped face down on the bed beside her. She turned herself around and pulled on a pale silk wrap, before heading for the bathroom, taking her phone from the table on the way.

She sat on the toilet, checking the message that had come in while she did so. It was Victoria, wanting to know about a playdate with Dmitri during half term. It suited her perfectly. Sacha was out most evenings, and Victoria had said she could even bring Dmitri home afterwards, meaning Matisse could ask Magda to let him in and not have to worry about being home either. She could spend an entire afternoon at the spa, or shopping, or maybe even a gallery and dinner.

She wiped, and stood up, a faint grimace of disgust as the remainder of Sacha's juices spilt down the inside of her leg. She put her phone on the side by the sink and got in the shower, scrubbing him off as fast as she possibly could. He'd been right: in the end it was about the money. If she left, she'd be cut off from everything, and she was damned if she'd let him do that to her after all this time. She thought he'd be dead by now, from a heart attack or killed by some thug with a grudge; she thought she'd be able to walk away with the cash, and the house, and be free of his bullish presence for ever. But here he still was, larger than life, and apparently invincible.

She wrapped her towel around her. She had Dmitri to

think about, of course. It was better for him to have stability, but the last thing she wanted was for her son to see Sacha as any kind of role model. Perhaps she was worrying needlessly, given the lack of enthusiasm Sacha showed for parenting most of the time. If he continued to stay at arm's length from her son – the way they both preferred it – Dmitri would hopefully decide for himself what kind of man to be, and learn from the people around him what the best version of himself looked like. The only thing to do for Dmitri right now was let him live as normal a life as possible, let him make friends, and hang out with ordinary families like the Turnbulls. She thought of Victoria, and the comical stories she'd told while they were baking, about her husband Chris, and their children. They seemed happy – not fairy tale exactly – but content. To her surprise, Matisse felt a little jealous.

But things weren't always as perfect as they looked. She of all people knew that. She was sure that Victoria and Chris had their own share of problems and secrets that they kept behind closed doors. Chris didn't look the type to have an affair, but maybe he had a mountain of internet porn stashed on his laptop like her own husband. Maybe Victoria was bored playing housewife. She was smarter than she let on, Matisse was sure of that. Matisse picked up her phone and started to reply to Victoria's invitation, making it as clipped and formal as she could. Making friends would be the best thing for Matisse as well, but she'd learnt her lesson long ago and kept herself to herself. She trusted no one, was friends with no one; except, she was lonely. She craved a normal life too.

Chapter Twelve

'I'm just dropping Dmitri home, Chris. I'll be about half an hour, okay?' Vicky grabbed her bag and slung it over her shoulder. 'Come on, Dmitri, get your coat on. I promised your mum I'd drop you back by seven.'

'It doesn't matter; she's not going to be there anyway,' Dmitri said.

'Well, I know, but I'm sure Magda will be waiting for you.'

Evie was getting her coat on too.

'Oh – no, Evie, you can stay here.'

'Why? Dmitri is my friend. I want to come.'

'I'm only running him up the road, Evie. You can say your goodbyes now and stay with Dad.' A manufactured playdate was one thing, but she had never intended her daughter to be around when she got down to the real reason for arranging it.

Evie frowned and threw her coat on the ground. 'Fine.'

'Evie, don't be like that. You've had a lovely afternoon—'

'Is there a problem?' Chris appeared at the top of the

stairs. He'd got home early for once, and was up on the PlayStation with Ollie.

'I wanted to go in the car with Mum, but she's saying I have to stay here.'

Vicky caught Chris' eye, imploring him to take her side. He got the message. 'It's just a quick car journey, sweetheart, and you need to start getting ready for bed. Say goodbye to Dmitri.'

'Bye, Evie. I'll get that game and give it to your mum, okay?'

Evie smiled. 'Thanks.' She turned to Chris, still cross with Vicky. 'Dmitri has this Harry Potter game for the PlayStation, he says it's really good and he's going to let me borrow it over half term.'

'That's kind of you, Dmitri. Thank you.' Vicky opened the door. 'Come on, off we go.' She ushered Dmitri out into the orange glow of the street, before calling back to Chris. 'See you in a bit.'

'Night night, Mummy, I love you,' came a little voice from the top of the stairs and she saw James wandering into view, clutching two toy cars. Vicky blew a kiss at her smallest boy, her heart full with love. He waved, farted and disappeared again, giggling. She turned to Evie and gave her a kiss. 'Don't be mad. I'll be home to read with you before bed, okay?'

Vicky and Dmitri got in the car and made their way to Wimbledon. The traffic was light, thanks to the school holidays, and Vicky was glad she didn't have to spend half an hour staring at brake lights in every direction.

'Did you have a good afternoon?' she said, trying to make conversation.

'Mmm,' came the response.

'That game sounds good. Do you like Harry Potter?'

'Yes, I do.'

More silence. She would be recommending to Jonathan that he recruit more eight-year-olds into the Secret Service from now on. They were very good at limiting the flow of information.

They reached the house and Vicky buzzed the intercom and waited for Magda to see them on the CCTV and open the gates.

Dmitri undid his seatbelt.

'I can go myself from here,' he said. 'I have a key.'

'Oh no. It's dark, and I promised your mum I'd see you to the door,' Vicky said, glad for once that she was telling the truth. The gates opened and she drove through and parked up at the front door.

Dmitri sprang out of his seat as soon as the car drew to a halt.

'Bye. Thanks for having me.'

'Wait!' Vicky hurriedly undid her own seatbelt and got out of the car. 'You need to get me that game for Evie, remember.'

'Oh, yeah.'

Vicky silently thanked her daughter for giving her a legitimate reason to spend a few minutes in the house. It would make what she had to do much easier. She followed Dmitri to the door, who ceremoniously unclipped a keyring from a beltloop on his jeans and let them in. He flung the key down on the table by the door, and chased up the stairs.

'Won't be a moment! I just need to find it in my bedroom.'

'No rush, Dmitri. I'll wait here.'

Vicky heard footsteps from below. She leant on the small

table where Dmitri had thrown his key and casually scooped it into her fist just as Magda's head peeked out from around the corner of the stairwell.

'Dmitri has gone up?' she said, climbing farther up the stairs towards the hallway.

'Oh, hello, Magda. Yes, he's gone to get a game to lend to Evie . . . sorry, I won't be long.' She paused. 'Actually, could I just use the bathroom? Do you mind?'

'As you wish,' Magda said. She was a woman of few words.

Vicky turned and headed into the cloakroom. Once the door was locked, she uncurled her hand, placed the key on the side of the sink, and quickly opened her handbag. She dug around until she found what she'd been looking for: an unopened rectangle of green clay. To the untrained eye, it looked like playdough, kept in her bag for a pre-schooler emergency diversion. However, sliced precisely in half and covered in baby powder, it wasn't intended for James. Vicky unsealed the clay and opened it up, before placing the door key inside and clamping down firmly. She released her grip and looked at the result. A perfect imprint, ready to make a copy of the Kozlovsky's front door key.

She flushed the toilet, washed her hands and came out clutching Dmitri's key inside her coat pocket. Magda was waiting, and Vicky, glancing at the clock on the wall by the stairs, gave a pointed sigh and made it clear she too was being massively inconvenienced.

'If you can't find it, Dmitri, don't worry; we can do it another time,' she called, stepping towards the stairs.

'I will get him.' The tone of Magda's voice told Vicky not to follow.

'Of course.' Vicky stepped back again in acknowledgement

of the unspoken instruction. She waited until Magda was out of sight and then gently placed the key back on the table. Moments later, Dmitri came thundering back down the stairs.

'Here you go,' he panted, passing her the disc. 'I couldn't find the case, sorry.'

'That's alright. Thanks. We'll bring it back to school on Monday, okay?'

'Bye, Mrs Turnbull.' Magda came back down the stairs to see them out. 'Thank you for dropping Dmitri home.'

'No problem at all,' Vicky said, 'I can do it any time.'

And now, she really could.

The next morning, she headed to make a dead drop. Ollie was at home and Evie was with her best friend Isobel getting a pedicure. Vicky fundamentally disagreed with the concept of children in spas, but wasn't about to say no to the free time it provided her. James was at the oversubscribed holiday camp at his nursery, thanks to a last-minute cancellation. Vicky wasn't sure if Jonathan had orchestrated it, but, either way, it bought her the time she needed to hand the key cast over without having to drive all the way to Gilbert House to deliver it.

It was a beautiful late autumn day, the sun low and bright, the trees lining the roads shaking off the last of their leaves to join the swirl of plastic bags and fag butts. The pub she headed into was quiet, but not completely empty, and a fire was lit in one cosy corner. Despite the temptation to take a seat inside, she ordered a lime and soda and a burger at the bar, checked her phone and went into the beer garden. It didn't raise any eyebrows – the pub was kitted out with patio heaters, blankets and fur-lined seats, all waiting outside for the great British smoking public.

She sat down in the corner that backed on to the rear wall of the pub, got out a pack of cigarettes and a lighter, a book and took a sip of her drink. There was no one else in the garden, but she picked up her book anyway, lit a cigarette, and lodged it in the ashtray. If anyone came, they'd assume she was smoking it.

After a few minutes, she glanced at the toilet windows that opened on to the courtyard. She'd heard someone lock themselves into a cubicle as she'd lit her cigarette, and now she heard a hand dryer. She waited until the bathroom door opened and closed again, the muffled sounds of the pub growing louder and then dimming. Then, taking the clay mould from her bag, she took a final sweep of the beer garden before hiding it carefully behind the planter next to the wall, where the trellis met the brickwork. Satisfied it was in the right place, she drained her drink, stubbed out the cigarette and went inside to eat her burger by the fire.

Wiping the last of the grease from her mouth, she looked at her watch and saw that it was nearly time to get James. As she did up her coat ready to face the outdoors again, she called home to check on Evie and Ollie.

'Hi, Ollie,' she said as her son answered the phone. 'Everything all right?'

'Yes, Mum. Everything's fine,' he replied. 'Evie's just got home. She wanted to go on the iPad so I said it was okay. I gave her a biscuit too, she said she was starving 'coz Isobel's mum had made them eat quinoa for lunch.'

'Thanks, Ollie,' she said, proud that, for once, her son had been responsible rather than winding Evie up and causing a row. 'I've just got to get James and I'll be home in about half an hour, okay?'

'Okay, Mum. Hurry up, though. I don't know how long I can bear being nice to Evie.'

She smiled. 'I'm on my way.' Out of the pub now, she headed into the train station. She stopped at the ticket machine – the one on the right by the entrance – and started the process of buying a travelcard she didn't need. Digging in her wallet for cash, she removed one of James's *Star Wars* stickers from the sheet inside at the same time and quickly stuck it to the side of the machine, while she waited for her ticket to print. She breathed a small sigh of relief as she took her ticket and headed to the platform. Her mission was complete and the sticker was the agreed signal that the DLB was ready to empty. One of Jonathan's team would retrieve the mould from the pub within a few hours and there'd be a meeting time set for her to get a copy of the key, plus all the other items she needed for the next part of the operation. Then the fun would really begin.

She took a look around the station while she waited for the train to arrive. Old training habits die hard; her earliest days in MI6, before her transfer to JOPS, had been taken up with endless memory test scenarios where she was asked to recall every single person in detail after a few minutes in any given location. She used to play it when Ollie was a baby, too, to keep her from the crazy baby fug she had wound up in those first few months after he was born. She'd had mild post-natal depression, the loneliness and lack of purpose after so many years running around with nothing but a gun and her gut threatening to overwhelm her at any given turn. To keep herself sane, she would imagine herself and her son into any number of life-threatening scenarios where the ability to recall a face would be what saved them from certain death. It made a refreshing change from singing 'Ring a Roses'. Today, though, the game was real. Jonathan was right about one thing – she would certainly be the last person anyone would suspect – but with Sacha set firmly in her sights she needed to be vigilant.

She took inventory of the platform opposite as well as the one she stood on; it was a quiet time of day for the London-bound trains, with only a few suits headed into town standing across from her: nothing to be concerned about. On her own platform, headed south, several people stood nearby in various states of smartphone oblivion. Near the stairs, a tired-looking woman gripped onto a toddler for dear life, in case he made a dash towards the platform edge. At the far end, a young man was reading a paper. The train rolled into the station and she got on, noticing as she did so that the man had folded his paper up to negotiate the gap between the platform and the doors. Now she could see who it was, and she recognised him instantly. *Jacob Zimmerman.*

She felt a flash of anger. What was the point in her going through the entire rigmarole of a dead drop if someone from her department was going to follow her around the whole time? She reached into her handbag for a burner phone, intending to call Jonathan and give him a piece of her mind. It was a waste of a phone, but seeing as he didn't seem to care about wasting departmental budget paying Jacob bloody Zimmerman to follow her, Vicky didn't really see why she should worry. He wasn't very good, now she thought about it. This was the third time she'd spotted him in plain sight.

Jacob sat down and opened up his paper again as the train started on its way. Vicky moved towards him slowly, the phone held to her ear. No signal. She swore and dumped the phone back in her bag. A mother sat with her toddler threw her dark looks.

'Sorry.' Vicky gave what she hoped was a placatory smile and sat down in a nearby seat, her view of Jacob partially obscured by a couple stood in the doorway with rucksacks on their backs. As they reached the next stop, they moved away from the door and she saw Jacob had folded the paper in half and then half again and thrown it onto one of the nearby seats. His eyes were closed. Vicky was furious. Was he that cocky, that he didn't even bother to *look* at her while he was tailing her?

At Parsons Green, their portion of the train emptied out, the mother and toddler thankfully getting off along with the rucksack couple. It was just her and Jacob now. The train lumbered towards the next stop; as they neared the station Jacob opened his eyes and stood up, checking around him and picking the paper back up. Vicky stood, half turned away as he came towards the standing area by the doors. In one swift move she spun and upended Jacob onto his back and forced his arm back hard enough to make him yelp. The paper flew across the floor.

'Ow! What the hell?' Jacob struggled, but Vicky held on tight.

'Stop. Following. Me.'

'Vicky? I'm not— I didn't— okay, stop!' Jacob used his feet to boot her away and she flew back against the litter bin. A coffee cup bounced out and onto her head, before rolling away across the floor.

'Gross.'

'Sorry.' He leant down to help her up; she took his outstretched hand and used the extra leverage to upper cut him with her other fist. The train lurched just as she was about to make contact and her arm flew over his shoulder instead, landing them in a rather awkward embrace. Jacob gently peeled her away from him and they both backed off to face each other, leaning against the Perspex walls either side of the doors. Vicky tried to control her breathing, feeling her face burning from the exertion. Jacob looked as pissed off as she felt.

'I feel like we may have got off on the wrong foot.' He smoothed his hair.

'I don't think so.'

The train stopped again, the doors opening. Jacob looked out.

'Got somewhere to be?'

'Actually, this is my stop. I live just on the other side of the bridge.'

Vicky narrowed her eyes.

'I just finished an all-nighter. I'm off home for a shower.' The doors began beeping to signal they were closing. 'Correction: *was* off home for a shower.'

She swallowed. 'You mean you weren't following me?'

'I told you – no. It's just a coincidence.'

'There's no such thing as a coincidence.'

The train started up again.

'Well, in this case, it's true. I told Jonathan you didn't need me interfering.'

'That's big of you.'

'Look, we don't know each other, and I know . . . well, I know you like to do things on your own. But I'm here – as back-up – or someone to talk to, bounce around a few ideas with. If you want.'

'Thanks.' She sounded sarcastic, but her anger was ebbing away.

'*Is* everything going okay?'

'It's fine. I'm just a little jumpy; I haven't done this in a while,' she admitted. 'It's harder than I remembered, sometimes. And lonely.' It felt good to talk to someone and say it out loud.

'You've been away for how long?'

'Fifteen years, give or take.'

Jacob whistled. 'It must be hard. If I take a couple of weeks' holiday it feels weird.' The train was slowing again. 'Look, I'm sorry about Jonathan, and all the cloak and dagger tailing stuff. But I'll be here if you need me, okay? Just don't attack me again.'

Vicky looked at him sheepishly. 'Sorry about that.'

The train stopped and the doors opened. Jacob looked out, both ways, and then jumped onto the platform. 'Gotta go! Need that shower. Bye, Vicky.'

He jogged away from her, moving quickly down the stairs and beyond her vision. Vicky got off too, and made her way to the station exit, rubbing her head where she'd hit it. Jacob hadn't been at all what she'd expected. She realised, reluctantly, it had been nice to meet him properly at last.

That evening, Vicky and Chris sat eating dinner together and Vicky temporarily abandoned all thoughts of spy work as they dug into a guilty pleasure of sausage, mash and beans.

'Everyone's really looking forward to Becky's party,' she said. 'Did you get anywhere with our costumes yet? Kate is dying to know what we're going as.'

A dollop of mash fell from Chris's fork. 'Oh shit, the Halloween party.'

'You forgot?'

'I'm really sorry, Vic. Work's been crazy, we're short-staffed still and with the lead up to Christmas we've got so much on. Can you sort us out something to wear? What about getting a Scooby-Doo costume from the fancy dress shop and I'll go as Shaggy?'

Vicky smiled. He was so predictable. 'Don't worry; I'll take care of it.'

'Maybe we should take a look online tonight and just see what's out there, for inspiration?' Chris was facing hours of work after dinner, and Vicky knew he was torn between wanting to get involved and having to focus on what he needed to get done for his meetings tomorrow.

'Chris – I've got this. I'll figure it out, okay?'

'Okay.'

He looked downcast and Vicky's heart melted. He was a daft idiot, but he was *her* daft idiot.

'But none of that miserable hardly-dressing-up-at-all nonsense. No Mulder and Scully, Vics. I like to stand out from the crowd.'

'I know you do.'

'What about The Incredibles? Or Batman and Robin?'

'I'll get back to you with some ideas that don't include Lycra, if that's okay,' she said. 'In fact, I'll get on the fancy-dress shop website and make a start right now.' She left the dinner table to go to the utility room and get the laptop, then realised her mistake and did an about turn.

'Are you keeping the iPad in the washing machine?' Chris chuckled.

'Very funny.' Vicky spied it on the kitchen counter. 'There it is.' She leant in to kiss him on the way to retrieve it.

'Must be hell in there,' he said, tapping her head.

142

'It's the menopause. I'm losing brain cells,' she said, airily dismissing the mistake.

'Maybe a glass of wine will help. At least then the brain cells will die happy.' He poured her a glass and she took it, picking up the iPad from the counter and heading into the living room.

'I'll have a little look for costumes while I watch *Homeland*,' she said. 'Enjoy your homework.'

Chris made a snarky face and settled back down to the table, opening up his own laptop to start his long night of work.

Chapter Thirteen

A few days later, the Halloween party was upon them. Chris had been in his outfit of overcoat, floppy hat and long stripey scarf since the kids' tea time, unable to contain his excitement. Vicky spent a little more time delaying the inevitable. She couldn't complain too much; after all, it had been her idea. But as she slipped the all-in-one Dalek outfit over the top of her black top and leggings, she definitely had second thoughts. Why couldn't she have been happy with a bit of Lycra and a cape?

'Wooo-eeee-ooooo, weeeee-oooooo, wah wah wah wah wah diddle ah . . .' The *Doctor Who* theme tune floated up the stairs and Vicky paused at the top, wondering if she'd make it down without stacking it.

'Exterminate! Exterminate! Bloody hell, watch yourself, Vicky.' Chris looked worried as she slid a couple of steps mid-descent. 'Can you see alright out of those slits?'

Vicky adjusted the top part of the costume. 'I don't think I'll be able to keep the head part on all night. I can't drink, for one thing.'

'We could get you a straw.'

'Very funny.' She heard the sound of laughter behind her.

'Mum, you look mental,' Ollie said, coming out of the living room.

'Thanks, Ollie. Did you say hi to Gran yet?'

'Yes, of course.'

'Good.' She turned back to Chris, who was busy with his iPhone. He was taking a selfie with her in the background, long scarf wrapped around his neck and a scared look on his face. 'Chris, is your mum all set and ready?' She poked her head into the sitting room. 'Hi, Maggie.'

'Hello, love. You look nice.'

The TV was blaring *Danger Mouse*, and her mother-in-law was already looking mildly harassed. Evie was showing her a dance and James stumbled in a two-foot radius around the television screen, clutching a sippy cup, looking for all the world like he'd raided the drinks cabinet. It occurred to Vicky that with a teenager and a toddler in the house, they should probably put the Grey Goose somewhere less accessible at some point, but, watching James trying to locate his mouth to drink and knowing that Ollie could barely find the milk in the morning, there probably wasn't any great urgency.

Vicky surveyed the room for her phone, so she could make a swift exit. She spied it in James's hand and cursed.

'James . . . Mummy needs her phone, please.' Her three-year-old began to cry as she prised the phone from his palms and put it in her back pocket. 'Oh, baby, please don't cry.' James's wails pierced her eardrums and she heard Chris call something from the hallway.

'What?' The noise in the room was unbearable.

'*Vicky!* We have to go.' Chris reappeared in the doorway.

'Leave this to Mum. Kids, do as Gran tells you – eat your dinner, no junk – and when she says "bed" you go. Okay?'

'Okaaaaaay.' Evie gave a loud snort, flopped onto the easy chair in the corner and flipped open a Harry Potter book.

Sighing, Vicky scratched at her hair. It was going to look a right mess by the time she got to the party. 'Bye, Maggie. Good luck. Bye-bye, my little one.' She kissed James on the head.

Chris ushered Vicky out of the room and towards the front door.

'So, you ready to walk round to Becky's?'

'Walk? I'm not bloody walking; it's freezing for one thing, and for another—'

'Don't panic, you great hunk of junk. We'll take the car and collect it in the morning.'

'Thank you.' Vicky retracted her arm from the lumpy tent structure that hung from her shoulders and pulled down her top that was riding up around her waist. 'Well at least I can eat and drink whatever I like – it's not exactly figure-hugging.'

'What have you got under there anyway?' Chris whispered in her ear.

'You're seriously trying to seduce me?'

He lifted her head dress and kissed her neck. Vicky felt herself go a little gooey.

'You *are* trying to seduce me.' They both laughed, the moment disappearing as quickly as it had come. Vicky was almost sad to see it go. Even if he was apparently turned on by a plastic plunger sticking out of her boobs.

'Are you two going or what?' Evie appeared in the hallway. 'Oh-emm-gee, Mum.'

'Blame your dad, Evie. I wanted to go as Mulder and Scully.'

'Who?'

'Mulder and . . . oh, it doesn't matter. Say goodnight and we'll see you in the morning, okay?'

'Goodnight. Please don't put photos on Facebook.'

'Too late.' Chris waggled his phone, showing his brand-new profile photo, and opened the door while Evie groaned in horror. 'Shall we, Head of the Supreme Dalek Council?'

'Exterminate! Exterminate!' Vicky edged out of the door backwards. Evie put her head in her hands and her mother-in-law waved cheerily.

'Have you got keys and some money for a taxi?' Chris asked her. 'I didn't think to bring anything except a bottle.'

'Don't worry, I've got a bag with me under here with all sorts of stuff in it.'

'Armed and dangerous, eh?'

'Something like that.'

When they reached Becky's house, the road was full to the brim with cars and they ended up parking around the corner and walking the last hundred yards or so. To the untrained eye, she really did look like she was floating down the road. The Dalek outfit had been the perfect cover for carrying the kit she needed for tonight: a torch, a screwdriver, her burner phone and a microscopic tracking pin all shoved into an innocuous cross-body bag. Jonathan had ordered Sacha's office phone to be tapped when they first picked up the case, and they'd had ears on him for weeks, but, due to the lack of relevant business calls, they guessed Sacha was using burner phones to get things done. Vicky had found out from Matisse that he often left his real mobile phone at home too. 'I can never get hold of him for anything,' she had said. It was causing them problems: not only did they not have ears on him most of the time, but, unless they went to the expense of tailing him 24–7, they had no way of knowing where he was either, prompting Vicky to suggest to Jonathan they needed to fit him with a tracker to trace his movements, with or without his phone. She was aiming to get one planted on him tonight.

While Vicky planted the tracker and kept Sacha and Matisse busy at the party, the JOPS surveillance team were going to the house, to bug Sacha's office with the aid of the newly cut front door key. Vicky had warned them about Magda, and the CCTV, but they'd arranged a diversion – a delivery of shirts from Moss Bros to the service entrance – and thanks to a hack on the cameras by Ops, they could slip through the gate and the front door unnoticed. Vicky was excited. Things were really happening now, and after tonight they would have eyes and ears on Sacha Kozlovsky from every angle.

They could hear the house before they reached it; screams of middle-aged delight came from every window, and the strains of nineties pop music resonated down the road.

Chris shook his head. 'Blimey, I hope they got rid of the kids for the night.'

'I think Becky's mum has them.'

'Thank God for grandparents, eh?' Chris said, as they

reached the house. The driveway and front porch were covered in fake cobwebs, carved pumpkins and inflatable ghosts. The door stood open, with a sign reading 'Trick or Treat?' above it. Becky was in the hallway, dressed as Wonder Woman. Vicky silently praised the two pairs of Spanx and the extremely good bra that she'd helped her friend procure the week before.

'Oh my God, Vicky, that is HYSTERICAL.' Becky caught sight of them coming in and immediately took a photo with her phone. 'Laura! Laura! Come and take a look at Vicky.'

Laura appeared from the kitchen dressed as Supergirl. 'Oh, Vicky, what did he make you do?' she said, leaning in to give Chris a kiss hello.

'Nothing to do with me, she was the one with the ideas this year,' Chris said, and headed for the kitchen. 'Is Steve in here?'

'Look out for Starsky. You'll find Hutch, a.k.a. Jon, in there too, I expect,' Becky said. 'The boys refused to do any Lycra, so they went all seventies on us.'

'Brilliant,' Chris said. 'Love it.'

'Did you want to stick your coat upstairs in the guest room?'

Chris patted his chest. 'Tom Baker never takes off his coat, Becks. You never know when you'll have to leave in a hurry.'

'Of course, Doctor, how silly of me.'

He disappeared off into the kitchen, leaving Becky, Laura and Vicky in the hallway.

'Was this really your idea?' Laura said.

'I know it seems unlikely, but it really was.'

'Well I think it's genius.' Becky gestured towards the living room. 'Shall we?'

They moved into the lounge where about thirty slightly sorry-looking crime fighters were already in various states of drunkenness.

'Vicky.' Kate was busy waving her hands to the S Club beat. 'Exterminate! Exterminate!'

Vicky grinned under her Dalek head. 'Hey, Kate.' Her friend was resplendent in a full-body black leather catsuit. She had been on an insane diet and workout combo since Becky sent out the invitations and Vicky had to give credit where it was due – she looked great.

'Hello, gorgeous,' she said. 'Michelle Pfeiffer's got competition, then.'

'So has Dusty Bin,' Kate replied, laughing.

'Well we couldn't all devote three weeks to protein shakes and CrossFit.'

'Truth be told, I wouldn't recommend it,' Kate said. 'I'm looking forward to a great big, fat burger tomorrow lunchtime.'

'Well I reckon you've definitely won sexiest woman in the room,' Vicky said, confident this would sate Kate's need to win, and rather glad she'd taken herself out of the running.

'Well, actually,' Becky said, 'I'm not sure Matisse didn't pip her to the post for that particular award . . .'

Vicky scanned the room, trying to place Matisse. Ahead, near the dining table, she could see Sacha. He was dressed in black tie and held a martini glass in his hand. Bond. James Bond. But where was Matisse?

'She's getting a drink,' Laura said, as if reading her mind. 'Oh my God, Vicky, but wait until you see her. I didn't think she'd have the balls, but, well, see for yourself—'

Laura nodded and Vicky turned around. Her jaw dropped and she silently thanked God that her face was hidden.

Carrying a bottle of vodka and dressed in nothing but a white bikini and a hunting knife, Matisse looked incredible. Her hair was gelled to make it look wet and her make-up was done expertly. She looked more like Ursula Andress than Ursula Andress.

'Bloody hell,' Vicky said, before she could stop herself.

'Told you,' Becky said.

'Hello, Victoria,' Matisse said. 'At least, I assume it is Victoria?'

'You look . . . wow . . . well, I . . . amazing!'

'Thank you.'

'Aren't you freezing cold though?' Vicky still couldn't quite believe what she was seeing. Did this woman have Dmitri by osmosis? Where were her stretch marks? What about her mum-tum? Vicky hadn't seen a body this perfect since she was . . . well, truthfully, she didn't think she'd *ever* seen a body this perfect.

'Well, I guess she's used to the cold,' Kate said.

'Don't be daft, she's French,' Laura said.

'Oui, but I have the Russian blood in me,' Matisse said.

'That's not the only Russian she'll have in her by the end of the night,' Kate commented. Laura snorted.

'It's a little cold for cigarettes outside, but luckily Sacha and I brought our big Russian coats,' Matisse said, ignoring Kate and pouring the neat vodka into a glass resting on the piano. She held up the bottle to everyone else, but they all shook their heads. 'He's in such a bad mood tonight; I am surprised he is even here.'

'I can't imagine he'd leave you alone to go out looking like that,' Becky said. 'He might be pissed off, but he can't take his eyes off you.'

*

Becky wasn't wrong. Sacha's greedy eyes watched his wife wherever she went, and Vicky saw he wasn't the only one. Matisse literally had the entire room's attention. Surreptitious glances, and one or two blatant lustful gazes, were coming from every direction – men and women. Vicky did her best to ignore her own jealousy monster rearing up inside. So, her swimsuit requirements included significantly more underwiring and tummy control. So what? She'd spent a lifetime mastering the art of being invisible, and if there was one thing she was good at, it was being indistinguishable from everyone else. She was here to do a job, one that she was good at. She'd take that over pert buttocks any day.

'I'm going to get a drink. Does anyone else want one?' She glided away from her friends and into the kitchen. Chris beckoned her over to where he was standing with Simon, Steve and Jon and passed her a bottle of Peroni. Vicky removed the Dalek head with relief and put in on a chair in the corner.

'I'm surprised you aren't in the living room with all the other mid-life crises gazing at our resident Bond girl,' she said to the four of them.

'Ah, I got my fast car last year, Vicky. I'm done,' Steve said.

'I'm more of an evil-overlord-with-plumbing-parts kind of a guy,' Chris said. 'That whole gorgeous girl in a white bikini thing is so last year.' He grabbed Vicky around the waist – or near enough her waist. To be fair to Chris, it was hard to tell where anything was in a Dalek outfit.

'She does look incredible,' Vicky said. 'But I must say, he makes a bit of an odd-looking Bond.'

'More like a Blofeld,' Chris said.

'Or that Jaws bloke,' Steve bared his teeth and growled, and everyone laughed.

'Yeah, he's hardly the Secret Service type, is he?' Jon said.

'Neither is James Bond,' Vicky said.

'Of course he is. He's the essence of a British spy,' Chris said.

'He really isn't, Chris. I mean, think about it, he sticks out like a sore thumb and wherever he goes people know who he is—'

'Argh! Get her away. She's spoiling the fantasy.' Simon put his hands over his ears in mock terror and Vicky grinned.

'Next thing you'll be telling me there's no such thing as Batman,' Steve said.

Vicky decided it was time to end the banter and put down her beer. She had work to do.

'Excuse me, chaps,' she said. 'I need to go to the bathroom.'

'Do you need any help?' Chris said, only half joking.

'No, I think I'll be okay. Send in a search party if I'm gone too long.'

She made her way into the hallway and up the stairs. The chatter dimmed to a noisy hum and she made one last check to make sure the coast was clear, then let herself into the darkened spare room where all the coats lay on the small double bed. Closing the door and sealing it shut with the door wedge, she lifted off her costume, threw it on to the floor next to the bed and opened up her bag to get out her torch and the screwdriver. If anyone tried to come in she'd have a few extra seconds while they forced the door past the wedge, which was really all she needed.

Tucking the screwdriver into her waistband and holding the torch between her teeth, Vicky rifled through the coat pile until she found what she was looking for a few layers down: two big, thick fur coats. She pulled them both out and laid them on top of the pile. Humming lightly, she checked the pockets of each coat and prayed she'd find what she was looking for, knowing if she didn't, that she had a much harder job on her hands. She struck gold as she searched the second pocket and her hand closed around Sacha's Cartier lighter, stashed with a pack of Marlboros in the larger of the two coats.

'Bingo.'

She pulled the light out and opened it up, getting a whiff of lighter fluid. Then, over the strains of Madonna striking a pose downstairs, she heard a voice. Someone was coming up the stairs. Vicky palmed the lighter, snatched up her handbag and turned off the torch. Her spare hand hovered over the screwdriver.

'Where?' a voice called. She couldn't figure out who it was, and hordes of people shouting about Marlon Brando and Jimmy Dean to the strains of 'Vogue' were making it difficult to assess which direction they were headed.

'Just up on the left-hand side.' Becky sounded impatient. 'Found it?'

Vicky waited a few long seconds.

'Yes, thanks!' came the voice, and the bathroom door closed and locked.

She breathed a sigh of relief. She switched the torch back on and eased the lighter out of its decorative gold casing. After unscrewing and removing the flint spring, she took the tiny tracking device from her bag and carefully slid it inside the spring. She put the lighter back together and got her phone out. Tapping something that looked a lot like the Google Maps app, she waited for the transmitter to connect.

When the little red dot appeared on her screen, right above where Becky's house was on the map, she tucked her phone away in her back pocket again and gave the lighter a quick rub with her top to get rid of her finger marks, before slipping it back inside Sacha's coat.

She had just stuffed the torch and screwdriver into her bag and thrown the Dalek costume over her head when she heard voices on the landing again.

'I need a word.' Sacha's voice was unmistakable. Vicky used the seconds of time the door wedge had bought her to stuff the coats back in the pile. She dived on to the floor on the far side of the bed and, as Sacha forced the door open, pulled a coat from the bed over her head. She tucked her feet and arms inside her Dalek costume and lay stock still, her heart pounding.

'Here? What's the matter, old chap?'

William? Why had Becky invited that idiot? More to the point, what the hell was William doing with Sacha?

Sacha spoke in low tones and Vicky could hear the stress in his voice.

'The deal is not going to plan. I might need to extend my credit line again while I divert the shipment and find a new buyer.'

'It's a big sum of money, Sacha. We've talked about this before. As your accountant, I'm not sure I can recommend doing that—'

William was Sacha's *accountant*? Did he know what a dangerous crook he was dealing with? William had four kids; he wouldn't put his family at risk like that. Would he?

'I know it's a lot of money,' Sacha snapped. 'It's that dick of a middleman, trying to screw me over, telling me the paperwork for the land transfer isn't ready yet.'

'You've still got a few weeks to go. I don't think there's much reason to panic.'

'What the fuck would you know about it? This isn't some small-time deal I've put together, William. I'm telling you, I can smell a trap.' She couldn't see a thing, but, by the sound of his voice, she could tell Sacha had made his way further into the room, towards her side of the bed. Vicky's heart lurched and she eased her hand down to try and find the screwdriver from inside her bag. Although what use a screwdriver would be if that great hulking lump of a man trod on her was anyone's guess.

'I've greased the palms of a lot of people to make this deal happen,' Sacha continued. 'But I didn't get where I am today by being a fool, and something isn't right about this jumped-up zhopa. I know other people who are like him. He wants this deal for himself and he's happy to let me take the fall in order to get it.'

'Are you sure, Sacha?'

'No one is going to screw this up for me. So, do what I pay you for and prepare to extend the credit line. If it comes to it, the goods will stay in Chinese waters until I can shift them elsewhere.'

'Your client won't be happy.'

'If that arsehole tries to fuck me over and my client is sitting waiting for a shipment that never arrives, they'll find him and pull his fingernails out one at a time until they get some answers. And if they don't, I will,' Sacha snarled.

'Steady on, old chap.' William sounded nervous and Vicky felt a flicker of sympathy for him. He was Sacha's accountant, and obviously complicit, but he'd got himself involved way over his head. She was starting to feel the same way.

'Just make the necessary arrangements, William.'

The bedroom door opened and closed. Both men were gone. Vicky waited a few minutes for her heart to stop pounding and then threw the coat off her head and lifted herself gently off the floor. She listened, then opened the door a crack to check the coast was clear. She'd just left the bedroom when Matisse came up the stairs.

'So, you managed to negotiate the bathroom with your costume then?' she said to Vicky, as they passed in the hallway.

Vicky glanced at the bathroom door, which was mercifully open to her left. 'Yes,' she said. 'It's all yours.'

'Oh, I'm coming to get our coats to have a cigarette in the garden,' Matisse said, working her way past Vicky.

'Well good luck out there – don't catch a cold,' Vicky said, and shuffled her way down the stairs as quickly as she could. She would have to report the conversation she'd overheard when she got home.

'Where've you been?' Chris said, turning around and shimmying his long scarf around her. 'Come and dance!'

'It was trickier than I thought, getting that costume on and off,' she said.

'I thought it might be.' Ricky Martin's horn section started up and the room began to shake to the beat of 'Livin' La Vida Loca'. Chris shimmied towards her like a giraffe with no bones and Vicky tried her best to join in, but she'd broken a sweat and was feeling thirsty.

'Jesus, this thing is warm. I might need to go and get another drink in a minute to cool down.'

'Why don't you just take it off?' Chris said.

Sacha and Matisse came back into the room, and Matisse peeled off her coat before beginning to gyrate her body across the dance floor. Vicky watched as Sacha snarled and headed back out again, presumably to put their coats back upstairs.

'Maybe later,' she said, feeling suddenly light and adrenaline-fuelled. Despite the close shave, she'd completed another successful covert operation and the night was hers to enjoy. 'After all, I never told you what was underneath . . .'

Chapter Fourteen

Vicky approached a bench in the park, flopped down onto it, and put her head between her knees. She'd decided to go on a post-Dalek, pre-Christmas health kick and was on week one, day three of the Couch to 5k app on her phone. She wanted to thank whoever invented it for highlighting the tragic state she'd got herself into and to point out to them that a minute and a half of walking time wasn't nearly enough to recover from sixty seconds of running. The lady shouting, 'You're halfway through!' just as she thought she was going to throw up was a dead woman if she ever got her hands on her.

In the app's defence, November wasn't the ideal time to kickstart a running career. It was freezing cold and damp, and Vicky was pretty sure she'd hate the process slightly less if she didn't continually worry about frostbite making all her toes fall off. Chris and the kids had fallen about laughing the first time she went out, wrapped up in every old piece of ski thermal she could find.

'You'll boil,' Chris said.

'I won't,' she said.

'When you're working up a sweat after ten minutes, you'll wish you'd worn less.'

'When I'm working up a sweat after ten minutes I'll be halfway across Putney Bridge and thinking about jumping in,' she said.

'Up to you, Vics, but, trust me, you'll be too warm.'

Chris maybe had a point. She caught her breath and felt sweat running down the smooshed-up cleavage formed by her sports bra. Her heart was thudding in her ears and her legs felt like burning lumps of ice, if that was even possible. And her hips – what the hell was that about? – they hadn't ached this much since her third trimester with James. She was a hot mess, and not in a good way. Still, at least she'd arrived at the meeting point early. Jonathan wouldn't be here for fifteen minutes or so, and she should have recovered her dignity by then, if not her breath.

In that moment, she heard a second set of panting and the face of a dog loomed into hers. She looked up and saw that Jonathan was squinting at her with his head cocked to one side, in a sort of amused disgust.

'Are you all right? Your face is purple.'

'Hi . . . yes . . . fine . . . decided to . . . get fit . . .' she squeezed out the words, and they sat in an awkward silence for several minutes while her face stopped pulsating. She took a few gulps of icy cold water that sent her into a coughing fit and, finally, when that was over, she could speak normally.

'What's the update?'

'We successfully bugged Sacha's office while they were at the party and we have tabs on him at all times thanks to the transmitter you planted. I also received your report on the conversation at the party and we're busy confirming the information and monitoring the accountant. Good job.'

'Thank you. So, what's next?'

'Surveillance are taking care of the rest and we'll action the rest of the plan once the deal's done.'

'What do you mean?'

'We don't need you to do anything else.'

'But what about—'

'We agreed no unnecessary danger, Victoria. You've done what we needed you to do, and you were lucky you didn't get caught, so let me take care of things now.'

'So, I'm off the case?'

'You can stand down.'

'Jonathan—'

'You've been a tremendous help in getting us access to Sacha, and uncovering valuable information, but the deeper we go into this, the more likely it is we will endanger you or your cover. It's better to keep you out of the next bit. You're too close to it all.'

'It's not my cover – it's my *life*, Jonathan.'

'Exactly. Better not to have any needless risk-taking, don't you agree? Or any nasty conflicts of interest at the crucial moment. We've been there before, remember.'

Vicky clamped her teeth together and took a deep breath to stop herself throwing a punch at her boss.

'I don't think you needed to remind me of that again, *sir*. And I think in the past few months I've proved I'm still more than capable in a high-risk situation.'

'No one's disputing your work to date, Turnbull.'

Vicky silently thanked her lucky stars Jonathan hadn't seen her cowering down the side of a bed in a Dalek costume.

'Surely there is something else I can do?' She really, *really* wanted to stay on the case.

163

Jonathan shook his head. 'I'm sorry, Victoria. I'm not putting you back on this operation. We can find you a suitable role, if you want one, something part time I assume. Maybe in Reports or Surveillance?'

'If I'd wanted a part-time desk job I could have come back years ago.'

'If you'd wanted a full-time ops job you could have come back years ago too. But you didn't, because it wasn't what you wanted.'

Jonathan was right of course. Glimpses of a life beyond her current one taunted and daunted her in equal measures.

'Is there no way to make something work part time?'

'Possibly. But you and I both know hardened criminals don't always work nine to five, three days a week.'

'But you'd consider it?'

'I think, given your circumstances, you need to tell your husband before I consider anything,' Jonathan said. 'It's perfectly fine for him to know – he *should* know – and you'd be surprised how much difference it makes to share the burden with your significant other.'

'I can't. Not after all this time. Chris would never forgive me for lying to him all these years. Even when we met, how we met – I'd basically be erasing our whole lives together . . . and the kids . . . I can't.'

'Then what do you want me to do?'

'I don't know.' Why was this so hard? If Jonathan hadn't dragged her back into service in the first place she wouldn't be feeling like this. Would telling Chris make a difference to anything? Would it make it easier? 'Oh, darling, just off to the Middle East to assassinate a bunch of terrorists. Can you make dinner?' No. It wouldn't.

Jonathan stood up and the dog pulled on the lead, happy

to be off again. 'Look, Victoria, the door's always open. But, like I've said before, you have to decide if you really want to walk through it. Decide what you want. Then talk to me when you're ready.'

'Yes, sir.'

'For what it's worth, your part in this operation was top-notch. Like you'd never been away.'

Vicky watched Jonathan and the dog walk away down the path and back towards where his car would be waiting. She sat for another few minutes, replaying his words in her head, and then stood up and began walking in the opposite direction, back the way she came. She felt empty, suddenly, the sense of purpose she'd enjoyed the past few months ripped away from her like a Band-Aid. She understood Jonathan's reasons, understood that she couldn't have it all . . . but to be dismissed as suddenly as she'd been bought on board made her feel used, rather than valued. She wondered if Jonathan had ever really entertained the idea of her coming back full time, or if this had been his intention all along.

As she walked towards the edge of the park her phone buzzed, and she pulled it out of her pocket to see a message from Becky.

Don't forget the Christmas Fair meeting tomorrow 9 a.m.

'Fuck it.' Fuck PTA, fuck Jonathan, fuck everything. She began to run across the park again, her feet grinding into the cold, hard pathway. An aimless, pointless run that no one cared about, not even her.

Chapter Fifteen

It was Thursday, two days before the Christmas Fair. Keeping up with the frantic WhatsApp messages from PTA committee members had become a full-time job and, in the end, Vicky had stuck the conversation on to 'mute' so that she didn't have to deal with the constant bleating of her phone every time someone had a comment to make about filling jam jars with teeth-rotting lollipops or the lack of crap unwanted birthday gifts donated for the raffle.

The one ally she had when it came to the relentlessness of the PTA, surprisingly, was Matisse. Despite Vicky's determination not to get too close, the more they got to know each other, the more she found they had in common. Well, not in common exactly – Vicky was never going to be ten years younger, a size eight, or French – but they shared a sense of humour and a love of art and the two things combined made the whole PTA thing just about bearable. Jonathan wasn't happy about it, of course. She'd been sent a curt message reminding her that Matisse was still under suspicion and to curtail her social interactions. She'd replied back, offering him her spot on the Christmas Fair committee. Things had gone quiet after that.

The operation hadn't, though. She'd taken a pre-Christmas shopping trip to the King's Road a few days back and was thinking about taking a break from buying precisely nothing when she spotted Sacha sitting outside a coffee shop, smoking and shouting into a phone in Russian. His lighter was on the table in front of him and Vicky knew that, thanks to her, JOPS would be triangulating the phone based on his current position in order to listen in. Well, she didn't have to be left completely out in the cold. She pulled down her woolly hat and sailed right by him and into the shop to pick up a cappuccino to go. He didn't even notice her; after all, this was the King's Road at Christmastime, and for every skinny blonde thirty-something carrying a hundred overflowing shopping bags (who he *would* notice) there was a dumpy housewife from Putney hoping to treat herself to something in Peter Jones. She stood in the queue for her coffee and listened to his rant. Fortunately, Sacha appeared to have no volume control when he was speaking in Russian.

'He wants *more* money? This bastard has been screwing around with me from the start.' Sacha stubbed his cigarette out in anger while he listened to the person on the other end of the call. 'I am not being blackmailed. We will find another buyer.' He paused once more. 'Oh, there is always another buyer, my friend. Prepare to divert the ship, we might need it to disappear for a while. Let's see how much this bastard wants his little pay-off when his low-life clients are asking where their goods are.'

He lit another cigarette and laughed. 'No. Fuck that. There is a better way. Let's see how much he wants it when he has to beg me for it face to face.' Sacha ended the call and immediately dialled another number. 'I need to book a flight,' he said, in English. 'Make it—'

'Can I help you, love?'

She'd reached the front of the queue. Vicky ordered and paid for her cappuccino and had to move to the far side to collect it. The coffee machine blasted and frothed, making it impossible to overhear the rest of the conversation, and, by the time she had her coffee in her hand, Sacha was gone. She cursed him, and then she cursed Jonathan. If she had still been on the case, they would be talking now, about what was happening and where that flight was going, and who was on the other end of the call in Russian . . . she swore again as it began to rain. Clearly, she wasn't going to get any shopping done today. She hailed a cab and got in.

'South Kensington, please. The V&A.'

She needed to go somewhere to think.

There was something soothing about the Victoria and Albert Museum. Vicky loved walking around the galleries there: the awed murmurs of hundreds of people echoing off the walls of the Sculpture Gallery contrasted with the muted sounds of the Fashion Gallery and the excited children in Silver, but somehow it all merged into an appreciative hum that snaked through the building like a trail of Bisto. Art students came to draw, old ladies came to lunch and tourists came to wonder at the plethora of goods inside this Victorian treasure trove. Vicky came to escape.

She was marvelling at the green and yellow Chihuly glass cascading from the atrium ceiling and plotting her route through the galleries when she saw a familiar, rather well-dressed woman glide into view.

'Matisse? What are you doing here?'

'Victoria. Hi.' She smiled and gave Victoria an air kiss.

'I can't believe you are here. What a coincidence!' There was just a bit too much of it going around today and it made Vicky uncomfortable. If Jonathan knew she'd bumped into Sacha *and* Matisse, he'd probably add her to the suspect list. Not that Matisse looked particularly thrilled to see her, either. Still, she needed to make the best of the situation. She noticed the ticket in Matisse's hand and made a snap decision. 'I see you're here for the exhibition,' she waved her own at Matisse. 'Me too. Shall we go together?'

'Oui, of course.' Matisse didn't sound overwhelmed by the idea.

'Unless you'd rather be on your own,' Vicky said. 'To be honest, I came here for some quiet time.'

'To be honest, so did I.' They both laughed.

'Well then, let's be alone together,' Vicky said. 'I always come here by myself. It might be nice to have someone to share it with for once.'

After they'd finished at the museum, Vicky had suggested they go to her old stomping ground for lunch. She had been talking most of the way around the exhibition, telling Matisse about her days working nearby and about how she met Chris, but it felt strange to be back in the same bar she'd met Anatoli, all those years ago, sipping champagne and laughing as if she'd simply slipped through time.

'I like that you brought me here,' Matisse said, as they

perched on stools with their drinks. Her usual immaculate style blended in perfectly with the Rolex-dangling masses that congregated with them in the bar. 'It shows me a different side of you that I did not know about until now.'

'I suppose it does, although I haven't been here in years,' Vicky said, feeling like a fish out of water perched on a stool next to a bunch of Hooray Henrys and trying to remember a time when she could lose herself in this crowd with a mere toss of her hair. 'I was pretty different before I had the kids.'

'Me too.' Matisse smiled, and this time Vicky watched it rise all the way to her eyes, before she suddenly burst out laughing. Vicky didn't know whether to join in or be concerned that Matisse had voluntarily creased her face into a smile. Can Botox break?

'What's so funny?'

'Oh, nothing . . . one day maybe I will take you to where I used to work before I had Dmitri, Victoria . . . then you will know why I laugh.'

Vicky pursed her lips. She had some pretty good ideas already. She wondered if Matisse was ashamed of her past life. She doubted it; as proved by Halloween, Matisse didn't seem the type to be embarrassed by her body.

They took longer over lunch than they had planned and travelled back to school by cab. The late November sky was so dim it felt like night already, even though it was only three-thirty in the afternoon. A few miserable raindrops were leaking out of the sky as they stood waiting for school to finish. The conversation turned inevitably to the Christmas Fair.

171

'I can't stand it,' Vicky said. 'I will be *so* glad when it's over. Why did I ever volunteer?'

'Why did you?'

The question had caught her unawares. 'Well, I . . . I—' Matisse was staring at her rather intently. Vicky remembered herself and relaxed. 'I was drunk,' she said, shrugging.

Matisse laughed. 'Is as good an excuse as any, I suppose. . . Well, we are nearly there, Victoria. We have our job, to bake the cakes and run the stall. We do not need to worry about anything else.'

'Yes, but I feel like people want me to worry. Those endless WhatsApp messages . . . James! James! Come back here please, Evie will be out in a minute.'

'They just want someone to say they are doing a good job, Victoria. We have our husbands, our children, but maybe it's not enough sometimes. I know it is not enough for me. I want to do something more with my life than just be Sacha's wife, or Dmitri's mother. All my life I have been nothing. For someone to say I am good at something, to say thank you, like you did when we baked the first cakes together, it means a lot.'

Vicky didn't know how to reply. To the outside world, Matisse seemed so self-satisfied, confident and so needless of the blessings of her peers. But she could see now, that it was really just a cry for attention, a way to compensate for her version of a disappointing life. There was a lot she still didn't know being hidden behind the mask that Matisse had created, and some part of her – the spook part – wanted to dig deeper in case there was something important they had missed. Vicky ignored the urge. Not only was it dishonest, there was no point. Jonathan had made it clear to stand down.

'Well that's one thing you are good at, for sure,' Vicky said. 'Talking of which, are you still up for doing some more baking before the fair?'

'Yes, yes of course I am. Thursday, yes? I will have everything ready for us.'

'Maybe I can do some mince pies as well, they're always popular.'

'Some what?'

'Mince pies?'

'At a cake stall? With meat in them?'

'No, no . . . it's a sweet thing, with raisins and suet and stuff. I'll bring some jars of it with me to your house, and some instant pastry. Christ, Matisse, where have you been that you don't know what a mince pie is?'

'Somewhere they don't make things from a jar,' Matisse said, pulling a face. 'Or have this thing you call "instant pastry". But maybe you can convince me they are better than they sound.'

'I'll try,' Vicky said. 'And if you're feeling really brave, maybe you can show me how to make my own pastry.'

They'd ended up baking all morning, until there wasn't a single inch of space left in the enormous kitchen to put any more cakes. Matisse buzzed around the finished products, humming, checking with wooden skewers to make sure they were done as they came out of the oven and turning them onto cooling racks with practiced expertise.

Sacha had appeared, on cue, the second the first batches were out of the oven; the smell of the baking too much for him to resist. Vicky had made him try a mince pie, which

Matisse said looked revolting in her opinion, but Sacha made sounds of satisfaction and went back for a second one before Matisse had time to stop him.

'They are for the charity bake sale. Leave them alone!' she said, placing a clean tea towel over them and patting his stomach, before slipping into Russian. 'Besides, Christmas is coming, and you need to take it easy or you'll never fit your trousers.'

'I won't need to worry about trousers,' Sacha replied. 'You can expect a call from the travel agent later. I decided we should get some winter sun.'

The flights were for all of them? Vicky wondered where they might be going at such short notice. She had a pretty good idea. She smiled at them both. They carried on, masking their argument with light voices and polite faces, oblivious to the fact she could understand every word.

'I thought we would be at home—'

'Well we aren't.'

'But it's better for Dmitri—'

'Stop being so selfish and try showing a little gratitude. I'm booking us a holiday in Dubai, for fuck's sake. I thought you would be pleased to show Dmitri where he comes from.'

'Shut up.' Matisse tried to hide the dull hatred in her eyes but Vicky could see it, plain as day. 'I'm so sorry, Victoria,' she said, in English, 'we are being rude, talking in Russian.'

'It's okay. Carry on your conversation. I need to get off anyway.' Vicky began gathering her things.

'I'll see you out.'

'No need, I can let myself out.'

'See her out, Matisse.' Sacha sounded menacing now, and Vicky wondered if she should stay after all.

'I'll ice the cakes later when they're cool,' Matisse said, opening the door for her.

'Are you sure?'

'It's better for me to be busy and out of Sacha's way, the mood he is in.'

'Matisse . . . is everything okay? You don't need me to stick around, do you?' She hoped Matisse was picking up on her cue.

'I'll be fine. Thank you, though.' Matisse nodded her head back towards the stairs and smiled. 'I can always garotte him with the cake slicer if he really annoys me.'

Vicky couldn't tell if she was joking, but it didn't look like it. She nodded, satisfied she would be okay without her. In another life, Matisse would have made a rather brilliant Bond girl.

Chapter Sixteen

'Magda!' Matisse called. Having seen Victoria out, she was back down in the kitchen. She stood face to face with Sacha, eyes not moving from his, like a pair of animals staring each other down before a fight.

'Yes, madam?'

She spoke English to the housekeeper, slowly and deliberately, so that Sacha was under no illusions about what she was saying. 'Magda, can you tidy up this mess and make sure my fat husband doesn't eat any more of the cakes, please?'

Magda didn't flinch. 'Yes, madam.'

'Thank you.' She spoke to Sacha now. 'So why are we really going away? Is this about a deal?'

'It's none of your business.' Sacha said, clutching his hand around her chin and squeezing her cheeks hard. 'It's a family holiday where you get to sit on your arse and wear very little. Understood?'

'Get off me.' She pushed his hand away. 'I understand completely.'

'I cannot believe I am taking you and your son to Dubai and you're pissed off with *me*? This must be a joke.'

'He's your son too, Sacha, and yes, I would have liked to be consulted.'

'Oh, let's not pretend, Matisse. We act like neither of us know the truth, but he is nothing like me. And never will be.'

Matisse sighed. 'Don't go there,' she said. 'You know I don't have anything to say on the matter.'

'Even after all this time, you don't want to admit it. But you know what I am talking about,' he replied, pointing at her with a singular stubby jab to the collarbone.

She wouldn't be drawn. It was always the same when she had a difference of opinion, when she challenged his authority. Always the accusations. What an insecure little man he was beneath all of that ink and big talk. She admitted that the identity of Dmitri's father was contestable, but that was hardly her fault. And what did it matter to him anyway? It wasn't as if he was Father of the Year.

They had only been married for only a few weeks when Sacha decided they should move permanently to Dubai. A haven for crooked Russians, he had spent increasing amounts of time there over the previous few years. He'd gone straight there from their honeymoon in the Maldives, while she'd flown back to Paris alone, but he'd called her after a few days to say he missed her; he didn't like them being apart. It would be better for them both to start fresh somewhere new, he told her, and ordered her to pack up and get the next flight out. She didn't argue. Dubai was an exciting adventure, a millionaire's playground; it was a place where Sacha could operate without scrutiny, and where she could live a life of luxury with her new husband, where no one knew or cared about her past.

Dubai was still a building site when she arrived. She wondered if it would ever be finished; they had been building non-stop for a decade already, but showed no signs of stopping. High-rise blocks jostled for space along the highway, with concrete skeleton neighbours waiting to be adorned with mirrored flesh. Cranes lined up along the skyline, twitching and twirling to the beat of some unheard drum. Street level, in contrast, was dark and motionless. It wasn't a pedestrian city. Matisse took it all in, as if systematically stamping the images into her memory would somehow make it seem more like home. But it didn't feel like it.

Their newly purchased villa was a true display of the wealth Sacha had at his disposal. The house was palatial. In the daytime it was flooded with light by the floor-to-ceiling windows in every room; at night it was lit by the huge chandeliers that hung from the high ceilings, like glittering demolition balls. She'd never seen anywhere so big. But, like everywhere else in Dubai, it didn't matter how big or grand the house was; great dusty bowls of sand blew hot and heavy over everything, and there was never any respite. Matisse grew tired of the view and wished she could walk down the vibrant Parisian streets instead of pacing the artificially lit shopping malls. And as summer turned to autumn the heat raged on, and still she knew no one save for her housemaid, driver and gardener, who barely acknowledged she was there.

She divided her time between the shopping mall and the

house, waiting for Sacha to appear, and then disappear, his life full of meetings and client dinners. Matisse's days were silent in contrast, punctuated by brief exchanges with shop assistants and deliverymen. The beautifully cut marble floors lining the opulently sized rooms echoed the sound of her footsteps as she wandered about the place like a lone sailor washed up on a desert island.

As winter approached, Sacha began to treat her as less of a confidante and more of an inconvenience. There were arguments, and tears; she was desperately homesick for Paris, and her friends. The passion leaked out of their relationship and he became irritated by her neediness and bogged down by her moods. It was cool enough that Matisse could get out of the house now, but she didn't know what to do and without Sacha's attention she found herself increasingly wanting to seek someone else's.

When Sacha was home, she hosted dinners and parties for his associates, and tried to seduce them with sly glances and the soft brush of her feet under the table, where Sacha couldn't see. But anything more than brief titillation was impossible. Men liked her and wanted her – she could read all the signs – but she was off-limits, untouchable; they seemed to know all too well what their fate would be otherwise.

Except one. A friend of Sacha's, who didn't seem scared of him, who sat with her in the kitchen drinking champagne while the others took care of business in the living room over poker chips and vodka. Who slipped her his number and asked her to meet him at the Burj Al Arab one sultry spring afternoon when Sacha had disappeared off to Moscow for a few weeks. Who gave her body what it was craving for over and over and then teased her heart back to life in the months afterwards with his conversation, his laughter and his love.

They were always careful. At the hotels where they met, she always arrived after him, left before him and ordered room service in advance, so they weren't disturbed, while he paid the clerk at the reception a small fortune to keep quiet in case anyone came around asking any questions. Later, when they sought each other's company outside the bedroom too, they only met where they knew they wouldn't be noticed: in out-of-town restaurants, walking the sands of Jumeirah Beach, or along the wide pavements next to the creek in the old town with only street hawkers for company. Often, she dressed in an abaya, the long, flowing robes and head cover acting as a convenient camouflage.

The idyll lasted a year, before things changed for ever. Their last afternoon together, Matisse had left the hotel as usual around sunset. It was a beautiful evening, the sun hovering on the horizon in a glorious moment of stillness before it fell out of the desert sky and into the ocean. She was dressed carefully in a green dress with a gold sequin trim, ready to greet Sacha when he returned home later that night. She felt the warm glow of satisfaction wearing it, knowing that it had so recently been peeled from her body by her lover while her matching gold sandals raked the back of his thighs.

Her sandals click-clacked across the marble floor of the hotel lobby as she walked out of the doors and into the lazy heat of the night. She didn't notice the sinister figure heading in as she left. If she had, she would have run back to the room there and then, to warn her lover of the danger.

It was at breakfast, the next morning, when the papers

reported a shooting at the hotel – right around the time she'd walked out the day before.

'Something wrong?' Sacha said, as she gagged on her toast.

'No, nothing . . .' She surveyed her husband. She knew him well enough to recognise he was enjoying the pain he was inflicting.

'I see you are reading about the man who was shot at the Burj Al Arab last night. A Russian man, they say, but they do not give a name. He was caught sleeping with some whore and shot dead. The authorities would prefer this was kept quiet, I think, and will not investigate. Such a shame that he did not keep his dick in his pants.'

She couldn't help it, the tears came to her eyes . . . he was dead, it was her fault. Was she next? She rose from the table, and Sacha grabbed her by the wrist, gripping hard and making her gasp.

'Don't worry, my Zolotse, there's nothing to be worried about. I know you are scared but there is no reason to be. You just forgot, for a little while, that I am your husband. I am angry, of course, but I understand. Once a whore always a whore, am I right?'

Matisse swallowed, and waited.

'Not everyone would be as forgiving as me, but I am willing to let you make this one mistake, just one, to understand what the consequences will be if you do it again. Dubai is obviously not a safe place, with men getting shot for sleeping with whores. I think, for your safety, maybe we should go back to France. What do you think?'

'You killed him.'

Sacha stared back with a cruel smile and a cold glint in his eyes. 'Yes, I did. Now, go and pack your things. The plane leaves in four hours. I'll be coming with you, of course. Being on your own, it seems, has caused some problems.'

He didn't leave her alone again after that. They returned to Paris, to their apartment, and when he wasn't there Sacha made sure the housekeeper reported all her comings and goings. It should have been unbearable, but the loss of love knocked the life out of her, so that she no longer cared enough about anything to be angry.

In the chaos of everything, she didn't notice that her periods had stopped until her clothes began to feel tight and she realised that the sickness she was feeling might not be just sadness. She did a test in their Paris apartment one morning about three months after she had arrived, which confirmed she was pregnant.

Sacha was suspicious; he tried to force the truth from her about her affair, but she always gave him the same answer: she had not slept with another man. She knew Sacha didn't believe her, but, instead of insisting on getting proof, he preferred to inflict cruelty on her, to show he had control. As her tummy grew round and her body heavy, he made her strip for him, dance for him and fuck him like the whore she had been when they first met. She complied, out of terror and self-preservation. But as the baby grew and moved inside her, she knew in her heart that it belonged to her lover, conceived on a date when she had worn a green dress with sequins and had blown him his last kiss goodbye.

When Dmitri was born, he had her looks, but her lover's eyes. She was as sure as ever who the father was every time he smiled at her. She thought of leaving Sacha, but she had nowhere to go, and, in any case, she didn't dare try, out of fear for her baby and herself. She tried to make herself useful and attractive to him again, keeping Dmitri out of sight and mind as much as she could, and, over time, they reached a precarious ceasefire. Sacha accepted Dmitri's presence in the house, and Matisse prayed he would grow up to look just like her. Magda was hired; it was clear from the outset that the housekeeper wasn't just there to keep the floors clean. Sacha had made good on his word, to make sure his wife was the epitome of the obedient and faithful: Magda was his spy, there to make sure she behaved. A prisoner in a gilded cage, Matisse accepted the status quo. There were no more children, no more affairs, and in exchange for her toeing the line, she had been allowed to live, and live well.

Matisse wasn't quite the scared young mother anymore, but she knew when she crossed a line, she would pay for it. Still, she couldn't let the argument go without having the last word.

'You want us to go to Dubai? Fine. Whatever you want, same as always. Just let's do it without the snide comments and a vice grip. It only makes you look a fool, not me.'

She felt the sting of the slap to her cheek almost before she registered his hand flying towards her. She staggered backwards, but didn't say anything. Magda continued wiping down the worktops as if nothing had happened. She was paid well enough by Sacha to look the other way when it came to his violent outbursts.

Matisse knew he was waiting for a reaction, but wouldn't

give him the satisfaction. He'd got his way; they would be coming to Dubai with him. He wouldn't be getting an apology on top.

Finally, Sacha turned and left the kitchen.

'Bastard.' She rubbed at her cheek.

She heard him grab his keys and slam the door, followed by the sharp sting of gravel in the driveway as he backed out and left in a cloud of dust. The dramatic exit, she knew, would be slightly marred by him having to wait for the gate to open.

Chapter Seventeen

When Vicky arrived at the Kozlovsky house early on Saturday morning, the cakes were iced, decorated and boxed up in Tupperware and neatly stacked in the hallway by the front door.

'Mama, Evie's mum is here,' Dmitri called, answering the door. He turned back to Vicky. 'By the way, I loved the mince pies. I tried one. They are delicious.'

'Thank you, Dmitri. I'm glad you appreciated them.'

Matisse was on her way up the stairs from the kitchen and Vicky grinned at the grimace on her face.

'All those cakes to try and he chooses those things. I am afraid the finer points of this English "delicacy" are lost on me, Victoria. Who eats fruit and beef suet from a jar?'

'Me! And Papa!'

'Okay, off you go, that's enough now,' Matisse said, and shooed him upstairs. 'I'll see you at the fair, okay? Papa will bring you, however much he doesn't want to.'

'I'll start loading the car,' Vicky said. 'I told Becky we'd be there by nine-thirty to set up.'

A phone rang. Matisse fished her phone out of her handbag and stuck it on speaker while she picked up a stack of cakes.

'Matisse speaking.'

'Oh, hello, Mrs Kozlovsky, this is Grace from Malachi travel agency. Your husband asked me to give you a call and go through your travel options with you. Is now a good time to talk?'

She sighed and picked up the phone, flipping it off of speakerphone. 'Sorry Victoria, I need to take this. I won't be a moment.' She turned towards the living room. 'I have five minutes.'

Vicky carried on ferrying Tupperware to her car. She occasionally caught a few words from Matisse, but nothing concrete. After five minutes, Matisse emerged from the living room, looking bored.

'Would you mind sending this on an email—' She cupped her hand over the phone and mouthed to Vicky, 'I'm so sorry.'

Vicky put her thumbs up and motioned that they were finished loading the car. 'I think there's one more batch downstairs,' Matisse said.

'I'll get it. Finish your call.' Vicky nudged her shoes off and went downstairs to the kitchen. At that moment, the buzzer rang for the service door.

'Magda, can you get that?' called Matisse from upstairs.

Magda didn't appear, so Vicky moved towards the lift. She saw on the CCTV there was a man outside. A courier. She peered at the screen. It was definitely not Jacob Zimmerman.

She buzzed the intercom. 'Hello?'

'Delivery for Sacha Kozlovsky.'

'Please place it in the lift, thank you.' Vicky buzzed the

door open to the lift and waited a few moments before hitting the call button. She listened to the rush of cantilevers, and when the doors opened again a small package sat on the floor. She picked it up and saw it was blank.

The courier turned to leave. She hit the intercom. 'Wait,' she said. 'Where did you pick this up from?'

'Leytonstone.'

'No, I mean, was it a company, or a private dwelling?'

The courier was walking away.

'Do you have a name? The person who paid for the delivery maybe? Hello?'

The courier opened the gate and disappeared from view. Vicky held the package in her hands, wondering if she should slip it into her handbag. Jonathan would no doubt thank her for uncovering a key piece of evidence – if it was one. Or he might just berate her for still acting like she was on a case she'd been told to stand down from.

'Victoria?' Matisse was standing behind her, still on the phone. 'Who was that?'

'Oh, it was a courier.' Her heart thudded heavily in her chest. Had Matisse heard her talking? She held out the package. 'I answered the intercom. I hope you don't mind.'

Matisse was still on the phone. 'No, I'm still here, Grace.' She shrugged and took the package from Vicky. 'Carry on.'

'He said it was for Sacha,' Vicky mouthed.

The corner of the envelope was loose and Matisse edged it open slowly. Vicky swallowed and looked over at the staircase. Sacha would go crazy at both of them if he found them opening his mail.

Matisse pulled out a cheap-looking card with *Merry Christmas* written on the front. She opened it up. Vicky could see there was something tucked inside but couldn't see what.

189

A notebook of some kind? Matisse scanned it and then folded the card shut, placed it back in the envelope and sealed it with a bit of Pritt-Stick. She glanced up at Vicky and put a conspiratorial finger to her lips. Vicky raised her eyebrows and pretend-zipped her mouth up. She could play along with Matisse, for now.

'Grace, I will have to call you back,' Matisse placed the package on the counter. 'I need to talk to my husband about his plans before we book anything.' She ended the call and turned back to Vicky. 'Let's go.'

'That sounded exciting,' Vicky said. 'Where are you off to?' She glanced at the package. 'I can't believe you just did that,' she whispered.

'Me neither.' Matisse was touching her hand to her cheek and looked flustered in a way that Vicky had never seen before. 'Come on. I want to go. Dmitri! We're leaving!'

'I told you I'd bring him!' Sacha shouted from upstairs in his office.

Matisse switched to Russian. 'Well what you say and what you do are two very different things.'

'I said I will bring him, Matisse, and I will. Did you talk to the travel agent?'

'I didn't see the point. You'll do what you want anyway.' Matisse swung her bag over her shoulder. 'The fair starts at 11 a.m. Don't be late. Oh, and you have a delivery. It's in the kitchen.'

Less than two hours later, Vicky was losing the will to live. Cliff Richard blared from a speaker in the corner of the school hall and the noise levels from crying toddlers, sugar-crazed children and their long-suffering parents had risen to way beyond acceptable. She looked around at the stalls lining the hall and saw that, just like hers, they were manned by a variety of hassled adults in comedy festive hats. The barely disguised frustration of stallholders crying, 'You have to pay for that if you want it' and, 'Please be careful, you might break it!' couldn't even be heard over the joyous screeching of children as they won jars of sweets, crap plastic toys and felt-tip pens of the permanent kind.

The Year Four bake sale was well underway, and the tasteful white, silver, and gold tables Matisse had put together heaved with donated cakes of all shapes and sizes. Their stall was towards the back of the hall, next to the patio marquee currently posing as Santa's Grotto, and, needless to say, it was one of the most popular stalls at the fair. When they'd arrived, Matisse had taken care of aesthetics and Vicky had priced the various fruit cakes, vanilla sponges, red velvet and chocolate cakes according to size and attractiveness, and adorned platters and plates with hundreds of cookies, brownies, Rice Krispies cakes, and gingerbread men. Matisse's own beautiful cupcakes were stacked in tiers on pretty stands she'd brought from home, their icing piled high like mini Kilimanjaro mountaintops and rice-paper Santas stuck at jaunty angles at their summit. As Vicky had predicted, there were mince pies aplenty. Their tantalising smell was making her feel permanently hungry.

She tried to keep tabs on her children as best as she could while she worked the stall. Ollie had disappeared off with his old friends – she could see him tramping around the playground outside with Becky, Kate and Laura's eldest, trying to out-cool each other. Evie was somewhere close by doing looms at the arts and crafts table.

James was hanging on to Vicky's leg, trying to touch every cake he could feasibly reach.

'James! Stop it. God, where is Chris?' Vicky said. 'That's four cupcakes and a brownie . . . James, please, sweetheart, let go of my leg . . . two pounds fifty please. James! Stop it.' James had nearly pulled her over by putting all of his weight on to her right leg, hugging it like a koala on a eucalyptus tree. She bent down to him.

'Look, James, I know you're bored but I'm going to find Daddy soon and—'

'Daddy!'

Vicky turned and saw Chris. Narrowly avoiding being hit by a flock of balloons a group of Year Fives were selling, Chris found his way to the stand.

'Thank God. Where have you been?'

'Out by the BBQ of course,' Chris replied. 'The bacon sandwiches are delicious. These pies look nice too.' Chris picked up a bronzed lump of pastry. 'Are they your handiwork, Matisse?'

Matisse wrinkled up her nose. 'Non, I do not understand these mince pies,' she said. 'They are definitely belonging to your wife.'

'Well, I'll definitely take one then.' Chris scooped up James from behind the table. 'Hey, dude! What's up? You want to go with Daddy and take a look around?'

'Want to play with Evie.' James looked wistfully over to where the arts and crafts table was.

'Well, let's go and see what she's doing, and then after that maybe we'll go and get a hot dog, yeah?'

'Hot dog! Yeah, Daddy, let's get hot dogs,' James said, all thoughts of his sister forgotten.

Vicky kissed her son and waved Chris off.

'Your husband is nice,' Matisse said.

'He has his moments. I'm lucky, I know it. So are you, though.'

Matisse laughed bitterly. 'In what way?'

'Well, you have Dmitri, and a perfect house, and, well . . .'

'Yes. I have Dmitri, it's true. And the house is very beautiful, of course. But there are things in my life that are not quite so perfect.' She looked down and fiddled with her wedding ring.

'What do you mean?'

'I think Sacha—'

'S'cuse me, what flavour are the green ones?' A little boy approached the table.

'They're vanilla with butter frosting. Did you want one?' The boy nodded, and Vicky took a cake and offered it to his outstretched hand. 'A pound, please.'

By the time the boy walked away, Matisse had moved to the other end of the table to deal with an enquiry about buying a whole Christmas cake and the moment between them was gone. Vicky dropped the pound coin from her cupcake sale into the money tin. She looked across as the Frenchwoman flicked her hair off her face and handed the Christmas cake over to its new owner. Matisse had been on the brink of telling her something. Whether it was important to the case or not she had no idea.

'Don't you have to go now?' Matisse came back over to her, tapping her watch.

'The next shift isn't here yet . . . but yes, Evie's going to be singing any minute . . .'

'Go. I'll manage without you.'

'Give me a text if my replacement doesn't turn up and I'll come back after the first number,' Vicky said. She'd have to wait to hear whatever it was Matisse had been about to divulge.

She began negotiating her way through the crowds. A sticky residue carpeted the floor, formed from wrapping paper and dropped Haribos. She stopped in disgust to pick a deformed cola bottle sweetie from the bottom of her boot, causing several other people behind her to tut. She finally made it to the entry hall where a chaotic graveyard of welly boots, coats, buggies and brollies lay. The traffic was quieter here, although the chances of getting snagged on one of the festive Christmas displays stapled to the walls was far greater. This year's theme was 'Christmas around the world'; as usual, everyone east of Greece rode camels, it snowed pretty much everywhere north of the equator, and the entire population of the world had assumed delicate pastel-coloured skin, courtesy of Crayola. There was glitter everywhere, shedding on to the shoulders of the passing foot traffic like disco dandruff. Vicky knew she'd probably still be finding the stuff sometime in February.

The choir would be starting the carol singing in ten minutes. Evie was front and centre and had been practising for weeks. She would never let them hear the end of it if either of them missed it, although it went without saying that she'd also given strict instructions not to stand at the front, cheer, take photos, or do anything embarrassing. Vicky had assured her that she wouldn't even notice they were there.

If she didn't hurry up and find Chris, they wouldn't make it at all. Vicky looked around outside and saw him wrapped up in his coat and huddled by the barbecue with a group of dads. The smell of cooking pork wafted towards her. She tried to get his attention by waving but, predictably, he didn't see her. In the end she went to get him.

'Chris, come on, the carols are starting in a minute and we promised Evie we'd be there.'

Chris waved to the other men. 'Duty calls,' he said.

'Where's James?'

'He's here . . . James!' Chris called out across the play-ground. Vicky looked in the same direction, scanning the area for her little dot.

'Chris, you can't just let him run about when there are so many people about . . . where is he? When did you last see him?'

'He was literally just here. Don't panic, he can't have got far.'

'James!' How could he have taken his eye off him like that? 'James! Shit, where is he?'

'I swear, he was a few metres away from me the whole time.' Chris was looking around with a slightly worried face. 'James!'

'Oh, for God's sake, Chris!' Vicky snapped, marching off across the playground. She could feel the panic rising in her chest and her temper rising at her husband. How could he have been so – so *neglectful*?

'Ollie? Come here a minute, I need you to help find your brother.'

'Seriously?'

'Ollie, come on! In fact, all of you can help me out and take a look around outside for him if you don't mind,' she said to the group of disgruntled teenagers hunched together like a coven of acne-ridden witches.

'Check the front gates first and the front playground too –

that's got a climbing frame and he might have gone there to play. I'll go and look inside,' Vicky said.

'I'll stay here,' Chris said. 'He might come back here to find me.'

Vicky didn't reply. She hurried inside, looking from left to right as she walked, trying to catch sight of her little boy. She couldn't tell Chris the real reason she was so worried, of course. In the normal course of things, James wouldn't be in much danger; there were loads of parents around who would soon know what to do if he was lost as well as volunteers manning the front gates to stop any errant little ones from leaving the fair without their parents. But Vicky was sick with fear. Who knows what her little trips to Matisse's house had sparked off; maybe Sacha had found a bug in his office and put two and two together . . .? She scanned the crowds, looking for faces she didn't know, stopping to ask mums she knew if they'd seen James, before she reached Becky in the centre of the hall. The choir were lining up ready to start the carols and Evie was staring at her with a furious glare, hardly able to believe her mum had gone against her request to stay hidden in plain sight.

'Mu-uuum . . .'

'Not now, Evie. Becks? Sorry, we've lost James, can you make an announcement?'

'Oh my God, yes, of course, hang on, I'll just get the microphone switched on.'

Vicky gave her the details while Becky tampered with a switch and tapped the microphone a few times. Once she was satisfied it was working, she spoke into the microphone 'Hello? Hello, can you hear me?'

Slade faded from the speakers and everyone stopped, expecting to hear the introduction to the school choir.

'We have a lost child, ladies and gentlemen, his name is James and he's three years old, he was last seen outside in the rear playground. Can everyone please have a look around them . . . James, are you in here, love? Shout for us if you're in here.'

Vicky nodded her thanks to Becky and headed back towards the door. Evie had her head in her hands. She caught her mother's eye and Vicky blew her a kiss before she left the hall. Becky continued on the microphone, 'Thank you so much for coming today. We're delighted to introduce the choir to sing their first carol this afternoon. Please come and drop a coin in the bucket to support them – all proceeds are going to charity.'

Vicky hated choosing between the kids at the best of times, and knew this meant a lot to Evie, even if she never said as much. But she couldn't stay to watch the choir. She had to find James.

She picked her way back through the stroller pile-up and out to the front play area. She met Ollie there. 'Anything?'

Ollie shook his head. 'Sorry, Mum. I asked the mums on the gate and they said they haven't seen any kids on their own wandering about.'

'But what if he wasn't on his own?' Vicky said, in a panic. 'Do you think he's been kidnapped?'

'No, no, I don't think so . . . I mean of course not,' she assured Ollie. 'Thanks, Ollie. I'll take it from here. Would you go and listen to Evie's singing now? At least then one of the family will have heard her.'

*

197

Ollie loped off and Vicky hurried over to the women on the gate, two Reception mums who'd drawn the short straw and were out in the freezing cold on meet-and-greet duty.

'We haven't seen your little boy. Sorry.' The first mum rubbed at her nose and stuck her hands into her pockets.

'Has anyone left in the past half hour?' Vicky said.

'Maybe a couple of people,' the other woman said.

'With kids?'

'Yeah, but we're pretty sure yours wasn't one of them,' the first one said.

'How do you know?' Vicky said, taking a step towards them. She felt her fists tighten and drew her right arm slowly back. 'If he's been taken, if you let him leave with some stranger—'

'Excuse me, there's no need to be rude; we would have said if we thought he had left with anyone,' the first woman said. The other mum was staring at Vicky's fists.

Vicky recovered herself. 'Sorry . . . sorry. I just want to find him . . .'

She heard quick little steps behind her at that moment and saw James running up to her. 'James! Oh my God, James, where have you been?'

'I found him trying to climb under the hedges at the side of the school,' a familiar voice said. Sacha. Vicky swallowed and stood up as the Russian approached, brushing bits of plant from his jacket.

'You know, you should be more careful. There are bad people out there, and you might not get so lucky next time.'

Vicky stared at him, not knowing what to say.

'James is lucky I found him first, though, eh, little man?' He pinched James's cheek, a little too hard for her liking. 'We had a nice chat, didn't we, about stranger danger?'

Vicky felt sick but put on a plastic smile and hugged James a little tighter. 'Thanks, Sacha.'

He nodded at her and disappeared into the school.

'James! What were you doing? You mustn't ever run off like that again, do you understand? Always stay where you can see me or Daddy. Always.'

'Sorry, Mummy.' James looked at her, his face a mix of upset and confusion.

'It's okay,' Vicky said. 'It's just, Mummy and Daddy were very worried about you. But you're safe now, and that's all that matters.' She gave him a series of kisses ending in his neck, which made him all tickly and giggly. 'Okay?'

James nodded, and Vicky put him down. He hesitated a moment before running straight to the play area, checking she could still see him, just as he'd been told. Vicky kept her eyes fixed on him while she fished out her phone and dialled Chris, hands still shaking. She thought about what she'd just said. She wasn't sure if James, or anyone else in the family, was really safe at all. Whether she was still technically on the case wouldn't matter to a man like Sacha. *There are bad people out there.* Was he saying that he knew about her? If he had found out, if he put two and two together . . . she knew he didn't mess around when it came to anyone who pissed him off. If he found out what she'd done, it would be her and her family in the line of fire, not Jonathan or any of his cronies. She needed to be prepared, needed her family to be prepared, and there was only one way of making that happen.

Chris picked up the phone after one ring. 'Found him,' she said. 'Let's go home as soon as Evie is finished. I need to talk to you about something.'

Chapter Eighteen

There was a long silence following Vicky's speech. Evie was watching TV, still furious that they'd all missed her singing. Ollie was in his room playing computer games and James had mercifully fallen asleep on the sofa. It was just her and Chris, sitting across from each other at the kitchen table, Vicky waiting for him to say something. She could see the emotions travelling across his face – anger, confusion, upset, shock – they followed one after the other after the other, and although she wanted to keep talking, keep justifying everything, she realised it was probably better to shut up and wait for the wheels to stop turning.

'So, let me get this right. All this time – right from when I first met you – you've been a – I feel stupid even saying the word – you've been a *spy*?'

'Well, no, not technically . . . I mean, yes, but when I got pregnant with Ollie, then I wasn't active anymore.'

'But you were still a spy.'

'No. Look, it didn't work that way . . . they agreed I'd stay on, but as a sleeper. I never did an undercover job again after that. It was another life, not important to me, or us.'

'Except that now it is.'

'It's only since September that I've been working again.'

'To spy on Sacha. Since September. Which was *four months ago*. Four months, Vic! How could you have not said anything for four months?'

'I didn't tell you because I didn't want you to be worried.'

'Worried about what? Should I be worried?'

'No!'

'So why are you telling me now then? Because it sounds an awful lot to me like I should be worried. You said you thought James had been taken by someone.'

'I was . . . I mean, I just thought—'

'For a spy, you're not getting your story very straight. If I don't need to be worried then why are you? Jesus, Vicky.'

'I'm sorry.' There was a long pause. Vicky felt a lump rise in her throat.

'Have you ever killed anyone?'

'What?'

'I said, have you ever killed anyone?'

'Chris, come on . . .'

'Well, have you?'

'I can't answer that.'

Anger flared up in his eyes. 'I supposed there's a lot you can't answer, isn't there?'

'There are things I can't tell you because they're classified or sensitive to an operation, but I can try to answer questions as best I can. I know this is a huge shock, Chris—'

'That's the understatement of the bloody year—'

'But you have to know I stopped doing all of this because of you, and Ollie, and then Evie, and James: I realised my family was more important. But then, when Jonathan called, it felt good. It felt like I mattered, like I had a purpose again – beyond the kids. Like I was doing something for myself, for once.'

'I get it, Vicky. But what I don't get is why you never told me. I mean, when we first met, or when we had Ollie, or even in September when you got recalled, or woken up, or whatever you call it – why didn't you tell me then? Is it because you couldn't, or because you didn't want to? Is it because you didn't trust me?'

Vicky was miserable. 'No! No. . . I don't know how to explain it . . .'

'Try.'

Vicky paused, trying to get what she wanted to say straight in her mind.

'When we met, it was just so nice, to see myself through your eyes. I was full of . . . sadness . . . I'd made a huge fuck up at work, no one liked me very much. *I* didn't like me very much. You didn't know all that. You didn't put me in a box or judge me.'

'So that made it okay to lie?'

'You saw me differently. It meant so much, Chris, to have someone see me differently.'

'I saw what you wanted me to see. What was I, just another target?'

'No! I never thought of you in that way.'

There was another long pause. She stared down at the table.

'I wanted to tell you, but I never knew how . . . we found out I was pregnant with Ollie, and my case had gone cold; my boss gave me leave for as long as I wanted it. By the time I was ready to tell you, or thought it was the right time to tell you, it didn't seem relevant anymore. We had a little baby and he was the important thing. I didn't want to burden you with something for no reason.'

'But it wouldn't have been a burden, Vicky.'

'Yes, it would.' Vicky leaned across the table to take his hand. She had to be honest with him – as honest as she could be. 'Chris, this job, it meant everything to me. I spent so many years pretending to be someone else that eventually I became her. I did dangerous things, dealt with nasty people and saw some very bad things, but I'd be lying if I said I didn't love it. When I met you, when I got pregnant—'

'Christ, tell me you didn't stay with me because of Ollie?' Chris said, ripping his hand away.

'By then I'd already made up my mind that I wanted to be with you,' she said. 'But I wasn't ready – we weren't ready – for me to tell you, and then when we were, I didn't think it mattered anymore. I had a family to love instead, and so I let my old life slip away into the shadows. I'm sorry. I was wrong.'

Chris looked at her.

'I feel like I don't know what's true or not anymore, about us.'

'It's all true. I love you. I gave up the service for you, and for our kids. I'm the last person who thought they'd ever be going back there again.'

'But you did it anyway, without telling me.'

'I'm sorry, Chris. Really, really sorry. I'm telling you now. Please, don't be angry.'

Chris met her eyes, his own filled with hurt and betrayal.

'Do you have to – Jesus, I can't believe I'm saying this – do you, did you have to "do" anything with anyone? Have you and Sacha been—'

'No! No. No. That's not what it's like. I would never do anything like that.' She winced inwardly. 'Not anymore. Maybe there was a time, before we met . . . look, with Sacha, it was just information gathering and reporting back. They wanted me to target Matisse to get in the house and plant a few bugs. That's all, Chris. I swear.'

'But you said you fucked up, before. What's to say that wouldn't happen again?'

'It would never, ever happen again.' Vicky felt tears prickling at her eyelids.

Chris remained stoic. 'Well, I'm sorry, but just saying it isn't good enough. I'm sure you're very qualified and I believe you when you say you'd never make another mistake. But it's not the driver of the car who's the risk. It's the drivers of all the other cars, the psychos and the criminals and the Russians *with a child at our school* – ' he realised he was shouting, and brought it down to a hiss, ' – I mean, for fuck's sake, Vicky, you had Dmitri here for a playdate, you treat Matisse like she's your best friend—'

'I did it to keep our kids safe!' This time it was her who raised her voice. 'I thought, if it was me working the operation, then I could make sure that nothing happened. And I would be the first to know, if anyone was in any danger.'

'But what if that person was *you*? The mother of our children. My wife. How would you feel if you were kidnapped, or killed, and our children were left with no mother? Did it ever occur to you to think about that?'

She thought about the past few months and how, although it hadn't felt like it at the time, she had compromised her own safety. She thought about the poison dart gathering dust at the back of the wardrobe; the gun waiting for her at HQ that she'd refused to pick up; her woefully out-of-date self-defence skills and lack of strength when she'd attacked Jacob. She shook her head miserably.

'You say the kids are growing up, that there'll come a time where they don't need you anymore. But that's not true, Vics. We all need you. We always will.'

'They're getting older. *I'm* getting older. When they're all grown up and gone, I don't want to end up regretting not having built a life for myself.'

Chris clenched his jaw. 'If you wanted to do something for yourself, then I can't blame you. If you want to do a job that you love, I want to support you. But this? Is this really the right choice for our family?'

Vicky swallowed. 'I'm trying to make the right choices for everyone,' she said dully. 'And . . . it's why I'm not going back.'

'I don't understand.'

'Jonathan didn't need me to be involved after I'd planted the bugs. He offered me my job back, permanently. He offered me a desk position too, but I didn't want it.'

'Why not?'

'If I'm going to do this job, it has to be in the field. It's what I love doing. It's where I'm best.'

There was a silence.

'You're best right here with us.'

'I'm best when I'm happy, Chris. It's not that I hate my life now; I love it, most of the time . . . but I can't be happy just doing the school run, the PTA and coffee mornings forever. Now James is bigger, and starting school next year, I want to do something else with my life. I'm nearly fifty, for God's sake.'

'You are not nearly fifty, Vicky.'

'You know what I mean. I haven't worked in fourteen

years. I'm basically useless outside of JOPS. I've got no work history, no CV, nothing. Jonathan wanted me back and maybe it *was* reckless, but I wanted to fix things and prove to him that I wasn't old and useless.'

'Prove to him, or prove to yourself?'

'Both, I suppose,' Vicky admitted. 'But honestly, Chris. It was nothing dangerous. I would never have done anything to put you or the kids in harm's way.'

'But you thought today that you might have. That's my point. Sometimes it's not in your control.'

'They stood me down. And I was trying to lead a double life, by not telling you the truth. If you'd known what I was doing, you'd have kept James closer maybe—'

'I shouldn't have to!' Chris exploded. 'Christ, Vics, what's wrong with you? Can't you see, even with the best of intentions, you're putting our family at risk?'

A tear fell down her cheek.

'You can't pretend it's not dangerous. You're not James bloody Bond, guaranteed to live so the franchise can continue.'

'I'm sorry,' she said, wiping her runny nose. 'I cocked up.'

'I'm beginning to wonder if making reckless choices is not just part of your personality – the bit that you kept so well hidden from me.'

Vicky smarted at the comment 'That's not fair, Chris. I'm not reckless. I'm not.' She wasn't sure she even believed herself anymore. Had everything she'd done, every decision she'd taken, been so irresponsible?

They both went quiet again. Vicky sniffed away the snot that threatened her upper lip.

'I just wish you'd said something before.'

'If I'd have told you, would you feel the same way?'

'I don't know. Maybe.'

'Because, if I was a proper part of the team, things would be different. I'd have back-up, surveillance, information . . . we'd all be protected. They'd look after us. Lots of people in Intelligence have spouses, families – they take it very seriously.'

Chris leaned over the table.

'But I need you to take it seriously, too.'

'I do.'

He sat back, deep in thought. Vicky watched him, wondering if she'd ruined their marriage for ever. She didn't know what to say to put things right . . . but maybe there was nothing she could say. Finally, he spoke.

'I'm not over this, Vics, not by a long shot.'

'I know.'

'So if you go back there, you have to be honest with me. I want to know if you're doing something dangerous; I want to know if we're vulnerable.'

'*If* I go back there?'

Chris sighed. 'I hate the idea that I'm stopping you from following your dream. Even if it's a nightmare for me.'

Vicky felt a glimmer of hope. 'I could see about part time. It would be easier, for all of us—'

'If you aren't honest with me after all this, if you don't talk to me, it's going to be very hard to come back from.'

'I understand.' She put her hand across the table and took his hand. 'So, can I call Jonathan?' she said.

'Talk to him. See if you can figure something out. But I mean it, Vicky. No more lies.'

'I promise.'

Chapter Nineteen

The following Tuesday, the Year Four parents' coffee morning was in full swing. Upwards of twenty mums were sitting in the cafe dissecting the events of the Christmas Fair and waiting more or less patiently for the young girl behind the counter to figure out their order of decaf skinny mocha mini espresso latte-ccinos, or whatever they had asked for.

Vicky sat next to Isobel's mother, Diana, who had somehow managed to get served already and was sipping smugly on a sea of froth and cocoa powder.

'So, what's everyone doing for Christmas?' Diana dabbed her coffee moustache with a napkin.

At the mention of Christmas holidays, the atmosphere grew tense and the women began sizing each other up like runners at a starting line.

'We're off to Rome for New Year's Eve,' one mum said, starting the bidding. 'Holly and Jackson are really looking forward to it.'

Vicky joined the chorus of 'ooo, lovely!', although she suspected if they were anything like her kids, Holly and

Jackson would rather be watching *Harry Potter* and stuffing their faces with Quality Street than wandering around collapsed bits of old stone in the rain.

Diana's attention turned to the seat opposite Vicky, where Matisse sat.

'What about you, Matisse? Bet you're booked somewhere nice.'

Matisse sipped her espresso, the only other drink to have made it to the table so far. 'Sacha decided at the last minute that we would go to Dubai for Christmas.'

Vicky hadn't seen her since Saturday's Christmas Fair, but, yesterday at Gilbert House, once she was reinstated, Jonathan had wasted no time confirming her suspicions about the Kozlovsky family holiday. Their trip coincided nicely with the date that the shipment of weapons was due to arrive there and Vicky had been wracking her brains trying to figure out why, if their marriage was as bad as Matisse had hinted at, Sacha would book a holiday for the family instead of going alone. Was he going to use them as collateral in some way? And if that was the case, who would protect them? Jonathan had said another JOPS agent was running point, with Special Forces back up, but she couldn't leave it to those clodhoppers to look after Matisse and Dmitri. JOPS orders had been to take Sacha out and take the terrorists down. There was nothing in there about protecting the wife and kid. She needed to be there, on the ground, seeing this thing through; she couldn't be part of another operation where someone got hurt because she didn't stop it. Not again.

'Oh my God, that is *such* a coincidence. We're going to Dubai, too!'

Jonathan was going to kill her. Followed swiftly by Chris. She felt a bit sick.

'Really? You never said anything.' Becky glared at her and mouthed 'What the hell?' in her direction. Vicky did her best to placate her friend.

'I only found out this morning, Becks. I was just about to tell you, I . . . I won a competition.'

'That's amazing!' Holly and Jackson's mum said, although she clearly didn't mean it. A free holiday to Dubai at Christmas definitely trumped three days in Rome.

'This is wonderful news.' Matisse, on the other hand, had genuine warmth in her voice. 'Dmitri will be delighted to have a playmate on holiday to spend time with – we can meet up at the waterpark, or for dinner, maybe? Or even Christmas Day on the beach. Where are you staying? We are at the One & Only on the Palm.'

'I don't know – I haven't got all the details yet.' Her brain was running at a hundred miles an hour as the reality hit of what she'd just done. 'I doubt it will be the same hotel as you though. It was a competition in a magazine – I don't think they'll stretch to the One & Only.'

'Still, a family holiday for five, at Christmas, for *free* – sounds too good to be true,' Diana said.

'Well, it's definitely happening!' Vicky did her best to look excited. She'd committed the whole family to being an arm's length from a case, just when she'd promised Chris she wouldn't get them involved. And she hadn't *exactly* cleared the trip with Jonathan before opening her big mouth. She hoped both the men in her life were still feeling supportive.

'I can't believe you didn't tell me before about the competition,' Becky said, on their way back to the cars. Vicky walked more quickly than usual, eager to avoid too much conversation and desperate to talk to Chris before she broke the news to Jonathan.

'Sorry, Becks. I honestly was going to tell you when I saw you this morning, but there were so many people around.' She spoke with punctuated breaths, puffing in and out as they made their way up the hill. She really needed to start using that running app again.

'So, are you going?' Becky said.

'Of course we are,' she sounded a lot more confident than she felt about that.

'How exciting! All that glamour and sunshine, you lucky thing. The kids are going to go nuts. There's that waterpark, what's it called, Atlantis, right, with the shark tank slide thing?'

'Sounds lovely.' Chris was going to be so angry he'd probably feed her to the sharks given half a chance.

'And the shopping, and the beaches . . . you won't need that duvet you've got on, that's for sure. Bikinis all the way.'

Horrific visions flashed before Vicky's eyes, of chasing Sacha through the streets while she wore nothing but a two-piece and a sarong.

'Do you have anything to wear in the evenings? You can't just throw on jeans, you know. When Laura went she said everyone looked like they came straight from a magazine.'

'I take it you mean *Vogue* rather than *Good Housekeeping*.'

'We'll have to do a massive shopping trip before you go.' Becky reached her car and got in. 'See you later – and bring the details with you – I want to see where you're staying.'

*

'You did *what*?'

She had decided it would be better to visit Chris at work, rather than call. Now half the office had heard Chris erupt through the glass doors of his office, she was regretting it.

'Vics, you promised me.'

'I needed to tell you before I confirmed with Jonathan—'

'*Tell* me?'

'Keep your voice down, for God's sake. Chris, I swear the kids – you – will be safe. I'll be safe. We won't be anywhere near the real action; I'll be where I'm most useful – keeping tracks on Sacha, Matisse and Dmitri, and maintaining my cover.'

'Your cover? Is that what we are now?'

A well-meaning assistant arrived at the door with two mugs of coffee. Chris shifted irritably in his seat while she placed them on his desk. They sat in silence until she left the room.

'It's not just the kids, Vicky. What about my mum?'

She'd hadn't thought as far as that. On top of everything else, they would have to abandon Maggie for Christmas.

Chris gestured at the mess of paper around him. 'And what about my job? Did it occur to you I might not be able to take the time off at this short notice?'

'It's always the "wrong time" whenever we book a holiday.' This, at least, wasn't easy to dispute. Chris was forever complaining about the inconvenience of taking a holiday close to deadlines that hadn't existed when they booked it. 'At least at Christmas everyone else is off work too. It's the ideal time, if you ask me.'

'Except you'll be working.'

'Only the first few days. We can stay on afterwards and really make the most of it.'

'It seems like I don't have much choice.'

'I'm not holding a gun to your head, if that's what you mean.'

'No. But you could.'

There was another long pause.

'Look, Chris, you said it was okay for me to go back to work. This is my work. I have to go where I'm needed.'

'I bet it was so much easier when I didn't know anything, and you could just manipulate your way into getting what you wanted. Right?'

'Chris—'

'I mean, you could have lied to my face, convinced me we'd won a competition. It would have been so easy, wouldn't it?'

'It's never been easy to lie to you—'

'So what's going to happen when we get to Dubai? I take the kids to the waterpark and you kill someone, or arrest them, or whatever it is you do, and then we all have Christmas like nothing happened?'

'Please be quiet, someone will hear.'

Chris glowered from behind his desk. 'Is that all you're worried about?'

'Given the situation, yes, I am. Chris, please don't make me regret telling you.'

Chris looked like he was going to implode. 'You promised me, Vics. You said you wouldn't put the kids in danger. You said you'd talk to me. Yet here we are again, with you making decisions unilaterally and expecting me to go along with it like it's perfectly normal. And it is far, far from normal.'

Vicky sighed. 'What do you want me to do, Chris?

Chris put his head in his hands. 'You've told so many lies.'

'Only one lie.'

'But a whopping great big one that I can't let go of. And you're so . . . cavalier . . . like I'm the one who's being stupid for worrying. And I worry, Vics. Since you told me, I worry all the time. The idea that I don't know what you're doing or where you are and how I'm going to be a nervous wreck if I get a call from school saying you didn't pick the kids up, or I'm going to get home and find our house burned to the ground . . . I worry about you – about me, our kids – and I feel completely helpless to protect any of us.'

She reached across the desk. 'I understand. But Matisse and Dmitri, they don't have anyone protecting them either. They could get hurt, and I can't – I won't – have them caught in the crossfire.'

Chris shook his head. 'All this danger . . . it's not how I see our life. It's not how I see you.'

'It's not how I see me either.'

'But some part of you must or you wouldn't be doing it.'

Vicky spoke through the silence. 'My job is to keep people safe. To keep us safe. And I'm good at it. That's all I'm doing in Dubai. It's the only thing I'll be *allowed* to do in Dubai. Jonathan is going to go crazy when I tell him what I've done. I've gone way beyond my jurisdiction. I shouldn't have said anything to Matisse without permission from him first to run with it. But the opportunity was right there, and I . . .'

'You took it.'

Vicky nodded.

'And that's the problem. You took that decision without even thinking about anyone else. About how it might make me feel.'

'But you said you would support me! I can't keep consulting you on every little thing.'

215

'Little?'

'Relatively speaking, yes.'

'So if this is little, what does big look like? I can't just give you a blanket "yes" on everything. What kind of husband and father would that make me?'

And what kind of wife and mother did it make her putting them in this situation? She hesitated. There was no right answer. She wanted to do the right thing by Chris and the kids. She had to protect Matisse and Dmitri. And, deep down, she knew a little bit of her needed it for herself, too. 'Please, Chris.'

'No, Vics. My answer is no.'

She felt a bit cross. 'I'm not asking for your permission,' she retorted.

'Then what do you want? My blessing? Because you're not going to get it.'

'Are you saying you won't come?'

'Possibly. I don't know.'

'But it's Christmas!'

There was another knock at the door. Chris waved at his assistant, who was waiting outside.

'I have to get back to work. We'll talk about this later.'

'But I have to see Jonathan, I have to tell him if we're going—'

'You've obviously decided that we are. You decided that before you even came here. You made it clear you don't need my permission for anything, Vicky. So who am I to stop you?'

216

Chapter Twenty

'You did *what*?'

Vicky watched Jonathan's face turned a nasty shade of puce for a few seconds before he recovered himself and picked up the nearest phone.

'Judith, in here now please.' He slammed down the phone. His secretary appeared at the door. 'Judith, I need you to get me five economy-class tickets to Dubai,' he snapped. 'Our brand-new employee here just decided to take a family holiday courtesy of Her Majesty's Secret Service.'

Judith gave Vicky a withering glance before turning her attention back to Jonathan. 'When for?'

'We need her in situ before the twenty-first. Maybe the sixteenth or seventeenth, that will give her time to meet with our JOPS officer on the ground there and get plans in place.'

'Actually, sir, I'll need to make it after the kids break up from school.'

Jonathan growled. Vicky took a deep breath and tried to look him in the eye. 'We'll need a hotel, too. Matisse said they are on the Palm, not the mainland. I did a bit of research and it's quite a trek, so it would be better if we were in the vicini—'

'Oh, for God's sake. Get them a hotel on the Palm, Judith, but nothing too fancy. Find out what's available that isn't going to bankrupt us.'

Judith nodded, and closed the door behind her.

'Next time you get a bright idea like this one, you might want to check it's not going to blow a planet-sized hole in my budget first,' Jonathan said.

'Sorry, Jonathan. But I thought it was important to take the opportunity by the balls.'

'Well you've certainly got me by them.'

'Oh, come on, you know this is the right thing to do,' Vicky said, a little put out that Jonathan wasn't warming to the idea. She'd already been through the ringer with Chris and really needed someone on her side.

'It isn't up to you to decide though, is it?' He buzzed Judith on the intercom. 'Judith, you got a price on those flights yet?'

'Four thousand five hundred and seventeen pounds, sir. And a minimum stay of seven nights in the hotels.'

Vicky felt all the colour drain from her face. 'Sorry, I didn't realise—'

Jonathan screwed his face up and banged his fists on the desk. 'For fuck's sake, Turnbull. *Five thousand pounds!* And that's just the flights. Judith, make it room only.'

'Yes, sir.'

Jonathan disconnected so hard Vicky thought the phone might sue for damages.

'I'll pay for everything. You can take it out of my salary.'

'You're absolutely right I can. Turnbull, if you're coming

back to work here, you should know you can't just go around pulling stunts like this in future. Things have got more complicated since you were here before – we're answerable to a lot more people about what we do and how we spend our budgets.'

'I am sorry. I acted on impulse, and I shouldn't have.'

'No, you shouldn't.'

Vicky thought about Chris, and the row they'd had. Maybe it would be easier just to stay at home and tell everyone the competition had been a hoax, hope that Chris would forgive her and Jonathan would forget. But Matisse and Dmitri . . . she didn't want them getting hurt because she'd put herself and her feelings first. She had seen how Sacha treated her, seen the bruises and heard the way he spoke to her. And she'd seen how much Matisse cared for Dmitri. If she was forced into a situation, if Dmitri was threatened in any way. . . Vicky knew the power that a mother's love wielded. Sometimes it could be the most dangerous of all.

'Jonathan . . .'

'What?'

'Something Matisse said, or nearly said to me. I'm convinced there's more to this trip to Dubai than meets the eye.'

'We're not missing anything that I can see.'

'Matisse knows more than she's letting on. If she didn't before, she does now.'

'We haven't picked up anything from surveillance. Please don't let your friendship with Matisse cloud your judgement on this.'

'I'm *not*. She opened a package meant for Sacha when I was there on Saturday, and it was a Christmas card, but I think there was something in it that caused a reaction. And then, afterwards, at the fair, she tried to talk to me about Sacha, but we got interrupted. Something has changed, I'm sure of it.'

Jonathan sighed. 'Fine. Get me something useful to help me figure out why the bloody hell everyone except me is going to be spending Christmas in Dubai. I want facts, dates, times and places. I want to know what that scumbag is going to be doing every single second of his swanky beach holiday.'

'Yes, sir.'

Jonathan got up and jammed a pod into the coffee maker. 'Want one?'

'Actually, I was just about to leave . . .'

'Sit down, Turnbull. There's one more thing we need to discuss.'

Vicky sat and Jonathan set a coffee on the desk in front of her. He took his seat opposite and opened the bottom drawer. Vicky heard the clink of glass and watched as he pulled out a bottle of vodka and two small shot glasses. She raised her eyebrow.

'God knows you've driven me to it this morning.' He poured the vodka and handed the drink to her across the table. Vicky was about to protest, but Jonathan didn't look like he was in the mood to be refused.

'Victoria, we need to talk about you and—'

'If this is about my ability to represent JOPS, I can assure you, I'll do everything I can to make sure I'm fit to be on the team. I'll liaise with the lead officer in Dubai and we'll coordinate with Special Forces to make sure that whatever Sacha is planning we're there, ready to take him and the terrorists down. I—'

'First of all, I can tell you right now that there will be no "we". You'll be there in an assist capacity only.'

'Yes, sir.'

'You're going to have to be careful over there. You've put yourself in a precarious position. If Sacha gets even the slightest whiff of what you're up to, the whole thing could blow up.'

'I'll stay well clear of any possible problems. I've got Chris and the kids to think of too, remember.'

'How's he taken it?'

'About as well as you.' She fished into her bag. 'That reminds me – he's signed the form. Your secrets are safe with him.'

Jonathan paused and fiddled with his shot glass.

'There's one more thing we haven't talked about.'

'What?'

'Anatoli Ivanov.'

'I know. You said he's in Dubai, working for Sacha.'

'Anatoli is making the land transfer of the guns for Sacha, from Jebel Ali Port to the Saudi border. But he's not working for Sacha. He's on our side. He's our eyes and ears, and he's getting us the proof we need that Sacha is cutting a deal with terrorists. It's his last big job for us before MI6 get him out.'

Vicky took a moment and let the information sink in. '*He's* our informant?'

'Technically, he's MI6's, but, when the case got transferred to us, we got him on loan. He's been working with them for years, feeding them information on Sacha,' Jonathan said. 'He must have got spooked enough about something to do it, but, what, I don't have a clue. I do know he's getting a new passport for his efforts. American, I believe.' Jonathan gestured to her shot of vodka. Vicky pushed it away.

'I've got to pick the kids up at three,' she said.

'He's a *major* part of the operation,' Jonathan said. 'And none of us can afford for you, or him, to be distracted by old . . . feelings . . .'

Vicky stood up from her chair. 'I can't believe you didn't tell me all this sooner.' She glared at her boss, trying to sort through her feelings on the subject. 'I can't speak for Anatoli, but I'm guessing he probably feels the same as I do. I'm all grown up now, with a husband and a family. I'm not about to go all doe-eyed and gooey about a target I fell for fifteen years ago. Give me – and him – a little more credit.' Anatoli was an *informant*. She of all people knew that would not have been an easy decision for him to make. So, what prompted it? 'Does Sacha have any inkling of what Anatoli's up to?'

'It's unlikely; Anatoli would be dead by now if he did.'

'Did Matisse know Anatoli? They must have met, surely?'

'They probably knew each other.' Jonathan drank his shot and poured another. 'But my primary concern now is you. I tried to keep you out of this because I didn't want you getting involved with Anatoli again – it was just too risky that something would go wrong. But you need to be prepared now, so that you don't screw up.'

'There's nothing to screw up, Jonathan. Whatever happened in the past, stayed there. You know that as well as anyone.'

After each date with Anatoli, Vicky had filed a report to keep Jonathan up to speed with developments. She was getting plenty of good intel about Anatoli's clients – many of whom were crooks on various watchlists, and some who were more specifically JOPS targets – and Anatoli didn't suspect a thing. It was perfect. Jonathan had been concerned to hear she'd begun a relationship, but she assured him she was in control of the situation. As time passed, though, Vicky found it more and more difficult to tell the difference between what was work and what was real life. She tried to remain focused by making sure that she asked the right questions, got the right information to report back and didn't reveal too much about herself. But the chemistry, the closeness . . .

She became convinced that their bond would be strong enough to withstand the truth and decided to ask Jonathan for permission to tell Anatoli who she really was and bring him on board as an agent working for JOPS.

'If you're sure he'll say yes, Victoria,' Jonathan said. 'Being an agent, betraying the people around you . . . it's not always straightforward.'

'He won't say no. Our relationship – he's invested – he'll help us, I know it.' She was sure she was right, and they needed him. Anatoli was close to the people they were after, with access to their homes and offices. It would make all the difference to be able to use him as a source once he knew what she needed rather than her gaining intel through a series of surreptitious questions and rushed glances at his phone.

They were at his rented apartment when she decided the time was right to approach him. It was late; they'd been out drinking and now they were lying on the sofa, their lips locked. A chillout soundtrack played from hidden speakers.

'We shouldn't be doing this,' she murmured. 'We've both got work in the morning.'

'To hell with work, Vika. Let's take the day off tomorrow and enjoy the time together before I go back to Moscow.'

Vicky sighed and gave in to the melting feeling inside her.

They began to strip each other's clothes away. Vicky ran her hands across his smooth chest and across his back and eased her fingers down to the button of his jeans as he worked his own way down her body.

She felt the nagging guilt of her duplicity. She liked Anatoli, she felt bad betraying him, but the job was important . . . if this was how she would secure him, win his trust . . . she opened her legs slightly to accommodate his hand as it moved further up her inner thigh.

'Wait. Stop.' She sat up. 'We can't do this, it's not right.'

'What do you mean? We've done it plenty of times before.'

This wasn't her; it wasn't who she wanted to be. She had to come clean with Anatoli, had to ask him right there and then to join her. He would say yes, she knew it. She could trust him.

'I have something I need to tell you.'

She told him about her job, about how and why they met and what she needed him to do. When she finished talking, he moved his hand from where it lay on her, got up, and began to dress.

'Anatoli? What's wrong?'

'You have seduced me into this – this relationship – to convince me to spy on my own countrymen, to double-cross my clients, to dance with death if I am found out?'

'It's not like that, Anatoli, I didn't seduce you, it just happened that way—'

'All this time, you've been using me. You've taken advantage, made me have feelings for you . . . I suppose you've been getting information from me this whole time without me even realising?'

Vicky blushed. 'Nothing that could lead back to you, I promise—'

'How much of this was real? Is anything between us private, or do you tell everything to your bosses, and laugh at me behind my back about how simple and stupid I am to trust you?' He looked around the room. 'Are there people watching us now? Have they been watching us this entire time?'

'Anatoli, please—'

'My answer is no, Vika. I am not this person. I cannot do this for you. We are finished.' He threw her the dress he had cast on the floor only ten minutes before, a disappointed and angry look on his face.

'Anatoli, no, look, you don't have to – we don't have to – I'll go back to them and say you won't do it, but please, I don't want this to end—'

'I think you had better go.'

Vicky could feel herself shaking. She'd blown it. Jonathan was going to be so angry with her.

'I will be leaving tomorrow,' Anatoli continued. 'I think it best if we do not have any more contact. I have a family – brothers, a mother – in Moscow. If anyone found out who you are, that I was . . . they cannot find out, do you understand? I will be killed. Please, Vika. Leave me now and don't contact me again.'

Vicky knew she was beaten. She put on her dress and shoes and headed for the door. 'For what it's worth, I'm sorry,' she said.

Getting annoyed with Jonathan years after the fact wouldn't help anything. But she wanted to be clear.

'Any feelings of a romantic nature – *any* – that I had for Anatoli, are dead and buried. Of course I reserve a fondness for him; he's part of my history, and I failed him, I failed Adam, and I failed at my job. But my priority is the objective *now*, to nail Sacha, eliminate the buyers and keep Matisse and Dmitri out of harm's way.' She stood up. 'And to be honest, I'm a bit fed up with people questioning my motives today. Between you and Chris—'

Jonathan prodded the paper she'd given him. 'I thought he was alright about you coming back to JOPS?'

'Well he's not. The Dubai trip – it's caused an almighty row.'

'If he needs reassurance that he's not the only one who's really pissed off about that, I'm happy to give him a call.'

'You're probably the second last person he wants to speak to right now,' she said, standing. They were done here. 'I'd like to see Mike before I leave. I need to ask him about a few things I need for the trip – and I need Ops to create the paperwork for the competition.'

'We'll have it couriered over to you later today.' He paused. 'Victoria, I had to ask. Letting feelings get in the way of your work – it cost us before.'

She looked at Jonathan. 'We all need to be very, very careful. But let me assure you *and* Anatoli that if, or when, we meet, I will be far more professional the second time around than I was the first. I failed you both last time; it won't happen again.'

Chapter Twenty-One

There was a short silence around the dinner table.

'Dubai?' Evie said.

'Cool,' Ollie said.

'What's Dubai?' James said.

Chris offered a glimmer of a smile in Vicky's direction. There had been another row and several days of cooling off before they'd finally agreed the trip was on, for everyone. With Jonathan's permission, Vicky had shared the details of her side of the operation with Chris, and, seeing that she wouldn't be directly involved with the takedown, he had agreed to a truce. She wouldn't say he'd completely come around to the idea, but they were telling the kids, which Vicky took as a good sign.

'We're staying at the Sofitel on the Palm,' she said. 'It's two interconnecting rooms, so you kids will be in one room and we'll be in the other.'

'Are we near the waterpark?' Evie asked.

'It's about five minutes away by taxi,' Chris said. 'I've booked a family pass to go there on Christmas Eve.'

Gasps of excitement escaped from the mouths of both Evie and Ollie.

'Is that the one where you go on a slide through the shark tank?' Ollie said.

'Yep.'

'Awesome.'

'We can't do dune bashing because James is too small, but we're going for Christmas Day lunch at a hotel in the desert and there'll be camel rides there,' Vicky said. She was going to be paying this trip off until next Christmas at this rate.

'Can Dad and I go quad biking?' Ollie said. 'And can we do that indoor ski slope? Joel went there last year and said it was really cool.'

'Maybe.' Chris threw a look in Vicky's direction. 'Let's see how much time we have to fit everything in. Your mum has some things she wants to do, too.'

'There's always the kids' club for Evie and James if you want to do something with Dad,' Vicky said, keen to keep both Chris and Ollie happy.

'Mum, I'm not a baby; I'm not going with James to a kids' club,' Evie said.

'There's a separate area for the little ones, Evie; you'd be with the older kids. There's loads to do and see while we're there,' she continued. 'Everyone will get their turn. Maybe one of the days we'll go and see Dmitri and hang out with them on the beach—'

'Dmitri's coming?' Evie's eyes were glittering.

'He certainly is,' Chris said.

Vicky ignored Chris's mild ironic undertone. 'His family are booked in a hotel just down the road from us. I found out from Matisse when I told her about winning the competition.'

'No way!' Evie looked delighted at the news. Vicky was

happy too. If Evie and Dmitri wanted to hang out, she would have a good reason to meet with Matisse.

'It's all going to be great,' Vicky said, 'but now it's bedtime.'

'I'm on it,' Chris said. 'Come on kids, let's get upstairs.'

Chris herded Evie and James upstairs to get ready for bath and bed, their excited chatter continuing all the way. Ollie helped her clear up the mugs from the coffee table and take them through to the kitchen.

'That's so cool that you won the competition, Mum,' Ollie said.

She hated lying to the kids. 'Yes, luck like that doesn't come along very often.'

'Will you still do all the Father Christmas stuff for James and Evie?'

'Of course we will. We'll just have to be a bit more creative about how he delivers the presents, that's all. And buy gifts we can fit in the suitcases, I suppose.'

'Mum . . . will I be able to Facetime from Dubai?'

'I imagine so. Why?'

'Nothing.' Ollie moved out of the kitchen with all the speed a teenage sloth could muster. Vicky let him go, but she was curious as hell. Facetime? Who would he want to Facetime? A girlfriend, maybe? She ignored the desire to poke around his room to see if there was any evidence. Not that he'd ever know she'd been in there; however, it was one thing to spy for a living and another thing entirely to do it to her own son.

Vicky washed the pots and pans from dinner while Chris got Evie and James ready for bed, and then she began to make plans. Listening to bugged rooms, hacking computers and tapping phones had told them a lot of a story, but the missing piece that would make all the difference more often than not, came from inside a person – from somewhere you could never reach with technology. Matisse had been so close to confiding in her at the Christmas Fair. She was sure, if she just got Matisse in the right place, at the right time, that she would reveal something more to her that would pull everything into focus. Vicky pulled off her rubber gloves and draped them over the tap to dry, then pulled her phone from her back pocket and sent Matisse a message to see if she fancied meeting up in the morning. This time, she hoped her intuition was right.

Vicky and Matisse sat at coffee the next morning and discussed their various plans for the trip. Vicky hedged as hard as she dared.

'I just hope Chris puts down his phone and computer for long enough to actually enjoy the holiday.' In truth, as hard as he worked, Chris believed a holiday was a holiday. Vicky had never checked, but she bet that he still put the out-of-office reply on his email when he was away.

'I am expecting I will be alone with Dmitri for much of the time,' Matisse said. 'Sacha is . . . well, Dubai is a place of business for him. He will no doubt have some things to attend to, and people to meet. But it doesn't matter too much. Dmitri and I will be fine on our own.'

'Matisse, is everything all right with you and Sacha?'

Matisse stared into her espresso. 'When I was younger, he was attractive because of his power, and his money. Now I wonder if any of it matters . . .'

Vicky put a comforting arm out towards her.

'Well, we're around. I know Evie was really excited to find out that Dmitri would be there.'

Matisse nodded. 'I know, thank you, Victoria.'

The two women finished their coffee.

'Well, I must go. I have shopping to do for our trip, and some banking to do as well,' Matisse said. She put on her cream leather jacket, flicked her hair out from inside the collar and zipped up the front against the cold. Vicky shucked on her big blue duvet and a woolly hat.

'See you at the carol concert tomorrow?'

'Of course. Sacha and I will both be there. Dmitri is really looking forward to it.'

'Evie too. Sacha's coming then?'

'Oui. I tell him he must come to this, the last concert, for Dmitri.'

'Last concert?'

Matisse faltered slightly. 'Of the year, I mean.'

Everything became clear to Vicky then. The two women exchanged a kiss on either cheek and she watched the Frenchwoman sashay down the high street towards the taxi rank. She reached inside her bag and called Jonathan.

'Sacha's going to Dubai, but I don't think it's just to oversee the deal. I think he's planning to run.'

'With a wife and a kid?'

'That's my point. The marriage is over. I think Matisse realises he's planning to leave her – she all but said it.'

'So, where's he running to? Does she know that as well?'

'Possibly. I doubt it. But maybe there's something at the house that might give us a clue. Something we weren't looking for before.'

'I take it you have a plan, Turnbull?'

'Of course I do.'

Chapter Twenty-Two

The surveillance team was watching the front door from inside a van somewhere down the street. The security cameras had been successfully accessed and a live feed on the van monitors showed the Kozlovsky family leaving their house. The tracking device inside Sacha's lighter confirmed as much.

'Stand by, Ops One.' Vicky heard Jonathan's voice in her earpiece.

'Standing by,' she whispered, and flexed her ankles and shoulders to get her circulation going again. She'd been lying amongst the bushes outside the Kozlovsky's main gate since it got dark and was not at all sure she'd be able to get back up without making a bunch of old lady sounds for the crew to snigger at. She blew into her hands, rubbed them together, and checked the time. 6.27 p.m. The carol concert was due to start at seven, but she'd asked Jonathan to arrange a few delays to the Headmaster's journey to the church, to give her a bit more time at the Kozlovsky's and still get to the concert herself. Still, she didn't have long.

The gates eased open and she saw Sacha, Matisse and Dmitri pass by in the car, their faces lit by the security light. Once they were through, the gates began to shut. Vicky moved to a crouch while she waited for the car to disappear around the corner. With seconds – and inches – to spare she nipped through the closing gate.

'Ops One in position.' She crouched behind the tree near the front door, masked from the house, and waited for her next instruction.

'Stand by, Ops One. Cameras switched to pre-recorded footage. Courier go.'

Vicky heard Jacob's bike rev around the corner to where the service door was situated and stop. The 'courier' had a parcel for Sacha, which would divert Magda from hearing Vicky open the front door.

'Ringing the buzzer now.'

The buzzer rang through her headset and she waited for Jonathan's command. She heard the intercom, and Magda's voice.

'Diversion successful. Entry secure. Ops One go.'

Vicky eased herself out of the bushes, went through the gate, and let herself into the house as silently as she possibly could. Time check. 6.31 p.m.

'I'm in.'

The house was quiet but fully lit. She could hear Magda getting irate with Jacob, who was stalling to give Vicky the maximum time possible, asking for Magda's signature and having technical problems scanning the parcel. Vicky started a quick check of the ground floor, looking in the few cupboards she could find and behind the art on the walls for any hiding places where evidence might be lurking. It was the first time she'd really seen the living room. It was less overtly opulent than she'd been expecting, given the extravagant kitchen, but no less exquisite. The art on the pale grey walls had been carefully chosen: a large slab of acrylic-on-canvas rectangles hung behind the sofa, and either side of the fireplace were two beautiful butterfly foil block prints – unmistakably Damien Hirst – stunning in their simplicity. The coffee table housed a Chihuly Macchia in brilliant aubergine, turquoise, and magenta. Vicky would have loved more time to look at each piece but had none.

She heard a door close downstairs.

'Courier is out. Ops One, get yourself upstairs.'

'Roger that.'

She crept out of the living room and back into the hallway, stopping for a moment to make sure Magda wasn't headed her way. Vicky heard the closing and locking of the house-keeper's bedroom door. Magda wouldn't be coming back out again on her night off without a good reason.

Vicky trod carefully up the spiral stairs to the first floor. 6.37 p.m. Inside Sacha's office, she shut the door and relaxed a little.

'I'm in the office,' she said, and began a more thorough search of Sacha's desk drawers and the panelled walls, looking for anything which might give a clue to what he was planning – tickets, a passport – anything to prove her suspicions right. She looked in the bin.

'I've found the Christmas card.'

'And?'

Vicky opened it up and was instantly disappointed. 'It just says "Merry Christmas" and no signature. There's nothing else inside it.' She dug into the bin. 'The envelope it came in is here too. But—' she turned it over in her hands '—it looks from the indentations like it had something more than a card in it.'

'Bring it back with you, we'll send it to Forensics. Keep searching. There has to be something.'

'Office is clean,' she said, after another three minutes.

'Are you sure?' came the response.

'Yes,' she hissed. 'There's literally nothing here. He's cleaned out. Whatever he's planning, he's made sure nothing got left behind.'

'Okay, pull out.'

'Roger.' Vicky moved back down the stairs and headed for the front door. She was nearly out when she remembered something.

'Wait a minute,' she said. 'There's a door in the kitchen that I've never seen inside. Maybe there's something in there. Do you have access to the floorplan?'

'Vicky, I said get out.'

'Just tell me, do you have access?'

'Hang on.'

She waited for her team to locate a plan of the house.

'It looks like a small room – maybe a walk-in food store or something.'

'No, it's on the wrong side of the kitchen for that. No one would keep their food that far away. I'm going down.'

'Victoria, stop, we said—'

'I'm going down, Jonathan. Can you hold up the concert for another five minutes?'

'You've got no back-up if the housekeeper comes out and finds you.'

'She won't. I'll be in and out before you know it.'

Vicky put her head over the railings and checked for any

noise. She could hear the faint strains of a television game show coming from Magda's room, but the lights in the kitchen were off and there was no other sign of life. She took a few steps down the stairs.

'*Shit!*'

The sensors did their job and lit up the entire staircase like a fairground ride.

'Vicky? Come in, Ops One. Report!'

'Nothing . . . it's nothing . . . I'm carrying on down the stairs.'

She pelted down the stairs and held her breath at the bottom, waiting for the last motion sensor to turn off and plunge her back into darkness again.

'Okay, I'm downstairs,' she whispered.

She made her way across the room to the door by the table. It was locked, but Vicky had bought a little bag of tricks with her this evening and pulled out her lockpicker from the bum bag strapped to her waist. It didn't take more than a few seconds until she heard the click to tell her she was in. A small sliver of light came from underneath the door, and she made one last check towards Magda's room before opening it up and slipping inside.

An innocuous table lamp sat on the desk, its gentle glow lighting the small office laid out before her. This room looked different to the rest of the house. A little more . . . real. There were books stacked on a shelf to the right; the books were about fashion and travel and interior design, with a beautiful Missoni candle sitting in a central space on the shelf nearest eye level. Lower down the shelves were a set of small storage boxes, and at the bottom a set of file boxes conveniently labelled with things like 'MAISON', 'VACANCES' and 'DMITRI'.

It must be Matisse's office. 6.44 p.m. Just enough time to take a quick look.

On top of the desk was the usual pile of paperwork, bills and bank statements – more money than her and Chris would ever see in their bank account even if they worked until they dropped dead. She continued down to the two desk drawers slung beneath the table top and opened the top one to find two passports, Matisse's and Dmitri's, and the family's travel documents for Dubai. Nothing unusual, three return tickets. Maybe she'd got it wrong. There was no passport for Sacha, but then Chris held on to his own passport too while she kept hers with all the kids' in a plastic envelope on a shelf in the spare room. It wasn't anything she could hang her hat on.

'Time to go, Turnbull.'

'Just a couple more minutes,' she whispered to Jonathan, and continued down into the bigger bottom drawer of the desk. It had more files in it – insurance, more bank statements, visa applications, marriage and birth certificates. She took a couple of photos of the tickets with her phone and checked her watch again. 6.48 p.m. She really had to get out of there. Just a quick look inside those boxes on the shelf . . . she grabbed one and slid it gently on to the desk, not realising that her phone had been shifted along towards the edge. It fell to the floor with a clatter.

Shit. When had she got so clumsy? She heard Magda's door open and quickly moved to a position just behind the door, hidden from sight unless Magda came all the way into the room. She pressed her back to the wall behind the door, slid out the stun gun from her bum bag and clutched it in her right hand, holding it out, ready to strike.

She heard Magda come into the kitchen and pause to listen. Vicky held her breath. She didn't want to electrocute Magda if she didn't have to and was relieved a few seconds later when she heard the older lady mutter what she assumed to be several Hungarian profanities, shuffle back to her room and shut the door again. Vicky relaxed and put the stunner back in her pack. Then she picked up the box and opened it.

Matisse's phone pinged, and she fished it out of her handbag to several disapproving looks. 'Move up, I need to save some seats.'

'Who for?'

'For Vicky. She messaged to say she's running late.'

'Why couldn't she get here on time like the rest of us?'

Sacha reluctantly shifted himself along the pew a few inches and she did the same. The church was bursting at the seams with eager parents all waiting for the service to begin, and Matisse had to throw her bag and coat quickly into the newly created space to discourage anyone from nabbing the seats.

'She's waiting for James's babysitter. Chris had to leave her waiting and bring Evie by himself.' Matisse saw Chris appear in the crowded vestibule of the church and waved. 'There's Chris now.'

'Hello,' Chris said, reaching where Matisse and Sacha sat. Evie ran to find her class. 'The babysitter didn't turn up on time, what a nightmare.'

'Ollie is not home?' Matisse asked.

'He's gone on a date with his girlfriend,' Chris said, a

239

nervous grin on his face. 'Of course, we're all pretending it's not a date, but they're off to Pizza Express and then back to her house afterwards to play computer games until we pick him up. We've managed to confirm at least that her parents are home, so there's no chance of anything getting out of hand . . . not that, well, you know, he's only thirteen . . . oh, hello, Sacha,' Chris had gone bright red.

'Christopher,' Sacha said, nodding.

Chris turned back to Matisse. 'How come they haven't started yet?'

'Vicky isn't the only one who is late. The Headmaster is also held up,' Matisse said. She got out her phone to take a quick photo of Dmitri and saw he was chatting away to Evie and the pair of them were laughing. She took the shot and showed it to Chris.

'Look at our two. Thick as thieves,' she said.

Chris looked at the photo and Matisse saw a flicker of disapproval pass across his face. 'Well, I suppose I'd better go and sit down,' he said.

Matisse motioned Sacha to move along the pew some more. 'We have space here for you.'

'Thanks . . . but I think I'm going to sit at the back so I can save a place for Vicky when she arrives.' Chris backed away from them towards the rear of the church. 'Evie prefers us to be unseen and unheard anyway. See you afterwards for a mince pie. Oops, sorry!' He crashed into the Headmaster who had just arrived and was making his way to the front, apologising along the way. Matisse put her phone on to silent as the Headmaster lumbered past her.

'Ladies and gentlemen, and children, I'm so very sorry I'm late,' he boomed, ignoring the many parents giving pointed looks at their watches and tutting with displeasure as he spoke. 'I was held up at some roadworks rather suddenly placed at the end of my road, and then on my way here there was a problem with my rear tail-light and the police stopped me to caution . . . anyway, the point is that we're all here, and it's Christmas, so I do hope the spirit of forgiveness is with you and that your enjoyment of what promises to be a wonderful evening isn't hampered by my tardiness. The children have been practising very hard, and we are extremely proud . . .'

The Headmaster droned on and then the service finally started. Just as the first reading began, Matisse saw her phone light up with a message from Vicky to say she'd made it. She turned around and saw her slide in next to Chris, giving him a peck on the cheek and muttering something. Chris pointed at Matisse, caught her eye, and they exchanged a small wave, Vicky rolling her eyes while she mouthed, 'Bloody babysitter.' She looked even more dishevelled than usual.

'The Angel Gabriel visits Mary,' came a voice from the front. It was Dmitri, beaming at them while he did his reading. Sacha nodded and smiled in return, and Matisse took another photograph before placing her phone in her bag. She wanted to enjoy this brief sense of family unity before it disappeared, along with her husband.

After the concert, the children were given gingerbread men and squash, while the adults scoffed mince pies and drank tea and tried not to look like they all wanted wine instead. Becky, Kate and Vicky congregated in one corner of the refreshments area. Becky was keeping a beady eye on her PTA volunteers and making sure none of them skulked off before everyone left and they could clear up the rubbish and leftovers. Vicky was doing her best to avoid Sacha and Matisse so that she didn't have to look either one of them in the eye. She saw Matisse making her way slowly through the crowds towards them and began to make her excuses to the girls. She really didn't want to talk to Matisse right now.

'I have to run and get back for the sitter,' she said to her friends.

'Why? She was late enough getting to you. Come and have a drink at the pub instead,' Becky said.

'I can't . . . Evie needs to go home. . .'

'Let Chris take her home,' Kate said. 'Come on, it's been ages since we all went out together.'

'No,' Vicky said. 'I nearly missed Evie's singing again tonight. I need to go home and spend some time with the family.'

Becky and Kate both looked disappointed. 'We understand,' Becky said, 'It's just we feel like we never see you anymore,' Becky said.

'That's not true, don't be silly.'

'You're always running off doing something else lately – if it's not meeting friends in town, it's baking with Matisse.'

'Well, if that's true you only have yourself to blame.' She tried to keep her voice light and jokey. Part of her really did want to go for a drink, but everything felt different now and she wasn't sure how to fix it. She'd put distance between herself and the others because it was easier than lying, but she was going to have to figure out how to manage things better if she wanted to keep her friends.

And her husband. Vicky spied Chris waving at her from the door. 'Look, I'm sorry, Chris and Evie are waiting for me and we're due to pick up Ollie from his girlfriend's. I have to go.'

'Ollie's got a girlfriend?' Kate said. 'We really haven't talked in ages.'

'What about the clearing up? In case you forgot, you're part of the PTA too,' Becky said.

'I can't. I'm sorry, Becks, I'll make it up to you . . . and we'll arrange a drink before I go, I promise.' She backed off and turned to catch up with Chris and Evie just in the nick of time and headed off to the car.

They walked in the cold, damp evening hand in hand with Evie.

'That was a lovely evening, Evie. The carols were beautiful and you sang really nicely.'

'Thanks, Mum. Me and Isobel did all the harmonies for "Hark the Herald Angels", did you hear us?'

'You did brilliantly,' Chris said. 'I had no idea your singing had got so good, Evie. It was an evening of revelation.'

It certainly was.

Chapter Twenty-Three

It had taken her only a few moments to put two and two together.

The first box she opened after Magda had gone back to her room was full of photos of a very young Matisse. The pictures showed a chubby, happy girl with two rather strict-looking parents, the images depicting what Vicky guessed was Matisse's childhood home in the South of France. She'd flicked through them fairly quickly; after all, Matisse wasn't the target and photographs from her childhood weren't likely to be relevant.

She grabbed the second box and placed it on top of the first. More photos. This time Matisse as a young woman – early twenties – with a wedding band on her finger, expensive clothes and the more familiar detached look in her eyes. A few were posed with a younger-looking Sacha – still imposing, but fewer lines and without the gut. They certainly made a handsome couple, but Vicky couldn't detect much chemistry between them, or even that they particularly liked each other. For newlyweds – which they must have been, she looked so young – they didn't seem to be very much in love.

Vicky moved through the pictures, thumbing them like a Rolodex. After the first third of the box, Sacha didn't seem to feature any more. Photos of the couple by the Eiffel Tower, by the banks of the Seine and by the Louvre were quickly superseded by the blue skies, palm trees and sand dunes of Dubai. And in all of them Matisse was on her own.

She was way over the two minutes she'd promised Jonathan, but she was onto something important, she knew it. She went back to the photos at the top of the pile to compare and found that Matisse was looking remarkably happier in the photos further into the box. Why? She'd left behind her home, her friends, her family, to move to Dubai. So, what was bringing the light back into her eyes? Or *who*? Someone was taking those photos and she'd bet good money it wasn't Sacha.

Time was running out. She had to hurry up and get out of the house and get to the carol service. She stopped suddenly, and pulled out a photo of Matisse grinning wildly, her chin pointed upwards to a man who was not her husband.

Vicky blinked and took another look at the photo. Anatoli's laughing eyes gazed into Matisse's and they were holding hands, the Burj Al Arab Hotel resplendent in the sunset behind them. As incredible, as unlikely, as horribly coincidental as it might seem, there was no doubt that Matisse and Anatoli had been together and had been in love. Vicky checked the date stamp on the picture – 2007 – and looked at their faces again. She pulled out Dmitri's birth certificate and took photos of both. If her suspicions were correct – which would certainly seem to be the case, given the date of the photo – then Dmitri was not Sacha's son at all. He was Anatoli's.

Vicky met Jonathan after drop-off the next day for her debrief, in a Clapham cafe near the common; it was busy and buzzy enough to mask their conversation, but Vicky wasn't planning on staying there. She grabbed her coffee, made a pointed U-turn, and headed back out of the shop towards the common itself.

Jonathan looked surprised she hadn't sat down and got up from his chair, swigging his coffee with one hand and holding the dog's lead with the other. She used her hand mirror to check he'd followed her from a safe distance and after five minutes or so, when they were well away from security cameras and busy streets and they could relax a little, Vicky found a bench to sit on. Jonathan let the dog off the leash to run across the wide expanse of common and joined her.

'So, come on then,' he said. 'What's the big secret?'

'I'm pretty sure it's not relevant to the actual case. We know from surveillance that Sacha suspected Dmitri might not be his. But his true paternity might be very relevant to the operation in Dubai.'

'Go on.'

'I discovered this in Matisse's office last night.' She handed over her phone with the timestamped photograph of Matisse and Anatoli and then swiped to show him the image of Dmitri's birth certificate and the photo she'd taken, of Dmitri and Evie on their playdate. Jonathan looked at it and sucked in air through his teeth.

'Jesus. Didn't see that coming.'

'You and me both. I'm pretty certain Dmitri is Anatoli's son. The timing works out, and . . . well, they have the same eyes. It's unmistakable once you make the connection.'

'How did we miss this? We knew Anatoli and Matisse had contact in Dubai, but I wasn't aware there had been a relationship between them, never mind a child.'

'I'm not sure Anatoli knows about the child, either. Given Dmitri's birth date, and the timing of Matisse's departure from Dubai, I'm not sure she would have even been aware she was pregnant when she left,' Vicky said.

'So maybe she never told him.'

'She's never talked to me about Anatoli. I didn't find anything to suggest they've had contact since she left Dubai.'

'It's a nasty conflict of interest . . .'

'With respect, sir, it was a long time ago—'

'Not you, Turnbull. Anatoli.'

Vicky flushed red and shut her mouth.

'We can't tell him.'

'Why not?'

'He's already under a lot of stress. It could compromise the operation if he knew he had a child,' Jonathan said. 'He may decide to contact Matisse to warn her, and make sure she and Dmitri aren't put in any danger . . . but he'd be doing the exact opposite. Sacha isn't a fool. He would know something was up, and it wouldn't take him long to get it out of Matisse, and then God knows what would happen, to her, to Dmitri, to Anatoli, to the whole deal. The whole thing would be a complete shit show.'

'So, what are you suggesting?'

'I think we need to recommend to MI6 that we take Anatoli out of the equation.'

'You want to kill him?'

Jonathan shook his head. 'No! I want MI6 to put him on that plane to America, just like he wanted.'

'But he's the one who has the relationship with Sacha. He's our man on the ground. We need him,' Vicky said.

The dog came bounding back towards them with a stick in its mouth. Jonathan got up from the bench and wrestled it away from the dog, then threw the stick back across the grass. Vicky stood too, and they walked slowly across the common as the dog ran off again to fetch.

'Anatoli's already putting himself at huge risk. Not made any better, I have to say, by the prospect of running into you.'

'At this point, I'm the least of your worries.' Vicky thought for a moment, then continued. 'I still don't understand how Anatoli ended up as an MI6 informant. He was so adamant he wouldn't help us when we asked him to. Something very serious must have happened to make him change his mind.'

'MI6 believed Sacha's business dealings had given him reasons to be nervous. He's an art dealer by trade, not a gun runner and he was getting too involved.'

'No, that's not it; it's not enough.' Vicky stopped walking. 'What if it was personal?'

Jonathan met her gaze.

'What if Sacha knew Matisse was seeing someone?' she said. 'He's not stupid; maybe he suspected all along that Dmitri wasn't his son. He isn't a man who would forgive his wife's infidelity easily.'

'So, he found out about the affair and threatened Anatoli? Sacha doesn't seem like the kind of man who'd leave it there, much less trust him with the biggest business deal of his life.'

'Okay . . . so what if Sacha knew Matisse was having an affair, but got the wrong man?'

'Airdrop me that photo.' Vicky silently thanked Mike for his coaching and once Jonathan had received the file, he tapped a few keys on his phone and held it to his ear. 'Judith, can you look up something for me? I'm sending you a photo with a timestamp on it. I'd like to know if there are any reported incidents in Dubai around that time. No, I'll wait.'

Vicky occupied herself with the stick and the dog while Judith supplied Jonathan with the information he was asking for. He put the phone down and slipped the leash back on the dog before telling her what he knew.

'There was a shooting reported in the news the day after the photo was taken. It was at the Burj Al Arab. The victim was a Russian national, suspected contract killing, the hitman was never caught. It might not be related, but—'

'Oh, it's related.' Vicky pointed to the image. 'Look where the photo of Matisse and Anatoli was taken. You can see the hotel behind them. Sacha must have had the wrong man killed.'

'How would that happen?'

'Wrong place, wrong time for someone. Matisse is an attractive woman. I'm sure there were plenty of admirers he could have thought were after her.'

'Okay. So, for argument's sake, let's say Sacha doesn't realise the mistake he's made. No wonder Anatoli wants a new passport and is willing to do anything to get it. He must live in constant fear of Sacha finding out the truth.'

'I'm guessing he was terrified of Matisse being punished as well. That's why he never contacted her, to let her know he was alive. He wanted to protect her.'

Jonathan nodded. 'Seems likely.'

'So, after she's left Dubai and gone back to Paris, Matisse finds out she's pregnant. She thinks the real father is dead, so she isn't going to confess and suffer the same fate; she convinces Sacha the child is his, to protect herself and her baby and continue living the good life she'd become accustomed to.' Vicky paused. 'What *did* Matisse do before she met Sacha?'

'They met in a strip club in Paris,' Jonathan said. 'She was a dancer. And more.'

Vicky digested this new piece of information.

'Psych evaluations say it was a symbiotic partnership: he got a beautiful woman on his arm who knew how to keep secrets, and she got money, prestige and a way out of a life she didn't want to live anymore.'

'So, what if that's changed?'

Jonathan screwed up his face. 'What do you mean?'

'Dmitri's eight years old; he's still a boy, but I remember when Ollie was that age, you could already see what he'd look like when he was older. His face is changing, he's got big teeth growing in, his jaw is squaring up, and soon enough he'll be a man who looks nothing like the one who is supposed to be his father. He might not have made the connection to Anatoli yet, but, even so, Dmitri is slowly turning into a permanent reminder of Matisse's infidelity. That must make Sacha angry, and, worse still, humiliated.'

'All this is very interesting, Turnbull, but as you said, it's not really relevant. We haven't really learnt anything new and there's still no proof he's going to run.'

'Not proof exactly, but if you add up all the circumstantial evidence . . . Matisse says he's leaving her. There are return tickets in the house for all three of them, but no passport for Sacha. Matisse isn't an easy read, but those photographs alone tell me she's not going anywhere. There are boxes of them in that room of hers . . . I used to think she was callous and unfeeling, but I know that's a façade; the real Matisse has a big heart sitting behind closed doors – literally – she couldn't leave all those memories behind. It's my guess that Sacha's getting ready to ship out alone. And Dubai is an easy place to run from – he could easily get to Iran, and from there he could disappear altogether. It would explain why he's overseeing the deal instead of staying away – to collect the cash and get out, all in one go.'

'We'll need the evidence. We need the shipment to exchange hands, we need to track where the money is before he tries to run, and we need to make sure we stop him,' Jonathan said.

'He's good, though,' Vicky said. 'We need a distraction to put him off his game.' She paused. 'When was the last time Anatoli and Sacha had face-to-face contact?'

'Anatoli says they've met in person maybe once a year in the past three years, but they've mainly communicated by phone or email.'

'It's probably not been enough for him to have put two and two together so far, but with everyone in the same place and a little nudge in the right direction . . .'

Jonathan's eyes widened slightly. 'If Sacha realised he'd been right all these years about Dmitri, and that his closest ally is his greatest enemy, that would be a huge distraction.'

'Maybe he'd be surprised and pissed off enough to let his guard down and make a mistake,' Vicky said.

Jonathan spoke with a hint of agitation in his voice. 'This is a very delicate operation we're talking about.'

Vicky nodded. 'What about Anatoli? Do we tell him about Dmitri?'

'No. It could compromise things. I want him focused on setting Sacha up for the fall, and if he's thinking about his son, he might not want to take the risk.'

'Sacha could kill Anatoli if he guessed the truth. And it puts Matisse and Dmitri in more danger than we realised.'

'That's where you come in, Victoria. We've teamed up with MI6 to make sure there are plenty of eyes on Sacha, but your job, now more than ever, is going to be to make sure his wife and child get out of this unharmed. And Anatoli.' He handed her a set of numbers written on a Post-it. 'Mike asked me to give you this. It's the combination for the safe in your hotel room. Everything you asked for will be in it, plus a weapon, standard issue.' He put his hand up to stop her speaking. 'I know, you don't want a gun. But, given what we know now, you might need it.'

'What about Chris and the kids?'

'What about them?'

'I need to be able to tell Chris something, to reassure him.'

'You have my word, Victoria. I will make sure your children are kept out of harm's way.' He continued, not giving her time to respond. 'Details of where to report will be handed to you when you check in. Our lead officer's name is Tariq.'

'Thanks.' Relief flooded over her as she realised she was finally going to get the closure she'd wanted. She was going to Dubai, and she was going to be able to put right the wrong of so many years ago. She would protect her friend, unite Anatoli with his family, restore her professional pride and prove to Jonathan – and herself – that she was up to the job . . . and, finally, show Chris that she and the people she worked for could be trusted.

'Be vigilant and flag if you think we've got problems. MI6 have a lot of people over there, but you're the one that knows all the players in this game; you'll be the one best placed to recognise any shifts in relationships or behaviour on Sacha's part. Keep close.'

'Yes, sir.'

Jonathan glanced at his watch. 'We should go.' He called the dog back over and got up from the bench. 'Merry Christmas, Turnbull,' he said, and walked off back over the grass towards the tube station.

Chapter Twenty-Four

That afternoon, when Matisse got home, Sacha was snoring in his office. She watched him from the door of the study with her lip curled and then went upstairs. What she'd ever seen in him was anyone's guess. Revolting, fat man. She couldn't wait for him to leave her.

Since she'd taken delivery of his fake passport tucked inside a cheap, anonymous Christmas card, she'd veered between being furious, relieved and terrified. There were no fake passports for her or Dmitri; whatever he was planning, it didn't include them.

Of all the ways she thought things would play out, she hadn't factored in blatant abandonment. She'd played his game carefully enough over the years to regain some of his trust – enough that is, to ensure she didn't end up dead in a gutter. But this was a literal slap in the face to everything she'd suffered to stay with him.

She made her way to the bedroom and let her shopping drop to the floor. Maybe she was wrong. Maybe she was going to end up dead in a gutter. She didn't think so, though;

even Sacha wouldn't kill a child, and if he was going to kill her, he would have done it by now. But why hadn't he? He'd loved her, in his own way, before he'd found out about the affair. Maybe, deep down, he still had feelings for her? No. Matisse didn't think love was the reason. It was more likely he had chosen to let her live because it suited him somehow. Which meant that, one day, it might not suit him anymore. The thought wasn't very reassuring.

She went into the dressing room to get some hangers. There was a bright side. She'd always been afraid of what might happen if she left him. But if he left her, she and Dmitri would be free. She could finally tell Dmitri who his real father was. Not the whole truth; it would be difficult enough for him to handle the news without telling him Sacha was a murderer too. Whether he was a good father or not, Sacha was the only one Dmitri had ever had, and his absence would weigh heavily on her son. But at least he would know the truth, at last, about where he came from. She hoped that he would forgive her, in time, for hiding it for so long. Maybe she could finally forgive herself too.

She began pulling at the bags and draped her new clothes on the bed, creating a patchwork quilt of designer wear. 'Mutton dressed as lamb,' Sacha would say, but she knew it was the green-eyed monster talking. She could still pull it off. She looked at the tight white Hervé Léger bandage dress lying nearest the pillows. Her eyes travelled over the sexy Pucci bikinis, a flowing nude Valentino maxi dress, and enough Oscar de la Renta to buy a terraced house in Barnsley. If he wanted a show – or a showdown – in Dubai, then she'd certainly be dressed for it.

On her return from the dressing room she saw Sacha

standing by the bed. She jumped, her cool composure slipping for a moment.

'I thought you were asleep.'

'I see you did some work on my credit card.' Sacha picked up a bikini top with one finger. 'I hope it makes you feel better about yourself.'

Matisse threw a less-subtle insult of her own. 'I bought you a new pair of shorts from the fat man's section in Harrods. They are in the dressing room.'

Sacha growled. He balled up his fist and shook it by his side, the irritation obvious by his tensed, whitened knuckles.

'Something the matter?' She slipped a dress onto a hanger and walked back to place it on the rail.

'Maybe it's time you got a job and learnt to live on your own money instead of mine.'

'Maybe I *should* get a job. At least I wouldn't have to answer to you anymore.'

'Who'd hire you? Your only qualifications are shopping and blow jobs.'

'You didn't seem to mind at the time.'

'Yes, and look where that got us. To this happy, happy place.'

Matisse flung down the Gucci skirt she was holding. 'Well if you're so unhappy, why don't you just go . . .' She hesitated. If he knew she had seen the passport, or that she had guessed his plans to leave, maybe she would be at more risk than pretending to know nothing.

Sacha stepped towards her. He was close enough now to hit her. 'Go?' he said. His phone rang.

'Go fuck yourself.'

Sacha pushed her onto the bed, face down, and held her

by the back of the neck. 'You seem to have forgotten that's what you're here for.'

The phone continued to ring.

'Shit!' Sacha released her and pulled his phone from his pocket. Matisse lay still on the bed and tried to stop herself from shaking.

'What do you want?' he spat the words out as if they were poison.

Matisse heard the Russian voice speaking on the other end in urgent tones, but couldn't make out what was being said. Whatever it was, whoever it was, she was very grateful for the interruption. And even more thankful when Sacha's scowl turned into a wide grin.

'So he decided to play along. Excellent. I'll see you on the twenty-first, my friend,' he said, and ended the call. He tapped a new number in and put the phone back up to his ear. 'This isn't over.' He pointed at Matisse, then walked away from her, heading downstairs. 'William? I have good news. Everything is ready. Stand by.'

Chapter Twenty-Five

The guttural Arabic blasted from the PA system, asking Vicky to secure her belt and place her bag in the overhead locker. She checked Ollie was belted in beside her and looked over his head to smile at Chris, who sat with James and Evie just across the aisle. He grinned back. The plane began its descent, and she watched Dubai spread out beneath her. As they turned inland, the skyscrapers stretched like blinking vines towards the darkening sky, and, between them, the winding rivulets of road exploded in a million glittering directions, carving their way through the city and off into the smoggy unknown.

Vicky looked down at the city in wonder. Now a huge tourist destination, the last time she'd been in active service Dubai had been a tiny dot of a place, a discreet stop for Russian prostitutes and occasional reports of child smuggling. Not any longer; in and amongst the celebrities and footballers' wives, the bankers, the traders and the property tycoons, the city was crawling with dubious businessmen of all shapes and sizes, all searching for legal loopholes to rinse their cash through the inflated real estate market and spending the spoils of their ill-gotten gains on fast cars and designer clothes. The perfect place for Sacha Kozlovsky.

The arrivals terminal was vast, spotlessly clean and deadly efficient, despite being one of the busiest airports in the world. Vicky and her family were processed through Passport Control swiftly and with the minimum of fuss. Pristine and bordering on belligerent, a customs official dressed in traditional white robes stamped their passports and motioned them on while he chatted in Arabic to his friend in the next cubicle about the football. Vicky pretended not to understand, although she was pleased at how quickly the language came back to her after years of neglect.

At the luggage carousel, she herded the tired kids around her while Chris went off to collect a trolley. Evie stared at the many local women waiting for their bags.

'They look beautiful, don't they?' she said.

Vicky joined her gaze. Their robes wafted, and expensive-looking shoes poked out from beneath the black folds, while designer handbags hung from the crooks of their arms. Stunning young faces peeked out from abaya, eyes immaculately painted with kohl and slender, ring-adorned fingers skimming strands of hair or refastening loose scarves. It was a reminder of the new world they had arrived in. They were playing by different rules now; an altered universe where one false move wouldn't just affect her, but her whole family, and Matisse's too. She needed to get her bearings quickly.

They left the terminal and were ushered towards a waiting car by a driver bearing a sign that read TURNBULL. The driver grinned.

'Hello, Vicky.'

Vicky laughed. 'Hi, Jacob. I guess Jonathan really is the only one not coming to Dubai.'

'He wanted you to have someone here you could trust.'

'And who better than the person I assaulted on a train?'

'You did what?' Chris had caught up with them, James in one arm and a suitcase trailing in the other. 'Hi, I'm Chris.'

'Jacob.'

'And this is James.'

'What's up, fella?' Jacob high-fived James, making him giggle. Evie and Ollie ran to catch up with them and introduced themselves to Jacob. Chris was smiling, more at ease than Vicky had seen him for days.

'So, you're our driver for the whole holiday?' Evie said.

Jacob nodded, catching Chris's eye. 'I'm here for you 24-7, whatever you need.'

'Thank you, Jacob.' Vicky looked at Chris, to make sure he understood. Jacob was their protector; Jonathan had been good on his word.

As they reached the car, Jacob handed Vicky an envelope. She slipped it into her bag and got into the front seat, while Chris piled the children into the rear. They pulled away in the black SUV, the chaos of the airport traffic giving way to the sleek lines of the city, and the effervescent glow from the lights hugging the skyscrapers against the darkness beyond. Vicky craned her neck to see the Burj Khalifa, the tallest building in the world, lit up white and strong against the black sky. High-rise quickly gave way to low-rise as they drove onwards, the familiar sail-shape of the Burj Al Arab changing colour as they passed by, and the twin towers of Atlantis glittering in the distance. Jacob made a turn on to The Palm and Vicky caught her breath. It was an enormous feat of engineering, to have dredged this tree-shaped island out of the sea and built so much on top of it. It took them nearly ten minutes to drive to the end, where they turned right and began the short drive around The Crescent to their hotel. They passed hotel after hotel on the way; each place more glamorous and alluring than the last.

'Oh look, Mum, there's a sign for where Dmitri is staying,' Evie said, pointing. Vicky knew exactly where the hotel was situated, of course. They carried on driving for another few minutes before pulling into their own hotel's fountain-strewn reception area.

'Here you are,' Jacob said. 'I'll drop you here and leave you to get settled.'

'Thanks, Jacob. Will we see you later?'

Jacob shook his head. 'Not tonight. But I'll check in with you tomorrow.'

Vicky nodded. 'Thanks.'

They got out of the car, a porter already helping with the bags from the boot.

'Wow,' Chris said.

Wow indeed. The hotel lobby alone was like nothing they'd ever seen before, stretching upwards and outwards and onwards in a never-ending sea of cream marble.

'Something else, isn't it?' Chris said. 'Vics? You with us?'

'Mmm.' It was an operational nightmare. So many pedestrian entry and exit points, although seemingly only one way in and out by car. She hoped it wouldn't come to that, of course, and that the operation stayed very firmly elsewhere. But if they needed to get out fast, then maybe a boat would be a better plan, if there was a jetty—

'You'll have to buy Jonathan something nice to say thank you.'

'What?'

'Are you even listening?' Chris lowered his voice. 'Is everything okay?'

'Yes . . . yes is it. Sorry. I was just—'

'Welcome, ma'am, sir.' The sing-song voice belonged to the receptionist who wore an enthusiastic smile and a smart black suit. 'Mr and Mrs Turnbull? A great pleasure to meet you.'

Vicky nodded at the greeting and, out of the corner of her eye, saw Jacob pulling away in the car.

'Thank you,' Chris said.

'Oh, yes, thank you.' Vicky was distracted; she needed to scope the place, quickly.

'We have taken the liberty of upgrading you to a suite during your stay,' continued the receptionist. 'You will be in room three eight—'

Vicky quickly focused her attention back on the receptionist. 'Oh no, no upgrade necessary, thank you.' The hotel safe in her room contained everything she needed, according to Jonathan. A last-minute room change could prove to be complicated. 'We are very happy with the rooms we have.'

'I was told you might say that,' the receptionist said. 'Your friend, Mr Tariq, is a good client of ours. He called this afternoon, to ensure we would be looking after you, and sent a gift basket with his driver, to be placed in your room. When we told him about the upgrade, he asked that his gift be moved immediately, and your butler be made aware.'

Confident Tariq had somehow facilitated a successful safe contents swap, Vicky didn't argue any further.

'Well, thank you, that's very kind,' she said, taking the room keys.

'You're welcome. Have a nice stay. If you want details

of kids' clubs, or other activities, please go and see the concierge and he will be happy to help you. Merlando is your butler for the duration of your stay. He will show you to your room.'

'Thank you.'

They made their way to the lift and Merlando held the doors for them until they were all in safely.

'First time in Dubai for you all?' he said.

'Yes, yes, it is,' Vicky replied.

'Lots to do . . . lots of waterparks for the children, and shopping and spa for you, madam,' he continued, babbling on happily about giant malls and slides with sharks in them as they rode upwards. They reached their floor and he guided them towards their room. 'Here we are, madam, sir. You like the room?'

Double doors opened on to a small hallway and Vicky looked either side as the children poured into the room amidst plenty of 'ooos' and 'ahhhs'. Merlando piled the suitcases in the hallway.

'Don't worry, I'll get the kids sorted out,' Chris said, and went through the doorway on the left. He poked his head back inside again after a moment, grinning. 'There's a whole bloody living room in here. It's bigger than our house.' He was gone again. 'Come on, kids, let's take a look at where you're sleeping.'

'I want the bed by the window!' 'Can James sleep nearest the door so that he doesn't wake me up in the morning?' 'Where's your bed?' Vicky heard her three children move into the bedroom area that led from the sitting room and she followed Merlando into her and Chris's half of the suite.

'This is your room, madam,' he said. She looked at the expanse of bed in front of her and gasped.

'If we get separated in the night we'll never find each other again,' she said. Merlando smiled.

'I'll be here for anything you need, madam,' he said. 'Oh, and here is your gift from Mr Tariq.' Merlando gestured to the huge basket that sat on a small coffee table in the corner of their bedroom. 'The room has been swept and your package is in the safe.'

'Thank you,' Vicky scrambled for some money from her wallet to tip him. 'Hang on, are you—?'

'This is very generous, thank you, madam,' he said, handing her a card and winking. 'I'll be nearby if you need anything, just give me a call. Enjoy your stay.'

He must be MI6. Jonathan really had done as he promised. Vicky waited until she heard the main door closing, and then went across to the basket. Fruit, dates, and a bottle of fizz . . .Vicky saw a note was lodged next to a box of Arabic sweets, the small corner of white card poking out from behind the packaging. She slid the note out and read it:

Dear Mrs Turnbull. Congratulations on your competition win! We trust you arrived safely. We look forward to seeing you tomorrow at 10 a.m. for our winner's photoshoot. A car will pick you up outside the hotel at 9.45 a.m. Anything you need in the meantime, please ask Merlando. Best wishes and enjoy your stay in Dubai!!

She cast the letter to one side and headed for the safe. She tapped in the six figures Jonathan had given her and the door popped open to reveal a phone, a plain white room key card, binoculars, a stunner, a gun and a box of ammunition. She took out the phone and put it in her bag, then shut the safe again.

'Mum! MU-UM!' Ollie came into the bedroom just as she had closed the safe door. 'Can we get something to eat?'

'Of course, yes. Come on, let's go and find something.' Vicky ushered him out of the room. 'Just let me have a wee and brush my hair and we can go and get dinner. Tell Dad.'

'I heard you,' Chris said, making an appearance. 'Wow,' he said again, catching sight of their room, and seeing the enormous basket of goodies waiting for them from Tariq. 'You'll have to enter one of these competitions again, Vic.'

Vicky threw him a look. 'Come on,' she said. 'Get the kids and we'll go and find somewhere for dinner.'

As soon as they finished eating, Chris took James up to the room. Evie and Ollie ate their dessert and asked Vicky if they could go for a scout around the hotel grounds. Vicky hesitated, and then relented. It was only six o'clock in the UK. Merlando had their backs. It was perfectly safe.

'Stay together please,' she said, handing them a room key. 'And don't be too long. It's already gone ten o'clock and it might not feel late to you because of the time difference, but we all need an early night or we'll never get up for breakfast.'

'What are we doing tomorrow, anyway?' Ollie asked.

'Well I thought you might want to head straight for the waterpark,' Vicky said, smiling as her two eldest children fist-pumped the air.

'We won't be late, Mum, we promise.' Evie grabbed Ollie. 'Come on, Ol, let's go!'

*

Vicky let herself into their room quietly so as not to disturb Chris putting James into bed, got out her laptop and the envelope the driver had given her from her bag and went to sit on the expansive balcony. Lights from the high-rises twinkled in the distance, and a cool breeze blew on to the balcony from the Gulf waters below. She took an extra moment for the view to sink in before going inside to retrieve her sweater from the sofa where she'd left it before dinner. As she grabbed it, the champagne caught her eye; their turn-down service had been in and placed the bottle on ice while they were at dinner. It seemed rude not to open it.

She wondered what Anatoli was doing this very minute, and whether he was alone. She felt sorry for him. Nearly a decade had slipped by and he had missed all the amazing, emotional bits about being a father that she knew he would have loved. She hoped he would be able to get to know Dmitri after all this was over. They both deserved that. She had to make sure it happened.

Sitting back down on the balcony and logging into the VPN with a glass of fizz bubbling away next to her, she sent a quick message to Jonathan to let him know she was in situ and that all was well. She left out the bit about the upgrade and the champagne. No need to rub it in. He'd been annoyed enough with her in the first place, and anything tantamount to her having a good time while she was here would mean she was never again allowed out of London.

There were no messages for her on the phone or in her email; but thanks to the brief from Jacob she was able to get caught up on JOPS' latest intel. The Kozlovsky family were booked into a very private beachfront villa on the far side of their hotel, facing away from the mainland and staring into the dark Gulf waters beyond; Tariq's operatives reported that Sacha had offered an extraordinary amount of cash upon check-in to ensure he got it. They also noted a package containing new clothes, a soap bag and a fresh supply of American dollars had been waiting for Sacha at the hotel reception. She scanned the remainder of the report for any details pertinent to her part of the operation. Dmitri would be attending the kids' club every morning from 10 a.m. until 1 p.m.; Matisse had a facial and a massage booked at the spa during the morning on the twenty-first of December. Sacha did not.

She took the laptop and report back inside and then wandered back out onto the balcony to drink her champagne. The conflict she felt was intense: on the one hand, she was itching to get on with things and get Sacha in cuffs, but, on the other, she was sorely tempted to go directly into holiday mode.

She sent a quick WhatsApp to Matisse from her real phone.

OMG we got upgraded! Check out the room!

Vicky snapped a quick photo from the balcony, looking back into the living room of the suite. With a bit of luck Matisse would reply with a picture of her own, of her accommodation. People took holiday snaps without paying attention to detail a lot of the time. A reflection, papers left out on the coffee table, an incongruous personal item: Vicky hoped for anything that would give her some scraps of information without Matisse even realising.

No such luck. Matisse replied after a few minutes, in text only, to tell her that their hotel was beautiful too, to enjoy their holiday, and they would see about meeting up in a few days. Vicky breathed heavily in annoyance. She couldn't message again; she didn't want to arouse suspicion.

'Well this is pretty all right, isn't it?' Chris cut through her thoughts and came to sit next to her, a glass in hand. He put his arm around her and they took in the view together. 'Did you get everything sorted?'

'Yep; I'm being picked up tomorrow morning at nine-forty-five,' she said. 'Can you take the kids to the waterpark and I'll join you there for lunch?'

'Sure. Ollie will be okay to wander by himself, and Evie can stay with James and me,' Chris said. 'There's a really cool kids' area they'll both enjoy, and a lazy river. When you arrive, I'll hand them over and take Ollie on the shark slide thingy.'

'Sounds good.' Vicky slid a little lower in her seat. Her phone bleeped. It was Matisse. Another message, with a photo included after all.

Guess who we just bumped into?

Vicky waited for the photo to download. She groaned.

'What's the matter?' Chris said.

Vicky held up a picture of William, the former PTA Chair, his wife, and their insufferable children, who were all smiling like little William clones along with Sacha and Dmitri. Chris had a confused frown on his face.

'What's the matter?' Vicky said.

'William doesn't have any kids at the school any more, and Matisse didn't start doing the PTA until this year, after he'd gone. How would they even know each other?'

'Well,' Vicky said. 'I know how, but I shouldn't really tell you.'

'William's *involved*?'

'Yes. No. Kind of. It's not really his fault . . . I didn't expect him to be in Dubai, mind you.'

'Neither did anyone else by the sounds of it.'

'The problem is, we should have. It was sloppy that no one picked this up.' Vicky dialled Jonathan, but it went straight to answerphone. She left a short message and banged the phone down in frustration.

At that moment the door opened, and Evie and Ollie piled in. Vicky threw the laptop under a cushion on the sofa and casually flicked at her phone. The kids sat down either side of her.

'Mum! Dad! The pool is amazing, it goes right on to the beach, and there are ice-cream and pizza stalls and kayaks and stuff down by the sand, it's so cool,' Evie said, over-excited and flushed.

Her phone bleeped. It was Matisse again, with a photo taken at the waterpark. Dmitri and one of William's kids were holding a giant ring next to the lazy river, with the caption underneath: The kids loved Atlantis! Another message followed: William and Sacha playing golf tmrw. Want to meet up?

Evie glanced at the phone and saw the photo. 'Is that Dmitri? Are they here already?'

'Yes, they are; we're sorting out when we are going to meet up,' Vicky said.

'Is that Alex? Are they here too?' Ollie peered at the screen over her shoulder. Alex had been in the same school year as Ollie; they'd got on well, both big fans of anything involving a ball, although they hadn't seen each other since they'd gone to separate senior schools and Vicky hadn't exactly encouraged a continuation of the friendship.

'Yes, it would appear they are staying at the same hotel

as the Kozlovskys,' Vicky tried not to grit her teeth too tightly. William's presence complicated everything even more.

'Awesome!' Ollie said, pleased that he'd found a playmate to hang out with for the holiday. 'Can I message him and tell him we'll be at the waterpark tomorrow?'

'You're supposed to be helping me look after your brother and sister at the waterpark tomorrow,' Chris said. 'You can meet up with him in the afternoon, if you want to see him and his parents say it's okay.'

'Cool,' Ollie said, and disappeared off with his own phone in his hand to unearth Alex's messenger details and make arrangements.

Vicky sighed. It had been a very long day. 'Evie, it's bedtime,' she said.

'It's not fair; if Ollie gets to see Alex tomorrow, why can't I see Dmitri?'

'Oh, for goodness' sake, all right. I'll message Matisse and we'll see what we can sort out about going over to see them, okay?' she snapped. She was tired, and fed up, and the holiday feeling she'd got close to earlier had dissipated like dust in the wind.

'Okay, Evie, why don't you go to bed and we'll sort it all out in the morning.' Chris's soothing voice guided Evie into her room and she heard him tell her to get ready for bed quietly so as not to wake James.

Vicky poured herself another glass of fizz and went back out onto the balcony.

'Golf?' she said to herself. 'Really?' She could no more imagine Sacha discussing handicaps than William shattering kneecaps. There was sadly no doubt, though, that William was up to his neck in Sacha's crap. How that lily-livered wannabe would manage imprisonment was anyone's guess.

Ollie wandered out onto the balcony. 'I think I might go to bed now as well, Mum,' he said.

'Sounds like a good idea, Ol, I'll be following you any minute,' she replied, and blew him a kiss. She put her glass down and went to check on Evie.

'When Ollie gets in bed, it's time to turn that thing off,' she pointed at the iPad in her daughter's hands.

'Okay, Mum, I will. Night.'

'Night.'

Ollie came into the bedroom, still clutching his phone.

'Don't make it too late, Ollie.'

'All right, Mum, I won't,' he whispered.

Chris and Vicky said a last goodnight, left the room and shut the door.

'I think I might go to bed as well,' Vicky said.

'Shall we have a bath before we turn in?' Chris said.

Vicky looked at the large circular bathtub plonked in the middle of an en suite nearly the size of her living room.

'Well . . . it would be rude not to, I suppose,' she said, smiling.

Chapter Twenty-Six

The buzzing of alarm clocks rang out from what seemed to be every corner.

'Jesus!' Chris sat up and knocked over the glass of water on his bedside in a bid to stop the hotel phone next to it from ringing off the hook. 'Shit!'

Vicky's mobile phone was also bleating. 'Where the hell is my phone?' she staggered out of bed and tried to locate the noise. 'Ow! OW! Ah, my toe. I've just broken my bloody toe.'

She gripped her stubbed toe and hopped towards the table that had Tariq's basket on it, hoping her phone would be there as well. It was, and she turned off the alarm and then turned her attention back to her foot.

'What did you do?' Chris turned on the bedside light. 'Christ, they don't mind a blackout curtain in this place, do they?'

'I stubbed my toe on the edge of the bed, it really hurts,' Vicky said, examining her toe. 'Oh my God, it's swollen up already. Ouch. Ouch. Ouch . . . it really hurts.'

'I'll get a flannel and see if there's any ice left in the champagne bucket.' Chris got up and opened the curtains a crack. 'Woah, it's sunny out there.' He disappeared into the living room. Vicky looked at the clock. 9 a.m. It felt like the middle of the night.

'Here you go,' Chris said, bringing back a cold flannel to pack her toe with. 'No ice, but the water is still cold.'

'Thanks.' Vicky wrapped the flannel around her toe and prayed it would stop throbbing. She had forty minutes to get ready before the car picked her up to take her to Tariq. The last thing she needed was a sodding broken toe.

'The kids are still asleep . . . shall I wake them up?' Chris said.

'If they slept through all that, maybe leave them for another fifteen minutes.' Vicky hobbled to the bathroom and inspected herself in the mirror. 'How formal do you think I should be?'

'I don't know,' Chris said. 'You're the expert. Where are they taking you?'

'No idea,' she said. 'It could be anywhere.'

She limped into the rain shower and luxuriated for a few minutes. Getting out and drying off, she heard James's little voice through the sliding doors, talking to Chris.

'Are the others up yet?' she called.

'Just getting them now,' came the reply.

Vicky suddenly remembered she'd stuffed her laptop rather inelegantly under a cushion in the living room the night before. 'Just a minute,' she said to Chris, and having retrieved it, limped back into the bathroom to check if Jonathan had replied. He had, to say he'd passed on her information about William and to try to keep tabs on the accountant whenever possible. Vicky was worried; now she had two lots of wives and kids to keep safe.

She turned her attention to the more immediate task: getting ready for her meeting with Tariq. She decided on a pink-and-white-striped dress, down to the knee and with cap sleeves. Fine for the beach, but she'd probably get away with a cardigan thrown over the top if they went anywhere inside. She brushed her hair and applied some mascara. The dress managed to show up every lump, bump and bulge and she had a zit coming on her chin thanks to the long-haul flight. Not exactly perfect, but it would do.

She winced with pain as she slipped on her flip flops. They weren't made for broken bones and every time she took a step it was agony. She took them off again and grabbed a couple of plasters from her soap bag and some cotton wool from the glass caddy by the sink. Once her toe was splinted, she slid her foot into a pair of roomy espadrilles, instead of the flip flops, and sighed with relief. At least she could walk now.

Everyone piled down to breakfast, the kids chattering about the day ahead and Chris shepherding them along the way. Vicky looked at her watch. It was already nine-thirty.

'I'm going to grab a coffee and then I need to run,' she said.

'Not with that toe,' Chris said. His smile disappeared. 'Good luck. Be careful.' He gave her a kiss.

'Don't worry, it's just a meeting; there's not much that can go wrong,' Vicky said, not sure if she was reassuring him or herself. She felt nervous, suddenly, about leaving Chris and the kids behind.

'Go,' Chris said. 'Merlando's got our back.'

She nodded, slurped on her strong filter coffee and waved at her children. 'I'm off to do a bit of shopping. See you later, be good for Dad.'

Jacob was already waiting for her, this time driving a smaller sedan with blackout windows. Not as noticeable here as at home, she thought, looking around at the other cars, which all had various shades of darkened glass. Jacob opened the door and she got in, placing her bag next to her on the back seat.

'You must be Vicky,' came a voice from the other side of the car. She swung in and stuck her hand out.

'Tariq? Good to meet you.'

Tariq was younger than her, in his thirties, and ridiculously good-looking. His dark hair was long on top, swept back from his perfectly symmetrical face by a slick of gel that was just on the right side of lothario. His teeth were even and pearly white, and his skin was a clear, tan colour with just a hint of stubble around his jaw. His body, as far as she could tell, embraced the theme of physical perfection; the fitted blue shirt he wore skimmed a clearly toned torso, and the belted beige jeans sat snugly with no discernible love handles in sight. If he wasn't a spy, he could have been a model. No use in London, where he would have stuck out like a sore thumb, but in Dubai, land of the beautiful, he melted right into the crowd. In comparison, Vicky felt hot and awkward, fulfilling her role beautifully as 'Brit Abroad'.

'I thought we'd grab a coffee and go for a walk along the beach,' he said.

'That would be nice,' Vicky replied. 'We only arrived last night, so some fresh air and sunshine would be nice.'

Tariq chuckled. 'Fresh air. You don't hear people saying that about Dubai very often.'

They drove past the Burj Khalifa, the famous sail-shaped hotel.

'Beautiful, isn't it?' Tariq said. 'Hard to believe that twenty years ago this place was considered an out-of-town destination. Now it's right smack in the middle.'

'This city is unbelievable,' Vicky agreed. 'It looks just as amazing by day as it did by night.'

'It certainly has a way of bewitching you,' Tariq said. 'Be careful, Vicky, you may end up wanting to stay.'

Vicky thought of London, and the grey dull skies, the traffic, the smell, the endless relentlessness of it all. 'I'm already sold,' she said, smiling.

They turned off the main road into a side street, heading towards the beach. As they slowed to a halt, she summoned up the courage to ask the question that had been on her mind since she woke up that morning.

'Will anyone else be joining us?'

On cue, Jacob pulled up at the dead end, facing the blue waters of the Gulf. A pale-suited figure stood by the boardwalk, smoking a cigarette.

'Ah, Anatoli,' Tariq said, opening the door. 'You're early.'

Vicky felt her heart speed up as she climbed out of the car to stand with the two men. If it was possible to feel lumpier and more middle-aged than she did now, standing between her ex-lover dressed from head to toe in Ralph Lauren and the chiselled, coiffed, Ryan Gosling body double that was Tariq, she didn't know how. She pulled her dress down, doing her best to iron out the creases, draped the cardigan over her arm and tucked a sweaty bit of hair behind her ears. Thank God she had her sunglasses with her, to hide some of the wrinkles.

'Vika?'

Anatoli looked surprised, although whether it was her mere presence or the state of her, was debatable. Quite frankly Vicky was amazed that he recognised her at all. She didn't know what to do. The last time she'd seen him, he'd thrown her clothes at her and walked away, leaving her ashamed, embarrassed and disappointed. So much had happened since . . . she blinked the memory away and forced the years to roll forward. From the silence, Vicky guessed he must be going through similar thoughts, but his sunglasses masked his eyes, making it impossible for her to read him. She realised she had hers on too and was thankful he couldn't see the tears in her eyes.

Tariq broke the silence. 'I believe you two have met.'

'Yes, I believe we have.' Anatoli's mouth broke into a small smile and he held out his hand. As she took it, he pulled her into him to kiss her on the cheek. 'It's been a long time.'

She laughed and accepted the embrace. 'Yes, it certainly has. Although you wouldn't know it, looking at you.'

'You look great, Vika. Like you are having a good life – one filled with family and love. You have a family, yes?'

'Yes, yes I do.' The tension was replaced by relief. She brushed an escaped tear away. They were still the same people. But they were both older and wiser, and with hearts that belonged to other people. She smiled up at him. 'Three kids and a very nice husband,' she said, thinking of her family and feeling proud, suddenly, that she had accomplished this amazing feat. 'You?'

Vicky's smile faltered and she cursed inwardly at her

idiotic knee-jerk reaction to their exchange of pleasantries. The last thing she wanted to get into conversation about with Anatoli was family.

'I have not been so lucky,' he said.

'So,' Tariq said, taking the lead on the conversation and interrupting Anatoli before it got any more awkward. 'Let's walk.'

Vicky hobbled along between the two men and tried to ignore the stabbing pain where her toe used to be. Tariq and Anatoli slowed down their pace to meet hers, although graciously neither mentioned anything.

Tariq began talking. 'Vicky, we need to get you up to speed on the takedown plan, and I thought it would be good for you to hear it straight from Anatoli.'

And reassure Jonathan she wasn't going to blow the whole thing wide open at the sight of her ex, no doubt. 'Good idea. What's the latest news at the port?' she said.

'The ship arrived a few hours ago from China,' Anatoli said, as they walked along the beach.

'Once it's completed the docking formalities, the customs officials will process the paperwork for the containers it is carrying.'

'The cargo's been shipped from China using false paperwork, and we're planning to let it go landside without a hitch,' Tariq said to Vicky. 'Sacha believes Anatoli has successfully bribed an officer to process it without a stop and search, so, once they have the all-clear, the two containers will continue their journey by road.'

'The transfer is taking place a few kilometres from the Saudi border,' Anatoli continued. 'Sacha has asked me to oversee it personally; he's not letting the load leave the country until he has his money. He's asked me to stay on the phone while the exchange takes place, and he'll give me the signal when the money is in his account.'

'The National Crime Agency are standing by in London to follow the money,' Vicky said. 'They'll start the trace the second the transfer is confirmed so that we can follow the money through the maze that his accountant will have created.'

'The sum we're talking about should create a blip somewhere in the system,' Tariq said. 'If we can tell them when to look for it, it won't be long before the guys at the NCA find out where.'

'How are you going to know exactly when the transfer takes place?' asked Vicky. 'It's too dangerous for Anatoli to wear a wire, surely, in case the buyers decide to search him.'

Tariq turned to Anatoli. 'We're giving you a listening device you can wear that we'll only turn on when the money transfer has been made. That way, it won't be picked up if they search you when you arrive at the exchange but we'll still be able to hear what's going on. If there's any trouble, we'll be tailing the trucks all the way from Dubai and we'll have cover at the border, so you won't ever be on your own.'

'Are we making arrests at the exchange?' Vicky said.

'The drivers this side are clean. Pakistani, no links, they'll probably be let go at the border and some heavier duty grunts put in place for the drive through Saudi. We believe the end buyer is waiting in Iraq, near the Syrian border,' Tariq paused. 'Special Forces will execute a drone strike once there's visual clarification that they've arrived at their final destination.'

Vicky stopped walking for a moment. 'What about Sacha?'

'This is where it gets complicated. We have to keep Sacha in play until the guns reach their destination; we don't want any alarms raised before we have the chance to take down the bad guys buying this shit as well,' Tariq said.

'So, we are going to have to hope Sacha sits tight once the deal is done, until the containers are delivered to their rightful owners,' Vicky said.

'That's where you come in, Vicky,' Tariq said. 'You have a good relationship with Matisse. We need you to keep tabs on what the family are doing and give the red flag if and when Sacha shows signs of bolting.'

Vicky nodded. She glanced at Anatoli. She detected a slight change of pace in his step as the conversation moved towards Matisse. Did he still have feelings for her?

She continued the conversation, watching Anatoli more carefully now. 'Any leads yet, on where Sacha's planning to go?'

'We found a fake passport in his hotel safe last night, while the family were out at dinner,' Tariq said. 'Name of Igor Petrushev. Our best guess is he'll head for Iran first, then maybe China, but if we let him get that far and he swaps passports again we could easily lose him.'

'What about Matisse?' Anatoli asked.

Ah. So, he did still hold a torch for her. He'd kept his tone casual, but she could tell he was far from relaxed as he reached for a pack of cigarettes from his back pocket.

'She's not your concern, Anatoli.' Tariq's tone was firm, intended to shut down this line of enquiry.

Anatoli lit a cigarette. His hands shook a little and he took a long drag. To stop himself from saying something he'll regret. . . Vicky remembered it from years before and motioned at Tariq to let her talk. Anatoli needed reassurance, to feel like he had some control. He was not a man who would be happy with 'need to know'.

'As far as we can tell she and her son aren't in on the plan and Sacha's made no moves to include them in it. But we are being cautious in case that changes and I'm going to keep them under surveillance throughout the operation.' Relief flooded Anatoli's face and Vicky gave him a small smile. 'It's what I'm here to do, Anatoli.'

Anatoli shook his head. 'I still can't believe you know each other. It is a small, small world.'

'Some might say not small enough,' Tariq said. 'Kozlovsky is staying in a villa with boat access so you can't do this on your own, Vicky. We'll have him and the family on twenty-four-hour surveillance and once the deal's done we'll have Special Forces standing by on land and sea.'

Anatoli raised his hand.

'It is true, what you are saying, that he could leave at any time. But I know Sacha,' Anatoli said, 'he is a showman at his heart. He won't want to leave without a big celebration, a fanfare of sorts.'

Vicky considered what Anatoli was saying and nodded her head. 'I agree; Sacha isn't a man prone to subtlety. I think we can expect some grand gesture before he makes a run for it.'

'Well, whatever he is planning, we need to make sure you are both invited,' Tariq said.

Vicky smiled. 'I think I can wangle an invitation.'

Anatoli smiled with her. 'She used to be pretty good at getting herself places she shouldn't be.'

Tariq looked at them both and then settled his gaze on Vicky. 'Just keep me posted,' he said. He looked at his watch. 'It's time to wrap this up.' He passed Anatoli a box. 'Here's a belt for you to wear; the buckle holds the listening device. We'll have eyes and ears on you from the moment you leave Jebel Ali Port with the trucks and will be waiting at the rendezvous with a car to get you safely back to Dubai. In case of trouble, say "I need some water" and we'll make sure we get you out of there.' Anatoli nodded and pocketed the belt. Tariq continued, his attention turned to Vicky.

'We need you to report back on Sacha's movements as much as you can, as often as you can, especially once the deal's been done. We'll send you a signal once the money's been transferred, and we'll put around-the-clock surveillance on Sacha to make sure he goes nowhere. But if you get even the smallest hint that he's on the move, then let us know so that we can be prepared to move in and stop him.'

Vicky nodded. 'There's one more thing,' she said. 'William Rogers, Sacha's accountant. He's here with his family. Matisse sent me a photo of them last night.'

Tariq nodded. 'Jonathan passed on your message. We think he's here as insurance as much as anything else, but he could be useful after the arrest if we offer him a deal to corroborate the evidence.'

'Insurance?'

'When the money is put into Sacha's account, he wants to make it as invisible as he can, quickly – and he won't want any ambitious accountants skimming off the top while he's vulnerable like that. He knows he'd be too far away to do anything about it,' Tariq said.

'So better to keep William in his sights so the poor bloke is too scared to do anything but follow orders,' Vicky said.

'Or unless he really can't be trusted,' Tariq said.

'I dislike William as much as anyone, but he doesn't seem like someone who'd have the guts to scam Sacha.'

'We'll soon find out, I guess.'

They walked back along the beach and reached the point where the car dropped them off. Tariq gave Anatoli a quick shake of the hand and clapped him on the back before opening the car door.

'Your help means a lot, Anatoli,' he said. 'Once we've got Sacha, you've got your ticket out of here, I promise.'

'Thank you, my friend.' He nodded his head and waited for Tariq to get into the car before leaning into Vicky.

'It was very nice to see you again, Vika.' He pretended to kiss her on the cheek, whispering in her ear with his smoky breath as he did so.

'Keep her safe,' he said.

Vicky nodded and pulled away from him. He'd placed the trust she'd lost all those years ago back into her hands. If he only knew the enormity of the truth . . . she hesitated. She owed him the truth, this time. But Jonathan was right; if they told him about Dmitri, it would change everything. This time it really was a 'need to know'.

'It was nice to see you too, Anatoli.' She got in the car. As they drove off, Vicky watched him through the tinted windows.

'Does it feel strange, to see him again?' Tariq asked. 'Jonathan told me you had some history.'

'No, it doesn't,' Vicky said. She looked squarely at Tariq. 'He's a good man, doing something brave; something he couldn't bring himself to do when I knew him last. I think he is driven by something far more real than we ever had, though. I think he really loves her, even after all this time. I could see it when we were talking just now.'

'Does she know he's alive?'

'No, I don't think so.'

'We need to keep it that way, make sure this doesn't all

284

blow up in our faces. There will be plenty of time for family reunions after all this is over,' Tariq said.

'For their sakes, I hope you're right.'

Chapter Twenty-Seven

On the monitor, Vicky and Tariq watched Sacha pad about the office of his hotel room in his swimming shorts, two phones on speaker in either hand. Tariq's team had done a great job of bugging the room and they could see and hear everything from their own room on the other side of the hotel.

'The agreed sum has arrived in your account by wire transfer,' William's usually pompous voice sounded a trifle nervous. 'That's an awful lot of money, old chap.'

It was an awful lot of guns. Vicky held her breath and waited for Sacha's next move.

'Thank you, William,' Sacha said. 'Start transacting and get rid of the trail.' He cut William off and put the phone in his right hand down on the desk. He lifted the second phone to his ear. 'Anatoli? It's done. Hand the trucks over.'

'Will do.'

Sacha put the phone down without saying goodbye and wandered over to the sofa. Vicky fist-pumped the air. The transfer had gone without a hitch and they had him. They had Sacha.

Tariq activated the listening device on Anatoli's belt. There was heavy static, but Vicky could hear Anatoli making a brief exchange in English with a man with a heavy Arabic accent.

'That must be the agent,' she said.

The meeting point had been just off the main road, somewhere they wouldn't be disturbed by passing traffic. Over the drone of the motorway, she heard two doors slam.

'Okay, they're on their way. Let's pick up Anatoli.' Tariq was about to speak into a walkie-talkie when Vicky stopped him.

'Hang on. I can hear shouting.'

'It's Urdu,' said Tariq. 'It must be the drivers of the trucks.'

'What are they saying?'

'They're asking why they must leave their vehicles.'

'They sound scared.'

'It's as we expected; the agent is swapping them out for his own drivers.'

Anatoli's voice rang out through the speaker. 'Stop. Where are you taking them?'

Vicky could sense his agitation and gripped her chair.

'Wait, no – NO!'

Three shots rang out followed by rustling and a thud at close range.

'Anatoli?' She felt sick. Had they shot the drivers? Had they shot him too?

Tariq spoke urgently into his walkie-talkie. 'Shots fired, repeat, shots fired. Do not engage. Charlie One stand by to follow the trucks. All other units stand by.'

'Wait – aren't you going to help them now?' Vicky stared at Tariq.

'We need to let the trucks go. They have to reach the buyers or the whole operation is compromised.'

'But what about Anatoli, you can't just leave him—' She hung her head. She'd promised herself there wouldn't be blood on her hands this time. Now three people were dead—

'Can anyone hear me?' A whisper came from the surveillance followed by more rustling and the sound of gunfire again. 'I *really* need some water.'

'He's alive,' Tariq said. 'Delta One, try to get a location on Ivanov. Proceed to extract with caution.'

They kept Anatoli's feed live and listened into the comms from the rescue team. There was another spatter of gunfire, followed by shouting in Arabic.

'He must be hiding somewhere. They're going to find him if we aren't quick.' Tariq got back on the comms to the rescue team. 'Update me.'

'We have him in sight, sir. Shall we go in?'

'Hold your position.'

'Why can't you just shoot?' Vicky tried to keep her emotions at bay, but she was too terrified and too angry. Yes, the operation was important, but they'd put Anatoli in this position. He'd *trusted* them—

'I told you – we need those trucks to get to the buyers. Hang on—' Tariq held up his index finger. 'I think they're leaving.'

Anatoli spoke again, to everyone's relief. 'They've gone. Please, come and get me.' His voice was thin and shocked. 'I think I'm bleeding.'

'Delta One?'

'Trucks are en route, sir. Area is clear.'

Tariq gave the command to move in and Vicky waited for the rescue team to make contact again. Finally, a message came over the comms.

'Got him, sir. Headed back to base.'

'He's okay?' Vicky couldn't help herself.

'A little shaken and a surface wound from a bullet graze, but, yes, he's okay. He's calling Kozlovsky now.'

On the monitor, Vicky could see Sacha propped on a sofa in his hotel room, having poured himself a drink. The phone on the coffee table rang and Sacha's face screwed up in annoyance as he hit the speaker. 'Hello?'

'Your agent is a fucking dog. He shot the truck drivers, then he tried to shoot me,' came Anatoli's breathless voice.

'You got away?' Sacha said. 'What happened?'

'Hid in the scrub while they put a few bullets around the place, but they gave up after a while and got into the trucks. I waited until they left, then ran back to the main road and thumbed a lift. I'm on my way back now.'

Vicky shuddered. She could hear the truth of the story in his voice.

'Who are you in a car with?' Sacha said.

'It's a van; some Egyptian guy. Don't worry, he doesn't speak any English, only Arabic,' Anatoli said. 'I told him my friends had left me for a joke, he believed me.' He paused the conversation and spoke to the driver. 'Joke. *Nokta.*'

'*Nokta, modheka awi,*' they heard the agent say, and both men laughed. Yes, it was very funny.

Vicky wasn't sure Sacha was finding it so funny. She watched his face closely.

Anatoli's laughter faded. 'I left the bodies in the desert, Sacha.'

Another pause. Sacha bent forward to get a cigar from the box on the coffee table. He lit it and puffed heavy smoke into the room.

'They are nameless, faceless men in this country; it will be some time I'm sure, before anyone realises they are gone.'

'It could have been me too.'

'But it wasn't.'

'No. But it was way too close. I think my days of helping you out are over after this, my friend.'

'Don't worry, Anatoli, they are definitely over.' Vicky wasn't sure, but she thought she detected a slight menace to Sacha's words. Before she had the chance to dissect what he'd just said, a change of mood came over Sacha suddenly, like sunshine after a storm. He gave a huge grin they could see even from the monitor.

'We should celebrate. With a party.'

'Anatoli was right,' Tariq murmured to Vicky. 'He wants to make the grand gesture.'

Vicky was getting annoyed with Tariq. He didn't seem to have heard Sacha's implied threat. Or maybe he didn't care; Anatoli was just collateral damage to him – he had been willing to let Anatoli be fed to the lions once today already.

Anatoli seemed to be as wary as Vicky. 'I'm not sure I'm in the mood, Sacha. I was nearly killed just now.'

'Don't be so miserable, Anatoli. You are alive, and I am rich,' his voice rose. 'It is Christmas, and I have friends here – you should meet William finally – and you haven't seen Matisse in so long, either. Please, don't make me force you to come.'

There it was, that menacing tone again. This time, it was loud and clear.

'You hear that?' Vicky said to Tariq. 'Something's up.' No doubt he thought she was letting her emotions get in the way, but he didn't know all the players like she did.

'Of course, Sacha. I will be there.' She could hear, even though he tried to hide it, that Anatoli was worried too.

On the monitor they could see Sacha downing his drink and levering himself off the sofa. 'Excellent! Then shall we say, let's meet at the marina tomorrow night? I will send you directions of where to go. And thank you, my friend. *Nothing* you have done will go unrewarded.'

Sacha ended the call, stuck his cigar between his lips, grabbed his room key and left.

'Target on the move,' said Tariq, into his headset. An affirmative came back, from one of the operatives disguised as hotel staff, that they would keep him in their sights.

Vicky glanced at her watch. 'I have to go. The spa treatment I was supposed to be having only lasts an hour. I need to get back to Matisse.'

'Go,' Tariq said. 'See what you can find out about this celebration. And make sure you get an invitation.'

Vicky left the hotel room and walked along the corridor to the spa. She was emotionally wrung out and took a moment outside the entrance while she rubbed lemongrass-scented oil into her face, arms and legs and scraped her hair off her face to process the past hour's events. Anatoli was alive, at least. But they hadn't even reached the hard part yet. She slipped a bathrobe around her, borrowed from the MI6 surveillance team room. She needed to draw a line under what had just happened and focus on what was going to happen next.

Matisse came out of the spa. 'How was your massage? You didn't want to wait inside for me?'

'It was amazing. I think I blacked out from sheer joy at one point,' Vicky said. She waggled her phone. 'I decided to message Chris and tell him I was finished. Poor bloke is probably run ragged by now.'

'It was very kind of him to look after all the kids while we went to the spa,' Matisse said, as they headed to the lift. 'Sacha would never dream of doing that for me.'

'Chris might never do it again unless we get back to rescue him,' Vicky said. 'What's the quickest way back to your room?'

'We'll get a golf buggy; they'll call one for us at the front desk.'

They got in the lift and headed to reception. When the doors pinged open Vicky got out and headed straight for the main entrance. Matisse was following her, tapping something into her phone, when Vicky caught sight of Sacha with his back to her, headed towards the expensive jewellery store in the lobby. She guided Matisse around the back of a large marble pillar to avoid him seeing them and moved them quickly across the lobby to catch the cart.

'Oh, look, there's one already outside,' Vicky said. 'Come on, let's grab it.'

'Good afternoon, Mrs Kozlovsky, and her friend too,' the driver said with a smile. 'To the villa, I assume?'

'Yes, please,' Matisse said, still busy with her phone. 'Sorry – I'll be done in a minute. I just needed to send a couple of messages.'

'No problem.'

'Everyone ready? Hold tight.' The driver hared off towards the Kozlovsky's villa. As they pulled into the parking bay, he gave a quick wave to a man in a hat who was sitting under the shade of a palm tree in front of the opposite villa. It was Jacob. God, Tariq hadn't lied about the twenty-four-hour cover; his people were everywhere.

*

293

The kids – Ollie, Dmitri, Evie and James – were all splashing about with Chris in the pool at the Kozlovsky villa, the warm Gulf waters lapping on the shore behind them. The afternoon sun was weak and disappearing at a rate of knots, but they didn't show any signs of getting out.

'You okay?' she called to Chris.

'Oh hi! Yes, never better,' he replied, splashing Evie and Dmitri with a wave of water. 'You?'

'The spa was perfect – just what I needed,' she said, hoping Chris would get the message that everything was okay.

Chris picked up James and bombed him into the water while the others screamed with delight. He shivered a little. 'It might be time to go soon. It's getting pretty chilly.'

'Kids, you heard your dad,' Vicky said. 'A few more minutes and then it's time to get out.'

The kids all ignored her and carried on playing. Out of the corner of her eye she sensed movement and turned to see Matisse sashaying her immaculate body towards the lounger next to her. She handed Vicky a cocktail and Vicky took a big slurp. It was the best drink she'd ever tasted.

'Thanks, Matisse. And thank you for inviting us to hang out here today. This . . . it's really very beautiful,' Vicky said.

Matisse nodded. 'Dmitri is loving the infinity pool, especially now he has friends to play with. It's good for me, too. Sacha is spending the day working,' she laughed, 'but, in any case, I prefer your company.'

Matisse removed her hat and tossed her hair over her shoulders. Vicky studied her through her sunglasses. She still couldn't quite believe Matisse was real sometimes. She was wearing the same bikini as she'd worn to the Halloween party, and it looked just as good on her in broad daylight as it had done in Becky's dimly lit living room. Vicky shifted her kaftan to cover a few inches more of her dimpled thighs and sighed.

'What is the matter, Vicky?'

'Honestly, Matisse, one day you're going to have to get old and fat like the rest of us. It's lucky I enjoy your company because I'd hate your guts otherwise.'

'Sometimes I wonder if it is more trouble than it is worth, to look this way. People have a very strange perception of you when you are attractive, as though you may not have any brains, or any feelings. Both are very untrue.'

'Well, I don't think of you that way,' Vicky said.

'Non, but you did,' Matisse replied, and Vicky flushed in shame, knowing her friend was right. And they were friends now, she realised. No matter what differences and secrets lay between them.

'Well they say you should never judge a book by its cover, but it's true, people do it all the time,' Vicky said. 'I mean, look at me; I *look* like a slightly overfed housewife who baked too many cakes for the PTA.' She wished she could tell Matisse the whole truth. Maybe once it was all over, she would. 'I hate that people think that about me, that there's nothing more to me than that,' she continued. 'William, for example, I know he's Sacha's friend, but he was such an arsehole. He always dominated everyone when he was on the PTA. Some of that was being a man, and a misogynistic one at that, but I think a big part of it was that he had a job and was surrounded by stay-at-home parents, and that somehow gave him a sense of superiority that I hated. And it wasn't even that he put himself at the top of the ladder; sometimes, it was more that I hated being judged by what he *saw*, not what I knew about myself.'

295

'This is exactly what I mean, Vicky,' Matisse said. 'Even my own husband cannot see beyond what is in front of him. He cannot see that there is more to me than this body, or these good looks; he cannot perceive that I may have grown and changed and learnt something in the many years since we met. One day he will regret that he didn't look a little closer.'

'Matisse . . . I may be way off base here, and you can tell me to mind my own business . . . but have you ever thought you might be better off without Sacha? You seem so unhappy.'

'Ah non, in fact I am *very* happy at the moment,' Matisse said, smiling and stretching her body along the length of the sunbed like a cat on a carpet. 'I was not, it is true, but right at this moment, I am feeling extremely *content*—' she pronounced it the French way, '—and for once it is my husband who has made me feel this way.'

'How come?'

'Sacha has been working on a very big deal, Vicky. I don't know what it is, but I do know that it will make him very rich. Too rich. When it is done, he is going to—'

Sacha poked his head out of the patio doors.

'Ah, you are back,' Matisse looked uncomfortable, but Sacha seemed oblivious to what she'd been saying. 'Where have you been? I thought you were still in the room on your phone, but when I went to find you, you were gone.' She sniffed the air. 'You smell of vodka.'

'I had a drink and went to Reception to make some arrangements for tomorrow night. I just closed my deal . . . I thought a little celebration was in order.'

Matisse looked at him suspiciously. 'What kind of celebration?' she said.

'The surprise kind.'

'We're having a surprise?' Dmitri said, from the pool. Kids and their bat ears. You could ask them to get their shoes on for school a hundred times and they'd never hear you – mention the word 'surprise' one time and they're like a dog straining at the leash after hearing 'walkies'.

'Yes, Dmitri, that's right; we're going to have a surprise party tomorrow night.'

'Can Evie come?'

Chris stood in the pool and looked anxiously towards Vicky. 'Well I'm not sure if that's—'

'Well, we'd be delighted if you could all come,' Matisse said. 'Right, darling?'

Sacha extended his arms out to encompass her entire family. 'Of course, you are all more than welcome.'

There was no way their children would be going to this particular party. Vicky thought quickly about an attractive alternative.

'How about you kids have your own thing – if that's okay with you, of course,' she offered, looking in Matisse's direction. 'You can do a big sleepover at our hotel room, we'll get a sitter, and then us adults can have a good time without worrying about looking after you all.'

'Good idea,' Matisse said. 'But how about they all come to our villa instead? We have the pool, and a nanny, and it is a nicer hotel than yours.'

Vicky smarted a little at the comment, and then nodded. It had been obvious from their visit today that the villa was under constant surveillance, and fully protected by some of the finest men and women on the planet. 'Sounds good. Does that sound good, kids?'

'You can drop the children at Reception and a nanny will

297

bring them to the villa. Matisse and I will meet you at the hotel jetty. Come tomorrow at 7 p.m.,' Sacha said. 'Then we will ride by boat to Dubai Marina.'

'Well, if it's not an intrusion,' Chris said, catching Vicky's eye. She nodded imperceptibly. It would be fine. She would make sure of it.

'We'd love to join you,' Vicky said. 'A celebration, whatever the reason, is always good in my book. And it's nearly Christmas too.'

'Oui, all the more reason.' Matisse settled back into her lounger. Vicky did the same, and the two women chinked their glasses. 'To our surprise celebration,' Matisse said. 'Whatever it may be.'

'To surprises,' Vicky said. She wondered who, out of them all, would be getting the biggest one.

Chapter Twenty-Eight

Matisse threw a brightly coloured silk dress over her head and watched in the mirror as it clung to all the right places on its way down her torso, coming to rest finally, perfectly, perched on her breasts and her hips. The hem draped delicately around her lower thighs. She slipped on a pair of gold Manolo Blahniks and fastened a gold and diamond bracelet around her wrist. The bracelet was new: Sacha had bought it from the jewellery store inside the hotel that afternoon. She wasn't sure why he was still buying her gifts, and he would certainly stop if he found out what she'd done, but she didn't care. Her husband was in a celebratory mood, and that meant only the best would do, for him, for her, for everyone invited on this little jaunt of his, even though she knew he really couldn't give a shit about any of them.

She wondered what the catch would be. There was always a catch: Sacha always found something on which to focus his aggression, even in the face of glory. But this time, she didn't care. Whatever he had planned, it was nothing in comparison to what she'd accomplished. She'd won. She'd taken a huge amount of money from him and he didn't even know it, and it would be too late, by the time news reached him, for him to do anything about it.

William had been so easy to intercept; he'd been won over in a matter of minutes by a few weak compliments and a trail of light fingertips. She'd accosted him months ago, at the fancy-dress party, guessing that he was as vulnerable to a beautiful woman in a white bikini as any other man she'd ever met. She had pressed herself close to him, seen his arousal plainly through his ridiculous Batman Lycra, and brushed her fingers lightly across him as she put her request forward. William had been putty in her hands.

She'd waited until now to put the plan into action. William had taken his time with setting everything up, to make certain there would be no mistakes; he'd required a little more persuading than she'd originally thought, but by the time she discovered the fake passport and realised Sacha was planning to leave her, everything was ready. Matisse put the finishing touches to her lipstick, before popping it into her bag along with her phone. The thing that would hurt him the most, was for him to realise his money was gone, right when he needed it. William was teed up to drain his accounts of everything just as Sacha was making his escape; his entire fortune was destined to disappear before he spent a penny of it.

'One more night of playing the whore,' she said, and turned, satisfied, towards the door.

Chapter Twenty-Nine

Vicky and Tariq stood outside the door of Anatoli's apartment. His shoulders slumped when he saw them.

'You look like shit,' Tariq said

'I don't want to go,' Anatoli replied. 'I'm done.'

He was sweaty and pale, and Vicky could see the strain of the past twenty-four hours had been too much. She put out her hand and gently touched his bandaged arm. 'You have to, Anatoli. I'm sorry. But this is the most important part of the whole operation. We can't have him suspect anything is wrong.'

Ali handed him a suit wrapped in a plastic dry-cleaning bag.

'Take a shower and freshen up,' Tariq said. 'A driver will be waiting to take you to the marina.'

'Is my paperwork ready?'

Tariq reached inside his own jacket and handed him an envelope. 'Ink is just about dry on the passport. But you have to keep your cool, Anatoli. Kozlovsky needs to be in handcuffs before you go anywhere.'

'I'd rather you put him in handcuffs when I'm not there. Sacha's not just prone to grand gestures, he's prone to grand violence.' He looked at Vicky, who was ready for the evening, dressed in white flared trousers and a halter-neck top teamed with white trainers that hid her still-bandaged toe. 'You shouldn't be there either.'

Vicky's phone buzzed. 'It's Jonathan. Excuse me for a minute.'

Tariq nodded.

Vicky listened as Jonathan relayed the latest information. Special Forces drones were on their way to take out the trucks that held the guns. It was only a matter of minutes before they went up in smoke, along with everyone involved.

'I'll text you final confirmation, but you have the green light on Kozlovsky.'

'Thanks, Jonathan.' She hung up and spoke to Tariq and Anatoli.

'The trucks have arrived at their final destination. We can make our move on Sacha tonight.'

Tariq checked his watch. 'I need to go. Vicky, I have something for you too.' He fastened a brooch to her top.

'A wire?'

'So we can hear what's going on. Wherever you are, we won't be far away. Good luck. I'll be in touch.'

Tariq left the apartment and Vicky stood to go as well. 'I have to go and meet Chris,' she said to Anatoli.

'I'm not coming. You can't make me.'

Vicky looked at him. 'No, we can't. I am not going to try and force you. Last time, that didn't end well for anyone. But there's so much riding on tonight.'

She could see there was something more he wanted to say.

'Matisse . . . I . . . we were—'

'I know.'

'I haven't seen her in nine years.'

'It's going to be a big shock for you both.'

'What do you mean?'

It was no good. She needed to rip off the plaster and tell him. 'Matisse thinks you are dead.'

'I know,' he said, miserably.

'*What?*'

'I knew Sacha was onto Matisse; I'd heard him on the phone to his henchmen a few days previously. I laid a trail, led him to the wrong conclusions . . . that day, the last day we were together, I saw Sacha's men coming into the hotel. They killed a man, a Russian, he was a no-good crook but still, I knew it should have been me. I was . . . relieved . . . to be alive . . . I wanted to protect myself and her. I didn't dare contact her. I thought he would kill us both.'

'You spent all of these years knowing she thought you were dead?'

'I thought – hoped – that maybe Sacha would mention me in passing and she would know I was alive, even if we couldn't be together.'

'You obviously loved her very much.'

'She loved me too. Part of me hopes she still does. It's why I decided to help MI6 in the end. He's an evil man, and I want him to pay for what he did. I wanted to try and reconnect with her. Ask her to be with me. But I fear it's too late. She has a child; she's moved on with her life. And in a few hours, I will be on my way to a new life, like I never existed in this one at all.'

'That's not true, Anatoli. And if you come tonight, you'll at least get to see her.'

'I'm afraid to see her. I'm afraid that she won't feel the same way as me, and that all this will have been for nothing.'

Vicky tried again. She had to get Anatoli on this boat. Without him there, Sacha would smell a rat, and the whole operation could come crashing down.

'When I was searching their house, I found old photos of you both, hidden away. She wouldn't have kept them if she didn't still care.'

Anatoli shook his head. 'It's not enough. It doesn't prove anything.' He sat back down. 'No. I will not go.'

Vicky took a deep breath. There was only one thing left to do. It was a massive break of protocol, but Jonathan and Tariq could kill her later.

'There's something else you need to know. About Dmitri.'

When she had told him, she sat quietly next to him while he cried. She understood. To miss out on years of making happy memories, to miss being with the person you loved and being a family together. . .

'I'm sorry, Anatoli. You understand why we didn't want to tell you. It was too emotional, too personal. We are worried enough about you as it is.'

'I am not worried about me. I have told enough lies to Sacha already. One more hardly matters.'

'We didn't want you to feel vulnerable.'

'Vulnerable? Vika, how do you think I have been feeling for the past nine years? The man I work for tried to kill me. He murders, he lies, he takes what is not his. He thrives on other people's fear, on his strength and money and power. I have watched him crush people and kill the ones who got in his way. I chose to betray him because I was tired of being scared, and tired of feeling vulnerable. This news, that

I have a son, it makes me sad, because I do not know him, and because he has grown up thinking this bastard is his flesh and blood. And because Matisse has done it all alone when we could have been together. It makes me want to kill Sacha myself, not leave it to you and your people.'

'To be clear, it's not an assassination—'

'I don't care what it is! Again, Vika, people are not telling me the truth. How long have you known about Dmitri? How many times did you think to tell me and then decide not to?'

'I had my orders, Anatoli.'

'Just like before.' Anatoli's voice went cold. He got up and headed to the door, holding it open for her. 'I think you'd better go.'

'No. Not like before.' Vicky stood up, but made no move to leave. 'This time is different. You aren't the only one to consider in all of this. Did you stop to think about how Matisse will feel when she sees you? When she realises that you are not dead? She's lonely, Anatoli. She hates Sacha. She's afraid that tonight he will try to do something to her and to Dmitri.'

Anatoli looked alarmed. 'Will he be here – Dmitri – tonight?'

'No. The children are all safe at the hotel, mine included, with enough guards to protect a small country. But Matisse doesn't know that. Whatever Sacha does tonight, she will need you there, Anatoli. And when all this is over, she will need you then too.'

'She has you. It sounds like you can protect her better than I ever can.'

'But she doesn't love me!' Vicky was exasperated and time was running out. She had to get back to the hotel.

'Please. Have a shower. Put on the suit. Come to the party and be with Matisse.' Vicky pressed her hand against his chest. 'You will regret it if you don't.'

She removed her hand slowly and looked at him. His eyes melted and he shook his head.

'Okay. Okay. I will be there, Vika. For her. For my son.'

'And I will be there for all of you.'

The taxi dropped Vicky outside the One & Only hotel and Chris met her in front of Reception with Evie and Ollie.

'There you are. The nanny your boss sent is waiting,' Chris said, gesturing at a woman in a golf buggy a few metres away who looked particularly buff for a nanny. 'But I thought you'd want to say goodnight to the kids before we go.'

Vicky kissed her older children. 'Sorry I'm late,' she said. 'I got caught up in something.'

'Do Gucci have a sale on, Mum?' Chris had told the kids she was at the mall.

'Very funny, Ollie.'

'I'm Liz,' the nanny said. 'No little one?'

'No. He's at the hotel with a babysitter. Well, two, actually.' Chris had insisted that James stay at their hotel. They had an actual childminder looking after him and Merlando on guard at the door. Despite wanting them to stick together, Vicky agreed, in the end, it was the best option. The other kids would keep him up late otherwise and they would all pay for it the next day.

Liz the nanny smiled. 'Well, you've got me at the villa, but there's a couple of butlers on hand for any room service we might need. We'll be fine.'

'Thanks,' Vicky said, and meant it. She knew that the

kids would all be safe here. 'I love you,' she said to Evie and Ollie.

Evie gave her a hug. 'You too, Mum.'

'Behave yourselves. Stay in the room. Do as Liz says, okay?'

'Later, Mum.' Ollie said. They trundled off towards the Kozlovsky villa. Vicky watched them until they went around the corner, out of sight.

'Ready?' Chris said.

'Let's get this over with.'

Chapter Thirty

They made their way through the hotel grounds and down to the gangplank where the concierge had told them the boat was waiting. She groaned as she heard the familiar voice of William barking instructions to his wife.

'Come along, Helena, don't be such a wet blanket, it will be fun. Get in the boat.'

'Great. William's here too,' Chris muttered. 'Pompous arsehole.'

As they approached the jetty, Vicky could hear the strained tones of William's wife trying to reason with him.

'William, you know I'm not the biggest fan of boats . . . I do think it would be better for everyone concerned if you left me behind. I'll only be a burden.'

'Helena, please just get in the boat.' Vicky detected a hint of desperation in William's voice. 'Sacha's been good enough to invite us all and it would be incredibly rude to say no.'

'Where is Sacha anyway?' Vicky said, as she reached the boat and saw that William was already seated on board, while Helena stood frozen on the side. 'Hello, William, Helena.'

William looked distinctly ruffled. 'He's just on his way: said he needed to sort a few things out before he left. Hello, Vicky. Long time, no see. And this must be . . .?'

'Chris. We've met before. Several times. At the school.'

'Ah yes, of course, sorry old chap. Terrible memory. So, how are you finding Dubai so far? Hope this wife of yours isn't filling your days with shopping and spas like mine is.'

'Not exactly,' Chris said, his lip curling. 'Anyway, I wouldn't mind if she did. She's earnt the break.'

'Hmm, well yes,' William said. 'I suppose anything to keep them quiet, eh?'

Wondering how long it would be before Chris tried to throw William overboard, Vicky turned to Helena. 'You don't like boats?'

'William informs me it might be more than a quick jaunt to the marina,' Helena said.

'Oh?'

'Well I don't know for sure, but Sacha mentioned bringing our sea legs; sounds to me like dinner might be taking a nautical turn.'

'Maybe he just meant for the speedboat ride.'

'Maybe. But we are going to the marina. Why pick a marina if you're not getting on a boat?'

William looked smug and Vicky hated to admit it, but he was probably right. Vicky felt inside her handbag for her phone. Tariq was no doubt on high alert now thanks to her hidden microphone, but she just wanted to be sure; until now, their focus had been on the mainland around the marina and the area near their hotel on the Palm, but if Sacha was planning to take them further afield . . . it sounded a lot like he might be using them as cover for his escape.

'Just need to send a quick message to James's babysitter,'

she said, and tapped a text to Tariq. She put the phone back inside her bag and heard the reassuring twinkle of a return message coming in. She peeked at the text before she closed her bag and saw that Tariq was on the case. Satisfied, she turned to Helena.

'Come on, Helena, I'm not all that great on boats either, but we'll make the best of it, okay?' She got onto the boat and held out her hand to the other woman. Helena took it, reluctantly, and stepped on board.

'Now all we need are the hosts,' William said.

'Speak of the Devil,' Chris said.

'Ah, good, you are all here already.' Sacha strode down the gangplank, Matisse bringing up the rear. Her heels click-clacked on the wooden slats as she picked her way towards them. 'Hurry up, Matisse, or we'll leave without you.'

Once they were loaded on board, Sacha clapped his hands on the shoulders of the driver. 'You can take us to the marina now,' he said.

Vicky tried to relax and enjoy the ride. James was with Merlando. The remaining kids, William and Helena's four, Evie, Ollie and Dmitri, were all safely in the care of the second undercover officer, Liz, and surrounded by back-up if it was required. Tariq had her back, on land and sea. They were as safe as they could be given the circumstances.

But the circumstances were not good. William was a bag of nerves. Matisse barely said a word and kept checking her phone. Anatoli . . . well she still wasn't sure he could hold it together when he arrived. Vicky thought back to Sacha's conversation with Anatoli, and Sacha's gleeful anticipation of this evening. They'd not had enough time to prepare. There was so much that could go wrong. What if she'd made a huge mistake? She clutched on to her bag and tried not to wish too hard that she was back in the hotel room eating popcorn with the kids. She needed to be on her game to make sure there weren't *any* surprises tonight.

The speedboat slowed down, and Vicky looked around her as they pulled into the marina. It was a truly impressive sight; the backdrop of high-rise buildings reflected in the water and mega yachts moored all around. She couldn't believe the size of the boats; they were twice as big as houses and a gleaming white that reflected the lights of the skyscrapers above.

They pulled up alongside one of them, and the driver got out and tied a rope to the jetty. William had been right.

'We're here!' Sacha grinned and put his hand up to the yacht that sat next to them. Its hull rose out of the water far beyond their heads and Vicky thought she could make out at least two decks above. *Bond Girl* was painted in large letters down the side.

'Welcome to dinner,' Sacha said, and began helping everyone out of the speedboat. 'Come on board, come on board!'

'As suspected, then.' Helena grimaced. 'Honestly, William, I really don't think that I—'

'Shut *up,* Helena,' William said.

He really was obnoxious. Vicky wondered what he would do if she took out her gun and said the same thing to him.

'I think you'll be all right on this one, Helena,' she said. 'We're not going anywhere while we eat, are we, Sacha?'

Sacha shook his head. 'We'll take her for a spin after dinner though,' he said. 'After all, can't have a beauty like this for the night and not take her out cruising, can we?'

Helena looked relieved. 'I'll stay for dinner then, and get

a taxi back afterwards,' she muttered to Vicky. 'But for God's sake, don't tell William, he'll only make a fuss.'

'Of course not,' Vicky said, building a timeline in her head for Tariq and wondering if she could get Chris off the boat at the same time.

'He'll have drunk too much wine to care by the time he realises I've gone,' Helena said.

'Not much he can do about it once we've set sail. I'll just tell him you're in the loo while we're casting off,' Vicky said, conspiratorially. 'Talking of which, I must pay a visit to the ladies once we've had the tour.'

They climbed on board the yacht.

'Goodness gracious,' William said. 'Helena, will you look at this?'

'Oh dear God.' Helena looked green.

'Fuck me,' Chris said, to no one in particular, as he stopped dead to look around at the acres of deck that stretched before him. Vicky felt much the same way. On the lower level she could see two jet skis parked, ready and waiting to be launched into the water. A possible escape route, but not really Sacha's style. Still, better Tariq know about them . . . she whipped out her phone and took some photos, remembering to 'ooo' and 'ahh', just like everyone else.

As they ascended to the next floor, they were welcomed by liveried staff and told to make themselves comfortable. Vicky stopped to take in their surroundings; the polished teak of the on-deck dining table almost completely hidden by the plates and glasses laid ready for dinner, complete with white-gloved waiters standing to attention. Vicky walked past them to peek inside, and gasped. The entertaining area was enormous: a large lounge with an L-shaped American-style leather sofa and a cinema-sized screen opposite; further back there was another, more formal dining room, reminiscent of one you might find in a French stately home, a casino area complete with roulette table; and last, but not least, a fully stocked cocktail bar. Beyond this room, no doubt, lay cabins for sleeping. Vicky looked down the hallway and guessed there must be at least six or seven bedrooms in total, all with their own en suite bathrooms. She took photos of it all and went back outside to wander about the deck. Around the front of the ship, she could see the captain, his face lit up by the screens in front of him. She took a photo of him, and went to find Chris.

They were guided upstairs to the top deck where another waiter handed them a glass of champagne. Another fully stocked bar, DJ decks, and sun loungers surrounded a sizeable hot tub. The deck beyond was a sea of sofas and candles.

'Well, what do you think, everyone?'

William looked overwhelmed. Helena looked sick. Sacha turned to face Matisse, whose usual cool demeanour had been whipped away from her by everything she saw before her.

'Sacha . . . this is . . . unnecessary . . .' she began, but Sacha waved her words away with a flap of his hand.

'It is not about necessary, Matisse. You should know that. Come, everyone. Let us enjoy. Cheers!'

The group raised their glasses and drank. Vicky, anxious to get the photos to Tariq, asked one of the waiters to direct her to the nearest bathroom. Once down the stairs and locked safely in a ridiculously opulent toilet stall, she spoke quickly into the microphone in her brooch as she tapped in a message.

'I'm sending you photos of the yacht plus mugshots too. There's a crew of five, plus captain and kitchen staff, not sure how many of them.' She hit a button on her phone and waited for the photos to show as sent, and then got an immediate reply.

Ivanov?

She spoke quickly. 'Not yet. Had a bit of a hiccup after you left. Expected shortly. I'll check again later, I have to go now. Over and out.' She needed to get back. She had no idea if the crew were white-gloved waiters or paid guns for hire who were assisting Sacha's escape, but she couldn't afford to arouse suspicion this early in the evening. She flushed the toilet, ran the tap and then gave a decent number of seconds before leaving the bathroom and heading back upstairs.

'Madam?' A member of the crew who had been on the main deck before called her from outside the bathroom.

'Yes?' she said, her heart thumping.

'You left your champagne, madam,' he said, handing her glass to her.

'Oh, thank you, silly me,' she said, taking the glass and smiling. He nodded. As soon as she got upstairs she dumped the glass at the end of the bar and motioned to the barmen.

'Do you have sparkling water?' she said. 'I'm feeling a bit too thirsty for champagne right now.'

Chapter Thirty-One

Vicky watched Sacha lean over the side of the boat. Matisse sat next to her, watching him too, her face pulled into a frown. She looked like she was about to get up and give him a big, hard push.

'Hello, my friend. Just in time.' Sacha was speaking to someone on the gangplank, waving his cigar around in the air. 'Come on up and meet everyone.' He turned to Matisse. 'Come, darling, come and meet my special guest.'

Matisse stayed where she was. Sacha disappeared down the steps and Vicky heard him greet a man in Russian. A few moments later, Anatoli emerged onto the deck. He took the glass of champagne offered to him and sipped it slowly, his eyes scanning the boat as Sacha spoke to him, introducing William and Helen before making his way towards them. His eyes stopped on Vicky first, before locking on Matisse.

Vicky heard Matisse take a small gasp, and she watched her set her champagne glass down, hand shaking.

'You remember Anatoli, Matisse,' Sacha said. It wasn't a question. 'You look like you've seen a ghost.' He laughed and slapped Anatoli on the back. 'And you're the ghost! How funny is that?'

Vicky swallowed hard. *Sacha knew.* Of course he knew. Their plan had been to throw Sacha off balance, make him emotional and irrational and therefore more vulnerable to mistakes. But if he'd come prepared, that changed everything. Sacha had outplayed them all: Matisse and Anatoli weren't potential collateral damage anymore; they were in the direct line of fire.

Vicky's hand moved slowly towards her bag. She didn't think he would try anything now, while they were docked in the harbour, but there was always a chance. She hoped Tariq was picking up on all of this.

Matisse's eyes held on to Anatoli's. She looked like she was going to be sick. 'It's been a long time,' Matisse said. Vicky saw tears in her eyes.

'About nine years, by my count.' Sacha continued to turn the screw, looking like he was enjoying every minute of it.

Vicky stood suddenly, diffusing the tension, and held her hand out. 'Hi, I'm Vicky. And this is my husband, Chris.'

'Nice to meet you,' Anatoli shook hands with Chris and nodded at Vicky. He looked grateful for the interruption and she gave him what she hoped was a reassuring smile. He looked as sick as Matisse did, and Vicky suspected he knew exactly how much trouble they were in.

Sacha, on the other hand, was enjoying himself immensely. 'You two must have so much to catch up on,' he said, putting his arm around Anatoli and gripping him vice-like around his neck. 'My friend, you must think my wife terribly rude for not keeping in touch. You two being so close, before.'

'Excuse me a moment,' Matisse said. 'I must visit the

bathroom.' She turned and bolted, wobbling slightly on her heels as she left.

'Well, Anatoli, you certainly made an impact,' Sacha said, watching her go. 'Do you have this effect on all women? Or is it just the ones you've slept with,' he hissed.

Vicky pretended not to have heard him and turned her attention to the dark waters of the marina. Somewhere out there Tariq and Special Forces were waiting. She hoped they weren't too far away.

Sacha headed towards the stairs that led to the bridge. Vicky thought about Matisse. Her face had been etched with shock as she'd run past her to the bathroom. When exactly Sacha had put two and two together was anyone's guess – he hadn't said anything before now that surveillance had picked up on – but it certainly made sense of the attempt to kill Anatoli at the exchange. Could he have known all along? Vicky held on to her bag and felt the reassuring shape of her handgun.

'Well, I think I'll go and check on William and Helena.' Chris gave Vicky a kiss on the cheek and headed to the back of the boat, where William and Helena were sitting near the hot tub.

Anatoli drained his glass. His hands were shaking too. 'This was a huge mistake,' Anatoli whispered to Vicky, looking around him. 'He knows about me and Matisse, I don't know how he knows, I don't imagine Matisse said anything—'

'Matisse thought you were dead, remember,' Vicky said. 'He must have found out some other way.'

'I should have seen this coming.'

'Yes, well now we know he knows, it changes things a little. We need to get you off this boat and away from danger.' She spoke into her brooch. 'Tariq, if you're getting this, we need to figure out an extraction plan for Anatoli—' She paused, feeling a slight vibration under her feet.

'We're moving!' Anatoli sounded panicked. 'What's going on?'

The landscape in front of them was shifting as the boat backed out of its mooring spot. 'We're headed out to sea,' Vicky said. 'Don't worry. Tariq's got this. We have boats waiting to intercept. All we have to do is—'

'I decided we should have dinner somewhere else, after all,' Sacha said, coming back up from the lower deck and heading towards the hot tub. 'Come back here everyone, sit and enjoy the view.'

With no choice but to shelve the conversation, Vicky and Anatoli got up from the bar and joined Sacha, Chris, William, and Helena. Matisse was still nowhere in sight as the yacht powered out of the marina. It took a wide sweep to the right, around the top of the Palm, as the guests sipped on their drinks and took in the view.

'This is quite something,' William said.

'I hope it doesn't get too choppy,' Helena gripped on to the edges of the sofa until her knuckles were white.

'It's just a few little waves,' Sacha said. He spoke into a walkie-talkie and the yacht pulled to a graceful halt on the far side of the Palm. The city stretched out in front of them; to their right, the Palm and the high-rise blocks of Dubai Marina, to the left, the financial city centre and the Burj Khalifa, stretching high into the clear starry sky. The Burj Al Arab was directly in front of them, the sail-shaped hotel lit up in greens, reds, yellows, and purples and the strange little sky restaurant sticking out like mission control at the very top.

'I wonder why people eat there at night,' William said, looking up at it. 'Absolutely nothing to see except the dark of the ocean. Worst view in Dubai.'

'But the best hotel, eh, Anatoli?' Sacha gave a dirty laugh. 'Aha! Here's the missing piece of the puzzle. How are you feeling, my dear?'

Matisse picked her way up the stairs and perched on the corner of the sofa next to Sacha. She looked like she'd been crying.

'I just realised,' he continued, 'that the last time you and Anatoli saw each other must have been in this very hotel.' Sacha put his arm around her, looking every inch like a spider about to snare its prey. 'In fact,' he said, 'I've asked the captain to stop here, so we can have dinner looking at the wonderful place where all the magic happened. We can relive the old times while we eat.' He moved his arm and patted Matisse's backside a little too hard, before turning to the rest of his guests. 'Let's get some more champagne while we drop anchor.'

He clicked his fingers. Four waiters appeared with champagne and trays of canapés. Vicky got up and walked past them towards the stairs, grabbing a smoked salmon blini as she went.

'Where are you off to, Vicky?' she could hear the desperation in Matisse's voice.

'I just want to get some photos.' Vicky stopped and faced them all. 'In fact, why don't I get one of you all before we all get too drunk and fat. Say cheese!'

'Ah, this is the life,' William said, seemingly oblivious to the tense atmosphere all around him. 'Cheers, everyone.'

There was a clink of glasses and a pause in conversation while they all took a glug on their fizz. Vicky backed away from the group again and pretended to be photographing the view.

'It's a shame the children didn't come after all.' Sacha lit a cigar and took a puff. 'It would have been nice to have them here. I don't believe Anatoli has yet had the pleasure of meeting his son.'

William looked confused. The remaining colour drained from Matisse's face.

'Sacha, now is not the time—'

'Oh, now is *exactly* the time,' Sacha said. He got his phone out and turned it around to show everyone a close-up photo of Dmitri from the Christmas concert. 'Remind you of anyone? It's not difficult to see once you've got the bastard right in front of you.'

Helena gasped out loud, while William muttered, 'Good God.' Sacha was right: when you saw an image of both next to each other, the resemblance between Anatoli and Dmitri was unmistakable.

'Shall we give him a quick call, so his daddy can say goodnight?'

'Sacha, stop—' Matisse stood up and Sacha squared off against her, his face boring into hers while he waved his phone around in his hand. Vicky took the moment to drop down the stairs and hide from sight, where the conversation continued above her.

'Oh, you don't want that, Matisse, for your son to finally know the truth of who he is?'

'How did you know?'

'You keep a door locked, I know you are hiding something behind it. When I first found the photos of you and your lover—' he spat the words out and spittle landed on Matisse's face— 'my first instinct was to confront you there and then.'

'So why didn't you?'

'Because I had other plans for you. I didn't want to just leave and have some messy divorce and half my money gone out to you and your bastard son because a judge said so. I wanted to be able to disappear completely, with everything, and leave you with *nothing*.' He waved a passport in the air. 'So that's exactly what I'm intending to do.'

'What about me?'

'Anatoli.' Sacha smiled. 'Yes. What about you? I needed you to finish this deal, of course. I figured I could leave it to my clients to put a bullet in your head when you'd outlived your usefulness, but they fucked up. And then, I thought, what a wonderful opportunity. I can get both traitors in the same place, and have the satisfaction of seeing their faces when they realise they are both completely fucked. And better still, let them play it out in front of their son.' He hit a button on his phone.

Matisse lunged for the phone. 'Do not call him, Sacha. I am warning you, if you do, I swear I will—'

'You will what? Tell him how you slept with someone else and covered it up so I'd never find out?'

'Maybe I will tell him how the pig I am married to pretended to have killed his father before he was even born.'

'Oh, it wasn't pretence, believe me. My people made a mistake, they got the wrong man. Do you think I would have let Anatoli live if I'd known it was him? Do you think I will let him live now?'

Someone – Matisse or Helena – gasped, and Vicky heard the familiar click of a gun cocking. Then another one. Then another one.

'Tariq, you need to get on board *now*,' she whispered, fishing the gun out of her handbag.

Sacha spoke again. 'Phones. Put your phones in this bowl, all of you and move to the back of the boat.'

'What do you want from us?' Helena sounded terrified.

Anatoli's voice sounded shaky too. 'Sacha, it's me you have the problem with. Just let the rest of them go. They didn't do anything, they—'

'Where's Victoria?' Sacha said.

'Who?' Another man, one of the crew, spoke up.

'The other woman. She's not here. Go and find her; and watch yourself. She's more trouble than she looks.'

Vicky moved to hide behind the door of the living room. She crouched low, by the curtains, and scrambled in her bag. A gun would alert the remaining crew to her position and she didn't want that. Thank God she had been furnished with a veritable arsenal of tools. She found what she was looking for just as the barman who'd served her the water earlier appeared. He had a gun tucked into the waistband of his trousers and was reaching for it when Vicky jumped on him from behind with a super-human speed she didn't know she was still capable of. As he struggled against her, she pulled his arm up his back and jabbed him in the neck with a stun gun. The barman wobbled for a moment until he fell forward and stopped moving.

'One crew member down. I'm fine.' She hoped Tariq could still hear her. She tucked her stun gun back into her bag and, with some effort, dragged her would-be assailant behind the sofa before cable tying his wrists and ankles. She was knackered, and sweating, and wishing she still had her combat pants when she felt the boat lurch. They were on the move again, faster this time. She made her way to the deck outside and stood in the shadows, trying to catch a hint of what was going on upstairs. Minus the one she had just knocked out, and assuming the other waiters were armed, that left four of them, plus Sacha and the captain, and the kitchen staff.

'Where are we going?' Chris spoke loudly, and Vicky guessed he was hoping she could still hear him. Which she could, just about. The wind was in their favour.

'We're taking a little ride to international waters,' Sacha said. 'I need a bit of privacy to deal with my friend Anatoli, and my ride will be waiting for me after, to take me on to a new life.'

'I knew it,' Matisse said. 'Where is it you're going to? Iran? Moscow?'

Sacha laughed. 'If I tell you I'll have to kill you,' he said. 'And I wouldn't want to leave Dmitri an orphan. He's a good kid, even if he's not mine.'

'Listen, Sacha, old chap, my wife's really not looking all that well,' piped up William. 'And I'll be honest, the guns are making me a little bit nervous.'

'You have no reason to be nervous,' Sacha said. 'As long as you sit still and don't do anything stupid. But, William, I know already that you are not the kind of man to make any grand gestures. You do not have the balls.'

Vicky heard Matisse mutter something but couldn't catch what she said.

'What did you say?'

'I said, he has plenty of balls from what I could tell.' Matisse spat the words out, sounding less nervous than before.

'Are you blushing, William? Tell me that she didn't fuck you as well?'

'William?' Helen's voice was raised now, hysterical.

'No, of course not,' William blustered. 'I mean, she's an attractive lady, but I could never – *would* never—'

'See, Anatoli? That's a real friend,' Sacha said. There was a pause. 'Where *is* Victoria?'

'She's probably being held prisoner by that crew member you sent down after her, you bastard,' Chris said.

'Shut up.' Vicky heard a thump and Chris groaned. 'Go and make sure she's secure,' Sacha said, presumably ordering a second gunman down the stairs.

Vicky hid behind the treads as a pair of heavy feet came down them. As the gunman rounded the corner, she picked up a small fire extinguisher from the mounted collection next to her and bashed him over the head with it. He crumpled to the floor, onto a pile of beach towels, making barely a sound. Vicky took his gun and placed it on the tread of the stair nearest to her, then lifted a couple more cable ties out from her bag and fastened them about his wrists and legs, finishing the job with a large piece of gaffer tape to the mouth. She rolled him out of the way of the staircase, then piled all the towels on top of him so that he couldn't be seen. Two down, three to go.

She was just about to go back up the stairs to see what the situation was up there when she saw movement from inside the boat. She grabbed the gun from the stair and, arms outstretched, waited.

Two men came out of the door, armed. The kitchen hands.

'Vicky! Don't shoot!'

It was Tariq and Jacob. She released her grip on the gun and tucked it into the back of her trousers. 'Christ,' she whispered, 'I nearly shot you. Things are getting heated up there. I guess you dealt with the kitchen staff.'

'It got a bit heated down there too,' Tariq grimaced. 'So, what's the deal?'

'Three crew remain upstairs, all armed, plus Kozlovsky.'

She lifted the towels to reveal the gunman and nodded towards the inside of the boat. 'There's another one in there. We have to move quickly. Sacha's going to know something's up when I don't reappear.'

'We're still headed out to sea.' Tariq motioned to Jacob. 'Get up to the deck and stop the boat.'

'Yes, sir.' Jacob disappeared immediately into the darkness.

'Let's put this to bed,' Tariq said. 'Come on.'

'We can use the bar as cover.' Vicky took her gun from her handbag and left the bag on the floor. Both poised to fire, she and Tariq crept up the stairs.

Chapter Thirty-Two

Vicky risked a peek to assess the situation and immediately wished she hadn't.

One of the crew was pointing his gun at Chris, whose head was bleeding from the knock he'd been given. He looked pale and frightened. She nearly cried out but forced the noise back inside her. She'd made a promise that they wouldn't be in any danger and now she had to get Chris out of harm's way; getting emotional wouldn't help.

Taking a deep breath, she quickly scanned the rest of the group. A second gunman had his weapon trained on Matisse, and a third held William and Helena. Sacha was holding a knife to Anatoli's throat.

'Friends. We were friends, you bastard. I help you to build your business, I put my trust in you, I paid you good money . . . I thought they'd kill you at the Saudi border, then you wouldn't be my problem anymore, but you are like the cockroach. So, what will you do once I am gone? Screw my wife again when I'm far away and you think it's safe? No, no, *no*. I do not think so.'

Vicky felt the boat slowing down. Jacob must have taken control of the helm, which meant that Sacha and the three gunmen they had eyes on were the only ones left. She gripped her gun and braced herself.

Sacha didn't seem to have noticed the drop in the wind, although a glance between Anatoli and Chris suggested they might have.

'Just get it over with, Sacha,' Anatoli said. 'I am not afraid to die.'

'Don't talk shit, Anatoli,' Sacha said. 'I can feel you shaking.'

Tariq motioned to Vicky and they made their way to the two pillars that stood either side of the bar, flattening themselves so as not to be seen. Vicky hoped her arse wasn't sticking out too much.

Matisse cleared her throat. 'Sacha?'

'Oh, she speaks at last. What's the matter, my Zolotse? Scared I'm going to hurt your pretty boy lover?'

Matisse addressed Sacha in a cool, collected voice, the one Vicky remembered from the bar after paintballing, before they became friends.

'I think you should let him go.'

'I'm sure you do. But I've got no intention of doing that. Certainly not for you.'

'If you let him go now, you can have your money back.'

Tariq looked over at Vicky, who gave a small shrug. She had no idea what Matisse was talking about. Neither did Sacha, obviously. He loosened his grip on Anatoli slightly and gave Matisse his full attention. 'What?'

'I said, if you let him go, you can have your money back.'

'What money? If you mean the house, it's yours, I can't be bothered to go through the effort of getting you out of it. Although when I found those photos of you and your lover-boy over here, I thought about it.'

'Oh, I don't mean the house; it goes without saying that is mine. No, I'm talking about the money that's busy being transferred out of your many accounts and as we speak.'

'You're bullshitting me.'

'Oh I'm not. Right at this minute, every single penny you ever made from your crooked "transactions" is being wired to the National Crime Agency. Isn't it, William?'

Vicky adjusted herself behind the pillar. She had a clear line of sight to Sacha now, and could see he had lowered the knife away from Anatoli and was pointing it at Matisse, his face contorted in a mixture of disbelief and anger.

Matisse continued, supremely confident. 'You see, I had plans of my own, Sacha. Your dear friend William didn't take much persuading when I asked him to help me. I think maybe he realised it was better to be on the right side of the law. Or he liked my white bikini.' Sacha snarled, and William whimpered. Matisse continued, undaunted. 'Your money, from this deal, and all the other little deals you've done over the years, is currently with the authorities. I planned on letting you find that out once you were gone already, but you've forced me to reveal my hand a little early. No matter. At least I get the pleasure of watching your face when I tell you of the gloriously *legitimate* millions William has very kindly wired to me. I'm pretty sure I have enough to get by.'

Sacha let go of Anatoli and lunged for Matisse.

'You little bitch—'

Vicky saw Tariq signal her, but she was already out from behind the pillar.

'Freeze! Don't move!'

The gunman holding Chris released him and took a shot at Vicky. He didn't manage more than a single badly aimed round, though, as Tariq opened fire in return. Vicky watched the gunman recoil in pain as the first bullet glanced off his arm. A second shot to his leg brought him down to the ground. Not a fatal shot, but enough to keep him down.

'Chris! Run!'

Chris took flight as Tariq fired at the second gunman holding Matisse. Confident of Tariq's aim, Vicky spun to aim squarely at the gunman holding William and Helena, who was, in light of everything that had just happened in the last five seconds, looking very unsure of what to do next. Vicky used his lack of a decision to make a snappy one of her own.

'Get down!' she shouted at William and Helena, and then she fired. It wasn't the cleanest hit she'd ever made, but it was enough. The gunman staggered back clutching his shoulder, dropped his gun, and fell over the side with a loud splash. The water around them lit up like a Special Forces Christmas as Tariq shouted into his comms. 'Suspect overboard. Get a recovery team in the water, now!'

Vicky turned her attention back to the deck as Special Forces went to work in the water. William and Helena were clinging onto each other for dear life, Helena looking like she really was going to throw up any second. Matisse was a shade paler than usual. Anatoli had picked up one of the guns from the deck, although he didn't look like he knew how to use it. Sacha and Chris were nowhere to be seen.

'Chris?' She did a frantic sweep of the deck. She hoped that he would appear from somewhere then, so that she could ignore the feeling of dread that was growing inside her. 'Chris?'

'Tariq, where's Sacha? Where's Chris?'

Tariq looked around. 'Shit.' Vicky could hear the urgency in his voice as he spoke into his comms again. 'Suspect on the move, check mid-level and lower decks. Armed, possibly with a hostage.'

She heard gunfire from below. 'Tariq!' She was desperate.

'Go.' He trained his weapon on the injured gunmen. 'I'll take care of things up here. And you?' He looked over at William, shivering and snivelling in a corner with his wife. 'Come here so I can arrest you.'

Vicky rushed down the stairs. 'Chris!' With no sign of him on the main deck, she carried on, stopping dead as she reached the lower deck and surveyed the scene before her. Jacob was there, a rifle trained on Sacha, the little red dot marking out his aim on Sacha's forehead. Sacha was backing up towards the jet skis, with a gun pointed to the side of Chris's head.

'Chris!'

'Don't move!' Sacha tightened his grip on Chris and Vicky gasped.

'It's okay, Vics . . . I'm okay.' Chris tried to smile, but she could see he was shaking all over. They were running out of time. She gently placed her gun on the floor and pleaded with Sacha. 'Let him go. He has nothing to do with this.'

'Tell him,' Sacha said, motioning to Jacob. 'Tell him to put down his gun too.'

'Put your weapon down,' she said to Jacob.

'Vicky, it's not the way to—'

'That's my husband and I'm telling you, Jacob, put your weapon down!' She turned her back to him, to give him a full view of her gun she'd taken earlier, still tucked into the back of her trousers. Jacob laid down the rifle and put his hands up.

'You made this too easy for me,' Sacha said.

Vicky met her husband's eyes and tensed her back against the gun in her waistband. 'Ditto,' she said.

In the moment before she pulled out the hidden weapon, Chris lunged at Sacha's legs, taking them all by surprise.

'No!'

Jacob sprinted towards the two men as they toppled backwards and began wrestling on the deck. Sacha's gun flew out of his hands and Chris scrabbled at his arms to try and pin him down but was overpowered in a matter of moments. The fat Russian rolled over to sit on top of Chris and threw a heavy punch.

'Chris!'

Chris slumped against the side of the boat, his nose bleeding, just as Jacob launched himself at Sacha. The two of them rolled away across the floor, Jacob being the quicker to recover, but Sacha being the more fortunate, landing within reach of the gun. Jacob, unarmed, tried to grab at Sacha's hands, to force his point blank aim up and away. But Sacha was a powerful man, and Jacob wouldn't be able to hold him for long. Vicky steeled herself to take aim. There was no way she would have another operative sacrifice himself because of her.

The first bullet hit Sacha squarely in the back of his shoulder, the gun flying away from him for a second time. The second and third shots hit his left leg. He fell to the ground, a pool of blood forming around him as Jacob, exhausted, reached across with cuffs and secured him.

Vicky put down her gun, ignoring the bile in her throat, and ran towards Chris. She crouched down in front of him and cupped his head in her hands.

'Chris, Chris! Are you okay? Can you hear me?'

Chris moaned again and opened a swollen eye. 'Ouch,' he said.

The boat docked, and Vicky could see a heavy military police presence on the walkways and in the surrounding waters. Unmarked cars were parked up, waiting to take the prisoners to their next destination: a less-than-salubrious Dubai prison for the ship's captain and his crew, and the airport for Sacha and William.

She was tending Chris's injuries with an ice-wrapped tea towel when Sacha appeared on the lower deck. He was still bleeding, although Tariq had tied a tourniquet around his leg using once-white towels from the hot tub. The guards taking him towards the gangplank seemed largely unconcerned.

Sacha stopped in front of her. 'You.' His voice was weak and watery, but full of hatred. 'You shot me. Again.'

Vicky shrugged. 'Not much different to paintball. To be honest, I thought you'd be harder to hit.'

He raised his handcuffed wrists and shook them at Tariq, who was standing nearby. 'You can't just arrest me. You don't have any proof I did anything illegal – and Dubai doesn't even have an extradition treaty.'

'You underestimate us, Mr Kozlovsky,' Tariq said. 'We have all the proof we need. Although I must admit my favourite part was blowing it all up a short time ago, along with your terrorist buyers.'

Sacha looked shocked. 'You knew who they were?'

Tariq nodded. 'We know everything. We have witnesses,

too. And with regards to your arrest, well, the Dubai authorities were very interested to hear about your bribes and your blatant disregard for their rules and regulations – and how you took out a hit on someone in one of their landmark hotels nine years ago.' Tariq held up an evidence bag with a passport inside. 'What was your plan, "Igor Petrushev"? Run to Iran, get to Russia, and then where?'

'You can't take me. They will want me here, to make an example of before they send me back to Russia.'

'Despite your desire, I'm sure, to spend a few months behind bars here before you can pay your way out and wait for another passport to be printed, Dubai have been very accommodating when it comes to taking you back with us. Frankly, you're lucky my colleague here didn't put a bullet through your head.' He nodded to the men holding Sacha. 'Take him to the plane,' he said.

Sacha snarled and looked at Vicky, his eyes suddenly narrowing. 'You *knew* about all of this. You're one of them.'

Vicky smiled back at Sacha. This was going to feel good. 'Let's just say, all those days spent baking cakes at your house weren't a total waste of time.'

'I should have known you weren't there because you actually liked my wife. Or did *she* know? Did that bitch rat me out?'

'Matisse didn't know anything.'

'But she stole my money.'

'She knew you were leaving her. She told me as much before we came to Dubai. She might have taken your money, but she wasn't the one who betrayed you.'

'So, who is the one who gave you all this proof then? William?'

'No, not William. His liaison with Matisse and the NCA was just as much of a surprise to us as it was to you.'

'*Anatoli?*' Sacha's face was sick with realisation. He spat at the ground. 'That bastard! Three times I had it in my power to kill him and three times he has escaped, and each time I learn more about how he's fucked up my life.'

'I think you'll find you did that all by yourself, Sacha.' Vicky said. She waved. 'Have fun in prison.'

'I hope you rot in hell.' The men guarding him pulled roughly at him and he began to limp away.

'You, my friend, are the one who will rot. Oh, and thank you for the money,' Tariq called after him. 'Seems your wife was telling the truth. We've just received details of a rather large anonymous deposit made to the NCA.'

An hour or so later, the yacht bobbed in its moorings, the magnificence of Dubai Marina rising up all around. Tariq had asked Vicky to stay for a debrief, and she had agreed as long as they had access to a very large glass of something and a few packs of baby wipes to get off the worst of the blood. The top deck had been sealed off, but the bar inside the boat was still accessible. Chris and Vicky made their way to it and poured themselves a drink, before going back outside to sit at the long-forgotten dining table.

'God, Vics, you were amazing,' Chris said, wincing as he sat down. 'You saved all our lives. I didn't know – didn't . . . I mean, if you weren't . . .'

She took his hands in hers. 'I'm sorry, Chris. After everything I promised, you were the one with a gun to your head.' She put her head down. 'I didn't save you. I failed you.'

'No.' Chris lifted her chin with his finger. 'You promised you'd protect me, and you did. When I saw you, when Sacha had that gun pointed at my head, I knew I could trust you. I knew that whatever your reasons were for wanting to do this insane job, that you wouldn't fail.'

He leant into her and gave her the most enormous kiss. Vicky melted into it, feeling the love and offering it straight back to her wonderful, brave husband. They separated finally.

'Did you check on the kids?'

'They're all fine. You kept your promise to them too.'

Vicky held on tight to Chris. 'I always thought I'd failed before, because I got too emotionally involved. That it was a weakness. But maybe this time around, it was a strength. Maybe having you and the kids to worry about – and Matisse and Dmitri, and Anatoli – it gave me a clarity and determination I've never felt before.' She looked up at him. 'I always thought it was better to work alone. But I don't think I could have done it without you.'

'Are you saying I'm your faithful sidekick?'

'Let's just say, next Halloween *we're* the ones going as Batman and Robin,' she grinned.

Chris nodded towards the couple embracing in a dark corner of the deck. 'What about them? What do you think they will do now?'

Vicky looked to where Matisse and Anatoli stood, lips locked, oblivious to everything around them. 'I have an idea,' she said.

'Ahem, ah, sorry, excuse me.' Helena appeared, looking pale, her eyes and face swollen with crying. 'I just wanted to say thank you, Victoria. I don't know how you did it, but you saved my life. You saved all our lives.'

Vicky smiled. 'You're welcome, Helena. How is William?'

Helena's face crumpled. 'He's being detained. He did a good thing, in the end, even if he was seduced by *her* into doing it . . . but he's been Sacha's accountant for a long time and there's a lot of tax evasion and money laundering charges he still needs to answer for . . . I can't believe he was so mixed up in all of this.'

She started to cry again, and Vicky reached out to give her a hug.

'I thought he was a lot of things, but I didn't think he was a criminal,' Helena moaned. 'I knew we should never have got on this boat. What will I tell the kids?'

'I think you have to tell them the truth.'

Helena sniffed and nodded. 'They've told me I'm free to go.'

'Well that's good.'

She broke away from Vicky and wiped her eyes. 'Well, goodnight . . . and Happy Christmas.'

'Helena?' Vicky took a deep breath and squeezed Chris's hand. 'Would you and the kids like to join us for Christmas lunch? We're going to a resort in the desert, there will be camel rides and dancing and a big pool to hang out by. I know it's not going to be a great Christmas for you, but—'

Helena's face broke out into a weary smile. 'That would be wonderful, Vicky. Thank you for the offer. But I think we'd better go home.'

She turned and made her way down the stairs to the lower deck. Chris let go of Vicky's hand and poured them another drink. They clinked glasses and looked out at the skyscrapers twinkling, their reflections bouncing off the dark water.

'I have to debrief with Tariq,' Vicky said.

'Actually, I've agreed with Jonathan you can do that when you get home,' Tariq said, appearing from the upper deck with Jacob. 'I think it's high time you got off this boat and went home to your kids.'

Jacob waggled a set of keys. 'I'm driving. You've had too much champagne.'

'What about them?' Vicky said, nodding towards Matisse and Anatoli. 'Will Matisse be able to come too? Our kids are in her villa.'

'We'll take care of Matisse. Ollie and Evie were taken back to the Sofitel at 10 p.m. by an officer, once we'd radioed in. You can go straight back there.'

'What about Dmitri?'

'Don't worry about Dmitri, or Matisse right now,' Tariq said. 'They'll be fine.'

'Come on,' Chris said. 'Let's go and hug our children. Whether or not they like it.'

'Sounds good to me,' Vicky said.

Epilogue

Matisse packed up the last of the bags and brought it down the staircase to sit by the front door with the others. On her way, she passed Sacha's office. She glanced in at the blank walls, wondering where the cameras had been, where the bugs were planted, and if they had been removed before she and Dmitri had flown back from Dubai. Vicky had assured her they would be gone before the next owners took up residence. No one would ever know.

Matisse continued down the winding staircase and into the kitchen, her footsteps echoing. The rest of the house looked as empty as the office, the bare bones of the place that used to be their home, now that the paintings and personal effects, such as they were, had been boxed and put on a shipping container. The cold January light seeped through the patio doors. She went to the cupboard for a glass and then remembered there were none; there was just a single unwanted mug on the draining board that she upturned and filled, taking a long gulp.

'Dmitri, do you want a drink before we go?' She called up the stairs again, her voice echoing in the emptiness.

'No thanks.'

A last check that all the doors were locked and the windows closed. The sound of her heels on the floor reverberated all around as she walked. She checked the laundry room and saw a package on the side, for Sacha, that must have been missed by the movers. More shirts, she supposed; she'd leave them for the next people to do what they wanted with them. Where Sacha was, he wouldn't be needing them, not for a long time.

Upstairs, she called to Dmitri.

'Come along,' she said. 'We'll miss our plane.'

'I wish we could stay here, Mama,' said Dmitri. 'I still don't understand why we have to go now. I didn't get to say goodbye to any of my friends.'

'You said goodbye to Evie, and we've been through this, Dmitri. It's not safe for us here. I wish it wasn't true, but it is. Papa – Sacha – knows a lot of bad people, and we need to go somewhere where they can't find us.'

Dmitri's eyes filled with tears. Her heart did the same.

'Will *he* be there, in America? I don't want him there. I don't want to see him.'

'Dmitri, this isn't the right way to speak about Anatoli. I know everything is new and difficult, but believe me, he is a good man. There is no rush to feel love for him, but I hope that in time you do. Please, trust me that it will be okay.'

The thought of Anatoli filled her with warmth. After Sacha and his men had been arrested, they had spent hours together on the boat, oblivious to everything but each other. Late into the night, they finally said their goodbyes.

'I have to go now.' She'd kissed Anatoli gently. 'I need to get back to Dmitri. Tomorrow will not be easy for him.'

Anatoli kissed her again. 'Is it too soon to say I love you?'

Matisse closed her eyes and felt him tight against her. 'Never.'

'I'm going to America,' he said. 'They promised me a passport, if they got Sacha. Come with me. Both of you. You'll be safe, somewhere he'll never find you. We can start a new life, the one we were supposed to live.'

She kissed him again. 'I need some time just for Dmitri and I first, and to think about what is right for him. All this will be very hard for him, you understand?'

'I understand. And I will wait for as long as it takes for you both to be ready.'

When she got back to London, to the house, Matisse knew that no matter what happened between her and Anatoli, she couldn't stay there. She decided they would go to America, but that Anatoli would live in his own apartment until such time as Dmitri was ready for them to be a family. Anatoli had been set up in a small town on the West Coast that seemed like a good fit for all of them, and so, without wanting to waste any more time, she'd begun the process of putting the house up for sale and leaving their old life behind.

It all fell into place very quickly. A man called Jonathan had invited her to meet for lunch, where he informed her that she and Dmitri would be offered witness protection and handed her new passports and visas for her to travel to the States. Between the proceeds from the house and the money Matisse had transferred from Sacha's bank accounts – which had been mercifully left alone by the security services – it would be enough for her and Dmitri to live on for the rest of their lives. Dmitri would keep his name; hers, and their surname would be changed. The school would be notified that Dmitri would not be returning for the spring term. His records had been altered and forwarded to his new school in America, where a place had already been secured. Matisse would give evidence in Sacha's court case via video, to save her appearing in person. Her paintings, her clothes, her boxes full of photos, would all be shipped to her new address in the next few weeks. Vicky had kindly offered to collect any post and make sure the house was left tidy and clean for viewings.

Victoria Turnbull. Matisse smiled again. She had known there was something about her friend that was different, but she'd never guessed it was because she was a spy. She'd come over after breakfast the morning after Sacha's arrest, and confessed to bugging his office, accidentally uncovering her deepest secret hidden in a box of photographs, and faking a competition win to Dubai so she could catch Sacha in the act of an illegal arms trade. Matisse found herself laughing like she hadn't laughed for years, at the ridiculousness of it all.

'You mean you joined the PTA as a cover?' she said. 'All those cakes, those meetings, the Christmas Fair . . . all in the name of national security?'

'You'd be surprised the lengths I'm willing to go to.' Vicky joined in the laughter. 'Christ, I even joined the WhatsApp group.'

She and Evie had come over again yesterday, when the removal company had left, to say goodbye.

'Thank you for bringing Anatoli back into my life,' Matisse said, as they embraced at the door. 'I know . . . he told me, before, about a woman in London who he loved but let go, that she was a spy, that he was too afraid for

344

himself and his family to do the right thing. I think, now, that it was you.'

Vicky nodded. 'It was difficult and destructive and wrong to get involved; I don't blame him for walking away when he did. And I'm glad he met you and I met Chris. That's the way things were supposed to work out.'

'Well, they nearly didn't work out at all,' Matisse said.

'But they did in the end. That's the main thing. Good luck, Matisse. I hope that your new life brings you happiness. I hope Dmitri settles okay. Send me a postcard, yeah?'

'But of course I will,' she said. They hugged then, and kissed each other on both cheeks, and two sets of eyes filled with tears as they knew it was time.

'I have something for you, before I go.' Matisse presented her with a large, rectangular package.

'What is it?'

'Let's just say it is a little thank you from me,' Matisse said.

Vicky picked up the package and walked towards her car. 'Bye, Matisse.'

'Bye, Vicky. I will miss you.'

'I'll miss you too.'

She'd gone then, leaving Matisse to finish her packing and prepare for the long flight west. They were flying to Los Angeles before hiring a car and taking the two-hour drive to their new home. Somewhere along the way, Matisse would become as invisible as Vicky.

'It's time, Dmitri, let's go.' She took one last look and shut the door, putting her arm around her son as they left the old world behind them.

*

Vicky sat facing Jonathan again, barely recognisable as the woman who'd first walked into his office six months previously. Her hair was cut into a newly sharpened bob that accentuated her cheekbones. She *had* cheekbones. Running had proved to be therapeutic – great thinking time – and she'd found herself going further and faster during her holiday, taking in the unfamiliar sights and sounds of Dubai as she jogged along the beach road each morning. Her skin, usually pasty, was tanned and, dare she say, a little tauter than before. She was relaxed, happy and confident – three things she hadn't felt in a very long time.

'You had a good holiday then, by the looks of things,' Jonathan said.

'Well, we decided to extend our stay and ended up there until New Year's Day,' Vicky replied. 'It was lovely, Jonathan. Honestly, you should see the place. I mean, it's like some kind of Disney on steroids, there's so much to do and see and it's all so *clean* and everyone seems to smile all the time, and it's—'

'Yes, thank you, Victoria, I'm sure it's great.' Jonathan sounded a bit pissed off. Vicky changed the subject.

'So, what did you want to see me for anyway, sir?' she said.

'Well I don't want to beat about the bush. I know you wanted to come back to JOPS,' Jonathan said, 'but I wanted to make sure, after all that happened on the boat, that you still meant it.'

'I had a feeling you'd ask me that,' she said. 'I want to . . . but I think I have to say no, after all. I thought about it a lot while we were away. Chris is super supportive, but I can't do it. It's not fair on him, or me . . . or you. And the kids . . . James is still so young, and Evie and Ollie, well they need me more than they think, even if it's just as a glorified taxi service.'

'I had a feeling that would be the case.'

'Sorry.'

'It's just, you're a natural. Even after all those years, you get results.'

'Maybe it was dumb luck in Dubai.'

'I don't think so.'

Vicky sighed. 'Neither do I, to be honest. But I can't do it. Full time would be impossible – and, as you said before, part time doesn't make any sense.'

Jonathan leaned back in his chair and sipped his coffee. 'What will you do instead?'

'I guess I'll stay doing some PTA stuff . . . spend time with the family . . . I don't know, Jonathan, I've got a lot to figure out. Matisse and Anatoli are lucky in a way: they get to build their whole lives from scratch, reinvent who they are, and live a life free from all the things you get saddled with over the years that shape the way things are for you.'

'They have to start again, build up friendships and shared history from the very beginning, in a place where they don't know anyone or anything, without any support. That's a lot of work.'

'I know. Starting over isn't the easy choice.'

'Neither is giving up what you love.'

'No.'

'So, how about we figure out a way for you to still be a school mum and a spy too?' Jonathan said. 'I'd like to offer you a deal, Turnbull. We'll keep you on a contract where we bring you in on an assignment basis.'

'As in, I get to choose what I work on and when?'

'Not quite. Look – there's no point in either of us pretending you're the same person you used to be. You don't look the same, and you sure as hell don't act it. But we need versatility, we need people to blend into every situation. And your age, your looks, your experience – they're all things we can use to our advantage. Not every time. But I'd certainly like to call on you when we need to.'

Vicky paused. 'And I could say no, if it didn't work for me?'

'You could. But I imagine you won't. Because from what I can see, you appear to be a far happier, stronger and confident person since you came back to work than the one you were before.'

'I suppose I am.'

A wood pigeon had found its way to the streets of Putney and was 'hoo-hoo-ing' outside their bedroom window. Vicky wished she had a baseball bat handy to shut it up. It was far too early, and a Saturday, and she didn't have to get up and do the school run or take James to nursery. As the pigeon continued its aural assault, Vicky tossed and turned and tried to imagine a scenario where the cooing was soporific instead of just bloody annoying, and failed. She sighed. She was *so* tired. Today was the PTA's big Easter egg hunt and she had so much to do. Becky had put her in charge of music, which was a merciful reprieve from cake baking, but she still had a thousand things on her to-do list before the hunt that afternoon.

The sun streamed through a gap in the curtains. She gave in and sat up, careful not to wake her sleeping husband,

and swung her legs onto the floor. At that moment, the doorbell rang.

Chris mumbled something in his sleep and turned over.

'I'll get it,' Vicky said. She took a quick look at the clock. It was early for a Saturday. Unusual. Not unheard of, but she couldn't think of a good reason why anyone would be ringing the bell at this time in the morning. She threw on her dressing gown and went downstairs.

She opened the door and saw that it was a delivery of flowers. They looked and smelt amazing.

'For a Mrs Turnbull?' the delivery man said.

'Thank you! They're beautiful.'

She shut the door, read the card, and smiled. *To my friend Vicky, with love,* it said. She knew it was Matisse, letting her know they were doing fine. She'd had three similar bouquets since January, one each month; her friend's way of communicating that she was safe and well.

Vicky wondered if Matisse was happy. She hoped so. Even on the other side of the world, would she still be looking over her shoulder once in a while, to check no one was watching? No matter how relaxed she appeared, Vicky was still on high alert most of the time. It had taken years to kick the habit of trusting no one after she left the service the first time. This time, with a family, she doubted if she could let her guard down fully until it was time to dig her a hole in the ground.

Vicky padded into the kitchen, flicked the kettle on and put the flowers in the sink, before going back upstairs to brush her teeth and go to the bathroom. She was awake now; she might as well go and make a cup of tea and enjoy the peace and quiet.

On a sudden impulse, she decided to poke her head into

James's room before she went down. Her youngest son was snoring softly; the image of his daddy, she thought. She moved on to Ollie's room and opened it, the smell of teenage feet, sweat and farts nearly knocked her down. She smiled, closed the door, and made her way to the final room. She saw a light was on under the crack in the door and gave a light tap.

'Morning, Mum.'

'Morning, Evie.'

'Who was at the door?'

'It was a delivery of flowers, from Matisse.'

'Does that mean they're okay?'

'Well I'm guessing it means they are happy and safe, yes.'

'Are they living with that man now?'

'You mean Anatoli? I don't know, petal. Maybe.'

'He and Dmitri look like each other. They have the same eyes.'

'Yes . . . yes they do.' Observant girl, she thought, smiling to herself. 'Come down for breakfast when you're ready, okay?' She kissed her daughter lightly on the forehead and went back downstairs for a cup of tea. Her beautiful children.

The kettle boiled, and she poured hot water into the mug. As it stewed, she cleared last night's dinner into the dishwasher and gave the table a wipe down with a cloth. She heard the letterbox open and something land heavy on the mat. The postman was early this morning, too. She took a sip of her tea and then went to the door again. A plain brown envelope was on the mat, with her name on the top, no address, no stamp. It wasn't the postman then.

She took the envelope into the living room and sat on the sofa. A pair of Damien Hirst butterfly prints now proudly hung either side of the chimney breast, and Vicky paused to admire them and silently thank her French friend once again for her generous gift. She turned her attention back to the envelope. Inching her finger under the envelope seal, a set of files fell out with blurred close-up photos of a woman and a man and a Post-it stuck to the top. 'Are you awake?' it said. She drank her tea, read the files, then headed to the utility room. She rifled through a pile of ironing in the basket on top of the washing machine until she found the phone she'd been looking for.

WIDE AWAKE

Acknowledgements

When writers come to mind, you imagine them as solitary beings tapping away in a shed, miraculously coming out after six months with 400 empty biscuit wrappers and a fully-formed novel. It couldn't be further from the truth! Writing takes a village, and I have an incredible village.

Firstly, my thanks go to my amazing agent, Davinia Andrew-Lynch, who believed in me and in *Tinker, Tailor, Schoolmum, Spy* enough to help shape it – and me – into a credible piece of work.

Huge thanks to Helen Lederer and the whole of the Comedy Women in Print team, for championing an award that recognises comedy writing as a craft in its own right and for their continuing support of all the witty women who have become part of the family; and to the 2020 judges of the Unpublished category – Yomi Adegoke, Fanny Blake, Kate Bradley, Grace Campbell, Kirsty Eyre and Jennifer Young – for selecting *TTSS* as the winner.

Thanks to Kate Bradley for making *TTSS* a reality, and to all the team at HarperCollins for their help and support guiding me through the publishing process (never easy for a first timer!). It is truly a dream come true to see Vicky in print.

Thanks to Julia Crouch for your invaluable critique and to Susy Marriot at PWA for your guidance and support. To Caroline, Eira, Gayle and Sarah, thank you for suffering through that early draft. I hope you like the results! Thanks also to my Falmouth cohort – Alison, Deana and Jane – it has been a pleasure trading writing war stories with you over Sunday-night cocktails on the Southbank. Long may it continue.

My sincere thanks go to all my wonderful friends and family around the world: in particular, to my Courtyard Playhouse family, for their friendship and laughter, and to Cheryl, who gave me the courage to write in the first place. Thank you also to Nathan: your pride and excitement at having an 'author Mum' means everything. The biggest thank you, though, must go to Steve, without whose patience, encouragement, and love absolutely none of this would have happened. 'I think I'd make an amazing spy,' I said to him one night, while drunk at a dinner party. 'You'd make a better assassin,' he said. Everyone else was shocked; we both erupted in laughter, and *TTSS* was born. Steve, this book is because of you.

Finally, thank you to every reader who decided to take a chance on a debut author, and to every bookseller who helped make it happen. I'm very happy and honoured that you did.

Read on for an interview with the fabulously funny Faye Brann, winner of the 2020 Comedy Women in Print prize.

Congratulations on winning the Comedy Women in Print prize, what did that feel like?

Surreal! The longlist was announced just after the first lockdown began in March 2020 and instead of getting to go to a swanky awards party, I found out I'd won by Zoom and got my Hussie (as the CWIP trophies are fondly called) in the post. Regardless, the excitement of sitting on a call with HarperCollins and being told I was going to be a published author was a very, very special moment. It sounds corny to say it was a dream come true, but it really was.

Did you write *Tinker, Tailor, Schoolmum, Spy* with the prize in mind?

Not at all. I started writing *Tinker, Tailor, Schoolmum, Spy* about four years ago and was in the process of searching for an agent when I first entered the CWIP Prize in 2019. I didn't win that year, but I did find an agent. Davinia gave me copious notes on my manuscript and helped me bash it into shape before we went out to publishers. Around the same time, CWIP dropped me an email encouraging resubmissions for the 2020 prize, but only if I had a significantly reworked manuscript. I decided to give it another whirl – and I'm very glad I did!

Had you written any books before *Tinker, Tailor, Schoolmum, Spy*, or is this your first full-length novel?

While I was living in the Middle East I studied for an MA in writing and wrote the opening chapters of a narrative non-fiction book about life as an expat wife (known back then as 'trailing spouses', UGH). Anyway, when I had completed the MA, I decided to carry on researching and writing the book. I haven't ever done anything with it in terms of trying to get it published, but it wasn't a wasted effort. Getting 80,000 words down on paper gave me the confidence and stamina to try my hand at an actual novel. I had a few ideas about what I wanted to do and made a few false starts, but *Tinker, Tailor, Schoolmum, Spy* was my first full length work. I learned a huge amount in writing it and I'm really proud of the result.

What advice would you give to anyone thinking of entering next year's CWIP Prize?

Go for it! CWIP is the mastermind of Helen Lederer and though only in its third year, it is gaining momentum all the time. Quite rightly, too. I think funny books can often get overlooked as being significant, even though we all love a bit of a giggle. The CWIP family is a hugely supportive and growing network I'm so happy to be a part of – they really care about their witty women writers and are great cheerleaders long after the competition is over. I think something like ten books have been published since 2019 (when the prize started) by debut authors who made the long and short lists. In two years, that's a pretty good track record.

How did you get the idea for Vicky, juggling being a special op with being a suburban mum?

Well, the initial idea for the book was about being a woman returning to work after years raising a family. I don't think it's a secret that picking up a career again on the 'wrong' side of forty-five with a great gaping hole in your CV can be challenging. But middle-aged women have so much to offer! So, really, I wanted to show that we can be awesome and use our age and experience to our advantage; and to capture that energy and elation at being your own person again while also exploring the frustration and guilt that many of us struggle with in trying to 'have it all'. In terms of Vicky being special ops, I always fancied being a spy and I thought it would be a fun mash-up of genres, to smash together the world of James Bond and *Desperate Housewives*. And so, Vicky was born.

The book opens at a paintball birthday party. Did you do any spy training to get into the mind of your characters?

Not really, unless you count doing a Couch to 5k. I read a few 'kiss and tell' spy books for procedural tips and tricks and spent a lot of time googling MI5 which was fairly fruitless (they are called the Secret Service for a reason), researching illegal arms trading, modern day spyware and how to procure a fake passport. I probably have a drone parked permanently over my house as a result.

If you were a spy, would you want to be behind the scenes or in the field?

Definitely in the field. Although my husband says I'd make a better assassin than a spy, and he may be onto something. Like Vicky, I did go clay pigeon shooting once, and was commended for my sharp shooting. I'm also a Slytherin and enjoy sitting still for long periods of time. It ticks a lot of boxes.

Have you also tried live comedy, and was it difficult?

I've never tried stand-up, but I've done a lot of improvisation comedy, which is very different. Not least because in improv the audiences are usually rooting for you – there's no heckling and it's really supportive. With stand-up, audiences are more 'I paid to see you, now entertain me'. Terrifying! Improv comedy is completely unscripted and I love the madness of it, that you arrive onstage with no idea what's going to happen and can create something funny, sad or beautiful from a word, a gesture or a few notes on a piano. It helped me become a better writer, too. It taught me a lot about what works in a story, about how to use detail and call it back later, and most importantly, about letting go of ideas that are not working.

How hard is it to be funny?

Creating comedy in any form is a bit torturous. You do spend a lot of time thinking 'what if people don't find me funny?' But I try to ignore that little voice as much as I can. Learning and teaching improv helped a lot with accepting that sometimes you're going to fail; but when you get it right, it's glorious. Humour is always in the truth of a situation. If you giggle while you're writing because you can identify with a particular character or moment in time, it's a reasonably safe bet that someone, somewhere, will giggle while they're reading it.

Do you have a favourite comedy writer?

I started out reading Janet Evanovich when I was younger, and I still really enjoy her books. Stephanie Plum was my favourite beach read for years. Ben Aaronovitch is another author I really like – the *Rivers of London* series is a great combination of police crime, fantasy and comedy. I think I was influenced a lot by both authors. For learning about comedy, Keith Johnstone's books are never far from my grasp. He is a pioneer of comedy improvisation and in his late eighties now; I did a workshop with him a few years ago and it was extraordinary.

Have you always wanted to be a writer?

Deep down, probably, although I don't think I really realised it until about ten years ago! I have always loved the theatre, so I suppose you could say I've always wanted to tell stories. I started blogging after my son was born as a kind of therapy, but the blog became quite popular and I realised other people enjoyed my writing, too, so I signed up to do a master's degree via distance learning at Falmouth University. Between that and the blog, I wrote almost every day for two years. After that it just became part of my life.

As a debut author, what was the most exciting part of having your book published?

Well, it's all pretty exciting! Seeing the cover for the first time was thrilling. Sending off the final proof was a big moment, too. If I had to choose, I suppose it's got to be seeing it for sale in a bookshop. Or rather, seeing someone pick it up and put it in their basket at a bookshop. Or maybe it's not that either . . . I think simply having it in my hands, as an actual book, thumbing through the pages I wrote – I think that might be the best thing of all. I'll let you know!